Wingwalkers

Wingwalkers

TAYLOR BROWN

ST. MARTIN'S PRESS

NEW YORK

First published in the United States by St. Martin's Press,
an imprint of St. Martin's Publishing Group

WINGWALKERS. Copyright © 2022 by Taylor Brown. All rights reserved.
Printed in the United States of America. For information,
address St. Martin's Publishing Group, 120 Broadway, New York, NY 10271.

www.stmartins.com

Design by Jonathan Bennett

Library of Congress Cataloging-in-Publication Data

Names: Brown, Taylor, 1982- author.
Title: Wingwalkers / Taylor Brown.
Description: First edition. | New York : St. Martin's Press, 2022.
Identifiers: LCCN 2021051027 | ISBN 9781250274595 (hardcover) |
    ISBN 9781250274601 (ebook)
Subjects: LCGFT: Action and adventure fiction. | Romance fiction. | Novels.
Classification: LCC PS3602.R722894 W56 2022 | DDC 813/.6—dc23/eng/
    20211022
LC record available at https://lccn.loc.gov/2021051027

Our books may be purchased in bulk for promotional, educational, or business use. Please contact your local bookseller or the Macmillan Corporate and Premium Sales Department at 1-800-221-7945, extension 5442, or by email at MacmillanSpecialMarkets@macmillan.com.

First Edition: 2022

10 9 8 7 6 5 4 3 2 1

For my father, the pilot.

For Dr. Hubert McAlexander of Holly Springs, Mississippi,
the greatest English professor who has ever lived.

When [Faulkner] appeared at the Bradfords' early Sunday morning, he looked ravenous and hung over. After he consumed a large breakfast, he launched into what seemed to Mary Rose a disjointed, nightmarish tale of accepting a ride from two motorcyclists, a man and a woman. They were aviators at the meet, and he had joined them in drinking, flying, and carousing.

—JOSEPH BLOTNER, *Faulkner: A Biography*

Non est ad astra mollis e terris via.
(*There is no easy way from the earth to the stars.*)

—SENECA THE YOUNGER, *The Madness of Hercules*

How do you know you're not dead?

—WILLIAM FAULKNER, "Ad Astra"

Book I

1

The Balloonitic

*T*he courthouse elms were dew-black with dawn when the Balloon-itic came rumbling into the Square aboard his mule-drawn buggy, one wheel wobbling out of true. An ancient driver sat at the reins with the surly airman hunched alongside him, his boots propped dusty and seam-busted on the splashboard. A brown mountain of canvas loomed from the bed of the conveyance, dwarfing the odd pair of itinerant wagoners. The fabric was crumpled and creased, the geologic panes etched with the soils of distant hills and pastures and bogs. The bleached white facade of the county courthouse stared down at the soiled heap passing before it, unimpressed.

Carnival tents were sprouting in the Square like overnight toadstools. There was the snake charmer, the bearded lady, and the wild man from Borneo, who gnawed on white clubs of ox bone, his ankle shackled to an iron stake driven deep into the earth beneath his tent. One might have witnessed any of these marvels for a dime. But the three brothers who followed the wagon across the Square, marching along the dark, dew-cut streaks of its passage like tightrope walkers—Billy and Jack and

Johncy Falkner—did not come for such lesser wonders. They came to watch a man die.

The buggy halted, and the Gypsy balloonist and his helper stepped down and went to work removing posts and planks from beneath the piled canvas, erecting a crude framework of sawn pine in the middle of Oxford Square, before the four-sided clock of the courthouse, whose faces rarely agreed. Over this, they draped the canvas gasbag, tugging and coaxing corners like men making up a bed, and the helper set a skillet of hot coals beneath the flaccid shroud. The Balloonitic lifted a five-gallon can of coal oil down from the bed of the buggy and, kneeling, slung the first dipper of oil onto the coals. The skillet flashed and crackled, belching black balls of oil smoke into the open maw of the balloon.

He would sling the dipper again and again, twice a minute until, two hours later, the canvas had begun to swell ever so slightly, bulging here or there. By this time, the two younger brothers, Jack and Johncy, had wandered off to pitch rings over the necks of milk bottles or dunk their heads for apples, to gaze upon the prize pumpkins and potatoes in the farmers' stalls. The streets were alive with horses and carriages, and townsfolk clacked back and forth along the board sidewalks that fronted the two-story brick and stucco facades of the Square's storefronts, many with balconies or cast-iron columns. Only Billy, eleven years old, stood fixed on the lawn, watching the coal fire fill the shoddy lung of canvas.

By noon, the gasbag had swelled lopsided over the wooden frame, like a sick cloud, and the Balloonitic could stand upright beneath the burled canvas. With each flash of coal oil, Billy saw him silhouetted against the soiled sailcloth walls, his poses strange and rampant, like some shade of man wheeling about the storm of creation, stoking its fire. Suddenly his mustachioed face ducked from beneath the canvas, sooty and red-eyed, wreathed in the blackest smoke.

"Brandy!" he yelled at his helper, who nodded and fetched a pint bottle from the throat of his boot. The Balloonitic took the bottle and unscrewed the cap and sucked on the spout, then pointed the bottle at

Billy. "Fetch them little brothers of your'n, and whichever else of these little pie-faces can make themselves useful."

Billy rounded up ten boys from the shooting gallery and the ring toss and from behind the bearded lady's tent, where they sat smoking pilfered tobacco and daring one another to lift the flap. They each held one of the mooring lines that dangled from the balloon, watching the sullen globe form beneath the braids of hemp. It flickered and belched, emitting black gouts of smoke, and Billy felt his own chest swelling in unison. Soon a man would ascend into the Mississippi heavens, high enough to see the university, the rail depot, the lazy scrawl of the Tallahatchie River. He would hang amid the clouded aeries of gods and eagles, and then he would fall, returning to the red clay and cotton fields of the state, living or dead. Either was miracle enough.

By five o'clock, the autumn sky was crumbling, laced with fire, and the balloon was huge above them, straining at its moorings. It threw a shadow the size of a house, and the boys were buoyant beneath its power. They were lifted onto their tiptoes again and again. Billy looked at his little brothers Jack and Johncy, who were small enough to be tugged from the turf for long, lazy seconds, their faces soft with wonder.

Now the Balloonitic emerged from his hide, soot-faced as a smithy or coal miner or fugitive from Hades, his cheeks slashed with tears. His helper came scurrying to him, carrying his parachute like an offering, a giant silk dress folded inside a croker sack. The balloonist heaved himself into the straps and buckles, carefully adjusting his testicles to the gasped dismay of the finer ladies in the crowd, and the helper tied a static line of grocer's string to a trapeze dangling beneath the mouth of the balloon. This was meant to rip open the chute. Few noticed, as Billy did, how the man didn't so much as check the knot.

The man settled himself onto the crossbar of the trapeze, wiggling his butt into place, and the balloon bounced and lolled like a drunkard's head. His booted feet hung short of the earth, like a child in a kitchen chair, and he looked across his gathered flock. Sunspotted farmers in from the fields, their faces sculpted pale by the morning's straight razor, and fat-cheeked country wives holding babies against their hips, toddlers clung slobbering to their skirts. White-haired captains who fought in the First Mississippi Partisan Rangers or Second Mississippi Infantry, who still wore their battle grays to reunions, the waists of the britches taken out by town tailors in armbands, and their great-grandsons, this motley assortment of boys who held the balloon to the earth.

The Balloonitic's eyes, red with smoke and brandy, roved this crowd, as if he knew what terrible secrets pumped through the numbered chambers of their hearts.

He looked at the underweight eleven-year-old who'd watched him all day with smoldering black eyes—eyes that looked like they could burn a hole through his canvas moon. "What's your name, boy?"

The boy stood taller, as if called to attention. "Billy Falkner, sir."

The Balloonitic gestured the boy forth, clapping a soot-stained hand on his shoulder. "All right, Billy Falkner, tell these slobbering little pie-faces to turn her loose."

Billy looked to the other boys, wearing the man's sooty handprint like a badge of honor. "All right, boys, you heard the man. Let slip the lines!"

They did. The braided hemp moorings slithered from their opened hands as the balloon leapt from the rig. A gust of wind shoved it sideways, the swollen canvas bobbing drunkenly across the white face of the courthouse—built after General Whiskey Smith burned the original building in 1864. The crowd gasped as the black elms of the Square threatened to rake the balloon from the sky. The trees missed, their naked clutches falling just short of the dangling man, and the balloon rose and rose, freed of entanglements, rising higher than the courthouse clock. Now the brothers were running, chasing the balloon as it bobbled across town. They hurdled the iron hitching chain that lined the Square, causing horses to stamp and rear, and went skittering and scrambling down the street, between the rowed offices of dentists and attorneys, past the site of the First National Bank of Oxford, where their grandfather, the Colonel, would one day feel entitled, as bank president, to throw a brick through the plate glass window after a night of hard drinking out in the country.

The balloon bobbed above a dusking foreground of steeples and flag-poles and oaks, ever climbing, shrinking, floating high enough to catch the last planes of sun, burning like Mars against the iron sky, and the boys' lungs were searing as they ran and ran. Billy led them, jumping creeks and ducking clotheslines, dodging barking dogs. His heart was a bloody planet, banging with thunder, threatening to burst from his chest, to follow the fleeing balloon into the dying autumn sky. He realized it was heading for South Second Street, where they lived with their mother and father and grandmother Damuddy on the old Johnny Brown place.

They passed before a row of castlelike Victorians, their lordly turrets bearing iron weathervanes and lightning rods, and they cut through the rattling weeds of an unmown lot. The balloon was threatening to escape them, to wink out of existence against the sheer immensity of sky, when they saw the man detach from his perch. A mere speck, sprouting limbs as he fell, wheeling and flailing through the twilight. A ribbon of silk came streaming from his back, rippling and fluttering for long, fatal seconds that tocked like eons in the skulls of the watching boys. Farther and farther he fell. He was just above the treetops, his death certain, when the canopy exploded into bloom, a patchwork bulb of tattered, hand-stitched panels that yanked him short of the earth.

He dangled in his harness, busted fragments of the chute fluttering about him, while the unweighted balloon went streaking across the sky above him, scrawling smoke against the clouds like a charcoal smudge. Now it curved downward, an amateur meteor diving for the ground.

"It's headed for our house!" cried Billy. "Hot damn!"

Then all was lost behind the trees. The boys turned up their street and flashed through the bricked gate columns of the property and up the gravel drive, running around the big, many-chimneyed house and scrambling over the panel fence in back. They rose on the far side, black-kneed, to see the chicken coop crushed beneath the smoking wreckage of the balloon. The roof was caved, the gaped planks spewing forth a squawking blizzard of outraged hens, their shorn feathers curling and slivering through the air like confetti.

Billy was about to order Jack and Johncy to chase down the fleeing poultry when there came a roar from the pig lot. He looked to see the Balloonitic rise cursing and flailing from the crumpled remains of his silken canopy, bursting as from the belly of a giant beached jellyfish. He was coated in goo and shit and pig slop. An orange rind stuck to his cheek; ringlets of curdled cheese adorned his head. There were chicken bones pasted to his knit cotton jersey. He raged while the hogs shuttled themselves to one corner, squeaking and coy, like schoolchildren at their first dance.

"Shit a bag of brownstones!" he screamed. "Fuck my ass with a horse-head cane!"

The oaths echoed off the back of the big house, where the chimneys were smoking, and Billy looked to see their father stride square-jawed from the back door. Murry Falkner was a former coal-shoveler and railroad engineer who once survived a pair of shotgun blasts at the counter of Herron's Drugstore, where a man he'd beaten with his fists returned with a slug-loaded 12-gauge and blasted a hole the size of a baseball in his back with one barrel and unloaded the second into his mouth, failing to kill him.

"Country slop-eaters!" roared the Balloonitic, brandy-drunk, staring down the huddled pigflesh. He pawed at the buckles and straps of his harness. "Hell-spawned, chap-lipped, mud-mouthed fornicators!"

Murry Falkner stood at the edge of the lot. "Sir, there's a Christian woman inside this house. I won't have her scandalized by such foul language."

The Balloonitic didn't seem to hear him. He kept fumbling with his straps and risers, cursing in cadence. A foul, vivid stream. Billy had never heard anything so sublime. The man cursed the sky that quit him, the earth that received him, the sun that was going down. He cursed his father for siring him, his mother for birthing him, his brother for not strangling him in his crib. He cursed Jesus, Mary, and Joseph. The Father, the Son, and the Holy Ghost. He cursed the Valley of Death, the Gates of Heaven, the Halls of Justice. The Sons of Liberty, the Communion of Saints, the College of Cardinals, the Fraternal Order of Police. The Fathers of the Church, the Daughters of the Confederacy, the Mothers of the Twelve Tribes. The United States of America, the state of Mississippi, and the town of Oxford. He cursed the owner of this pig lot.

Their father turned and walked back into the house. In his right hand, when he reappeared, was a single-action Colt's revolver, long-nosed and nickeled like a fancy watch. He strode toward the pigpen.

"Uh-oh," said little Johncy.

The boys watched their father step over the hip-high fence without breaking stride. He stood at the edge of the crumpled parachute, about to level the pistol when the warp-wheeled buggy came rattling and skidding around the side of the house. The helper was at the reins, the bed full of greasy carnival men. They leapt down and rushed the pig lot. They surrounded the Balloonitic, placating him with a swarm of helping hands, unbuckling the harness and sliding down the straps and picking the cheese curds from his hair. Someone handed him a bottle of brandy. They surrounded Murry Falkner as well, smiling and chattering in soothing voices, throwing their arms wide in explanation, in demonstration of good nature and universal brotherhood. One extracted a sheaf of soiled bills from his pocket, licking his thumb.

Ten minutes later, the canvas balloon had been piled into the buggy, the parachute heaped like whipped cream on top. The Balloonitic sat on the buggy seat, head back, snoring. A worm of saliva crawling from the corner of his mouth. Their father stood as before, the long iron finger of the pistol held against his leg. In his other hand, a strangled wad of bills. They could see his chest moving up and down, heavy as a bellows. His eyes were on the shattered henhouse, the scattered hens, the drunken airman snoring amid such calamity. The balloonist's helper climbed into the buggy, released the hand brake, and Little Johncy started toward their father.

Billy caught him by the collar of his shirt. "Leave him."

Instead, one of the hogs was first. A red Duroc shoat, newly weaned. She waddled toward their father, braver than the rest, and snuffled at his backside like a friendly dog. Murry Falkner raised the pistol and shot her between the eyes.

The balloonist snorted at the report, then turned aside. His helper slapped the reins.

"What's a fornicator?" asked Johncy.

2

Della the Daring

GEORGIA COAST, 1933

Della the Daring stood on the right wing, one hand on the banshee wire, the land a patchwork of green one thousand feet below. The wind skirled through the struts and guys, the sky itself threatening to rip her from this audacious contraption of wood and fabric and wire that dared its power, that buzzed high among its white cathedrals of cloud. It was a Curtiss Flying Jenny, a two-seat biplane that once trained the aviators of the Great War—men like the one who sat begoggled in the rear seat, a white silk scarf strung like a vapor trail from his neck, a pint bottle of bootleg whiskey huddled between his knees, nearer even than the control yoke.

Her husband.

He screamed over the clattering engine, the shriek of wind. "Hat trick!"

She nodded.

They were over Georgia somewhere, another nameless hamlet whose dusty streets lay flocked and trembling with the pink handbills they'd rained from the sky that morning, the ones that announced the coming of DELLA THE DARING DEVILETTE, who would DEFY THE HEAVENS, shining like a DAYTIME STAR, a WING-WALKING WONDER borne upon the wings of CAPTAIN ZENO MARIGOLD, a DOUBLE ACE of the GREAT WAR, who had ELEVEN AERIAL VICTORIES over the TRENCHES OF FRANCE.

Zeno dipped the wing toward the field of spectators, their faces sprung round beneath the sun, their mouths stove black with awe, and the devilette watched the shadow of the machine rip across them like something come wicked from the sky, a beast to pluck them bloody and rootless from the fields. She walked farther out on the wing, kinking her silver-clad body through the maze of wire trusses and interplane struts that divided the airfoils.

She was wearing her silver lamé jumpsuit, her show name stitched blood-red between her shoulder blades—DELLA THE DARING—and she wore a leather helmet and knee-high riding boots polished to an arrogant luster. She didn't wear a parachute. The slipstream slung the metallic fabric of the one-piece suit hard against her, tight against her breasts and hips, streamlining her.

Her nails were sharp, unpainted, and the outermost bracings sang like piano wire in her hands as she knelt on the ribbed surface of the wing, then lay down flat on her belly. She could feel the spruce spars and ribs trembling against the cloth that bound them, against her own body, the whole wooden skeleton of the machine threatening to jump its skin. She removed her leather flying cap and stuffed it down the neck of her suit.

The wings bore wooden skids designed to prevent the craft from catching a wingtip and cartwheeling during a rough landing. They dropped in half hoops from the outmost struts, like the curved rails of bentwood rocking chairs, and Della the Daring slid her legs over the leading edge and hooked them cross-ankled in the spruce hoop, climbing down so that she hung monkeylike from the underside of the wing, her bottom flashing silver over the upraised faces of the crowd.

She knew, as she always did, that some part of them wanted her to die. She could almost feel their eyes pulling her to earth, the compounded force of their wills, the dark curiosity of what she might look like skewered in the crown of an oak or busted like a watermelon on the hood of a T Model Ford. But when the machine roared upward into the sun with her body dangling from the wing, Della knew she was pulling their red hearts high into their throats, and it was their own blood they could nearly taste on their tongues.

The sun roared across the heavens, the green world wheeled and righted, and Zeno banked again for the field. This time Della hung only by her ankles and a single hand, the other plunged low in the slipstream, her fingers clawing through the wind. She'd removed the pin that bound her hair, and it tore in flaming tongues behind her, a banner of fire.

In the middle of the pasture, there stood the boy she'd paid a quarter to hold his hat doffed, waiting. Zeno lined him up as if for a strafing run, nosing into a dive, and the wind came shrieking through the wings. The earth rose beneath them, like the swell of a vast green sea, and Della watched the spired pines at the edge of the field whip past her—more than once she'd felt the brush of such trees, a cloud of needles torn fluttering in her wake—and now the blades of pasture grass were singing beneath her.

She had eyes only for the hat.

It was a tweed flatcap, doffed high like a salute, and she raked it fast from the boy's hand as she passed overhead, like a hawk ripping a mouse from the field. Zeno blasted them nearly vertical from the ground, and now it was not only the crowd but the weight of the earth itself that tugged so hard at her body, jealous perhaps of her leaving it so freely, and she held fast to the bend of spruce.

Higher and higher they rose, clawing skyward until the machine slowed, its power spent, and hung there, a black cross pegged against the white face of sun. Della cast away the hat. It tumbled and slid earthward, strangely slow, an object newly anointed with power. She knew they should make these farm boys pay them for the privilege of standing afield instead of the other way around. After all, from this day forward, that cap would be hallowed. Every girl in the county would want to touch it, and every man would tip his own hat to the boy who'd held it. The boy's children and grandchildren would be told of the day he stood unmoved beneath the fell swoop of the flying machine, and years later, looking at the hat hanging from a tack on the wall or sitting on the mantel, he would believe the story of his own daring—he would forget he'd been struck too rigid with fear to do anything else.

What was the price of that?

In the relative quiet of the stall, as Zeno heeled the near motionless machine back toward the earth, she could hear him yelling from the cockpit. "Death hang!"

When they again crossed the field, she was hanging upside down by only her knees, her arms dangling, her body limp as something on a meat hook.

How loudly they cheered.

"Eight dollars?" asked Zeno. He looked around. The crowd was gone, the Jenny parked behind him like a pinned moth, his old terrier leashed to one of the struts. "You're telling me I had my wife crawling all over that paper-and-matchwood crate at one thousand feet of altitude with no parachute for eight goddamn dollars?"

The man offered the hat upon a pair of upturned palms. It was a tatty flatcap not unlike the one Della had snatched from the boy in the field.

"I done what ye said," he said. "It's full, ain't it?"

The man wore a set of hard-beaten overalls, the denim worn thin and colorless against a washboard. That morning, after landing, they'd found him in a neighboring field whipping an ancient mule that looked made solely of dust.

Zeno pointed at the hat. "Who, when told to pass a hat, passes one of these? You pass a top hat, or a bowler at the least. Something with some size to it, some depth."

The farmer spat. "Ain't got a top hat."

Zeno still had on his belted leather coat, the fur collar hackled about his mustachioed face. He snatched the cap and stared into it. A nest of dirty coins and dander and pocket lint, laced with swirls of gray hair from the farmer's own spotted pate. "Where's the paper money?"

The man sniffed. "Wasn't none."

Zeno's eyes scoured the man, the bandy legs, the face like dried tobacco leaf. "Designs on a new mule, friend? Is that it?"

The old farmer seemed to grow taller before them, his spine straightening, His eyes went white-lipped, round. "Are ye saying I stoled ye money, son?"

"How 'bout you empty the pockets of them dungarees and show me different."

"I never emptied my pockets for no man. Specially not no Gypsy."

Zeno grinned, his smile wide as a knife. "Well, there's a first time for everything."

Della, standing beside her husband, looked down to see a crude blade in the farmer's hand, a yarn-handled shard of iron cut from the leaf spring of a Ford. Behind her, she could hear the low gurgle of threat starting in the old dog's throat.

"Zeno," she said, clutching his wrist.

Zeno seemed only to calm, smiling at the blade just inches from his belly. He folded the cap of jingle money under his arm and reached slowly into the chest pocket of his flying coat, extracting his pint bottle of whiskey.

"Best ye give me my cap back," said the old farmer.

Zeno had a long pull off the bottle, then belched through his teeth. His cheeks, swarthy already, were dusked with oil smoke. A paler band across his eyes, where his goggles had rested. "With the money still in it, I take it?"

The farmer nodded.

Zeno stoppered the bottle. "You one-gallused son of a bitch."

"Best ye hurry it up," said the man, "before I get antsy." He wiggled the knife.

Zeno nodded and pulled the lapel of his coat to stow the bottle. Della knew his long-barreled English revolver was hanging right there under his armpit, unseen. The same one he'd carried over France.

"Zeno," she whispered.

He tucked away the bottle. His hand emerged without the gun. "You cut me, you're gonna have to cut her, too." He cocked his thumb at Della beside him. "You think you could cut on a thing pretty as that?"

The farmer looked at her, his tongue skidding over his gums. His face fell to the cruel implement in his hand, as if he'd found it lying in the grass.

"No," said Zeno, "I didn't reckon you could. She ain't no hog like you're used to." He pulled a small burlap sack from the patch pocket of his flying coat and unfolded it. He poured the dusty silvers into the bag, then held out the emptied hat.

The farmer looked at it. "Where's my cut?"

"It's folded square in the bib pocket of them dungarees you're wearing, now, isn't it?"

The man snatched up the cap, holding it to his chest. "Take ye little she-devil and Brit dog and get out of my pasture."

Zeno looked back at his old dog, Sark, whose long black beard was going gray. He was sitting erect, ears up like a little soldier, his hair all mussed from an afternoon of strangers' hands.

Casually, Zeno re-extracted the bottle of whiskey. "He's a Scot, actually. A Scottish terrier. Descended of the old Skye breeds, reared by the Highland clans for hunting badger and fox." Zeno had a short pull off his bottle, burped. "Tough little buggers, they are. Earl of Dumbarton called 'em *diehards*."

The man stepped forward, nearly touching the tip of the knife to Zeno's belly. "The hell is wrong with you, son?"

Zeno's eyes were glassy, saw Della. A long ways off.

"Have you ever been on fire?"

"On fire?" asked the man.

"On fire," said Zeno.

"Cain't say as I have, no."

Zeno pulled again on the bottle. His breath came hot through his clenched teeth. "You had, you wouldn't be afraid of no leaf spring knife."

Della took him by the arm. "Let's go," she said, pulling him toward the machine.

His face was smoked dark, his eyes white. He walked backward toward the machine, watching the farmer, who stood there slump-shouldered and bowlegged, holding the knife and cap.

"One day I'll get me a Vickers gun for this old crate," said Zeno. "Just like I had Over There. When I do, I'm gonna come find all you little four-flushing cheats and make Swiss cheese of your clapboard houses and imploding barns, your mules too stubborn to die at the end of your whips. Ever you hear a buzzing in the sky, maybe it's me coming down on you."

The farmer continued to stand there, like some crownless tree grown warped from the field.

Zeno dropped the emptied bottle in the grass and scrunched his shoulders, holding his hands gun-shaped on either side of his face. "Tat-tat-tat," he said. "Tat-tat-tat-tat-tat."

"Get in the goddamn cockpit," said Della, pointing him on.

He grinned slyly and handed her the sack of change, then slipped the dog's leash from the strut. "Come on, boy!"

Sark leapt into his arms.

Zeno climbed onto the wing and swung his leg over the leather coaming of the rear cockpit and nestled himself into the pilot's seat, the black terrier in his lap. "Let's get your goggles on, old man," he told the dog. "Let's get your harness."

The farmer stood there watching, unmoved, like the boy in the field during the show. The shadows were growing long, the light smoky. The bullbats were up, skittering over the field on dagger-shaped wings.

"We need to hurry," said Della.

They'd been caught aloft after dark before, trapped in the sea of night. The earth dark and foreign, no way to tell if a field was furrowed or stumped or full of small trees that would shred their machine into a litter of sailcloth and splintered spruce, their bodies scrawled red over the broken ground. They needed to find another pasture or untilled field or country lane to set down. Another night spent amid the slab-sided cattle of the state, the sleeping plows and prowling farm dogs.

Della pulled on a set of fingerless gloves and approached the big propeller, hewn from a single piece of oak, the swept blades capped with thin sheaths of metal to protect them from flying debris. She cranked the propeller in half turns once, twice, three times, like winding the hands of a giant courthouse clock.

"Mag on!" she called.

"Mag on!"

"Contact!"

"Contact!"

She gripped the upper blade of the prop and kicked one leg up, eye-high like a dancehall performer, then brought the whole weight of her body down on the blade, spinning it clockwise to the hub. The engine erupted to life, belching smoke, the propeller stuttering into a clear drum of power. The twin heads of the motor were exposed through the open cowling, the rocker arms bobbing up and down like tiny pump-jacks, the exhaust pipes blued with heat.

Della climbed into the front seat under the roof of upper wing, her hair fired by the machine-wind, her face stung by shreds of grass and blown dirt. She pulled on her leather cap, buckled the chin strap, and set her goggles over her eyes. Zeno taxied downwind, the dog sitting tall in his lap. Della watched the old farmer, planted yet in the pasture, his cap clutched over his heart, his hand shining with the iron blade.

She twisted in her seat, looking back at Zeno over the low windscreen. "We needed that paper money!"

Zeno squinted one eye down the side of the fuselage, aiming them for takeoff. "Paper money? He's a groundling, baby. We don't need it bad as him."

3

American Boy

OXFORD, MISSISSIPPI, 1910

*T*he secret was here. *The American Boy* magazine—"The Biggest, Brightest, Best Magazine for Boys in All the World"—whose recent issue included plans for a scale-model airplane. Billy pored over the drawings for hours on end, sometimes before the flickering vigilance of candlelight. Somewhere within these crisply penned lines and angles was the secret of flight. When school let out for the summer, he began.

He and his brothers scavenged beanpoles from their mother's garden, secret as elves, and hoarded day-old newspapers taken from trash bins and burn barrels and the men's rooms of various businesses on the Square: Chilton's Drugstore, Patton Hardware, Neilson's dry goods. They pried rusty nails from old boards with a cat's-paw, their tongues stuck through their teeth, while Billy scribbled calculations with a pencil nub. The plans in the magazine were for a bi-wing model of 1:32 scale. They were not yet full-scale men, but they were larger fractions than that. Billy dragged little brother Jack, ten now, to the auction yard and made him hang two-handed from the iron hook of the hog scale.

"How much?" asked Jack, his face mushed between his hanging arms.

Billy stared a long time at the needle quivering over the stamped brass measurement plate. He chewed his bottom lip. "Seventy-eight pounds," he said.

Jack dropped to the ground. "Hey, that's pretty good, right? Lemme see."

Billy turned so his brother couldn't see his notebook. "You're going on a reducing regimen, Jack. I'll write it up."

"The hell I am."

"No gravy or fatback for the rest of the summer," said Billy, making notes. "I need you no more than seventy-five pounds. Half scale."

"What? What for?"

"So you can fly the damn thing."

"Me?"

"I'm too big, and Johncy's too young. His faculties haven't reached a sufficient stage of maturation for aeronautics."

"The hell they ain't," said Johncy.

Jack rubbed his hands together. "You said we were weighing ourselves to see how big we'd grow up. Said you had a chart."

"I lied."

Jack stepped closer. Despite their age difference, he was nearly as tall as Billy now. "How do you know you're too big? You ain't weighed yourself."

Billy stiffened his spine. "I'm two years older than you."

Jack eyed him up, down. He was big for his age, and Billy small. "So?"

Billy looked down his nose and sniffed. "If you're scared, little brother, just say so."

They worked in the carriage shed, where they were largely unbothered, and the flier began to form beneath their summer-brown hands. Billy had painstakingly drawn the plans with pencil and yardstick, boy-scale, upon long rolls of wrapping paper filched from a Christmas trunk in the attic, and they sawed and hammered and glued long hours over a sawhorse table. Their foreheads blistered with sweat, the blueprints spotted with drips. Billy could hardly sleep at night. He was too eager for dawn, when the cool sun would slash through the windows of the shed, illuminating the ribbed wings of his creation. He boiled pilfered coffee grounds over blue flames of canned heat, feeding the double-strong coffee to his yawning wing-wrights as they arrived each morning still knuckling the sleep from their eyes.

Mammy Callie, who'd been born into slavery some seventy years before and reared each of the Falkner boys in turn, arrived in her crisp apron and kerchief and polished high-button shoes, her lower lip packed with snuff. While their mother might not know what they were doing in the shed, Mammy did. She brought little Dean, her charge, to visit his big brothers. He was three now, a toddler, and he released Mammy's hand to wonder wide-eyed at the skeleton of beanpoles and baling wire they'd constructed, like the featherlight architecture of an enormous dragonfly.

Billy watched this littlest of their line, and his chest swelled with pride. "Dean Swift Falkner," he said. "I believe you'll make an aeronaut one day."

They skinned the beanpole bones with sheets of newspaper, brushing coats of flour paste over headlines of James J. Jeffries, PUGILISM's IDOL, losing to challenger Jack Johnson in fifteen rounds, and Cy Young, pitcher for the Cleveland Indians, recording his five hundredth win. They pasted over news of a train collision in Middletown, Ohio, that killed nineteen people, and a tornado in Italy that killed sixty-one. In London, the body of a missing actress had been found. They read the father of classical ballet had died, along with the inventor of the hoop skirt.

"First observer of the planet Neptune kicked the old bucket," said Jack, eyes switchbacking down the obituary. "He was niney-eight."

Johncy leaned both-elbowed on the table, tiptoed. "Says here Russia and China are dividing their spheres of influence in Manchuria." He looked up. "What's 'sphere of influence' mean?"

"What's Manchuria?" asked Jack.

"Goddamn it," said Billy. "This ain't the place. You can read the paper on the crapper like a man."

Johncy had turned to the funnies. "Y'all seen this one with the brick-throwing mouse?"

Billy slid his brush into the nearest can. "Nuh-uh," he said, leaning over. "Lemme see."

Slowly the flour paste hardened on the wings so they shone like eggshell. Soon you could no longer read the smudged patchwork of train wrecks and flash floods that skinned the craft; the gubernatorial nominations and celebrity murders and ninth-inning home runs were fading into history. The boldest headlines were but vague bruises beneath the white layer of dope. Meanwhile, Billy dreamed of his own exploits stamped in the papers:

MISSISSIPPI BOY-GENIUS SENDS HIS BROTHER ALOFT!

BILLY FALKER: AERONAUTICAL PHENOM!

MOVE OVER, WRIGHT BROTHERS: IT'S THE FLYIN' FALKNERS!

He dreamed of brother Jack strapped in the cockpit of their shed-built flying machine, soaring high over the hills and cotton fields, tracing the lazy scrawl of the Yockeney-Patafa River from one thousand feet.

In the afternoons, while the paste dried on the wings, Billy would visit the house of his schoolmate, Estelle Oldham. Often the girl would be sitting in the parlor, watching the comings and goings of the street while the maid curled lengths of her hair around a broom handle, again and again, a mass of auburn curls that bounced on her shoulders like brassy springs. Billy would wave through the window, and they would walk to Davidson & Wardlaw's, the bookstore on the north side of the Square, reading poetry and magazines on the velvet couches of the back room, where Billy would carve the paste from under his nails with a penknife. Sometimes he would give her fragments of verse he worked on in the shed, in the early morning when the canned heat was hissing and the coffee boiling and his brothers were still in bed. Verses full of fauns and shepherds and sylvan nymphs. Sometimes he gave her verses copied straight from the English poets, waiting to see if she could tell the difference between his own poetry and theirs.

She always could.

"Louis Blériot flew the goddamn English Channel in a monoplane," said Billy. "It don't need two sets of wings to fly."

"But the plans call for two wings," said Jack. "A *bi*-plane."

The four Falkner brothers—Billy, Jack, Johncy, and little Dean—were standing before the pole-and-paper craft. Billy, who'd put the final touches on the flier himself, had just whipped the cover from the finished product like a magician revealing a rabbit or dove or woman sawn in two. The undercarriage had been adapted from an old wheelbarrow, with a hickory-spoked wheel and iron skids, and the seat was a cane-backed chair with the legs cut down. The propeller was pedal-powered, the chains and sprockets salvaged from a pair of ancient bicycles. But there was only a single set of wings.

"Damn the plans," said Billy. "An upper wing ain't but more drag, bud. It's for show. A token comfort for men lacking in nerve."

Jack crossed his arms. "You just don't want to build the second set."

"Hell," said Billy, "I design and construct a flying machine that will make my little brother famous, put his name in magazines and newspapers all across the land, exhibiting his pioneering spirit and daring, and this is what I get for my efforts?"

In truth, he'd run short on materials for an upper wing. They'd scavenged every last soiled grocery sack, old newspaper, and roll of wrapping paper from their homes and the homes of their friends. Billy had been at the verge of despair until he stumbled across the story of Louis Blériot, the French aviator who'd flown across the Channel in a single-wing craft of his own design, crash-landing near Dover Castle after a flight of 36 minutes, 30 seconds—and making headlines around the world.

Jack frowned. "It ain't your head on the chopping block."

Billy slid one arm over his brother's shoulder. "Listen, Jack, if a single wing is sufficient for a man to cross the English Channel, it's plenty for this crate to fly, right? And if it makes you feel better, we'll knock out a couple planks to lighten the fuselage, and you can leave your cap and shoes on the ground for the maiden flight, even less weight." With his free hand, Billy gestured into the mote-filled air of the shed, as if arranging something out of the dust and light. "Then we'll find us a nice, high bluff to shove off from, and this here ship will find some of that good, solid, thick Mississippi air beneath her wings—and, bud, she'll rise just like a kite." He looked at his brother. "Child's play, Jack."

The boys stared into the air before them, openmouthed, as if their brother's very words might stir a wind beneath the wings of the ship, lifting it before their eyes. Even little Dean Swift seemed rapt, his face cast cherublike amid the swirling dust motes.

Then brother Jack shook off the spell. "It ain't your head on the chopping block, Billy. I'm the one has to fly this damn *monoplane*." He spat out the last word as if it were something foreign, despicable. Perhaps French.

Billy shrugged. "It ain't my fault that today, in the year of our Lord nineteen hundred and ten, you are exactly one-half the size of a full-scale, hundred-and-fifty-pound man, now, is it? This here is destiny, Jack. You cannot deny it."

"Except you were the one drew the plans."

Billy squeezed his shoulder. "And it was mortal men wrote the Bible, bud. Wasn't it, now?"

They stood on the bluff at the back end of the pasture, which ended in a sheer, fifteen-foot drop to the broken earth below. The airplane sat at the top of the slope, slightly cocked in the grass, the wings spread jaunty, and pilot Jack looked like a ghost. His face was paper white, as if he, too, were constructed of beanpoles and newsprint and paste.

Before climbing into the pilot's seat, he shook hands with each of his brothers in turn, even little Dean. Billy was last in line, bobbing on his heels with anticipation. When he took Jack's hand, he felt the clamminess of his little brother's palm and noticed the beads of sweat perched on his upper lip, but there was something else, too: the beady steel in the boy's eyes. The mettle. Billy's heart swelled like a balloon in his chest.

He could not send his brother over the edge.

He allowed Jack to climb into the cockpit and pull the goggles over his eyes and test the spin of the propeller, the oiled rattle of the bicycle chain. He allowed his brother to swallow his fear a last time and raise his right hand, beginning the countdown, while Billy crouched at the tail, ready to drive him with terrific speed over the ledge, into glory or dust.

"Three-two-one . . . Go!" cried Jack.

Billy pushed but weakly on the tail; the craft hardly budged on its iron skids. "Hellfire," he said. "Jack, I need you to get out and push. I ain't strong enough."

"Me?"

"I need those big horse legs of yours, pushing. You and Johncy both."

"Who's gonna fly her?"

"I am."

"I thought you were too heavy."

"You were all in," said Billy. "We all saw it. Now, get out and push."

The boy-built craft skidded and rattled toward the edge, Billy's brothers huffing and slavering with effort, Billy pedaling with all his might, the sprockets squeaking, the propeller blades lunging through their arcs. Then the grade steepened, the machine leapt down the slope, and his brothers fell away rolling in the grass. The edge roared toward him, the contraption's skids banging through the grass like a sleigh's, the wings shuddering, and then he was over the bluff's edge, into space, the air whispering against the hollow planes of the wings. His brothers were rising to their knees in his wake, willing him to fly, and he did, he did. For one long, glorious moment, he floated in defiance of everyone who would've said he couldn't do it. Who would've called his dream preposterous, too big for reality. He was the first boy in the state of Mississippi, if not the world, to fly.

Then the nose lurched downward and the wings folded and the ship plummeted beneath him, as if the hand of gravity or fate or God had caught up with him, swatting his ship from the sky. The red soil of North Mississippi filled his view, gullied and cracked like a broken heart. He felt a strange, giddy squirt in the dark of his chest just before impact.

The craft shattered like a hundredfold crunch of bones, and he was thrown tumbling and rolling inside his smashed dream, his mouth filled with dirt and newsprint and the tang of blood. Then stillness. He lay faceup, wreathed in wreckage, faded headlines and funnies and obituaries floating about him like white little birds.

Jack and Johncy came sliding and scrambling down the red face of the bluff. Soon they stood over him, their mouths hanging open.

"Guess he was too big after all," said Johncy.

Jack squatted, his legs bowed wide. "Yeah," he said. "Could be he's more of a man than we thought."

Billy hardly heard them. A dazed smile hung on his face; his goggles were skewed. He was staring up at the cloud-painted sky, the heights he'd nearly reached.

4

Coal-Holders

SOUTH GEORGIA, 1933

*T*hey flew west toward the descending sun. It was almost summer, oven-hot even under the dusking sky, the western clouds red-veined with light. The wash from the propeller smelled of gasoline and burnt oil; Zeno said the piston rings were starting to go. It was always something.

The earth lay beneath them in an irregular stitching of cotton and to-bacco fields, faint geometric shapes like patchwork. Denim-clad farm-hands were trudging home from the fields, strung like little blue ants along the sandy roads, heeding dinner bells. They paused and stared up, dark-faced and light, as if some miracle passed over them. It was 1933. Some had still never seen a flying machine.

The fields pushed up against slender swaths of longleaf pine, remnants of the virgin pine forests that had for centuries been ax-cut and assembled into colossal rafts, floated down the winding brown rivers of the state, and sold to the sawmills perched on the coast. Della was from one of those port towns, Darien, her family blood-tied to the original Scottish Highlanders commissioned by General James Oglethorpe, founder of Georgia, to establish an outpost in the 1700s to defend Savannah against Spanish raiders from the south. The Highland Rangers had originally named the settlement New Inverness, building a fort, clashing with Spanish and Indian forces, and petitioning the Georgia governor in 1739 against the introduction of slavery. When their early crop harvests failed, they quickly turned to cattle and timber. Della's forefathers had lived on these trees since the eighteenth century. They'd sold them as ship masts and shake shingles, as lumber and staves and naval stores.

But the flow of timber, once thought limitless, had dwindled from a century of overcutting, and the Georgia ports had starved. The old barons had lost their ships and warehouses and mills. They'd hanged themselves from barn rafters and fled in buggies in the dead of night, their creditors left to pick over the scraps. Her own father, Colonel Bain Mackintosh, had put a filigreed shotgun to his heart.

Della herself had heard the shot. Had been first to push wide the study door. First to see the crimson flashed upon the wall.

Now she shook the image from her mind, looking back over the edge of the cockpit. The falling sun caught on a vast field of new stumps, the sawn pines flaring like coals against the darker earth. There was a road torn through the clear-cut, the earth grooved by endless skids of timber mule-drawn to waiting trucks.

Della turned and pointed for Zeno to see. "There!" she said. "Wide enough?"

Zeno nodded and jabbed a wing toward the road. The craft began sliding from the sky, bouncing on the updrafts while the fields beneath them tilted and wheeled, the crude strip pivoting like the needle of a compass. The sun rolled along the horizon, striking them sidewise. The propeller blazed, a slow turning of scimitars, and Della watched the distant shadow of the craft undulating across the earth. Then they were out of the light, into the gloom of the lower world, and Zeno was frowning, working stick and rudder against the rough air, the road throbbing upward to greet them. Closer, she could see the once-forest littered with a wreckage of busted logging chain and leather harness, fractured ax handles and broken dog hooks.

Zeno flared the nose and chopped the power. The wheels banged once on the road, hard, then settled down, the thin tires bouncing through the ruts. The propeller jerked to a stop, cocked at a slant, and the craft seemed to wilt slightly as it slowed. Zeno was already clambering from the cockpit, Sark tucked under one arm. Soon he was standing wide-legged on the edge of the road, his scarf dangling in the breeze as he and the dog urinated side by side.

Della looked to the far tree line, set like a black wall against the dusked sky, and she saw firelight trembling in the piney hollows. Then there were men in the clearing, standing like a crop of tall-cut stumps while fireflies rose burning from the grass around them.

Zeno, seeing them, clapped his hands, rubbing them like a man whittling fire with a stick. "Let's see if they don't got a drop to drink."

They were timber cutters, Black men in billowy white shirts, their straw hats worn high aback their heads like fraying halos. They stood awestruck around the machine. Some reached out to touch an aileron or rudder or the great twin-bladed propeller. They had the smell of working men, sweat and smoke and saw oil, and the build of those who'd spent years in these woods. Their collarbones were yoked and capped with muscle, the fat bellies of their forearms twined with veins, their eyes sizing up everything for the fastest way to cut it to the ground. They invited the fliers to their timber camp pitched just within the tree line.

Zeno strode among them, already at their center, expounding on the rudiments of flight. Already a tin canteen had found its way into his hand, his mouth hissing after every swig. Della followed a little ways behind the band, watching the sawn pine float past her in the dark. Some of these trees had been green little bottlebrushes when the first European anchors dropped in the rivers and bays. They'd sheltered deer and turkey and quail, even the old tribes of which so little remained—the chance arrowhead turned up by harrow or plow, destined for a farmhouse mantel or study drawer.

The timber-cutters lived in green canvas tents set helter-skelter beneath the pines. Passing one, Della smelled the thick odor of mildew. The tents seemed to exhale it through their vented flaps. There was a slip-tongue skidder parked amid the trees, the man-sized wagon wheels rimmed with thin bands of iron. Nearby, a pack of mules in a crude corral munched their dinner of oat feed. The men's tools were stored beneath a large canvas fly strung between two arrow-straight trees, the green flaps pegged wide. The edges of felling axes and cross-cut saws gleamed in the shivering firelight.

The firepit, set in a circular jaw of stones, was surrounded by a ring of sitting stumps. The fire bobbed heavenward, an orange spear point tapping the underside of a cook pot hung from a tripod. One of the men removed the lid with a rag and doled steaming helpings of beans and fatback onto tin plates. They gave the first portion to Della along with a spoon. A young member of the crew conveyed the second plate into the outer darkness, a white napkin draped over one arm. Della watched him dissolve into the night.

Zeno was still talking. The men sat swabbing their food with tufts of biscuit, enthralled by this mustachioed creature dropped out of the sky. Soon a stone jug was circulating hand to hand.

"Bernoulli was a Swiss," said Zeno. "It's a simple law of fluid mechanics."

His big hands were cutting through the air, edged like wings, his plate forgotten on his knee. He was demonstrating the faster movement of wind over the curved top of an airfoil, creating an area of low pressure. Sark sat between his boots, his goggles hanging from his neck like a collar, his jaw slightly open. Lately, Della had noticed a slight cloudiness in the aging dog's eyes, but hadn't said anything to Zeno. Meanwhile, his master hadn't stopped talking.

"Now there's some people say it isn't Bernoulli's principle that explains it but Newton's third law of physics."

The jug reached Della. She hooked two fingers through the small curl of handle and swung the jug over the back of her arm.

Zeno, seeing her across the flames, stumbled midsentence. "That explains," he said, swallowing. "That explains . . ."

She lifted the heavy jug on the back of her elbow, letting the whiskey slide hot into her waiting mouth.

"*Lift*," said Zeno.

She knew the others were watching, too, her metallic suit glowing like lava against her skin, her white throat pumping the whiskey down. It was backwoods busthead, through and through, a noxious fulminate that seemed capable of detonation without careful handling. Still, her face did not skew or bunch; she loosed the hot fumes through her teeth, passing the jug to Zeno. He was through the rough outer bands of the night's drunk, sliding into the electric calm of the eye.

Her plate was mainly finished, a lardy curd congealing along the edges. She set it between her boots for Sark. Now that supper was done, the men threw extra logs on the fire. Firelight crawled the neighboring pines, and Della saw the trees here were catfaced—the lower bark stripped away and the trunks marked with V-shaped cuts, like the up-turned whiskers of a cat. They looked like carved totems of some kind, the god-beasts of ancient tribes. They'd been bled of their resin, used to make turpentine and pitch and tar. Now they awaited the ax.

"We're working our way west," Zeno told the men, wiping his mouth with the back of his hand. "Hoping to join up with a real flying circus or else make it into the movies."

His words alighted in Della's chest. To hear him say it, that they were destined west, for the Golden State, where her own mother, she knew, had dreamed of going, jumping from stage to screen. There, to hear it told, a woman could command the true value of her worth.

"*Goddamned sky tramps.*"

The words came stony and edged, flung meanly from the dark. A white man with a giant black beard followed behind them, holding an empty plate. His shirtfront was spilled open, his hairy chest shining with sweat. His suspenders looked hastily donned.

"Air Gypsies," he said, "suckling the dry teat of the South."

Zeno did not stiffen or jump. The corner of his mouth curled slightly up. "Gypsies," he said. "You say it like a slur."

The man sat on a stump on the opposite end of the fire. He was the foreman, it was plain. His beard was curly and wild, like the rich black hair between a man's legs. It haloed his face like a mane. It was a red face, Della saw, square and built like brick.

He summoned the jug to himself with two upturned fingers, short-cutting the line. "I bet it's petrol you come for, ain't it?"

Zeno's eyes shone like double bits of silver—a risen light. "If you're selling, we have."

The foreman raised the jug high on the back of his arm, never taking his eyes from Zeno. "I damn-sure ain't giving it for free."

"No," said Zeno. "We wouldn't want to tax your generosity."

The man swigged from the jug, then held it dangling between his knees, hooked on the end of his finger. The others looked longingly at the un-passed whiskey. The man looked at Della. "What you got to pay with?"

"Why, aeroplane rides, come morning," said Zeno. "It's too dangerous to fly at night."

Della felt the man's eyes roving her, sliding over the swells and valleys that made her.

"What if that ain't the kind a ride I'm after? What if a night ride is just what I need?"

The look on Zeno's face didn't change. His face was shining, wired with light. "Then you better look somewhere else, friend."

The foreman looked back at him, cocking his head. "What was you, aviator in the war?"

"That's right," said Zeno. "Lafayette Escadrille."

The squadron, formed before the United States entered the war, had been made up of American volunteer pilots whose aircraft, uniforms, and commander were all French. Their fighters bore the painted heads of Chief Sitting Bull in his feathered warbonnet, roaring into the wind. All in all, some two hundred American pilots would fly for the French during the War—thirteen became aces and fifty-nine died in combat. Several did both.

The man raised the jug, pointing with one finger. "I seen your kind, buzzing high up over the trenches in your little double-wing kites, flirting with your Vickers guns. Flying home to a hot supper in some country estate, drinking brandy and smashing every slit in France while we was sleeping cold in holes we dug, covered in lice and rats and shit, listening to the poor sons of bitches caught out in the barbwire, dying with their insides turned out."

"Oh," said Zeno, "I don't believe it was so fun as that."

The man sipped from the jug, a string of whiskey beads left quivering in his beard. "It was a sea of bodies down there. A black sea. After the rain, they'd start turning up from last week's charge or the previous spring's fool attempt to move the line. A crop of the dead spurting up, pale as worms, arms and feet sticking out. We had this hand come out of the trench wall, half clasped like it was holding a bottle. We used to shake it before going over the top. For luck. Meanwhile, there you was, high and mighty over it all. And here you are now, cock-poking clouds while the rest of us work the earth." The man leaned farther toward the fire, the snarls of his beard edged with light. "What you had up there was the clean death, while the rest of us died in shit."

Zeno leaned back, spreading wide his arms. "Ah, 'the clean death of a beast.' 'I would not give it to trulls who made a mockery of my mother— you sluts who lay with suitors.'"

"Say what?"

"So quoth Telemachus, before he hanged the dozen maidservants who'd lain with the suitors of his mother. *The Odyssey*, friend. That's where your words are from."

"The hell they are. What are you, some kind of a schoolteacher?"

"A student, merely," said Zeno. "A long time ago. An aspirant classicist."

"I never did know a poem-quoter with sand or sack."

Zeno leaned forward, still smiling, his mustaches spread winglike over his bared teeth. "I propose a contest. A test of will. If I win, you give us the petrol we need to fly far, far away from here, free to continue suckling the dusty pap of the rustic hordes."

The big logger set the jug between his boots. "And if I win?"

Della watched Zeno.

He looked at her, his eyes slit like little swords. "What do you think, my sweet?"

Della looked at the logger. She looked him up and down, her chin strong. "I wonder if his prick is as big as his mouth."

The men laughed into their fists even as the foreman tried to cut them silent with his eyes. He looked at Della. "It's big enough for yours."

The two coals were selected according to similitude. They had to be equally sized, from the same part of the fire, to ensure that neither man was given unfair advantage. Two stumps were set close together, and the men knelt before them, facing each another. The camp cook stood over them, a tonged coal the size of a pebble held smoking in each hand. Zeno removed his flying jacket, folding and handing it to Della, then began rolling up his left shirtsleeve, the curved handle of his Webley revolver wobbling in his shoulder holster. The logger, rolling up his own sleeve and licking his palm, eyed the gun.

When the shirt was nearly to Zeno's elbow, he hooked one finger under a nearly invisible seam on his skin and peeled a long, sheer, flesh-colored tube of silk from his arm, like the shed skin of a snake, revealing the cruel monstrosity of his hand and forearm. It was like an untended candle, the flesh melted and re-hardened into an irregular form. When he made a fist, it looked like a blackthorn shillelagh, gnarled and scar-hardened.

The logger's teeth flared from his beard. "What in the fuck is that?"

Zeno handed Della the silk glove. It had been intended, originally, to be worn with an expensive peignoir, a garment a woman would wear while brushing her hair or padding down the plush halls of an ocean liner or sleeping car in the dead of night, heading to a washroom or whispered bunk. It was the same color as his skin, nearly indistinguishable unless you knew to look.

Now he held the naked hand to the light, spreading the fingers like knobbed shafts of deadwood. "It's my arm," he said, looking at the logger. "You don't like it?"

"It ain't fair."

Zeno contemplated the once-melted flesh, pursing his lips. "No," he said. "Surely not."

"I mean it's a unfair advantage."

Zeno looked innocently at the man, and only Della could see the pleasure quivering at the corners of his mouth. "Did I not earn such advantage, sir?"

The logger's beard seemed wilted, down-pointed and long. He was looking around the fire for support, finding only a ring of blank faces. "Earn it?" he said. "You ain't asked for that to happen to you."

Zeno leaned forward. "You mean it was no consequence of my will? If I had lit my own self on fire, then, perhaps, I could rightly avail myself of whatever advantage it lent me in games of backwoods coal-holding? Then perhaps it would be fair? Like a pugilist who's thrust his fists against a fence post ten thousand times so that his callused knuckles will not break upon the bony point of another man's jaw?"

"Yeah," said the logger. "Yeah, that's about right."

Zeno sat back. "But did I not ask to be placed in the cockpit of a 'double-wing kite,' as you called it, made of matchstick wood and cradling an eight-headed stove one thousand feet in the air, full of hot oil and petrol, the wings doped with flammable nitrocellulose, while a searing hail of lead roared down from the sky and up from the earth? Did I not, like so many others, carry this pistol in case of just such eventuality"—he tapped the weapon under his arm—"so that I might remove myself from the burning cockpit, having no parachute?"

The logger leaned forward, setting his hand palm-up on the stump before him, as if awaiting the drop of an owed coin. "Maybe you should've used that gun."

Zeno set down his own palm, his unburned one.

"Zeno!" said Della, grabbing his arm.

He ignored her, his body heavy as stone despite her tug. He nodded to the cook, who placed the coals, white with heat, simultaneously into their waiting hands. The logger screamed through his teeth, the coal jumping from his hand almost instantly, while Zeno sat quivering for long seconds, his face bubbling with sweat, his eyes fixed on the seed of agony boring itself into his flesh.

"I was raised a Catholic," he said through his teeth. "I did not wish to trade this fire for hellfire hereafter."

Della kicked his arm, sending the coal flying into the night, flaring its red belly as it went.

"You stupid son of a bitch," she said, looking down into Zeno's up-turned face, which shone like a weeping child's.

"Baby," he said.

Zeno followed her through the trees and field of stumps, back to the airplane. His footfalls heavy, uneven with drink, Sark steering him like a tugboat at the side of a listing freighter. They slept beneath the wing of the Jenny, as they so often did, Zeno curled up like a great animal beneath his coat, blubbering sweetly to the dog of his wife's beauty, her daring, until he fell asleep, his bulk rising and falling with faint whistles. She lay on her back, straight as a corpse, her hands laced across her breast, looking up at the ribbed body of wing. Before falling asleep, she reached up to touch the hardened cloth, tracing her finger down the long, slender bone of spruce.

In the morning, Zeno stood on the far side of the fuselage, vomiting, as axes and saws sounded in the distant woods. His right hand was swollen and red, the palm bubbled. A pair of ten-gallon petrol drums sat on the side of the road, left in the night.

5

Snake-Lips

His mind was a storm, a blackish cloud of gnatlike machines wheeling and raveling in deadly abandon, tying their dark contrails into ever tighter knots of smoke. Each chattered and pulsed with machine-gun fire, spitting death through the pewter sky, and the names of the pilots burned like poetry in his brain: Boelcke and Immelmann, Ball and Bishop, Garros and Guynemer. These scarfed and goggled knights of the air, with their swagger sticks and riding breeches, their flying caps set on so bold. These men, their names stamped thick and black in the newspapers, who died in streaks of heavenly fire. Surely their boots rang loud on the planks of French taverns and wine cellars. Surely they had no shortage of women draped from their arms, their breasts mounded silver with the finest sheen of sweat—

"*Billy.*" His mother's voice.

He straightened. "Yes'm?"

"The man said to look at the camera."

The brothers were having their portrait taken by the town photographer.

"I was looking at it."

"He was off in the clouds," said his father, sniffing. "Like always."

The photographer retreated back beneath his dark cloth, removing the brass cap of the lens, and Billy stared into the glass eye of the device. Here he could see his brothers reflected in skewed miniature, sealed into a tiny world their own. They looked so soft in the lens, like a rash of flesh-colored ghosts. He stared hard, his head shaking slightly, as if he might shatter the glass with his eyes.

His father, in his rocker on the porch, roared with pleasure. In his hands was the sibling portrait, a black-and-white fortress of unsmiling faces. Still, there was a certain unity in the shot. Each visage a semblance of the other, like steeples of the same faith, and a similar rake of the shoulders. A pride evident even in Billy's own carriage—a boy who'd been made to wear one of those braces advertised in the back pages of the newspaper, a laced canvas vest intended to correct an adolescent stoop. There was Jack on one side of him, big as Billy despite his age, and Johncy on the other, thirteen now, smaller and handsomer than both of them. Lastly, there was little Dean Swift, a white-frocked angel of a boy, waist high, who seemed to radiate light. He was the best of them, there was little doubt.

Their star.

Of their faces, Billy's was the least clear. The most ghostly. It was as if he vibrated at a different frequency than the rest of them, a higher pitch, and this could not be captured so conclusively in the wooden box of the camera. The lower half of his face hung in shadow, his mouth a thin, lipless slit. Only his eyes were certain, coal-black and smoldering.

His father was tapping this eldest son's face with his forefinger, leaving an iridescent sheen on the photograph. "Look it here," he said. "Old Snake-Lips at it again."

Billy turned and walked from the porch. His fists balled hard at his sides, the pain scraping through the chambers of his heart.

Estelle had the freshest face, like the white flesh of a pear, and a slight upturn of the nose. Her hair was a kingdom, curled in turrets of honey and oak, and she shared Billy's love of the English poets. Keats and Swinburne and Houseman, whose volumes he carried belt-bound into

the woods, spending long days lost among sunny meadows and chattering birds and word-song—days he should have been in school.

Estelle was slightly older than he, but it had never seemed so until
these last few years. The hard breastless seed she'd been had budded,
bursting into the light. Her body had swelled with little hillocks and
valleys, a whole new country of pale flesh rising beneath her clothes.
How he wanted to send the sled-runners of his fingers across that landscape, to blush her skin with the heat of his breath. In her presence, he
felt like a red-breasted bird that could not speak; only sing or screech.
For so long, he'd had her all to himself. The long swings on the porch,
the afternoons in the bookstore, the days spent reading on the benches
of the Square. Nothing between them, no suitors or lost breath. All her
smiles just for him.

Now callers came like pilgrims to her porch, university men dog-
eyed with desire. They offered fraternity pins and rides in daddy-bought
roadsters, well-sleeved arms for weekend dances, and Billy watched her
smile upon their offerings. Her teeth like a knife.

Brother Jack, fifteen now, sat cross-legged in an aisle of the university library, Billy beside him. Giant Ole Miss annuals were draped over their
laps. On the glossy pages, gentleman suitors with gleaming black hair and
square white teeth. Sons of Mississippi, with names like Thad or Greer
or Finch. They were in their prime, beaming like newly anointed saints.
They seemed so sure of themselves, as if they could bend the world into
their orbit—even the kind of women they didn't deserve. Jack watched
his older brother, who stared into the yearbook with singular concentration, his head quivering ever so slightly, as if trying to ignite the paper by
force of mind. He'd dropped out of high school twice now—perhaps for
good this last time—and now spent his days haunting the Ole Miss cam-
pus, writing poetry and staring at the clouds.

The thump of a dropped book and Jack wheeled his head around,
looking for the brown-skirted librarian who might come to beat this
pair of town boys from the hallowed aisles of her domain. None came.
A cough in the distance, a turned page. He looked back to Billy, who'd

taken no notice of the sound, then down to the annual in his own lap. He turned the page and gasped, knuckling his older brother on the knee.

"This'n beats the band, Bill. Look." He pointed to the portrait of one Cornell Sidney Franklin, a senior law student from Columbus, Mississippi. Jack read the young man's chosen inscription aloud. "'I want to grow as beautiful as God meant me to be.'" He looked gape-jawed at his older brother. "You got to be shitting me, Bill."

Billy looked at the photograph briefly, then snapped his own book closed with a huff.

Jack scratched his head. "Is it just me, or have I seen this one up at the Oldhams' house, courting Estelle?"

Billy didn't answer. He rose, leaving the annual at his feet, and snapped his tie high against his throat, as if preparing for an inspection.

Jack was still staring at the annual. "Christ on a crutch, Billy. I didn't know God made jackasses of this caliber."

Billy held his chin high, perfecting the knot of his tie. His eyes flicked down at his younger brother. "All over hell and creation, Jack. Calibers you wouldn't believe."

"What are you going to do?"

"About the jackasses of the world?"

"About Estelle."

Billy smoothed the sleeves of his coat, straightened his spine, and stuck his finger into the small watch pocket of his vest, as if checking for something valuable, a jewel or ring. Then he marched out of the library, silent, like a boy going into battle.

6

Anything

*T*hey came storming across the country in the wake of the Armistice, a swarm of mayflies hatched in the aerodromes of France, featherlight fliers buzzing from field to field, town to town, looping and barreling in brainless mania, flying into trees and lakes and fields of cotton and corn, slamming into farmhouses and clocktowers, exploding before the heat-flared faces of the crowds. They died by fire, as they had in the war, or were ripped asunder in the violence of impact, goggled ex-aces who could find no way down from the high of combat save this. They traded enemy guns for hail and downpour, lightning and the crushing winds of anvil-shaped clouds. They died in legion, short-lived, while the cities roared, and when the country crashed, they flew only lower, faster, to draw their pennies from the crowds.

Zeno landed at the Mackintosh & Co. sawmill in the spring of 1930, and the saw hands and stevedores came stunned from their labor to marvel at his machine. It sat in the grass like a sailcloth wasp, the nose turned up, wearing a blond mustache of propeller, slightly skewed. Della was out there on horseback, surveying the grounds with a man from the bank. She was twenty years old. Her father was dead, buried in a narrow mahogany casket, the invoice yellowing beneath an ink blotter on his old desk, and her mother was more than ten years gone, killed in the influenza epidemic of 1919. The woman had been a firecracker to hear it told, a red-haired actress who'd performed on the stages of Savannah, her name in lights, and founded a theater for the children of the city's stevedores and mill hands—much to the chagrin of the town's society women.

Della's father, Colonel Bain Mackintosh, had served in the Third Georgia Volunteer Infantry in Cuba and maintained the last sawmill on the Darien River until Black Tuesday, 1929, when the market crashed and the credit dried up and the ink of ten thousand ledgers across the land ran red, the world toppling about him like a forest of sudden-cut timber. Perhaps the Colonel had looked out at the loyal bellies that depended on him—men whose grandfathers had ridden the great timber rafts down the snaking rivers, singing chanteys as they rolled the lumber onto three-masted schooners—and thought he owed them his life. His honor. Perhaps it was the only way to rid himself of the shame.

Since her father's death, Della had been trying to sit at his old desk, sized like one of the giant rafts that used to float downriver. The house was empty and dark and she was alone. Her only relations were a pair of widowed aunts who came on Sundays to cluck at the poor state of affairs and help themselves to their dead brother's gin. Women who raked too hard at the red rat's nest of Della's hair and whispered in her ear of widowers nearly her father's age, with lumped throats and trembling hands, who would love to wife a pretty young thing like her.

Her mother had hated them both.

More than once, alone at her father's old desk in that empty house, the ledgers and letters of creditors piled at her elbows, Della felt a coldness pass through the room. The ashes sat lumped in the hearth, unstoked, the dim blue house silent but for the pop and groan of old joinery. More than once, in the beadboard twilight of the room, Della listened to the croak of the chair as she spun slowly in place, waiting to see the red feathers of her father's heart flung yet upon the wall, his blood driven deep into the plaster. She was almost surprised to find the surface scrubbed clean, pocked like an acne-scarred face.

There wasn't enough lumber coming down the river, and even less credit to buy it. There was nothing to do but sign the petition of bankruptcy, surrendering the mill to what was left of the bank. Mackintoshes had worn tartans and fought Cuban grenadiers with two-handed claymores. They'd worked with axes and adzes, squaring beams of heart pine and dragging them to the riverbank with teams of oxen, floating them downriver in makeshift rafts held together with iron boom-dogs. They'd imported machinery for the first steam-powered sawmills, providing the lumber for the great sailing ships of the northern ports, themselves part owners in barks and brigs, schooners and steamships. The riverbanks were still lined with the stone ballast of those enormous holds. They'd survived hurricanes and fever and the burning of Darien during the Civil War. Staring at the paperwork, thinking of the unpaid debts and shrunken bellies, the decimated forests and giant clear-cuts, Della thought less and less of how her father could do what he'd done.

When the pilot stepped down from the cockpit, he had a small black dog clutched under one arm and a Health-o-Meter bathroom scale under the other. He promptly set the scale on a nearby stump. The bezel was dented, the red needle slightly drunk.

"Rides!" he called out. "Two cents per pound!"

The mill hands were turning out their pockets, picking through lint for stray change and crinkled bills. They were lining up before the stump, holding their hats in their hands, suddenly conscious of their weight. They spat and sucked in their guts, as if that would help. Some ran off to the mill latrine—anything to save a few cents. The world was going to hell; they would fly high above it all, if only for a moment.

Della rode to the head of the line, her riding boots bouncing in the stirrups. She looked down at this mustachioed pilot, his face dusked with oil smoke, his breeches rumpled and stained like those of an old hobo. He was the size of a three-door icebox. The small black terrier huddled close against his leg, long-faced and bearded like a creature of fairy tale, his black-bright eyes belying the gray in his muzzle. The man eyed her and the horse she rode, as if estimating their weight.

"If you want that specimen of horseflesh to sprout wings, like white Pegasus, it ain't going to be on the back of my aeroplane."

She stepped the horse forward, cutting him in half with her shadow. "These men work for wages. Who said you could take them from their labor?"

His goggles gleamed on his forehead like a second set of eyes. "You saying I can't?"

She looked down the long-assembled line of prospective air-riders, men with sawdust in their lungs and pine sap under their nails, their faces soft with wonder. She touched the envelope nestled against her ribs, so thin already. Her only money left in the world—her only savings— and yet.

She swung off the horse and handed him the reins. "How much for you to take all of them?"

The foot of the island was a forest of ship masts and boiler stacks, crisscrossed aerials and wind-strung signal flags: the fleet of tramp steamers that once carried whole tracts of milled pineland in their bellies. When her turn came, it all fell away, the ships shrinking to the size of washtub toys as the machine climbed high over the coast. The rivers and creeks shone beneath their wings, a thousand water snakes crawling through the brown-gold marshes and evergreen islands that edged the continent. Up here, the world opened wide, unfurling west, revealing a vast nation between the seas. A world so much bigger than she could imagine inside the crushing walls of her father's study, trapped between the ginny whispers of her aunts, telling her to latch herself to a man, to bow and serve or else she'd find herself alone, no roof over her head.

Her mother had dreamed of going to California, auditioning in Hollywood—an agent had even written her. There, he said, women were not just acting but also writing, directing, producing. Wielding power unheard of in other realms. Della's mother, reluctant to part from her husband and little girl and children's theater, had put off the journey again and again, only to die with her train already booked. Della didn't want to suffer a similar fate. She had to act. She couldn't be anchored to the earth, to a mahogany desk and scarred wall and her father's casket moldering six feet underground, right there next to her mother's. She knew she'd end up there, sure as they had, unless she got out.

She went to Zeno that night. She found him snoring beneath the wing of his machine, a pint bottle of whiskey empty at his side. The dog lay like a small shadow nearby, his muzzle resting on his paws. He raised his head, ears perked, but didn't growl. She pressed herself against this man from the sky, pushing her face into his neck, her knee into his crotch. He smelled of whiskey and smoke and the day's long sun, like the stable grooms and mill hands she sometimes fantasized about, slipping her hand beneath her nightgown.

She would fly from this place.

Zeno growled, coming awake, and she felt him harden against her thigh. Soon his tongue was swirling in her mouth, his mustache scratching her cheeks and throat. He ungloved his right hand and palmed her belly, then slipped his fingers under the waistband of her breeches. She turned onto her back and groaned, twisting and agonized. This was a first. Her suitors had been trembling boy-men with soft hands and pink faces, or else aging widowers in search of second wives. She imagined them sleeping in echoing bedchambers, reading their scripture before bed, setting their eyeglasses on the nightstand before blowing out the lamp.

Zeno snorted and sputtered like an engine, splitting her like a wishbone beneath him. She bit her thumb when it hurt. He squirted himself hot across her belly, and she was almost relieved, thinking it was done. Instead he slid down her belly, gently, arranging her legs just so. He lowered his face between her thighs. Soon she was arched beneath him, shuddering, her fingers snarled through his hair.

Afterward, she felt flushed, radiant. Her muscles twitching like a horse throwing flies. "Where in the world did you learn that?"

He lay on his back, eyes closed, his hands laced across his chest. One still gloved. "France," he said.

In the morning, she woke alone in the shadow of the wing. The sun was barely up, a watery light in the east, and Zeno was already dressed, his coat belted, his scarf dangling from his neck. He was circling the aircraft, tugging on wires and struts, working the rudder back and forth with his hands.

She sat up. "Take me with you," she said.

He frowned, looking at her. "With me? Where to?"

"Wherever you're going. Away from here."

He smoothed the bristles of his mustache with a gloved hand. "Why would I do that?"

"Last night. It doesn't have to be the only night."

He crossed his arms and leaned against the fuselage. "That's a very nice offer. Truly, it is. But I got more than that little thing to keep in the air. I got to keep this whole crate in the sky."

"I can help you," said Della. "I'll do anything."

His eyes glided over the long wing that shadowed her. "Anything?"

They were aloft again, higher this time. The wind shrieked, pummeling her, ripping the hair from beneath the leather flying cap that Zeno had given her. The coast lay two thousand feet below, the edge of the nation crumbled into islands and hummocks and bights, speckled with oyster boats and shrimp trawlers. There was the Altamaha, the great serpent of river that once fed the mills of her forefathers, and there the Port of Darien with its fleet of empty steamers. Zeno turned inland, the earth rolling beneath them like a globe, revealing cotton fields and farm roads, and Della felt a tap on her shoulder. She looked back at Zeno, goggled and scarfed in the rear cockpit, and he was pointing toward the wing.

Anything.

How easy to stay fixed in the dark nest of the cockpit, refusing to rise. To return instead to the huge desk in the cold office, the overstuffed chair that groaned like a ghost. The shot-scarred wall, soon to be bank property. The memories of a man who would have wanted, more than anything, to see her fly free of the world that had collapsed on him.

Della's fingers found the nearest wire. It hummed in her hand, singing with power, filling her with vibrations. She tore herself upright from the seat, standing into the full blast of wind, and threw one booted leg over the edge of the cockpit, onto the wing. Then, somehow, the other.

Fear, she'd learned, was much like physical pain or nausea or heartache. When it came, it was always worse than you remembered it. There was the willowy betrayal of your limbs, the cold scalpels of sweat, the fugitive pulse. The pounding nearness of death. Forgetting, she'd learned, was a gift. Otherwise, you would never go out on the high limbs of the world again, daring the wind—you would clutch the roots of the earth, trembling, waiting to die.

But when she first stepped onto a wing, it was like remembering. She'd been here before, it seemed, crouched in the cross-trussed eaves of this little featherweight house in the sky, looking down upon a world of dollhouses and cars that crawled like beetles, toy trains chuffing cottony tufts of smoke over the hobby board landscape, farmhands planted like tiny figurines.

The earth looked almost soft from such a height, hazed by altitude, as though, if she stepped from the wing and fell into its embrace, she would strike it through and keep on going, punching a hole through the layered eons of sediment. She would look up, as from the bottom of a well, and someone would throw her a rope. She would emerge earth-blackened and triumphant, smiling bright, receiving the thunder of applause.

Such were the illusions she must live by.

7

The Count

*H*e's *quair*, is what he is. Always was."

"*Daddy*," protested Estelle. "Be nice now."

They were watching Billy Falkner stride past them on the dance floor, clad in his twenty-five-dollar suit whose forked tails trailed after him like the tail feathers of an enormous swallow.

"How the hell does he afford a tailcoat like that, working as a goddamn bank clerk? Don't do nothing more than his granddaddy ever did, that old *colonel* sitting white-suited, puffing his cigar, watching the Square the day long. Boy's a dandy, is what he is."

Estelle twisted the golden ring Billy had given her. He'd had a Gothic *F* engraved on the inner side of the band, so he would always be with her. If her father only knew.

"He writes beautiful verse," she said. "Sometimes."

"*Verse?*" Her father snorted, watching the ballooned cheeks of the Black trumpeter he'd paid seventy-five dollars to come down from Memphis. "Verse. It takes more than pretty words to make a way in this world, girl. The sooner you learn that, the better."

She watched Billy on the dance floor. He was built short and narrow, his chin pointed small beneath high, hollow cheeks. His mouth narrow and tight, cut white-lipped in place. He was not a very good dancer, as if he must premeditate the movement of his every joint, but there was a dignity in his bearing, a stubborn poise. His spine was sword-straight, as if forged from steel, and he walked like a man who already bore medals on his breast. Increasingly, he spoke to her of "Immelmann turns" and "Split S" maneuvers, of the meteoric rise and fall of the great air aces, who were always being crowned or killed over the distant farmyards of France.

He'd written her strings of letters while she was away for a year at Mary Baldwin College in Virginia, cooped up in the blue folds of the mountains among the endless titter of beribboned girls. She'd torn open the envelopes with her fingers, braving paper cuts to read of Billy break- ing his nose in a game-saving tackle of Possum McDaniel or having his cheeks smeared with the hot heart-blood of his first bear, killed at the camp of General George Stone in the bottomlands of the Tallahatchie River. She could imagine those dark eyes of his blazing into the words he wrote, as if they might light the page afire.

"Thinks he's got something none of the rest of us is got," said her father. "The boy's putting on airs."

One story came to her from his brother Jack. He and Billy and a friend were playing the back seven holes of the university golf course on a Sun- day afternoon, keeping out of sight of the clubhouse since the blue laws restricted play on the Sabbath. Weeks earlier, their mother had hired the town photographer to do a family portrait, and their father, Murry, holding the resultant tintype, had had occasion to tease Billy, poking fun at his mouth, nearly invisible in the photograph.

Old Snake-Lips.

They were on the sixth fairway, eyeing the oiled sand of the green, which was fenced to keep the ranging cows away, when Murry Falkner came tearing from the bushes behind them, slashing the air with his blackthorn walking stick and spewing curses.

"You got-damn heathens, I *know* you ain't playing on the Lord's Day!"

Jack, telling the story, shook his head. "Me and the other boy, we snatched up our balls and ran. Not Billy, though. The crazy son of a bitch goes sifting through his clubs, real thoughtful-like, and pulls a long iron from the bag. Turns and addresses the ball, cool as a cucumber, and aims right for Daddy. Knocks one whizzing right past the old man's ear." Jack shook his head again. "Daddy don't even flinch."

"What happened next?" asked Estelle.

"Last I saw, Daddy had that walking stick raised, black and gleaming in the sun, and there was Billy just standing underneath him, upright, waiting for the thing to come down. That little smile on his face, like he was off in the clouds someplace—"

"*Estelle.*"

"Yes, Daddy?"

"Are you even listening to me? That boy is a truant. A derelict. He didn't even finish high school. No prospects. And here he is, prancing in tails. You know what people are calling him? Calling him the Count."

"That's not nice," said Estelle. "He's talented."

"*Talented*? Talent don't get you nowhere in this world unless you use it. Man's got to get up and work every day of his life. I tell you what gets you somewhere. Hard work, study, vocation. Family, that gets you somewhere, and associations, contacts. I'll tell you who has all that and more, in spades: Cornell Franklin. There's a man, there. President of his class at Ole Miss, captain of the track team. Law degree. Doing big things for himself in Honolulu, I hear. Assistant district attorney. I hear talk of a federal judgeship coming his way before long."

"I don't want to live in Hawaii, Daddy."

"And handsome. The Good Lord don't cut 'em like that, not often. No, ma'am. Tall, too. No little Oxford runt, born of a stableman. An up-and-comer, carving his name in the world. A face man, handsome as a Brahman bull."

Estelle looked at Cornell, home to visit his family. *To hunt for a wife,* whispered her mother. He was swinging a girl with brown braids across the dance floor, his joints oily and smooth, his polished shoes flashing like knives. He smiled at her, his teeth square and perfect, gleaming like the grille of a roadster.

He *was* handsome.

Her father watched, too. Cornell was the reason for this party, she knew. The reason her parents' very best china and silver lay glittering on the banquet table, subjected to the rare insult of being used, and the servants hurried about, wearing their starchiest whites. The reason a Memphian trumpeter was scrunching his shoulders with effort, his breath blown so beautifully through a kink of brass, his vest pocket bulged with folded bills.

Her father extracted a thin cigar from the pewter case engraved with his initials, his university ring winking beneath the overhead lights. He looked at her from the corner of his eye. "You don't want your younger sister getting married before you, do you, now?"

Estelle shook her head despite herself.

No, she did not.

The engagement ring arrived via post, a double diamond set in a finger-size halo of 14-karat gold. Included was a note from Cornell, written from Hawaii.

A marriage proposal.

Billy sat next to Estelle in the brush arbor behind his grandfather's place, holding the ring. He rotated it between his fingers, sparking light from the faceted stones. These twin treasures born in the unseen ovens of the earth, a hundred miles below the surface, belched to the upper world through glowing pipes of magma. These icy stones, unearthed in the cruel darkness of mines, cut and polished by the monocled diamantaires of Antwerp, shipped across oceans and nations and worn finger to finger through generations—all to steal away his sweetheart.

Estelle sat knee-clutched beside him, the bottom of her dress all soiled. Her face was twisted and flushed, like a pained rose, her cheeks dewy with tears.

"I don't want to marry him," she said. "I don't."

Billy set the ring back in her hand, carefully, wanting to chuck it into the woods. "Then don't," he said.

Estelle's hand closed hard over the ring. Her fist quivering, strung with the finest bones, and Billy wondered if blood would rise gleaming between her fingers.

"I have to," she said. "I have to."

He set her trembling fist in his lap, so she would not stain her dress.

Billy Falkner left Oxford in the winter of 1918, a month before Estelle and Cornell were to be married. He rode a northbound train, the cars rattling through the winter country, the dead lands hunched naked and gray under their pall of snow, the trees like stony crowns. He had twenty-five dollars in the pocket of his coat, plus a single thumb-worn nickel. He looked at the white sky, so pale and cold, as if he could escape his pain there. The troubles of the earth seemed so small from such a height, so storybook, as they must look to God.

8

The Hunters

*W*est," she said. "You always say that."

Zeno stood wide-legged in his flying breeches and sniffed, scenting the sky. "The winds are right this year."

"The winds? This ain't a sailing ship." She flipped her hand at the Jenny, parked nose-up in the grass, haughty. In the background stood the coffin factory, big as Noah's ark.

"I mean the winds of *fortune*," said Zeno. He looked at his bandaged palm. "The Mackintoshes, I believe, were never poets."

Della was kneeling, scratching Sark on the scruff of his neck. "They weren't too whiskey-soft of an evening for husbanding," she said. "That much I know."

Zeno turned to look at her, his mustache gull-winged in grin. "Hard-pricked those Mackintoshes, yes. But who of them had such a tongue?"

Della rose from the dog's happy wagging and put a hand on Zeno's shoulder, leaning close to his ear. "Perhaps you should use it for more than talking, Husband. Lately, you use it for so little else."

She didn't await his reply, setting off instead for the coffin factory. For three years they'd circled the South, following rivers and railways from hamlet to hamlet, pasture to pasture, sometimes striking upon towns with brick courthouses and heroes of local history cast in bronze upon green squares of mown grass, the belled spires of churches pricking the sky, topped with crosses as if to ward off aerial invaders. Waycross was such a place, set at the intersection of nine railroads and five highways. Earlier that morning, flying down out of the sun, she'd watched the web of iron and white-baked road converging, the railcars shuttling beneath them in rust-red convoys, the black road cars hounded by dusty ghosts of their own making. There were the planing mills smoking on the edges of town like giant steamships, two of them, and the great tobacco warehouses where the leaves were strung in late summer to dry, long garlands like for some humorless ball.

She'd strode down those aisles and others, down assembly lines and gangplanks and the corridors of fur markets, where the hides of alligators and raccoons hung like the flags of conquered nations, their heads still attached to their gutless, flattened bodies. Men would straighten from their stalls and stations to watch her pass, the silver pulse of her hips, the twin pump of her breasts. They stood gape-mouthed, slavered, as if she were something to eat. They would leave their work and turn out their pockets to see such a creature dangled from the heavens; they would bear the slaps and crossed arms of angry wives.

Sark bounced along beside her, his tongue long and loose with the heat, pink as a broiled salmon. He was Zeno's dog more than hers, loyal to his master long before she came along. On the morning they left her home in Darien, she'd knelt to pet the dog, reading the name etched into the quarter-sized metal tag.

"Sark?"

"Like Cutty Sark," said Zeno.

"The clipper ship?"

Zeno set his flask between his teeth. "The Scotch whisky."

"Oh," she said. "I think my daddy had a bottle of that in his cellarette."

Zeno lowered the flask, undrunk, and looked at the goggled dog.

His tongue rounded his teeth, as if gathering words. "Of course, there's the prefix in Greek: *sark-*. Comes from the noun *sarx*, meaning 'flesh, kindred.'" He gestured toward the dog with his flask. "Flesh of my flesh."

She looked at the dog. He was panting, his eyes bright with confirmation.

"Of course," she said, scratching him behind the ears.

Della didn't let the animal lick the crumbs from her face, as Zeno did, nor let him drink from the same tin cup, but often the dog seemed to prefer her, trailing her like a shadow. Sometimes she wondered if he really were some part of Zeno, keeping watch over her.

The coffin factory loomed. She'd never been inside. They tried not to hit the same place more than twice, for audiences were too quickly jaded—they felt cheated when you turned up months later, still alive.

The building was not constructed of brick like the mills. It was wood-framed, sheathed with long planks of gray-weathered siding. Stenciled in white script, slightly rain-bled, ran the company name: DIXON & SONS COFFIN CO. As she neared, she could hear the bang of falling hammers, the whine of saws. She didn't knock, just pushed through the door into the dimness of the front office. A pomaded clerk started to rise from his desk but froze, squatting there like a man surprised on the commode.

He held his hand up, thumb and forefinger touching, as if to pinch something from the air. "Ma'am?" he said. "Ma'am?"

Della kept on through the room, Sark scurrying beside her in escort. They pushed through a second door, into the din of creation. The ceiling arched high above them, raftered, and sunlight slashed down from dirt-hazed windows, illuminating swirling mobs of sawdust. Saucer-shaped lamps hung from the crossbeams, their bulbs caged in wire. Beneath the lights lay a vast honeycomb of yellow pine, coffins cradled openmouthed in their rows. Men were bent over them in canvas aprons, planing and sanding, blond curls of wood piling at their feet.

Della clopped down the three steps to the factory floor. There was a wide center aisle down which she strode, the heels of her riding boots hammering the concrete. Soon the men were straightening from their work, their hand planes and hammers clutched to their chests, listening to the words that leapt from the woman's tongue:

"Air show! Wing-walking and stunt-flying, loop the loops and barrel rolls!"

Della listened to herself, as she always did, and this was not her voice. This was the voice of a carnival barker or sermonizer or newsboy, the words hawked high over the crowd.

"See Captain Zeno Marigold, double ace of the Great War! See Della the Daring Devilette, who defies death, walking on wing and wind!"

The teeth of handsaws fell silent at her passage, the scratch of sandpaper. In one corner, the great iron piston of the drop stamp stilled, no longer punching quiltwork designs into sheets of tin. A Black man stood in another corner, gawking, a casting ladle gripped in oversize leather gauntlets, the molten lead shimmering like the suit she wore.

"Death hang and hat trick!" she cried. "Low-level inversion!"

She walked on, hawking her wares—her stunts and daredevilry—thinking all the while of the casket invoice crumpled beneath the blotter on her father's desk. She wondered if it was still there, unpaid, in a room flocked with the dry husks of receipts and reckonings and bills of lading. She wondered if they rustled and fluttered about the room, nudged by the breeze from a stoned-out window. Surely the old Mackintosh house would be the target of stone-throwing boys who wished to rouse the old ghosts huddled in the shadowy recesses of the place, to hear their stones rattle in the hollows of that once-bright house, now festooned in kudzu and creeper vines, their red blossoms splayed like the last of her father.

"After-show rides! Two cents a pound!"

The caskets floated on sawhorses to either side of her, fleets of them like open-decked ships, each awaiting its freight. They were nothing like the big whale of mahogany that shuttled her father into the earth. They were more like the pine boxes of the Old West, unlacquered hexagons propped upright to cradle the riddled bodies of outlaws for public display.

"No one flies lower or faster!"

Now came a long table of fittings stamped from tin and brass. There were ornamental backplates, like tiny shields for the fitment of coffin handles, sorted each according to design—convenient pickings for the carpenters—and there were sheaves of blank breastplates awaiting the names of the dead. Farther on, castings: baskets of handles for the gloved hands of pallbearers and crosses of every style and dimension, some strung with the tortured forms of Christ. The latter were for Catholics, of course. Mostly they had stringy arms, their bodies wasted with want, though she saw one batch that was neatly muscled, steel-drivers in thorny crowns who could splinter the crosses that bore them should they wish to un-martyr themselves. They were basketed each according to likeness, whole battalions of toy-size gods.

Despite herself, Della stopped before them. The figures were brazed to their crosses. She could see the little cushions of melt beneath their hands and feet. In some dark corner of this place, a man had the job of crucifying tiny Christs with torch and flux, day after day, wondering whether he was damned.

A tap on her shoulder. She wheeled about to find the pomaded clerk, his thumb and forefinger pinched before her face.

"You cannot be here," he said. "This is a factory. We have caskets to build."

She looked over his head. A hundred watching eyes, wide with wonder. She smiled, looking back at the man. "Oh, I believe the dead can wait. Or do you wish, sir, to work these men right into the coffins they build?"

Laughs from the crowd; the clap-thud of boots stamping in approval.

The clerk bent farther toward her, as if he would pluck a whisker from her chin. "The dead wait for no one."

Della, smiling wickedly, began to squat before him, sinking almost to girl-height. He leaned over her, glowering, and she sprang from the floor. He reeled backward, sprawling, as she landed on the table behind her, crosses and Christs shivering beneath the crash of her boots.

The man recovered, slicking back an oily hook of hair. "Get down from there!" he said. "Who do you think you are?"

Della strode along the edge, goose-stepping, her arms tilting like wings, her feet slamming heel to toe like a tightrope walker's. She looked out across the floor, seeing the upturned faces, boy-round with awe.

She pointed to a man holding a carpenter's rule. "You, sir, you look like you've sized up a woman before. What do you think of me?"

Now she twirled in place, tracing the outline of her body through the silver suit. She gestured to a coffin lying nearby. "Would one of these fit?"

The workers stamped their boots and roared.

The clerk looked over his shoulder, as if his own death were afoot, about to walk through the door. "Miss," he said. "Miss! Please, you must leave now."

Della whirled and looked down at him. "Truly, sir, could you turn away such a promising prospect of new business as I?"

The man tugged one of his sleeve garters. "I don't have the authority."

"No? Then who does?"

"Mr. Dixon," he said. "Or one of his sons, elsewise."

"And where can I find one of these Dixons?"

"The Dixon men, they bear hunt of a Saturday. Down in the Okefe-nokee."

Della squatted narrow-heeled on the corner of the table. "Down deep in the swamp, are they?"

The man looked at his shoes, nodding, while whispers slithered from the crowd.

Come on, Finney, just for an hour.

Old Man Dixon'll never know.

We're ahead of quota.

Did you see the lines on her, Finney? Did you?

Della coaxed him closer with a flick of finger. "Come now," she said. "You can even have a ride for free."

Della lay on her back in the tree shade, legs crossed, as Zeno buzzed high over the field, giving the workers their after-show rides. In the early days, she never wanted to come down. Up in the bottomless hall of wind she was home, in the shriek and light. She could see the world from on high, as God might. The minuteness of it all, the pattern and order. She saw not a single field of cotton but a land of it, a thousand fields littered like playing cards. She saw not a cluster of men but a nation, multitudes coming and going from their little forts.

But the earth was jealous. It was always tugging at your chin and breasts and boots, bending you toward it. It wanted you to see everything close up, so close you could hardly decipher it. The eye of a broken-legged horse, the tongue of a road-killed dog, the bright spray of blood against a wall. It wanted to draw you into itself, its black belly, to eat your bones and sigh your ghost. This force, she knew, did not rain from the heavens. Gravity came from the weight of the earth itself, the deepest core. Falling, you were not ousted from the sky; you were drawn to the earth. You were killed with desire.

Lately, though, she found herself more amenable to the pull. She lay with Sark's chin on her belly. The old terrier was dozing, his eyes hidden beneath his fluffy eyebrows. A little fire was crackling a few feet away. Soon she would heat a bartered can of beans, the treasure of someone's Saturday lunch box. In the meantime, she let herself be drawn into the warmth of the dirt, the whispering grass. She let herself be lulled, wanted. She closed her eyes, drifting into the early days, what seemed so long ago.

What days, though. The elation of flight, of being lifted free of shadow and earth, of standing high in a world of light, and the nights of tasting grass in her mouth, her body torqued palely in some lonely field, split and shuddering, her cries heard only by the cows and owls and crickets, perhaps the aging denizens of the nearest farmhouse. She liked to think some of them were inspired by such. More than once, she saw a new glow in the face of a farmwife come morning or a knowing wink, or she found a basket of fresh eggs waiting in the grass.

She was free, unbound. The pocked wall of the study was a long way gone, the gin-breathed aunts who would've pushed her to marry the first man of standing who'd take her, any man jack whose livelihood had not fully crumpled with the Crash. Zeno? She smiled, wondering what those women would think. He was nearly twice her age, his face dusky, his temples graying beneath his leather flying helmet. His pockets were empty, his prospects nil. He owned nothing save his dog and his airplane and his wits, and sometimes they owned him. He had luck, but nobody owned that, and he had a bellyful of stories, which he could readily exchange for food and did. He lived on the wing: no fixed base of operations, no home. He was blown like a moth on the wind.

When she first saw him without the mask of engine smoke, she was surprised at the swarthiness of his complexion, as if his face were sun-cured by whole ages aloft or successive generations of nomadic existence.

In a dark field, a week after they met, she asked about his family.

"Family?" The word seemed a pill on his tongue. "My father was an itinerant balloonist."

"Itinerant balloonist?"

Zeno stared into the fire, nodded. "A carnival man, just passing through." He paused. "A Gypsy, to hear it told, by blood and inclination both. People called him the Balloonitic."

"A real Gypsy?"

He nodded. "They say."

"And your mother?"

"Seventeen at the time. Parents bused her off to Connecticut to have the baby. A convent." He stared into the fire. "She died in childbirth."

After a succession of foster homes, he was sent to live with a distant family relation, a granduncle, in a derelict plantation house outside Savannah.

"The man was an eccentric, a scholar. The house was sinking back into the swamp. There were vines snaking in through the windows, lizards skittering across the floor, packs of mongrel dogs running wild. You had to check the toilet for spiders before you sat. Still, there were books. They were everywhere: on shelves and in teetering stacks and propping up furniture. My uncle cared for little else. Books and brandy. The classics, especially, and the works of the Church Fathers." Zeno shrugged. "So I read. Read and read and read."

He was at Oxford University, studying Latin and Greek on a scholarship, when the war broke out.

"Why did you go?"

"We couldn't imagine *not* going. It was the Big Show, after all. You were nobody if you didn't go. And there was the poetry."

"Poetry?"

"Sure. The Greeks, the Romans. I was fatted on the stuff. Everybody was, whether they knew it or not. Honor, glory, fame, awaiting in distant lands. *Dulce et decorum est*, like Horace said. How sweet and honorable to die for your country."

"But America wasn't even in the war yet."

Zeno spat into the fire, a bubbling hiss. "Seemed close enough."

Perhaps he might have become some soft-palmed professor—the kind her aunts wanted for her—had it not been for such poetry. She didn't know. She only knew she wanted to be bound to him. She wanted to spend her days in their tiny cage of wire and fabric dangling from the sky; she wanted to spend her nights nestled atop the warm bellows of his body, breathing the sweet reek of him, her fingers strung through the dark curls of his chest. But Zeno would not be married except by a priest, and no priest would marry a pair of itinerant fornicators who'd known each other only a month—and one of them a Protestant.

Finally they heard of a priest living on Jekyll Island, trying to dry out amid the sea turtles and Spanish moss, the beaches and winter cottages of Rockefellers and Vanderbilts that stood mostly empty now under the oaks. They found him in a beachfront hermitage, his cleric's collar wilted and yellowed like an old dog's, his jowls long, a silken scarf tied around his head like a bandage. It was crimson. "The color of Christblood," he said. "Like that which flowed from His thorny crown."

Zeno gifted him a bottle of bathtub gin. "Would you marry us, Father?"

The fallen priest cradled the bottle to his chest. "For this, my son, I would marry the fleas to a dog."

He led them down a narrow path meandering through the dunes. They emerged onto a beach wracked with giant ribs and cradles of driftwood, sun-paled like the bones of doomed ships or beasts. Above them, whole trees snarled dead-limbed from the sands, their crowns wind-bent and wild as witches' hair. Some of them were toppled, upturned, their roots spread thousand-fingered against the sky, the beach latticed with their shadows.

"The sea," said the priest, "it steals this island inch by inch. In a thousand years, perhaps there will be no island at all. Not here. The luck of this island will be gone, run out. It will have shifted into another form, another place, the sands redeposited upon some other shore. Perhaps this is not luck but the will of God, this flux, this amorphous shifting of the world. Canyons carved miles-deep by the tireless trickling of His will, whole islands risen atop mountains of His infinite time. Some say that we are not but islands ourselves, chance masses of cells each smaller than a grain of sand, bodies formed and unformed by wind and sea and earth. I say that may be so, but no island is truly an island. It is part of a chain, a submerged range. Such are men, not alone, but each bearing the sands of his ancestors, and all of us pulled together, together, by what but love?"

Here he touched them each on the shoulder, the three of them standing thigh-deep in the crash of surf, and the sky blazed and the wind whistled through the salt-white antlers of dead trees. The bloody islands of their hearts pumped in something like unison, and Della felt alive, alive, until she sensed a shadow in the water, pointed like the tip of a spear, and now a black fin broke the surface, gleaming like an upturned wing, and the beast was turning toward them, black as fate.

She awoke. Back in Waycross, at the coffin factory, in the shade beside the fire. A giant Ford phaeton—a topless tub with four doors—was bouncing and tearing across the field, a boulder of black fur lashed to the hood. The front seat bristled with white men and long rifles. In the rear, a pack of fawn-colored hounds, their tongues slung like pennants in the wind.

Sark stood beside her, rigid as a tiny cannon, growling.

"Hush," said Della, though she wasn't sure he should.

The queue of workers had broken; they were racing back to the factory now. The wire wheels of the car seized, the tires ripping through the grass, and the car lurched to a stop, the heads of men and beasts bobbing in unison. Now they were leaping from the black tub of the automobile, men and dogs, and here came Finney, the clerk, fighting his way against the fleeing tide of workers, his palms held out in plea.

A large man, round as a bear himself, was last to step down from the car. The machine groaned on its springs, unburdened of his weight. He was wearing a felt slouch hat strapped at the chin, one side pinned up like Teddy Roosevelt in Africa, and he carried a large-bore rifle that looked like a toy in his hands. His several sons stood behind him in various stages of miniature, each wearing the same hat, like the innards of a Russian doll. The hounds roiled and flamed about their boots, drunk on wind and bear's blood.

Finney stood before them. "I can explain, Mr. Dixon. It was to boost morale!"

Old Dixon squinted up at the buzzing airplane, as if to aim, then handed his rifle to the nearest son and smacked Finney in the face, knocking him to the ground with an open palm. His bulk loomed over the crumpled clerk.

"Goddamn Finkelstein," he said. "I should of known not to hire a Jew."

Christ-killer, said one of his sons.

Kike.

Old Dixon pulled a red kerchief from his back pocket and wiped the heel of his hand while the dogs swarmed and darted about the fallen man, long-tongued with glee. Now the big man turned in Della's direction, the heads of his sons swiveling in unison, and Della was already taking up the large faggot of green-leafed sticks she'd gathered, tossing it onto the fire. The greenwood popped and crackled, throwing smoke.

The men began marching in her direction, and here came the hounds bouncing and spurting through the grass, surrounding her, swirling like tongues of fire. Sark pivoted this way and that on his front paws, facing the boldest of the aggressors. His beard was long at the chin, shaped like a hatchet, but there were too many of the redbone hounds, smiling dumbly, nipping at his hocks. One of them darted in close, and Della kicked it squealing and skittering from Sark's flanks.

Old Dixon stood before her, his eyes slit, his cheekbones high and white as cliffs. "You kicked one of my dogs."

Bitch, whispered one of his sons. *Whore.*

Della listened to the green crackling of the fire, willing the smoke aloft.

"You don't strike me as a man afraid to kick something needs kicking," she said.

"Not man nor dog," said the old man. "Nor woman."

"There's some of them that kick back, you know."

The old man stepped closer. His sons, too. Their faces were white, their eyes like firing slits in bunkers of concrete.

The man rubbed his palms together and cocked his head, his tone suggestive. "All's the better," he said.

His chorus snickered.

"I lost half a day's production because of you," said the old man. "I'm owed."

"I'm sure Captain Marigold will furnish rides for you and your sons, free of charge."

The old man belched a laugh, throwing one hand toward the sky. "Rides? In some old birdcage like that, glued together with chewing gum and baling wire? We had a flying circus come through town last fall. Had them a big Ford Trimotor, nearly new."

Carried twelve passengers.

All metal, too.

The big man crossed his arms, stepping closer. "We all got to go at once." He winked.

The hounds were slinking, slack-jawed, their tongues loose. The hatted sons stood with arms crossed, too, each man cradling a gun.

Della lowered her voice, conspirator-like. "Where you want it?" She cocked her head. "Out in them woods?"

The old man thumbed the hairless promontory of his chin, cleft like a doll's ass. "It?"

Della stepped closer. "Me. That's what you want, ain't it? To *screw* me. You said you were owed."

The old man straightened slightly, as if pushed back by the word. "Well, I didn't say—"

"Oh yes, you did. You and your sons, too. It's what you were suggesting, wasn't it?"

The man's hands went fiddling about his waistband, as if he didn't know what to do with them. For the first time she could see his eyes: periwinkle blue. "Now?" he asked. "In there?"

"You can kill a bear in the woods. You can't have a woman, too?"

"Well—"

"We can do it orderly," said Della. "Firstborn to last. How would you like that?"

Old Dixon looked back at his sons for the first time, as if to see his concerns reflected. They weren't. Only a half dozen mouths cocked at just the same angle, waiting. When he looked back at her, his face was blotched red, blooms of blood shuttled up against his cheeks.

"What's the matter?" asked Della. She sized him up, lingered on the level plane of his crotch. "Can't get it up no more?"

His face fully colored, a scarlet balloon, and she could see the shame transforming inside him, balling into rage, his arm rearing back to strike her, but in the drama of the last minute, the men had forgotten their hounds. The animals were circling in place, crazed, their tails curled between their legs. Only Sark stood unmoved, awaiting what would come.

He knew.

The sky went sudden-dim above them and the sun burst apart, shadow-split into a thousand gleaming shards. The men looked up to see the shadows resolving, assembling, a machine shrieking down out of the sun like some winged killer of prehistory. They dived flat to the ground as the creature crashed overhead, the whole earth quaking beneath the roar, and Della was left standing tall in the whelm of remnant smoke, laughing at the men spilled before the toes of her boots. She laughed at their round blue eyes and gaping mouths, their scattered guns and rolling hats, their dogs who'd fled cowering into the trees, yipping weakly at the sky.

"Pantywaists."

The old man rolled over, groaning. Two of the sons started to reach for their guns.

"Don't," she said. "Not unless you want a flaming bottle of whiskey to land on your roof some dark night and burn this fucking place to the ground. Nothing left but cinder and ash and a bunch of angry ghosts come down like a wind, looking for their missing coffins, nothing to haunt but you and your generations since."

The Jenny had peeled sharply across the field, looping high against the sky for a second pass, and now—by a signal of her hand—it touched down lightly in the grass. A white-eyed passenger scrambled from the front cockpit and tumbled down the wing and went zigzagging toward the factory, dizzied by the aerobatics. The leather-clad ball of Zeno's head sat hunkered behind the rear windscreen, his scarf trembling in the prop wash. His big English revolver hung over the side of the cockpit, catching the sun.

Della strode toward the machine, her rickety island in the sky. She knew the Dixon men wanted to take up their guns and shoot her in the back, board her up in one of their pinewood coffins and sink her in the sandy white loam of the land.

They wouldn't.

9

Cadet Faulkner

A God-fearing young Christian gentleman," read the enlistment officer. "A young man of firm moral fiber and proper ideals, who wishes only to place his life in service of the Crown."

Bill stood full-lunged before the man's desk, his hands clasped behind his back, the slightest smile curling beneath his scant new mustache. The officer was reading from a letter of reference written and posted to his office by a Reverend Mr. Twimberly-Thorndyke of London, England. Bill had forged the looping flattery of the vicar's letter beneath the light of a coal oil lamp in a friend's cramped apartment and then mailed it to the sister of an English friend, who posted it back here to the Fifth Avenue office of Wing Commander Lord George Wellesley of the Royal Air Force.

The recruitment officer set aside the work of fiction, lifting another paper from his desk. The morning sun slashed down from a high window, clear and bright, illuminating the sheet like a sail that might just carry Bill abroad, aloft. Outside, the clop-clop of carriages, the clatter of motorcars.

"William Cuthbert Faulkner. Says here you were born in Finchley, in the county of Middlesex, into the Church of England?"

"Yes, Lieutenant," said Bill, pronouncing it *leftenant* in the Londoner's accent he'd been cultivating for the past several weeks. Trucks were *lorries*, jelly was *jam*. The government *were* a bunch of fools. "That's Faulkner with a *u*," he said. "Unlike the *colonial* spelling."

He knew his grandfather would have a fit at this, for the man still called the British "lobsterbacks" and told often of his own great-grandfather's exploits at Kings Mountain during the Revolutionary War, when a host of frontiersmen and sharpshooters from the far side of the Appalachians—Overmountain Men—laid waste to a thousand-strong militia of Crown loyalists.

The officer grunted. "And your mother resides in the town of Oxford, Mississippi?"

"As have I, *Leftenant*, since primary school. Just a little postage stamp in cotton country."

The officer, garbed in his powder-blue airman's uniform, cut his eyes over the sheet. "It seems you have retained your accent after all these years."

Bill leaned forward from the waist, dropping his voice. "I would not want to sound like one of these *continentals*, would I, sir?" Here he winked.

The Englishman's face didn't change. His flying cap hung from a hook in the corner. "Perhaps not."

He laid the paper aside and set both hands flat before him, pressing himself from his chair. Then he took up a cane and came limping around the front of the desk, rocking straight-kneed on one leg. Bill tried, unsuccessfully, not to gawk.

"Bloody Sopwith Camel," said the man, banging his cane against his wooden leg. "Devil's own machine."

Bill had seen the craft in photographs, a barrel-shaped fighter with stubby wings, synchronized machine guns, and a giant propeller.

The officer stood before him. "Offers a pilot three choices, does the Camel: Victoria Cross, Red Cross, or wooden cross." He tapped his leg again. "You see which I received, and lucky to have it." He swung out his hand, as if to shake, but instead pointed to a Detecto two-in-one scale set against the wall, which measured height and weight. "Now, let us make sure you meet the King's requirements."

Bill balked. These hated scales, his bane.

"Are you aware, sir, that the average height of a medieval knight, based on surviving suits of *armour*"—here he added the British *u* in his mind—"was but sixty-five inches from sole to crown?"

"Well, you had better be sixty-six to join the Royal Air Force. A man must reach the rudder pedals, after all. On the scale, please, and remove your shoes."

Faulkner chewed the inside of his mouth, looking from the man to the scale. He had tried everything to grow taller. Milk and spinach and bunches of bananas, even ginseng powder purchased behind the glazed and dangling ducks of Chinatown. Now he snorted in disgust and pulled off his shoes, a sharp-toed pair of Johnston & Murphy derbies he'd bought in Memphis for twelve dollars and a half, and stepped onto the device with first one foot, then the other, testing the surface like pond ice. The needle wound lazily toward the 120-pound mark but lost momentum, hovering at 113 pounds. The one-legged lieutenant drew a ruler from his tunic and held it atop Faulkner's head, tracing it toward the hash marks stamped into the measuring bar.

"You are standing on your toes, sir."

"I can't help it," said Bill. "I have very tight tendons."

"Stand flat-footed, Mr. Faulkner, and now."

His heels clapped down hard, jumping the needle, and the officer waited for the device to quit shaking before he took his measurement.

"Sixty-five and one-half inches," he said. "Half an inch short. I'm sorry, Mr. Faulkner, but I'm afraid you don't meet the minimum requirements of the Royal Air Force."

Faulkner leapt off the scale. "You must be mistaken, sir."

"All cadets must be at least five and one-half feet tall, or sixty-six inches."

"So round up."

"The RAF does not round."

"So fudge it. Surely you fudge."

"I'm sorry, Mr. Faulkner, but we cannot use you."

Bill felt his blood rise from the floor, his body gaining at least half an inch in pure outrage. "Can't use me? Well, we'll just have to find someone who can, won't we? We'll just have to see who else is in dire need of airmen at the moment."

The officer clasped his hands behind his back. "Mr. Faulkner—"

Faulkner stomped to the door in his sock feet and spun crisply on his heel, cocking one eye. "Tell me, *Leftenant*, which way to the German embassy?"

The flying officer met his gaze and held it, eyes keen, as if searching the sky for enemy fighters. After a long moment, Bill turned and grasped the door handle like a control yoke, casting his chin over his shoulder to bid the man adieu—along with his dreams of becoming an airman.

As he opened his mouth, the officer spoke. "It seems you satisfy the requirements of the Royal Air Force after all, Mr. Faulkner. You've the steel we need in pilots, I see." The man bent to his desk and scratched crisp black letters on an RAF document, then held out the paper. "Your signature, please."

Bill, buoyed by his own bluff, his belly tight as a drum, strode the five steps to the desk, took up the pen, and scrawled his name on the proper line. William Cuthbert Faulkner was to report for flight training in Toronto in one month's time, a "Cadet for Pilot."

Papers in hand, he turned to leave.

The officer rapped the floor with his cane. "Forgetting something, Mr. Faulkner?" He pointed at the pair of twelve-dollar shoes lying forgotten by the scale.

Bill looked down at his argyled feet, on which he would have gone slapping down the sidewalk of Fifth Avenue like a madman or tramp. He set to stamping on his shoes, using the backs of two fingers as a shoehorn.

The officer watched him. "And another thing, Mr. Faulkner. You can come off the bloody accent. A man need not be a British citizen, nor even a territorial, to serve in His Majesty's Royal Air Force. The next officer may not be so . . . *amused*."

10

Trembling Earth

*T*hey flew south out of Waycross, following the asphalt ribbon of US 1. The sun was rolling down the western sky, darkening as it went, and their pockets were sheafed with the dry leaves of bills that always blew so quick into the wind. There were cans of petrol and motor oil to be bought; cans of pork and beans and tomato soup. There were handbills to be printed and loosed like confetti over the next country hamlet, and tins of Cavalier Boot Creme and two-cent cigars and headache powders and the ever-present pint of bootleg whiskey that Zeno kept tucked in his flying jacket.

On the edge of town lay the railroad shops of the Atlantic Coast Line, the boilers and forges emitting slanted pillars of white steam and coal smoke. Locomotives, like giant iron slugs, jutted from the rowed maws of the enginehouses in various states of repair, sparks spraying from their axles and driving wheels. Men on elevated catwalks forked cakes of ice into the roof-mounted bunkers of refrigerator cars loaded with Florida citrus, destined for the lunch boxes of ironworkers seated on the skeletal crossbeams of skyscrapers high over Chicago or New York. Strings of boxcars lay in the diversion yard, awaiting engines, and everywhere railroaders in denim coveralls—mechanics and signalmen and train crews—made long shadows against the descending sun.

Della watched the Jenny's shadow skate across the web of iron rails, rippling and tumbling over freight cars and machine shops and coaling platforms. She thought of the Mohawks of Manhattan, a tribe of men seemingly called by the high steel of the rising metropolis, who walked the iron beams one hundred stories over paved streets swimming with tiny yellow taxicabs and suited executives ascending endlessly from subway stations. They'd worked on the Bank of Manhattan Building and the Chrysler Building and the newly completed Empire State, each successive spear thrust higher against the city skyline. People said the Mohawk were unafraid of heights, born to walk windy crossbeams like street curbs. They worked in four-man gangs, gunning red-glowing rivets with air hammers, and danced on thousand-foot-high skeletons for sport.

Della wondered if they were truly fearless, as many believed. She doubted it. Possibly they lacked the imagination to picture themselves exploding on the pavement of Fifth Avenue like water balloons, or they held with the scientists who theorized that a man, falling without a parachute, would pass out several stories before he struck the ground. Perhaps they believed, against all logic, that they would sprout wings and fly—much like she, falling, would pass into the soft heart of the earth, undestroyed. More likely they did the simplest, hardest thing in the world: they didn't think about it.

The rail lines crossed beneath them, an iron web spinning outward across the state, and they flew south, the rails fired forge-red by the falling sun. In other parts of the country, lighted towers and rotating beacons were being built, aiding passenger lines and airmail pilots, and Lindbergh had flown the first nonstop transatlantic flight in the *Spirit of St. Louis*. Transoceanic routes were opening, aided by sextants and celestial reckoning. But here, the rails and highways led them.

The earth began to transform beneath them, sliced and shattered with gleaming shards of water, and cypress trees clutched the mucky banks with their knuckled roots. Here was the edge of the Okefenokee

Swamp, Land of the Trembling Earth, inhabited by bears and panthers, white swampers and some said the ghosts of the Seminole. A wilderness of cypress and tupelo gum, where alligators cruised like gunboats. The rails skirted the edge, and Della was growing worried, darkness coming when the log structures of Camp Cornelia assembled beneath them.

Zeno cut a wing and slid them from the sky, floating down to a grassy strip hewn from the earth for the shiny, high-wing monoplanes of the old cypress barons come down to inspect their logging operations. Few now came. The field was empty, the windsock gone. A biplane lay balled and moldering at the edge of the woods like a wad of old parchment. Some previous barnstormer, perhaps, who looped too close to the ground. A pilot run out of luck. The machine had partly burned. Steel wires and spruce ribs stuck from the flame-eaten skin.

After they landed, Zeno stood with Sark under one arm, staring at the wreckage. He made the sign of the cross over his heart, small with his thumb, his hand still bandaged from the coal-holding contest.

Della came up beside him. "Hope it was quick," she said, "whoever it was."

"Aye, before it caught fire." Zeno blinked, grunted. "Come on."

They walked toward the camp. In seasons past, the swamp-cutters would come boy-faced to welcome the devilette and her captain. They would feed the aerialists twists of candy and fried alligator tail and backwoods brandy with the innocent giddiness of a Christmas morning. None now came. The little sawmill was silent. Spindly slash pines stood like scarecrows about the log-built structures of the place, the barracks and mechanic's shop and old office. The flagpole rang lonely in the wind, touting its striped rag.

Before them, the first leg of the Suwanee Canal gleamed rifle-straight into the swamp, like an oiled gun barrel. Here was the main avenue to the interior, hewn by a company of former Confederate officers, led by Captain Henry Jackson, who sought to drain the blackwater wilderness for cypress logging and turpentining and, with the trees gone, a vast array of rice plantations. They brought in steam shovels, gangs of convict labor, and veteran gold miners from the North Georgia hills, dredging a canal twelve miles through the halls of cypress, through malaria and snakebite and whole navies of alligators. But their shovels tore open dormant deep springs and the water flowed the wrong way, into the swamp instead of out. The Suwanee Canal Company folded like so much else. People called it Jackson's Folly.

"There's a light in that one," said Zeno, pointing to one of the outbuildings. "Come on."

Inside, a man lay flat aback an oaken desk big as a mortuary slab. His rubber boots were mud-caked, his fingers laced across his chest. He was fully clothed, wearing brown canvas pants and a green shooting shirt. A lever-action rifle stood propped against the desk. A felt hat covered his face, the brim tatty and serrated from long weeks in the swamp. It shook with his snores. Beside him stood a lantern, the flame glass-housed like an exotic moth. Della watched the light crawl twinned into her husband's eyes.

"Hardin!" he roared.

The man's body seemed for the briefest moment to rise levitating from the desk, yanked airborne by Zeno's voice, and he seemed to sit up in midair. His boots stomped hard-heeled onto the desktop, driving him upright above them, awake, his cupped palms catching his hat as it slid from his face.

He beamed. "Zeno!"

He leapt from the desk into the bigger man's arms, his muddy boots hooked around Zeno's waist, and the pair went careening across the room, Hardin holding his hat aloft like a rodeo rider, Zeno kicking a wastebasket clanging across the planks. Sark bounced after them, ears up. They crashed against the wall and busted apart on the floor, laughing, their cheeks awash in tears.

They'd met each other during the war, when Hardin crash-landed his bomber at Zeno's field after being shot up by German fighters over the Western Front. His aircrew had spent a raucous few nights with Zeno's squadron before their own unit could fetch them. Years later, their paths crossed again when Zeno landed at Camp Cornelia to perform for the mill hands and logging crews. Hardin had spent most of his adult life in the swamp, working as a timber cruiser, foreman, forestry agent, and now as the caretaker for the property—or what was left of it.

"Goddamn, Zeno. I thought you were dead."

Zeno's laughs caught in his throat. "Dead?"

Hardin sat up against the wall, chest still heaving, and drew a flat bottle of whiskey from his boot. "That burned crate out there, I was afraid she was yours. I came back from checking on the hunting cabins out on Floyds Island last summer to find the wreckage. Pilot was crisped, charcoaled." Hardin sipped from the bottle and shook his head, passing the whiskey to Zeno. "Not enough left to make an identification."

Zeno took the bottle, his face darkening. "That'll be me one day, most likely. Burned down to cinder." He took a long pull of the whiskey, exhaled. "Won't even need the crematorium."

Della felt a pain in her chest, as if his words had stabbed her. As if he cared so little about their life, the one they had and the one they wanted. She snatched the bottle from him and choked down a double swallow. It was busthead again, swamp-made, thunderous between the temples. Hardin watched her take it down, his eyes gone soft and round. "Hell, Zeno, I thought maybe this one here went and left you, and you done flown yourself straight into the ground for heartache."

Now Zeno looked up, the two men spraddled wide-legged beneath her. "Naw," he said. "She ain't left me yet."

"Well, she ever smartens up, I know a place she can come."

Hardin winked at her. Zeno reached out and wrung the man's neck, playfully, lovingly, and the two of them proceeded to tussle about like cubs on the floor.

That night, Hardin told the same story he always told when they visited him. He told of the maiden with the golden wings who'd come to him in a dream in the year 1911, when he first came to the swamp with a small crew to cruise timber for a logging interest. They'd been in the swamp for nearly a month, running survey lines through the wilderness, and he was worn thin. The veil between worlds had become threadbare, transparent.

"She come slicing through this line of cypress along the edge of camp, wheeling up against the sky like some joyous bird, those wings of hers flashing gold.

"I called out to her. Said, 'Teach me, please. Teach me too to fly!' She come down and hovered before me, and her skin was the color of pearls. She said to touch her shoulder with my one hand, lightly, and hold my other out wide, palm open, like so."

He touched Zeno on the shoulder, as for balance, his opposite fore-arm hanging from his rolled sleeve like an oaken club, a brutal imple-ment barbwired in veins, knotted in swamp-scars. He raised it hovering over the floor, dainty almost, like a man about to dance. His hard square hand was open, palm-up, ready to receive the gift of flight.

"I failed, though, that first time. She said I didn't touch the right shoul-der." At this, Hardin slipped quickly to Zeno's other side, as if in do-si-do.

Zeno watched him, eyes bright.

Now Hardin held out his opposite arm, elbow bent, as if to hug an imaginary friend. "That second time, she said I grabbed her too hard." At this, his fingers clawed into Zeno's shoulder, the veins rising like worms from the back of his hand. "I was too afraid, she said. She said you couldn't fly if you were afraid of falling. Said she'd give me one more chance. Said she'd fly past me, quick as she could, and if I could catch her in flight, she'd take me with her into the sky."

Hardin pushed up his sleeves, one after the other, and planted his heavy rubber boots, crouching like a wingback. He threw down his hat.

"She floated back from me and spread her wings wide, her every feather fixed in place, and it was so cool in the shadow she cast, so clean and blue, like the first dusk of fall, and then she rose and arched her-self into an S, like the body of a swan, and came shooting toward me in a streak of light, a bolt of golden fire, and I *snatched* for her!" Har-din's hand shot toward Della's chin, stopping just short of her throat, his fingers curled clawlike before her heaving tendons, and she felt a red blush across her chest. "But I missed, and I woke in a crumple of canvas, gripping the ridgepole of my tent to my chest." His eyes were red now, trembling with tears, and he held his fist against his heart. "She was gone, elusive as them Daughters of the Sun."

He was speaking of the legend of the lost hunters who encountered the maidens of an enchanted island in the swamp, who offered the men baskets of marsh hen eggs and tree fruit and pointed their way home, warning them to be wary of ever coming this way again, for their husbands would kill any men who so much as glimpsed their wives.

"She was some part of them, I think." Hardin looked at Della. His eyes had gone wide again, wet with drink or lonesomeness. "Maybe you are, too."

It was nearly midnight when they emerged from the building, swaying. Della could feel the white whiskey churning inside her skull, roaring like whitewater. Zeno threw back his head, cradling Sark under one arm, and sniffed the sky. A faint nimbus around the moon. "Storm coming," he declared.

"Maybe we ought to sleep in one of the outbuildings," said Della.

"Them old roofs are holier than the cathedrals of France," roared Zeno. "Holier than the basilicas of Rome!"

Behind them, Hardin snored on the slab of desk, the empty bottle of whiskey clutched to his chest.

Della looked back there, the moth of flame still fluttering inside the glass housing of the lantern. "He's sweet on me," she said.

Zeno smiled, belching through his teeth. "Aren't they all?"

Della lay her hand on his upper arm, leaning against him. "And you?"

He looked down at her, like something just remembered. "Of course."

He kissed her on the forehead, tender, and she could feel the tickle of his spit over her eyes, like the touch of a rose. Then he set Sark down at his feet, and man and dog walked off into the night, knowing she would follow.

In her dream, they floated high over a hill country red-gulched and dry, covered here or there in irregular patches of cotton, the unpicked bolls hovering like formations of tiny white-tufted clouds. There were columned houses, netted in vines, and tumbledown shacks and cross-roads cut like bloody symbols in the earth. There were strings of ragged figures shuffling along the country lanes, like the grand migration of beasts, and buggies and trucks barnacled with clinging riders, the roads fuming with their dust. Along the horizon, the great cities stood ready to receive them, hazed by distance, hovering like castles of smoke.

Now a great river came rolling through the land, black with the blood of fields, the spill of sewers and ditches and back-hovel creeks. The Big Muddy, where sternwheelers smoked like floating factories and passengers wore razors beneath their shirts, careful to keep their wallets close, and tugboats chugged upstream like paddling bulldogs, pushing long barges of manure or coal or salt or slag or pipe. This mighty river, where men had come to settle affairs of honor, taking to sandbars with pistol or sword or Bowie knife, killing each other over bird dogs or poker hands or fence lines, and the bodies of the drowned and murdered were flushed from the heart of the nation like used rubbers.

Past this lay the West, bright and golden, where the sun would go to sleep, speared bloody by a thousand converging highways and wagon roads and railroad lines. Where there were studios and celluloid, and Howard Hawks had made his film *The Dawn Patrol*, and Howard Hughes had made *Hell's Angels*—air spectacles whose biplanes swirled like black moths against the silver screen, each riding a shaft of machine-shot light. Here her feats might be seared onto film, recycled in black and white before the gape-jawed faces of the cinema crowds, and she might risk her life for more than a few scraps of paper money from the dusty pockets of field hands and tenant farmers.

This far shore loomed, and her heart rose like a winged thing in her chest, thumping her breastbone, and yet the machine on which so much depended—everything—began to sputter and shake beneath her. The motor backfired, emitting heavy knots of smoke, and the craft groaned under its skin. It seemed so fragile of a sudden, a folly of sticks and string and paste. How could such a shoddy contraption dare to cross a nation, floating free of the many dangers, the fangs and claws, the high cold mountains and wide fast rivers and legions of hungry, pistoled men?

The motor seized. The propeller froze, whistling like a giant knife.

Della looked back, and there sat Zeno at the stick, goggled, grinning as if nothing were wrong. And there sat Sark in his lap, ears perked, tongue out, panting that something surely was. For the craft was sinking now, unpowered, no longer kissed by the spirit of flight, and they would crash into the black slake of the river, driven like splinters into its tongue. And Zeno grinning as if this were the natural order of his world, and expected, and he was pleased to see its logic borne out. As if he were already dead, had been, and found but pleasure in this final confirmation of faith.

I'll show him.

Della rose from her seat. She grabbed hold of the upper wing and stepped high-kneed from the cockpit, climbing onto the ribbed roof of the craft. The wind clawed at her body, at her every limb and extremity, desperate to rip her free of this machine and whirl her through the vast, roaring blue and dash her brightly against the earth.

But she would not be moved. She rose to her knees, sliding the toes of her boots beneath staggered hoops of leather fastened atop the wing, and then she rose to her feet, leaning hard into the wind, one foot in front of the other, angled in her silver suit like the stainless gods adorning the long hoods of Packards and Duesenbergs. Her face hard and white, as if wind-carved. But this was not enough. She could feel a pair of blisters rising from the hard white clay of her back, blood-filled and burning, and they seemed to be crowding the air from her lungs. Soon they were the size of chicken eggs, swollen from her shoulder blades, and she could hardly breathe. Now ostrich size, and alive, trembling with power, as if she might hatch whole birds from the ribbed confines of her torso. Her stretched skin burning, shearing red-zagged over the risen muscle. In a scream of agony, a pair of wings burst forth from her ruined flesh, the silver feathers unfurling into the wind and light. Bright ribbons of blood streamed from the newborn pinions, like garlands, and she felt the sky itself caught beneath the arched shadow of her transformation.

The wings were giant, rivaling those of the machine, so that it became like a triplane, a triple-winged flier like the murderous red Fokker of Baron von Richthofen, who'd killed so many of her husband's comrades. She could feel the weight of the craft slung beneath her, so heavy, tugging her toward the earth, and she filled her lungs with wind, willing herself to fly, to carry them to the far shore. Her wing muscles ached. Her heart was stoked red as an ember, her blood burning against the hollow bones of flight, but she was lifting them, lifting them, until she smelled the smoke.

She looked down and the machine was on fire, long tongues of flame whipping and shivering from the wings, curling the skin black, revealing the skeletal underpinnings of spruce. Sark was barking, yelping, feeling the first fingers of fire, and Zeno was silent, prepared to die like one of his saints. They tore flame-tailed and smoking across the sky, as if cast from heaven, and her own heart was flaring in her chest, wind-bright between her ribs, and she worried her own love had set them alight.

Sark's yelps became louder and louder, as if he'd leapt from the cockpit onto the wing, then bounded onto her shoulder like a cat, perched there, barking right into her ear. His breath hot and wet, rattling against the soft pink ribs of his palate, and her whole body was trembling, straining to hold them together even as they rode their dark slash of destruction to the earth.

Della woke, bolting upright, striking her head on a spar of the bottom wing. Sark stood beside her, bouncing four-legged in the grass, barking his alarm, and Zeno had one great hand on her shoulder, still shaking her awake. She turned to look at him.

"Fire," he said, his eyes wide.

Behind him, the swamp glowed.

At first, the naturalists and newspapermen would theorize that a stray fork of lightning had come searing across miles of dark country, zigzagging beneath the stars like a serpent of fire to strike the dry grass at the edge of the swamp. After all, the only storm in the area had kept to the horizon, passing like a distant army in the night, and what other force might have sparked such mindless destruction?

Smoldering clumps of moss would descend on the streets of Waycross and Folkston like hellish snowflakes, the ground pocked with spats of fire, and barns and chicken coops fifty miles distant would go up like torches, beasts of burden screaming in the night. Backwoods believers would preach the end of the world, their figures cut dark before burning churches while the sky rained fire and their flocks cowered. The town beauty of Homerville, having slipped out her bedroom window to sleep in the arms of her sweetheart on the edge of Lake Verne, would have a flaming mass of Spanish moss land square on her back, leaving a scar, and the square-faced churchwomen would call it the wages of sin, while ponds all over South Georgia hissed like boiling springs.

One year later, a closer shadow of the truth would be known. The park superintendent would catch two boys poaching alligator amid the charred ruin of Dinner Pond. They were swamp-fed teens, stringy and hard, and they didn't want to go to jail. They confessed at the end of his rifle. A year before, they'd been fishing the selfsame pond with a boy named Strickland, a known killer of cats and stray dogs. They were hiking out of the swamp, their catches strung like silver medallions from their necks, when Strickland lit a cigarette and flicked the match into a dry bunch of grass at his feet. The swamp was dry that spring, parched like the rest of the country, and the flames sprang quickly, leaping from bush to bush like jackrabbits.

"What you done that for?" asked one of the boys.

Strickland stood with his thumbs hooked in the straps of his overalls, the flames dancing before him. He shrugged. "Wanted to warm my hands," he said.

Della and Zeno leaned against the tail and strut, turning the Jenny into the wind while Sark bounded up into the cockpit. The canal glowed like magma between the trees and tails of fire were floating down all around them, strangely slow. A single clump of flaming moss on the nitro-hardened fabric and their livelihood, their home, would ignite like the struck head of a match.

Della hurried to the propeller, cycling the blades in short chops, once, twice, again, working oil into the cylinders. "Mag on!" she called.

No reply.

She looked up, and Sark was standing alone from the cockpit, smoky-eyed, his paws perched on the edge and ears perked, looking back toward the old logging camp. She followed his gaze and saw Zeno standing silhouetted in the field, looking toward the red bubble of light, as if a great city lay just beyond the towering gates of cypress, the smattering of outbuildings.

He turned. "Hardin," he said.

Her heart thumped. This man, her husband, who'd risk everything for a fellow brother.

"Hurry!" she cried.

Della had to sit in Hardin's lap, in the front cockpit, while Zeno throttled them down the field. The Jenny bounced and bounced again, struggling with the added weight. Finally she lifted into the air, clearing the charred carcass of the other biplane and the trees just beyond it. Zeno turned them downwind, skirting the edge of the swamp.

The land pulsed and flared beneath them, belching smoke and flame, as if hell's gates had come unbarred. The very air had turned violent. Flaming debris danced around them, blown hundreds of feet high in the heat, and sudden slugs of fire shot past their wings like burning birds—maybe some were. The Jenny was caught in updrafts again and again, their bellies singing as the craft shot skyward on vertical torrents of hot air, only to plunge again in the downdrafts. Della saw a family of deer struck rigid in a clearing, nearly walled in by fire, the velvety knobs of their budding antlers glowing. She saw the armored snouts of alligators arrowing through the creeks and canals, diving for the cooler bottoms. She saw a lone black bear rumbling under trees of fire.

She was watching this destruction so closely that the hand which came sliding over her thigh felt almost natural, like the spread of flame.

The fingers moved up the inside of her leg, slowly, following the inseam of her breeches. Against her wishes, her body came alive at the touch, the blood tingling up the backs of her legs, scalding beneath her clothes. It seemed so long since she'd been touched, wanted. So long since Zeno even noticed. The hand edged higher. Here, now, above the flaming of the earth, inside the roar of her own whiskey-bent mind, the transgression seemed small, secret, safe. Hardin. A man she cared for, who'd always adored her, singing her praises to Zeno. A man who truly loved her husband, who might be drunk enough to think she was his maiden with the golden wings returned, a Daughter of the Sun. Before she knew it, his hand had found the buttons of her fly, thumbing them open. Had moved between her legs. How easy to lean back and open herself, to let the world burn.

Della placed her hand over his, firmly, and moved it aside.

11

The Ace

*C*adet Wing lay before him, a vast tent city on the shores of Lake Ontario. The slate expanse was cut with the wakes of steamers and racing shells. A scream of gulls fumbled on the wind above him, cast like scraps of paper, and the upper sky was full of training ships.

Cadet Faulkner was sun-browned, his hair kissed the color of rope. His body had been hardened on the parade ground, drilled to form by the hard barks of Flight Sergeant Tabernacle, and his head was full of lectures on wireless telegraphy, topography and mapmaking, and the intricacies of air law. He could cut the crispest salute, his hand whipping knife-edged to his temple, and swagger wide-kneed like a British officer, clicking the heels of his hobnail boots to attention. He could receive six words per minute on the wireless. He could identify every cloud in the sky and every man-made flier that chugged against those lofty white tufts.

He could do so much now, but he couldn't fly. Not yet. Beside him, on the end table, sat his overseas cap, still bearing the dreaded white band of the cadet. On his wrist he wore a silver identification bracelet,

WM FAULKNER stamped below the RAF seal. In his hand, a pen. He was working on a poem, set in the early hour of a dawn patrol.

"The Ace"

The silent earth looms blackly in the dawning
Sharp as poured ink beneath the grey
Mist spectral, clutching fingers . . .

He puffed on his pipe and peered out at the lake. Brother Jack had been shipped overseas, a private with the Fifth Marine Regiment. Bill envied the things his brother would see. London, Paris. The Continent, the Big Show. He worried the war would end before he, too, got his chance to go abroad. Even to fly.

Back home, little Dean Swift had just turned twelve, growing up like a weed. How much Faulkner missed his littlest brother, his shoeless brown feet and blinding smile, his tatty straw hat. A fishing pole or squirrel gun ever in hand. His face beaming, a little sun. Bill dreamed sometimes of sitting across the table from Dean at Mack's Cafe in Oxford, buying him plates of fried eggs and flapjacks while the kid told him tales of gigging bullfrogs by torchlight or stalking braces of grouse. His naked heels would be swirling over the floor as he spoke, and Bill would tell him of his exploits in the skies over France. He would tell Dean of pouncing on squadrons of Huns from the blind white eye of the sun, scattering their triple-wing machines like so many baitfish and watching them dive for the earth to escape his guns. Little Dean would be listening openmouthed, his tongue covered in yolk and crumbs, his eyes welled with awe for his big brother Bill, the hero.

Cadet Faulkner puffed again on his pipe, looking to the page.

The sunlight
Paints him as he stalks, huge through the morning
In his fleece and leather, and gilds his bright
Hair . . .

Estelle, he knew, was in Hawaii now, her body brown-baked by the Pacific sun, the fuzz of her forearms flecked with bright sesames of sweat. That double-diamond ring smiling on her finger, proud of its conquest. Her fingers and toes painted pink, like candy for his tongue.

He blinked the image from his mind, looking instead to the lake. There, he could almost see the ghost of a long-dead bull moose splashing in the shallows, chest-deep, the water streaming from the vast candelabrum of his antlers, and the elusive lynx or gray wolf slinking through pines etched against a dawning sky. He could imagine fleets of canoes slicing through the early mist, manned by feathered warriors of the Iroquois nation, ready to redden their hatchets with the blood of the Huron, and the lake edged with sleeping wigwams, pole-framed and sheeted in bark, each whispering a spire of smoke to the sun.

A century later, the flat-bottomed bateaux of the French would appear, their gunnels lined with silver-coated men, each in tricorne with musket readied, their bayonets glittering like teeth in the dawn. A huge Huron scout crouched in the bow, red-faced and furred, leading Montcalm's regiments to avenge the death of his ancestors. Then, in 1812, the twenty-gun sloop of war, HMS *Wolfe*, flagship of the British line—he could see her wallowing amid a churning storm of powder smoke, dismasted, her sails shredded by the carronades of an American corvette, her decks sloshed with blood.

After that, the great palace steamers of the antebellum North would reign, paddle-wheeling from port to port, their natty passengers sipping brandy beneath the sway of crystal chandeliers, and some of those liners destined to burn hissing into the depths, their passengers entombed in the cold stone of the lake.

So many ghosts. They rolled like mist across the water, like the palest fire, spirits released from husk and hull, from the giant coffins that littered the vast darkness of the lakebed. The past was alive before him, risen, and he wondered if that was how God saw the world, the everpresence of the earth burning beneath his eyes, a vast conflagration of specters and souls. He wondered if he, too, were but a ghost beneath the sight of heaven.

He set aside the poem of the dawn-gilded ace and began drafting a letter to Estelle instead, striking out attempt after attempt at an opening line:

~~Dearest Estelle,~~
~~The leaves are beginning to turn here and blood-red blossoms cover~~
~~the brick walls as though myriads of crimson butterflies have alighted~~
~~upon them.~~

~~Dearest Estelle,~~
~~I know now it is not under the Mississippi sun that my fate awaits,~~
~~but in the clouds over Europe.~~

~~Dearest Estelle,~~
~~I love you and I am going to fly away tonight to steal you from that~~
~~damnable husband of yours.~~

Cadet Faulkner struck out each scribbled assay into the white blankness of the paper, unable to find the lance of truth that would touch her heart. Finally, he growled and set the letter aside, returning to the poem. Here, a man would ascend to battle in the vast arena of the sky like some machine-age knight, not even the thin silk of a balloonitic's parachute beneath his bum. An ace. A man unlikely to return to earth, less by fire or fall.

Thus Faulkner kindled him, a creation his own.

12

Dawn Patrol

SOUTH GEORGIA, 1933

Zeno knelt on one knee beside the Jenny, as if genuflecting. He was throwing up. The sun had just risen in the east, a milky orb diffused through the yellow pall of ash. The burnt air stung their nostrils and raked their throats, and Della wished her tears were only from the smoke. She went to Zeno, his form balled beneath his leather coat, and placed a hand on his shoulder. His spasms sang up her arm. She could almost feel the wet rattle of his lungs.

This terrible ritual, every morning, like penance for the night's debauch. His right hand was still bandaged, curled like a red mitt against his chest, and his body quaked and quaked. Usually it disgusted her, the puddle of gut acid, the glistening filaments strung from his chin, but he'd just saved their lives. This man had flown them out of the firestorm and landed them in a pasture, gently at night, when the fuel ran out. She patted Zeno between the shoulder blades, and she had a sudden urge to climb onto his back, to hook her heels about his waist, her hands about his neck, and ride him like a giant animal, a bear from the woods. She would never let go.

He heaved again, then wiped his mouth with the back of his hand, laying his jaw sideways on his knee and looking at Hardin. The man stood dazed and canted, staring back toward the rising sun, where the swamp still burned. His lips were gummy and white. His eyes so wet, it might have been his own barn on fire, his own animals burning. He was holding his hat over his heart with one hand, his other hanging forgotten at his side. Sark stood beside him, sniffing excitedly at the tips of his fingers. The dog turned and looked back at them, head cocked and ears up, innocent, as if asking a question. Della looked down at herself, only to see the topmost buttons of her breeches still undone.

Her heart lurched.

Zeno had already seen. When he rose, he had his big English revolver out. "Hardin!" he roared. "You touch my wife?"

The man turned, his gaze fastening on the small mouth of the barrel. "What?"

"I ain't forgot that time in France," said Zeno. "That barmaid I fancied. You done me that way again?"

Hardin's face paled—perhaps he'd just remembered the act. His shoulders fell. "I, I was drunk, Zeno. I didn't know what I was doing. But she stopped me."

Zeno held the pistol straight from his arm, his body turned sidewise like a duelist's. "She shouldn't have had to."

"I'm sorry."

"You were a brother to me. I ought to kill you."

Della could see the pressure rising inside him, like air in a balloon. "*Zeno*," she whispered.

He cut his eyes to her. They were wet. He looked back to Hardin. "Start walking," he said.

"To where?"

"To where I can't see you no more."

Hardin turned and started toward the rising sun, the burning swamp. Once he stopped, as if he would say something, but Zeno only cocked the hammer on the pistol. Hardin seemed to nod, then kept walking toward the distant light.

"He started it," said Zeno.

"Yes."

"But you stopped him."

"Yes."

"And this was the first time?"

"Yes."

Zeno had held the pistol on the diminishing figure of Hardin until the man was long out of range. Now the gun hung against his thigh.

Della looked at it. "Zeno?"

"Yes?"

"I didn't stop him quick as I should have. Part of me didn't want to."

"Why not?"

Della looked down at her hands, so like paltry wings. Five-feathered, flightless. "Because I'm a coward."

Zeno lowered the hammer and slid the pistol back inside his coat. "The hell you are. That's one thing I know. Now tell me why."

Della felt the words hammer against her throat, wanting out. "I got nothing in this world but you. No home. Daddy's dead, my mama, too. And you could be gone any day. Sometimes I think you're already gone, or want to be. Sometimes I worry I've given my heart to someone who'd rather crash than fly. Somebody who'll destroy me, wreck my heart so bad there's no putting it back together."

He reached out and took her wrist. His thumb lay on the thin blue veins there, branched like rivers beneath her skin. "I'm here," he said.

Della looked at the ashen sky, crossed by fleeing birds, and the Jenny sitting smoke-stained and sloppy in the grass, like a wilted pan-ama hat. "Sometimes I think we're already dead. We're killing our-selves a little every day, using up our luck, racing toward the dark. I think maybe we're no better than Daddy. Least he had the grit to get it over with."

Shreds of debris floated about them, lazy as motes. Zeno pressed his thumb against her pulse. "If we're dead, we're in hell together," he said. "So it don't matter."

"You drink too much. It scares me. You drink yourself from the world. From me."

"I won't drink so much."

"You don't touch me like you used to."

Zeno nodded. He led her by the hand, away from the Jenny, toward the woods.

"Stay," he told Sark.

Afterward, they lay latticed in the shadow of the pines, notched like puzzle pieces on the spread pallet of their coats. The woods croaked and ticked, hazed with smoke, and Della was running her fingers over the hardened flesh of Zeno's burns, like a range of mountains risen welted and pink from the furred landscape of his arm and chest.

She knew the scars itched him sometimes or gave him phantom pains. She let her fingers, cool and white, trace the valleys and slopes, like soothing weather. Her knee lay over his thigh. It had been good, like the early days, when he couldn't seem to have enough of her. When it was like he loved her so much he might kill her, holding her by the neck, forehead to forehead, his thumb in the hollow of her throat. When he bent hungry between her thighs and she went outside herself, floating ten feet above, watching the pair of them writhe on the grass.

"Tell me," she said.

Her head was riding the gentle swell of his chest. His eyes were closed. "Tell you what?"

"What it was like." Her fingers pushed softly into the scar tissue. "When it happened."

Zeno turned his head and breathed into her hair, as if he could inhale her spirit from the top of her head. "You smell like smoke," he said. "You sure you weren't the one started this fire?"

"You're changing the subject."

"This hair of yours." He held up a fistful of bright red curls. "I believe you could set the world alight."

"Tell me," she said. "I stand to know."

"What it was like?"

"To go down," said Della. "To burn."

He inhaled, long and slow, filling the twin airships of his lungs. They swelled beneath her head, stayed rigid.

"I don't like to talk about it."

"I know you don't. But you think about it all the time. I can see it. I stand to know. I'm in that plane with you every day, up there." Her eyes searched for a break in the canopy, a space where she could scan the blue above, but she came up empty. "I stand to know, Zeno."

Zeno exhaled. His eyes were clear, empty of drink. He looked up toward the splinters of sky glaring down through the pines.

"Eleven days," he said.

"What?"

"Eleven days. That was the average life span of a new pilot on the Western Front. You know those bad mornings we have sometimes, when the air feels too thin?"

Della nodded. Sometimes they both felt it, sometimes only one. It came in the mornings, not long after waking up. A sting in the chest. The wind sharp, the veil thin. The sense of a dark shape out there in the sky, unseen, swimming close. Sometimes they canceled the show; usually, they had no choice but to go on.

"Well, it felt like that all the time," said Zeno. "Like there wasn't hardly enough air to fly, even to breathe. The Fokker Scourge had already come and gone, when the Germans first got the machine guns that could fire between their propeller blades, turning the Allies into *kaltes Fleisch*—cold meat. But then Richthofen and that fucking Flying Circus of his had come along. Names were being chalked off the board left and right. People were calling the Royal Flying Corps 'the Suicide Club.'"

Zeno breathed in, out, looking up through the trees again.

"It was one of those bad mornings, the day it happened. So cloudy you couldn't see the sun." He let his fingers catch in her curls, but gentle.

"Still, cloudy could be good. With a low ceiling like that, nobody could leap out at you from the sun."

He shook his head.

"I still don't know how they managed it. They dropped out of the clouds of a one, right in front of us, a squadron of *Dreideckers*—triplanes—like a cloud of bats. They were already shooting." He squinted, as if picking their shapes from the motes. "There's that moment between when you tell your hand to do something and when it does it, that was all it took."

He pulled his fingers from her hair, then smoothed it down.

"I seen MacMonagle, beside me, go up like a torch. I stabbed the rudder and yanked the stick, I don't even know what direction, and I was rolling and twisting toward the ground. I remember thinking how pretty it all looked, France, all those green and brown fields laid out like from above. Like the maps had come first, neat as plans, and it was all order and logic. Then I pulled out and Mac's body came streaking past me, on fire. He was flailing and thrashing, like he couldn't claw himself fast enough into the ground."

Zeno clenched his jaws, swallowed.

"I remember being glad it wasn't me."

The scars were sharp under Della's fingers, harder somehow, as if newly risen.

"Maybe it was that thought that done it," said Zeno. "That bad thought. Because a finger of fire came pouring out the port side of my engine, like it was looking for me. I raised my hand to shield my face and it went streaking up my left arm." He sniffed. "Sometimes I think it was God trying to scorch my insides, to show me how black my heart was."

"It wasn't," said Della. "You know it wasn't."

"I know why everybody jumps. Anything is better than burning alive. You'd do anything to get away. What saved me was the gun. I put it to my head, but I couldn't do it." He was looking far past the canopy of pines. "In that moment, burning alive, I believed. I knew there was a hell. I was there. Right then, I would have shot God himself between the eyes for putting me there, but I couldn't shoot myself. Instead I flew. Down, fast, like I could bore a hole to hell if I hit the ground hard enough."

Della could feel the rise and fall of his chest, track his heartbeat nearly in sync with her own. It never rose, never wavered. She realized he must have relived this moment—his own death—again and again, thousands of times, so that it no longer raised his pulse.

"Next thing I knew, I was lying on my back in a field. I could see the plane standing tail-up in a ditch, burning." He paused. "I could smell myself, like meat."

He let his fingers dip back into her curls, inhaled her hair. Improbably, his heartbeat slowed.

"Thing is, after you've been on fire, it's hard to feel anything else. The scale is off. Nothing else, no feeling is close. I never felt much of anything since then, till I met you. You were like fire in my blood."

"Fire goes out."

He took her by the back of the neck, his hand big enough to crush her. "Ours don't."

Della clung closer to him, the vast landscape of his body.

She believed.

The sun rose blindly over the land, the sky yellow-bellied, linty with floating debris. Their throats were raw, their faces creased with black lines of soot. The woods had become strangely quiet, as if calmed by the smoke. Zeno whistled for Sark.

The dog appeared from the haze, his black beard cutting through the brush like an ax.

"Water," said Zeno.

The dog seemed almost to nod, then stormed on through the smoke, the underbrush swaying behind his haunches. They followed, wearing only their boots, their sundries gathered under their arms. Soon the dog was barking, announcing his find.

Zeno tapped his watch. "Seven minutes thirty-one," he said. "Still got it, old man." Pride in his voice, as for a favored son.

The creek was tea-brown, lazing through the pines. Della squatted in the stream, balling herself, the current tripping over her shoulders, gathering in the little cups of her collarbones. She let it curl around her breasts, whisper between her legs. Zeno floated on his back beside her, his face and chest humped from the water, his toes pointed up. Their clothes hung drying in the trees, newly scrubbed, while their boots stood like tired old soldiers on the bank. Sark trundled back and forth through the bushes, maintaining a perimeter.

Della, still balled, strung her arm beneath the surface, cradling Zeno's head in her palm. He was so light, floating there, like something that could fly on its own. A Zeppelin or observation balloon. She scratched the back of his head beneath the water, her nails finding his scalp.

His chest rumbled, a sort of purr, and his eyes rolled closed. "You want something," he said.

"Is that wrong?"

"Not if you keep this up."

"I think it's a sign."

"What is?"

"The fire. It's telling us to move on. The past is over."

"It ain't ever, honey."

Della rose from the water. She could feel the slick white planes of her body, semi-sharp, shaped as if with knife and thumb. Her breasts small and firm, the nipples purple. The reddish wedge of her loins.

Zeno looked up at her.

"Here's your future," she said. "You want it or not?"

"Where will I find it?"

"West. California. It's time. I'm tired of circles. I want a line with an end."

"Careful what you wish for, girl."

"Don't act like I'm a child. You didn't just sweep me away, you know. I knew exactly what I was doing that first night I came to you, and I know what I'm doing now. That contraption we have out there, that *flies*, it was meant to go places. I don't aim to be a goddamn buzzard, circling the dead. I aim to chance the journey. I chanced it with you, and now I'm asking you to do the same with me. I know it scares you. It's the only thing that does, as far as I can tell. Living. You don't want to leave those boys you knew. The ones that didn't come home. You think you deserve to go down like they did, or worse. Not in glory, far from. It's like you want the shame of it, dying for eight dollars in a farmer's hat, leaving a scar in some field that'll never heal. Well, here's news for you, man. You don't. You're coming with me, and we're going West, and we're gonna live until we die."

Zeno reached up and took her wrist.

She wanted to kneel alongside him, to beg, but instead she stood there, rigid as a statue, while the current swirled around her hips. Zeno lifted his head, setting his cheek against her stomach. He'd shaved and his jaw was smooth, like some younger version of him she never knew. He rubbed his chin back and forth below her navel, his mustache tickling her skin. He looked up at her, his face rising sunlike over the pale fields of her body.

"West," he said. "I'm game. Wherever you are, I'll go. But the Jenny, she'll never make it that far. All the way across the country."

"The hell she won't," said Della. But she knew. She knew the machine had been flown hard for more than a decade, pulling loop the loops and barrel rolls, landing rough in field after field, lashed by rain and wind and snow. She thought of how it had looked that morning, sooty and withered, slightly out of true.

"We need us one of those Waco Nines," said Zeno. "With the three cockpits. One for each of us. Or maybe one of those new de Havillands, a Tiger Moth. I figure that'll do."

"It will, will it? Just where in the hell are we going to get something like that?"

Zeno kissed her below the navel, softly, then paddled back, stretching out in the current. He was smiling. "Where there's a will," he said.

Della looked along the bank. There hung their yellowed shirts and undergarments, their fraying socks and trousers and battered coats. There hung Zeno's holster, looped from the branch of a sapling, the handle of the gun curled crooked and black.

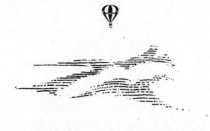

Book II

13

Count No-Count

OXFORD, MISSISSIPPI, 1919

Bill Faulkner strode down the sidewalk of the Square, chin high, shoulders square, a swagger stick tucked under one arm. He was limping slightly, clad in the powder-blue flying officer's uniform he'd been wearing when he stepped off the train in early December 1918, returning from Cadet Wing into the outflung arms of his family. Now it was February, and the uniform hung still tidy and blue in his wardrobe each night, resting from daily rounds of wear. A Sam Browne belt was lashed across his chest, polished a leathery gold, and the pips of a full lieutenant—twin Bath stars—rode high on the shoulder boards, catching the sun. He was wearing his overseas cap set rakish over one ear, his mustache trim and dark. A pair of aviator's wings fluttered on his breast, as if sprouted directly from his heart.

Behind him marched Dean Swift in his Boy Scout uniform, the pair of them parading high-chinned before the dour white face of the county courthouse, as before the bemedaled commanders of a review stand.

They were headed to the bank.

In the pocket of Faulkner's tunic was a check for $73.69, his discharge money, which would nearly cover the cost of the uniform. His service record stated he'd been discharged "in consequence of being surplus to R.A.F. requirements." The Great War, after all, had ended on the eleventh hour of the eleventh day of the eleventh month of 1918, when the Armistice was signed. Pursuit pilots were no longer needed. In France, surplus warplanes were being thrust into heaps and set alight, their skin curling from the blackened skeletons of their wings, their control wires glowing bright. In the States, you could buy a war-surplus Curtiss Jenny for $500, though it might as well be twenty times that much for William Cuthbert Faulkner, formerly of the Royal Air Force, with a heavy charge account at a big-city sutler.

"Bill!"

A tubby man in a rumpled suit came hurrying across the road, hailing him, his chin jiggling over his bow tie. His name was Harlan or Hubbard, perhaps Horace. A lawyer. Bill had gone to school with him. The man had missed the war because of a weak heart.

"Bill," he said. "I heard you was back." The man held a newspaper rolled in one hand, slapping it hard against his palm. "Hot damn, I heard you was a flyboy for the Brits."

Bill and Dean Swift stood stiff-backed, as if at attention.

"An aviator," said Bill. "That's correct."

"You see any action?"

"We beat the Kaiser before I got my chance at any Huns. But Armistice Day, that nearly killed me."

Dean Swift stood beside him, looking up, his chest swelled with pride. The man rolled the paper tighter in his hands. "Armistice Day, how's that?"

"Took up a Camel to celebrate," said Bill. "Snub-nose mother, all motor and smoke, runs on castor oil. The devil's own machine. Crock of bourbon between my knees, just to settle the tum. Executed some stunts for the boys. Chandelle, Immelman. But they wanted a loop. Could see them down them there, whirling their caps." He paused.

The lawyer held the rolled paper in both hands, tight as a control stick, his knuckles white. "And?"

"And I executed nine-tenths of a perfect loop."

"Nine-tenths?"

Bill nodded. "Hangar had the audacity to stand in the way of my per-fect ten. Flew right through the roof. Ended up hanging from the rafters, trying to drink my bourbon upside down." He shook his head. "No easy task, that. Too much goes up your nose, bud."

The lawyer slammed the paper against his thigh, hard. "By God," he said. "By God. Did you get hurt?"

"Cracked up my leg. Little limp is all."

"Well, by God. I reckon it could of been worse—"

"And my head," said Bill. He tapped the swagger stick to the brim of his cap. "Silver plate in my skull."

"*No.*"

"Oh yes." Bill leaned forward, turning his head and removing his cap, rapping the metal crown of the stick against his skull. "Can't you hear it?"

The young lawyer bent toward Faulkner, turning his ear to the sound, eyes squinty with concentration. He bolted upright. "By God, I hear it! They put a plate in your head!"

Bill replaced his cap, a jaunty tilt. "Only medal they gave me, bud."

The man started to say more, but Bill held up the swagger stick in a departing salute.

"Good day, sir."

He and Dean Swift strode on, leaving the man dazed in their wake, as if wand-struck, the rolled paper dangling from his hand. They were some distance away when Dean spoke up.

"I ain't know you had a plate in your head."

Faulkner winked at him beneath the high shade of his cap. "There's a lot you don't know, Little Brother."

A pair of old-timers sat on nail kegs in front of the hardware store, men gummy and chinless, a spittoon between them. At intervals, they leaned and rang the brass, their bullets black as tar. They were nearly eighty now, veterans of the First Mississippi Partisan Rangers, or so they claimed. Colonel W. C. Falkner—Bill's great-grandfather—had raised the regi-ment. Hard to know if these mossbacks had ridden with the Old Colonel or not. Their peers were all laid aground, wearing stone monuments on their chests.

"Look-it here," said one. "Yonder they come, the great-grandsons."

The other tugged on his earlobe, wagging his head. "The Old Colonel would roll in his tomb."

"Aye," said the first. "These his descendants, strutting like a pair of banty roosters."

Bill and Dean came within range.

"Where you boys headed to?" asked one. "Yon nursery, gone suckle you some teats?"

"You ain't need to be gussied up such for that," said the other. "No-sirree. They'd take you in your birthday suit."

The brothers stood before them. Dean's Boy Scout sash, studded with merit badges, lay across his chest at exactly the same angle as the gleaming slash of his brother's Sam Browne belt.

"We are going to the bank," said Bill.

"You walkin' with a limp there, Billy Falkner. Got you a cob in the ass?"

"Could be it's the *u* in his name," said the other. "I heard he come home with a queer letter wedged up there in his Falkner."

"Well now, there's a thought. I heard you was flying them air machines. Course in our day, we never had no *machines* to hide behind, no-sir. Kill a bluebelly, you had to see the whites of his eyes."

"Aye," said the other. "Run him through with your saber, or else bust a cap in his heart."

The first old man wagged his finger at Bill. "Your great-granddaddy had two mounts shot from under him at First Manassas, you know that? Killed him a chance of Yankees despite."

"Colonel William Clark Falkner," said the other, looking to the sky and closing his eyes. "The Knight of the Black Plume, he was, christened by Beauregard himself on the field of battle, charging Sherman's guns with a black feather in his cap. 'Men, follow yonder knight of the black plume and history may never forget you!'"

"Bless him," said the first. "They don't make men like that no more. Never needed no *u* in his name, now did he?"

The other old-timer opened his eyes and looked hard at Bill. "No, surely not." He leaned and thwopped a slug in the spittoon. "What do you propose to do with yourself, young namesake, now that your wings have been clipped?"

Bill straightened. "I propose to write."

The old-timers laughed. Wet, death-edged hacks, like something trying to chop its way out of their lungs.

"*Write*? You won't write nothing so grand as your great-granddaddy done."

"Aye," said the other. "*The White Rose of Memphis*. There was a book. Riverboats and romance, murder and masquerade."

The novel, written by the Old Colonel after the war, took place on a Mississippi steamboat during her maiden cruise. The murder-mystery had become a bestseller, subjected to multiple reprints and serialized in the Ripley *Advertiser*.

"They don't write them like that no more," said one of the mossbacks.

"Amen," said the other. "I believe the blood's run thin."

"The Old Colonel, he wouldn't brook a century such as this'n."

"No, surely not. He'd bust it a cap between the eyes, sire the world from scratch."

"He wouldn't brook no peacocking, neither, not from men of his command."

"We never flaunted ourselves such."

"No, sir."

"Never hussied about in our grays."

"No-sirree, nor flown our flags and banners."

"Not like the bandy-leg bucks of today, so full of piss and snot."

Bill stood rigid before him, the swagger stick held underhand, tucked under his arm. His black eyes danced, bright with flame. "But there is a singular difference, is there not?"

One of the old men spat. "What's that?"

"You lost."

The old-timers' mouths fell open. They were silent, as if gagged.

Bill turned on his heel and continued down the sidewalk, Dean trailing close behind him.

The old men watched, slack-mouthed, while the great-grandson of their commander limped away. Finally he was out of earshot.

One of them licked his lips. "High-flutin', that one."

"Thinks he's something special in the world, don't he now?"

"No wonder they calling him the Count."

"Count No-Count, more like it."

The other laughed, phlegmy and sharp. "Says he's going to write."

"Huh. That boy couldn't write a book if God whispered every last word in his wet little ear, like them prophets of old."

14

Daughters

Fuel," whispered Zeno.

Sark jumped at the word, starting through the woods. Zeno and Della followed, dressed now, pushing through the palms and shrubs of the flatwoods. It was nearly noon and the smoke had only thickened, so heavy you could stare straight up into the yellowed eye of sun.

"Don't do that," said Della.

Zeno looked down. "Why not?"

"You'll go blind."

"The priests said the same thing about self-abuse. Yet here I stand, eyes like a hawk."

"Not for lack of trying, I presume."

They kept on, and soon found themselves among catfaced pines, chevron-cut for resin, the freshest slashes bleeding sap into tin gutters. A turpentine grove. The catfaces hovered amid dirty rags of smoke, and Della could sense an edge of panic in the burnt air. Unknown birds wheeled beneath the sun, angling like bats, while gopher tortoises dragged themselves through the brush like living stones. Snakes whipped and skated through beds of straw. The entire forest was heading west, she thought, same as they would. The thought rose winged and burning in her chest.

Where there's a will . . .

Soon they were among turpentiners, Black men wielding long hacks like reaper's scythes. Their bony shoulders were hung with sun-beaten overalls, thin as paper, nearly white. They were cutting high streaks in the pines, nailing troughs to catch the bleed. They straightened at the sight of the white strangers, tipping the brims of their rumpled newsboy hats. Sark trotted on. The trees broke, and here stood the turpentine camp. Barrels of pitch and resin stood in soldierly rows, the wooden staves hooped in iron, the heads caulked by hand. Beyond this a miscellany of buildings, tin-roofed, swarming with men Black and white. Boilers chugged under wall-less roofs, distilling turpentine like whiskey through heavy coils of copper. Great vats of boiling water steamed, burning the hardened sap from used troughs. Men lowered and raised them with long iron tongs, as if engaged in some ritual of absolution.

The pitch had once been used to waterproof the rigging of sailing ships, to caulk the seams in their hulls. Della thought of the three-masted schooners and brigs that once sailed the state's timber to far points across the globe, the lumber laid flat as corpses in those enormous holds. She thought of her daddy, who'd watched those wooden ships turn to iron, their sails puff into steam, and the green army of virgin pine, so vast, fall finally before the iron blades of men. He'd been a kind man. His eyebrows were bushy and white, his hair, too, and his eyes were clear, bright as tiny ponds. He'd been quick to sit her on his knee, to tell her stories of Highland ancestors and Indian kings, of sea monsters in the dark slink of the river that fed the mills. He'd seen war in Cuba, she knew, and felt the burden of ledger after ledger of the family business, trying to keep the mill going for all the men whose families depended on it. He always seemed so brave, like a man straining to hold the world together. Smiling in apology, that he was not God.

"Della."

She looked at Zeno. "What?"

"You thinking about your old man?"

"No. Why do you say that?"

"You have a look, honey."

"Look like what?"

Zeno showed his teeth. He didn't want to say.

"Like what?" she said.

"Look," he said. Sark sat proudly before a Ford A Model truck, panting. Fuel.

By midafternoon they were aloft, floating mote-like beneath giant, slow-rolling boulders of smoke. In an hour, they'd outpaced the worst of it. The sky cleared to an iron haze and they picked up a freight line heading straight west, the iron rails bright with use. They passed melon patches, bunches of cantaloupe and watermelon balled hard and green on the vine, like newborn planets, and shacks slouched rust-roofed amid them, flea-specked with chickens and shoats and rag-clad children. Della wondered how their walls must shudder at the passage of trains.

They passed a small rail platform, the village roofs gathered before the planked altar of commerce. Men stood in the dirt among the buildings, in a circle, waving money like handkerchiefs. Before them, in their makeshift cockpit, a pair of red-waddled bantams wheeled and slashed, game for blood. Della saw the wicked glitter of their gaffs. One fell, flapping in the dust, and the cockfighter raced to his wounded bird. He knelt over the top of it, spitting into its beak, the muscles of his bare back banding with effort. Finally he rose, the creature bled out at his feet, while the winning cock strutted in the dirt. The man kicked the dead cock like a sack of meal, watching it tumble to the edge of the pit.

Della felt the Jenny swing beneath her, rolling knife-edged onto its wing, and they dived through the sky, racing half-inverted for the pit, as if called. Della could hear fury in the shriek of wire, in the mounting roar of the engine, and she knew Zeno was bringing the circle of men beneath the crosshairs of his imaginary gunsight. The bettors, seeing the machine plummeting toward them, dashed this way and that, tripping and crawling and rolling, their money clutched to their chests, and

Della watched one ricochet off a barred door, bouncing stunned onto his butt in the dirt.

Zeno swung the Jenny low across the rooftops, cutting hard across the rail platform, and Della looked back to see the men chasing their blown hats and bills. She could almost hear Zeno's belly laughs over the pounding of the engine. Sark was smiling in his harness, his tongue streaming from the side of his mouth.

In an hour, the sky had nearly cleared, bluing westward, and the city of Valdosta began assembling before them. It brought smoke of its own, pillars hovering wind-toppled over cotton and feed and planing mills, and the city was alive with traffic, motorcars strung like ants along the lanes. Bungalows sprang from green fronds of palmetto, each house square and trim, and Della pitied the people packed so close, who saw so little of the sky. The pines turned to oaks and the houses grew grander, as if sprung from larger seed. They were sided with white clapboard or brick, with heavy columns to suggest their weight, and azaleas blazed wild among the greening statuary of their gardens.

Soon a golf course slid into the view, the fairways crosshatched by mower blades. Zeno circled, lining them up on a straight par five that led to the foot of the clubhouse.

Della turned in her seat, yelling over the roar. "The hell are you doing? They'll have the police after us."

Zeno grinned and pulled the choke. The engine began to sputter and cough, drowning in fuel, leaving a trail of oily black smoke in their wake. "Engine trouble," said Zeno. "Couldn't be helped!"

Finally the engine died, flooded, and the propeller stopped halfcocked on the front of the Jenny. They whistled over a foursome clad in knickers and ties, men who stared gape-mouthed at the passage of the machine, and Della watched their shadow skate down the fairway, strange and angular as a pterodactyl's. Zeno yawed them away from a pot bunker and landed them on the mown grass with hardly a bounce, weaving back and forth to slow the brakeless Jenny before the elevated crown of the green. The flag snapped in the wind. Soon a cascade of men came down the steps of the clubhouse, clattering in their golfing spikes. They looked strangely similar to Della, almost identical. Middle-aged men like her father, each attired in knickers or plus fours, their ties tucked between the buttons of their shirts. Some wore vests or cardigans despite the spring heat, some plaid or woolen caps. But their faces, these were the same: gray faces, streaked and worn like old bars of soap.

They'd seen the propeller frozen on the front of the descending machine.

"What happened?" they asked. "Has there been a malfunction?"

There were shadows smudged under their eyes, and Della noticed how patchy the grass was under their warped shoes, how pale-worn the elbows of their sweaters and shirts.

She climbed down from the cockpit.

"Are you okay, my dear? Have you been hurt?"

They held out their hands, as if they might touch her, but did not.

Zeno set Sark on the ground between his boots.

"They have a dog," said the men.

"How handsome he is."

"A Scots terrier."

"A diehard."

"That's right," said Zeno. "Hardheaded as an ax."

"How can we help?" they asked.

Zeno stood on a stool they'd brought him. He held a wedge of ham sandwich to his chest, chewing, peering at the engine in mock concentration.

"Plug wrench," he said.

One of the men, his shirtsleeves rolled, handed up a long socket from the wooden box of tools carried from the club's machine shed. Zeno tinkered and cranked, the tool swiveling in time to his jaws.

"Pimento cheese or ham, miss?"

Della looked at the platter of tea sandwiches, the bread cut so white and trim. She could hardly believe how hungry she was.

"May I try one of both?"

"Of course."

The men watched her eat with apparent satisfaction.

"She is very hungry," they said. "When was the last time she ate?"

"Have another," they said. "Have as many as you like."

When a waiter appeared on the clubhouse steps with a second platter, the men fell over one another to fetch it themselves, along with fresh pitchers of water, tea, and lemonade, which they set on a folding camp table alongside the sandwiches.

"Would you like another drink?" they asked. "Tea, lemonade?"

"Sometimes we mix them," said another, as if in confession. "We call it swampwater."

They were already pouring her a glass of the mixture, holding the honey-colored drink before her like an offering.

"Like summer in a glass," they said.

"Thank you," said Della.

She ate and ate, watching Zeno's theatrics. He held a spark plug to the sun like some oily jewel newly excavated from the earth, twisting it this way and that. He tapped the intake and exhaust valves with the handle of a hammer, used a grease gun to lubricate the rocker arm assemblies. He filled and drained the carburetor bowls, ensuring there was no water in the fuel. The golfing men watched, feeding him tools and sandwiches and swigs of whiskey from tin flasks they carried. There was an immense patience among them, as if they were observing surgery on some giant wounded bird come down on the smooth grass to die.

Zeno finished his last wedge of sandwich, rubbing his fingers on the leg of his trousers, then straightened from the motor. "Okay, let's try her."

For effect, Zeno laid off the ignition booster with the first attempt. The engine only banged and rocked, belching a clot of smoke. With Della's second pull, the propeller kicked to life, a stuttering wheel of power.

Zeno laid his elbow over the side of the cockpit. "Who wants a ride?"

Della came around the other wing and hooked her fingers on the leather coaming, lifting herself to Zeno's opposite ear. "What about the show?"

Zeno turned to look at her. "We've given them one."

"I want to go up."

The golfers were assembling themselves into line, patting themselves to find their wallets and billfolds.

Zeno looked at them, then back at Della. "There's no need, honey."

"I said I want to."

Zeno chewed on the corner of his mustache. "Okay."

She knew these guy wires and struts better than the bones sliding along the backs of her hands, better than the balusters and handrails of a childhood porch. She swung and reeled among them, hooking them in the end joints of her fingers, kicking her legs high and wide, her body splayed over the scrolling map of the earth.

She knew the club men were breathless, moaning, grasping their own throats or frayed ties, clapping their hearts or hugging their bellies. She knew they had daughters her age, and she'd become them. She was their hundred daughters swinging over the void—clad in silver, sharply contoured, strutting on a stage high over the eyes of men, arousing terror and pride, desire and awe. She was swelled with these women, each so loved, as if her body had been poured full of new blood. She was filled to bursting when she crawled under the fuselage and hung from the spreader bar of the undercarriage, as if from a trapeze, her body blown long and hard and sleek over the green blaze of the land, over hearts swelled big as balloons.

She knew they would kiss their daughters' foreheads anew tonight, or squeeze their hands especially tight—feeling the thin, strong wires that strung their flesh—or they would simply stand at the doors of their bedrooms, watching them sleep, unable to believe what astonishing creatures had come of their blood. She knew, if she did not keep venturing onto the wing, time after time, she never would. The dread would come, heavy as lead, and she would fall.

15

Strawberry Harvest

OXFORD, MISSISSIPPI, 1919

A single stocking still hung from a nail on the mantel. It was March. The Christmas tree was gone from the corner, burned crackling in the yard. The old wingback chair had been set back in its place. The tinsel had been returned to empty biscuit tins, the ornaments swaddled in balls of newspaper and packed in boxes in the attic. The fruit trees were blooming now, the azaleas. Soon Christ would be whipped and harried through the aisles of ten thousand churches across the land, scourged by centurions in tinfoil armor, his understudies ascending crosses of mill-cut pine, as they did year after year.

Brother Jack had not returned from France. His letters had stopped. His Christmas presents were stacked in front of the fireplace, their bows wilted beneath the lone stocking. Bill and Johncy and Dean passed this shrine each day. Each evening they saw their father staring at the stocking over the top of his newspaper, the look of a wounded animal in his eyes.

"He'll be back," said their mother. "I know he will."

Bill was going to victory dances in his uniform, to the post office and the bank and the café. His father eyed the fine cut of the tunic and trousers, the lightning slash of the shoulder belt, the tiny pair of pilot's wings that spoke so loud. One evening, after weeks of Johncy's begging, Bill let his little brother try his luck with the uniform at a dance the next county over. Johncy returned well after midnight, shambled and lipstick-smeared, hardly noticing the shadowy form of his father slumped in a rocker on the porch, a crock of whiskey set between his feet.

His father's hand shot out and clamped his arm, hard enough to bruise. A croak in the dark: "I'm proud of you, Son."

Bill would wonder, always, if his father knew it was Johncy in that uniform. If the uniform was all that mattered.

Bill thought often of Jack. He thought of the specks of steel in his brother's eyes, that morning of their beanpole airplane's first and last flight, when Jack, despite his terror, would have piloted the flimsy craft straight off the bluff. There was iron in the boy's blood, sparking now and again in the portholes of his eyes, and Bill knew the brave were first to die. There were the Huns in their spiked helmets, raking tracer fire across the gray waste of the Western Front. There were rolls of razor wire, which caught young infantryman like flies, screaming for their mothers as they cradled their guts in their arms, and the incessant rain of shells, falling on men like God's own hate. There was hand-to-hand fighting, with bayonets and trench knives, when men cast out each other's eyes with their thumbs, and the shock that left them quivering in huddled balls, weeping, their hands jammed over their ears. So many horrors for these men who lived half-buried in the earth, as if in their own graves—men who had no wings to fly.

In April, a letter. Jack was in a hospital in Hyères, France. He'd been assigned to the Sixty-sixth Company of the Fifth Marines, hardened fighters who earned the nickname *Teufel Hunden*—Devil Dogs—at Belleau Wood, advancing into the very jaws of German machine-gun fire, their bayonets swimming through the wheat fields like fangs. His first fighting had come near the village of Saint-Mihiel, where the dewy hills and stone hedges seemed too pretty for war. There, his family knew, men had died in droves, son after son after son, as if their countries could never run dry of blood. He fought across the charred waste of the 1914 battlefields, where the tattered remains of French and German uniforms swung inexplicably from dead trees and smashed and punctured helmets littered the earth like the shells of killed tortoises. His war ended on the edge of the Forest of Argonne, in the first hours of November, when an artillery shell laid open his knee to the meat and a fragment of shrapnel punched through his helmet, burrowing its way against his skull.

So strange. Two wounds, which mirrored those that Bill claimed.

The limp, the plate in the head.

They met Jack at the train on a hot May morning, clasping his arms and swatting his back and throttling his shoulders. Dean buried his face in Jack's chest, imprinting the medals in pink geometrics against his cheek, while Bill hugged him around the neck, squeezing hard. The family gathered in the black tub of their Model T Ford and bounced home over the country lanes.

There, Christmas in May. Jack sat in the wingback chair in the corner, opening his presents. There was a new clasp knife, stag-handled, and a pewter stein with his initials engraved. A windproof lighter and a bag of saltwater taffy, each morsel wrapped in a twist of wax paper. Jack presented their mother with a gift of his own: the shell fragment extracted from his head, lying on a piece of bloodstained gauze.

That night, Bill and Jack bought a bottle of corn whiskey from the house of a bootlegger near the county line and rumbled from joint to joint, drinking until the stars grew tails and the moon doubled and the windows of nip joints winked like glow-bugs through the trees. Sometime after midnight, they accosted the Confederate soldier who stood eyeless and mustachioed on his marble pedestal before the courthouse.

"Soldier!" roared Bill. "Pa-raaade rest!"

The infantryman held the barrel of his rifle in both hands, the butt set just in front of his right boot. He was staring south, candle-white and lean, as if into the distant past or future. His shoulders and foraging cap were spattered with bird shit.

Jack, lying faceup on the nearest bench, belched. "Steady one," he said. "No fainting from parade for him."

"Soldier!" roared Bill. "What think you now, these two score and fourteen years hence, of thy Just and Holy Cause?"

Above the soldier floated the courthouse clock, ticking against the stars like a windup moon. A hot, dark wind rose from the Delta, moaning against the stone like woe.

"Couldn't have said it better myself," said Bill.

Dawn found them on a high bluff south of the train station, where they used to go as boys. Their tunics were unbuttoned, their ties skewed. The seats and knees of their trousers were stained. They wore their caps at silly angles, as if set that way by laughing girls, and maybe so—who could remember?

Jack stared into the wet eye of his bottle, hiccupped. "You know what kept me going over there?"

"What?"

Jack reached into the side pocket of his tunic. Out came a small black Bible, hardly bigger than a deck of cards but twice as thick. The corners were mashed, the pages rumpled by moisture. The ribbon was frayed like an old battle pennant. He opened the book. Bill thought his brother was going to read a verse that heartened him, that steeled his blood when the star-shells laid naked the dark hours. Instead he pulled a photograph tucked between the pages, handing it to Bill.

It was little Dean Swift, aged five or six, dressed in a white frock, his head haloed in the palest curls, like wisps of smoke. Bill felt the tears gather hot at the backs of his eyes.

"He's so beautiful," said Jack. "I thought about him all the time."

"Me, too."

"They don't make many like that."

"Damn few."

"The only one of us worth a damn, besides Johncy."

"Indeed." Bill touched the glowing figure in the photograph, lightly. "Our star."

A steam whistle crowed the dawn, high and lonesome, and they bellied their way to the edge of the bluff. Chuffed balls of smoke rose from the top of Thacker Mountain, some few miles distant, like a volcano threatening to blow. Soon a locomotive crested the peak, cannon-black and fuming, and the train went charging down the grade, searing along the rails, yanking car after car over the top of the hill. It was a fruit train, the open-topped cars loaded with mountains of strawberries, each like a tiny bright heart.

They watched slack-jawed, as they had as boys.

Jack licked his lips. "You think there's as many strawberries there as boys dead in France?"

Bill felt the sting again behind his eyes. "Eight million? I don't think so."

The rail cars continued to crest Thacker Mountain—one after another after another. The engine charged down the long straightaway toward town, blowing steam and coal smoke, an iron thunder they could feel in their bones. Jack's hands rubbed at the rusty clay of the land, as if burrowing for shelter.

He looked at Bill. "What was it like to fly? To be so far from the earth?"

Bill looked to the sky, dawn-bright and cloudless, and narrowed his eyes. A vast kingdom where it seemed he'd spent many an hour, or would.

"The thing is, bud, once you been up there, you never want to come down."

16

Fury

Summer found them on a peanut farm near the Alabama line, grounded. The Jenny sat in the middle of the barnyard, the half-dissected motor covered in a green tarpaulin. The sun was malignant, a white boil in the sky, so hot you could hardly breathe. Dogs lay deadened in the ticking heat, Sark among them. Chickens waddled beneath the wings, pecking stupidly at the earth, or alighted on the struts and wires.

The piston rings had gone. The motor had begun smoking so bad they had to fly with handkerchiefs tied over their faces, and still that wasn't enough. After all, castor oil was a purgative. Again and again, Zeno had to land them wherever he could, on byroads or ball fields or fairgrounds, so one or both of them could scurry into the woods to squat.

"This is why we never went up against the Boche without a flask of milk and brandy," he said, sipping from a bottle of bootleg cane liquor.

Della, cowering in a gulch nearby, wanted to tell him where he could stick his milk and brandy, but her teeth were clenched.

Over Bainbridge, Georgia, two of the plugs fouled at once, their electrodes too oil-blacked to spark. Nowhere to land among the huddled facades of old coach hotels and supper houses, so Zeno swung them toward the edge of town, aiming for the pasture of Harlan Custer, a peanut farmer who'd hosted their performances in years past. Zeno judged the wind by the orientation of the cows—they always faced into the breeze— banging the Jenny to the earth amid the lowing protest of the herd. They had barely enough money to cover the parts. Zeno ordered them from an aviation outfit in Memphis, who had to send for them from the Curtiss factory in Buffalo, New York.

They spent their days waiting, waiting, helping however they could. Watering animals and slopping hogs, shoveling shit from barn stalls. They walked the clay paths between field rows, inspecting plants for signs of peanut rust or southern blight. They slept on hay bales in the barn, listening to the scurry of rafter mice, the whisper of pursuing cats, their every breath attended by the maddening tick of hay. June turned to July, the days so long and hot. The sun so slow in its diurnal arc, moving west, ever west—as if only to taunt them. The roar of cicada filled Della's blood. She felt trapped, imprisoned in the windless vault of heat. She fought the urge to scream. She was grounded, clipped wingless in green oblivion.

Her only salvation was the summer storms that tumbled across the heavens like granite rockslides. Daily they came. The sky would turn violet, electric, and a steely blade of wind would come shuddering across the furrowed rows of peanuts. Soon the trees would be whirling about the barns and house, storm-throttled, and the land would be lashed with rain, horsewhipped like some beast of burden. Della would emerge from the hot mouth of the barn and stand alone beneath the roar, letting the lightning wire down from the sky, as if seeking the fiery crown of her head.

At first, Zeno tried to drag her back to the cover of the barn.

"Touch me, you'll be bumping nothing but gashed watermelons of a night."

That didn't stop him, but her eyes did, crazed and blue. He held up his hands, backed away, retreated to the porch alongside Cuss, who offered up the crock of whiskey between his boots.

He chuckled, a death rattle from his ancient throat. "She's a hot one."

Together they watched her, bound hair whipping like a foxtail in the wind. Zeno raised the crock two-fingered against the back of his arm and drank, exhaling through his teeth.

"Streak of fire, that one. Stranger to the ground."

Della lay beneath the mad blister of sun, her face flushed a strawberry hue. Grasshoppers zipped through the weeds; gnats spun in lusterless dizzies. Beetles tickled her skin, and she didn't care. In the distance, the black tatters of turkey vultures, riding the death-waft of a heifer in lazy eights. She felt close to the edge of something. A fall, perhaps, and yet here she lay, already aground.

"Girl, you dead or just lazing?"

Della bolted upright.

There stood Cuss, his face like a hunk of sledge-split stone. A forked weed hung from the corner of his lipless mouth and he was leaning his bulk on the knobby end of a shillelagh. He wore a leather gauntlet on his other hand, as a smithy might wear, and upon this heavy glove perched the statuesque form of a giant raptor, blazing brown and gold under the sun. The eyes were hidden beneath a feathered hood, the beak like the hooked blade of some terrible knife.

"Jesus, Cuss. You about gave me a stroke with that thing."

Cuss spat out the reed. "Come on, I got something to show you."

Della stood, brushing the beetles from her clothes. The bird must have been three feet tall. It had feathered legs and yellow toes and talons like curved pieces of obsidian, deathly sharp. Cuss's obsession was birds of prey, which he kept in a row of slatted mews behind his house, each with bathpan and perch and skylight. She'd never paid them much mind.

"What is he, a falcon?"

"She," said Cuss. "Her name is Fury, and she's a golden eagle. Three times the size of a peregrine falcon, and nearly as fast. She can stoop—dive—at over two hundred miles per hour. The Mongols fly them from horseback, use them to hunt wolves."

He had begun limping on through pasture, and Della found herself following him.

"Wolves?"

"Her eyesight is eight times better than ours. She can see the twitch of a rabbit ear from three miles."

"Miles?"

The eagle's shoulders bore white epaulets, like some martial insignia, and the white brush of her tail was brown-tipped, as if dipped in paint.

"Her heart bangs three hundred fifty times per minute," said Cuss. "Same's a machine gun. She's doubly alive compared to us."

Della watched her. She rode the gauntlet so still and tall, as if she were born to his fist. No sign that her blood was singing, her bones full of gas.

"Where are we going?" she asked.

Cuss didn't answer. He just kept walking. His right forearm bore the tattoo of a once-naked woman, kneeling, but she'd been dressed—a two-piece bathing suit inked over her breasts and pelvis—so he could join the navy. She pulsed each time he planted the shillelagh.

Soon they could see the dead heifer in the distance, toppled in the field. Her eyes were pecked hollow, her tongue curled blue. Flies glistened above her, crazed, and the vultures wheeled high above, their shadows scraping the earth. Their wings were broad and dark. They looked like birds of prey but for their bald bloodred heads.

Leather straps dangled from the eagle's hood like tassels. Cuss leaned and took one of these straps in his teeth, the other in his free hand, and slipped the hood. The eagle seemed to swell on her perch. Her head swiveled this way, that way. Her crown was bristly, like a tiny Indian warbonnet, her eyes yellow-gold. They seemed to see all, furious and unblinking, the pupils big as gun bores. Cuss wound back and cast his arm, launching the bird from his fist. Her great wings unfolded, thumping the air, and she sculled her way into the sky. Cuss watched her, shielding his eyes with the massive gauntlet.

"The old hawking books say a golden eagle is fit for an emperor, and no one the less. The French call her *l'aigle royal*. Me, I'd rate no more than a goshawk—goose-hawk—a yeoman's raptor."

Fury kept climbing, rowing herself smaller and smaller against the sky. Della felt her blood rising with the bird, as if the raptor's talons were buried in her heart.

Cuss leaned and spat. "Thing is, the boys wrote them books are dead as hammers."

Fury was higher than the vultures now, still climbing, her wings flung wide, edge-feathers spread like long fingers. Cuss watched.

"The Sioux, they worshipped this eagle. She was the most high of creatures, closest to the sun. Her talons had the power of a giant's hand. She was a holy bird."

There was a piercing sharpness in Della's breast. Her heart was tumbling over itself, and she was breathing through her mouth. Fury rose vertically, as if on a string, climbing straight into the sun. There she was burned from sight, her ascension complete. She might have flamed to ash or entered the kingdom of heaven. She was gone.

Della found herself angry that she couldn't even look at this ball of fire whose cycles ruled the earth. The sun, the likeliest of man's gods. She wanted to see Fury pegged wide-winged against its power, haloed in glory, her wings feathered in crown-fire. A creature that would be cast down only of her own will. Della closed her eyes; purple and blue planets pulsed in the black universe behind her lids.

"Girl."

Della opened one eye. "What?"

"Look."

The heifer lay dead as before. The column of vultures wheeled slowly between the earth and sun, black scraps cradled stiff-winged on the rising heat.

"Look at what?"

Cuss raised his shillelagh.

As if at his command, Fury dived from the upper light, her wings folded in stoop, her body blazing like a bolt of sun-fire. She corrected her dive by slight degrees, tail-steering, searing wingless into the very center of the vultures, flaring gull-winged at the final moment to hammer her victim from the sky. A black burst of feathers, glittering like knives, and the column of vultures exploded in hissing tatters, fleeing the stroke of death. Fury rode her victim to the earth, her wings arched like a parachute.

"An *unkindness* of ravens," said Cuss. "A *wake* of vultures."

In the field, Fury mantled her prey, her wings swelled like a shroud. There she stood stiff-necked, eyes burning, as if posing for a heraldic shield. Then she dipped her head and gutted the bird, lifting a string of viscera in the shining blade of her bill.

"God," said Della.

She felt her own heart had been pierced. Now the wounds were welling, the blood so new and warm it glowed. She turned, feeling eyes on her spine. There, on the distant porch, sat Zeno. He was watching open-mouthed, boylike, his hands clasped between his knees like a churchgoer's. Della widened the red slash of her mouth for him, smiling bright.

17

Body Flying

OXFORD, MISSISSIPPI, 1919

Faulkner stood on the Oldhams' porch, staring into the jaws of the brass lion on the door, which held the knocker ring in its teeth. A daylight moon, full and round, hung in the sky behind him. A handkerchief was tucked into the sleeve of his tweed coat, a cane hooked over his forearm. His tattered volume of Swinburne pinched under one elbow. His breath was ragged, his blood quick. The knocker hovered there before him like something that must be torn from the lion's jaws. Past this, in the belly of the beast, was Estelle. She was back from Honolulu. It had been one year since she'd left. He pictured her inside the house, sitting before the great piano where she'd once serenaded him, her fingers frozen now on the keys. The Chinese amah would be holding Estelle's baby daughter, whom they called Cho-Cho—"butterfly"—and the parlor would be silent, heavy with grief.

Estelle's younger sister—just twenty years old—had been struck with influenza.

She was dead.

Faulkner took the Swinburne volume in his hand. It was the Modern Library edition. The corners of the black leatherette cover were crinkled, the pages worn by his thumbs. He and Estelle had read the poems aloud to each other on this very porch, verses full of "snowbright breasts" and "nebulous noonshine," of "unkingdomed kings" and "tyrannous lust." The volume had kept him company in Canada, at Cadet Wing, when the first wave of Spanish influenza burned through the command and the aeronautics school was quarantined. Faulkner stood untouched among a city of the bedridden and fevered, who moaned beneath their twisted, yellowy sheets. The volume seemed a talisman of some kind, an artifact blessed with the power of their shared history. A protection, should the curse come to call again.

On the flyleaf, he'd drawn the RAF insignia, a pair of eagle's wings spread under the crown, and written his name. Beneath this, he wrote *S of A*—the School of Aeronautics, where they'd studied rigging and fired naked engines on wooden cradles—and *Borden*, the aerodrome where cadets took flight—a post he'd never reached, just as he'd never reached the pulsing chambers behind the white shield of her breast, nor the holy slick between her legs. At the bottom of the flyleaf, he left an inscription of fire and thunder, proclaiming his love.

Swinburne had given him the words, and Houseman and Keats and all the others who seemed to know him as a brother, his pains and wonders, and the rhythms that thundered in the dark of his skull. He straightened his spine, knowing whoever answered the door would be taller than he. Knowing, too, that stature was more than a matter of feet and inches. His eyes rose, burning into those of the brass lion that guarded the door. He reached out and grabbed the loop hanging from its teeth.

A month later, the moon was full again, and Bill, Jack, and another friend came thudding and rocking down the night-lanes in a black roadster, their ties pulled loose, their golf clubs rattling in the rumble seat. They were looking for a nip joint in the woods that bordered the Tallahatchie River. Estelle was on a liner back to Hawaii, heaving through the Pacific swells. The inscription he'd written her was in the chest pocket of his heather tweed coat. She'd torn it from the volume—neatly, he thought, so neatly, with careful crease and tip of tongue—for fear her husband might see the damning candor, the heart-wound bled black in verse.

She said she would not forget the words.

Bill now stared into the quivering mirror of the washtub, holding a dipper in one hand. It was white lightning, clear as branchwater but glory-struck. The starlight bled through the searing liquid; the moon throbbed out of round. Faulkner looked up to the night sky, making sure the stars were still there, fixed in their constellations.

A voice from behind him: "You lookin' at the wrong dipper, *Count.*"

Faulkner looked down from the stars, recalling the tin dipper in his hand. He ladled a full helping of corn whiskey from the zinc tub, then turned to look at the man who'd spoken. Faulkner had seen him in town. He was a foreman at the mill, overseeing the racket of the belt-driven presses, barking at men who poured sack after sack of surplus cottonseed into the hoppers. The man wore the gallused dungarees of his trade, the denim paled with wear, the bib stretched like a breastplate over his broad chest. He out-scaled Faulkner by a good six inches and forty pounds.

Faulkner raised the dipperful of liquor. "Let us see, sir, who can eat more lightning."

The man huffed. "Dandy little flyweight like you, it won't even be a contest."

Faulkner shrugged and raised the dipper. His throat pumped and pumped, sucking down the high-proof whiskey until twin jags flashed from the corners of his mouth. He finished in a single go, exhaling through his teeth, and wiped his mouth with the back of his sleeve.

"Round one," he said, holding out the dipper.

That night, they blasted home through the country lanes, the pines wheeling past like wagon spokes. The foreman lay whiskey-dumbed in the rumble seat, cuddling one of the golf bags, babbling sweet nothings into the ear of a one iron. The Tallahatchie River beamed and sparkled through the trees, like stars poured liquid from a jar, and Faulkner, victorious, rose from his seat, catching the wind in his mouth. The whiskey roared like glory in his skull. He was wearing his British riding breeks, with the leather sewn inside the thighs, and his green golfing socks were pulled up to his knees. His tie streamed from his neck, snapping in the slipstream, and he donned a pair of motoring goggles from the glove box. Here, rising into the starry violence and wind, the great Ace of his poetry.

The foreman sat up from his one iron. "The hell is he doing?" he roared.

Brother Jack looked over his shoulder at the foreman and shrugged, as if they were witnessing the most casual of pursuits. "Body flying."

Faulkner stepped over the door and onto the running board. The road raced silver beneath him, like water on stone, and he placed the worn sole of one six-dollar dress shoe on the fender, then climbed onto the metal barrel of the car's nose, squatting between the leather straps that held down the hood. The vibration tickled his toes. He crouched there duck-footed, his soles arched to hug the slope of the engine cowl, and slowly rose to standing. He spread his arms, winglike, feeling the wind whistle through his teeth.

The Ace took flight.

He banked with the turns, balancing on his bowed legs, the night-roads wheeling before him. His arms carved through the black, butter-thick air, slicing through silver wraiths of river mist. He was piloting a night-fighter over the Western Front, swinging his spotlights through the clouds, searching for blimps or bombers while fireflies danced before him like tracer fire. He was wind-blasted, his heart singing reckless between the trees. He had lost his howling loneliness in the thunder of flight.

A fork in the road, bright as branched lightning. He banked right, the driver left. Faulkner was launched wing-spread from the hood. Soaring, soaring, as he had in the beanpole flier—straight into a ditch.

Faulkner sat on a nail keg in front of the hardware store, his head swathed in white gauze. The pair of ancient soldiers sat on the other side of the brick-propped door, chuckling among themselves. Faulkner's approach had set them tittering.

"Look-it what this way comes," said one. "The Great Swami."

"Where's your crystal ball at, young Turk?"

"Lost it on that magic carpet ride of his, I reckon."

Faulkner had ignored them, entering the store and emerging with a pad of stationery and a fountain pen. Now he sat hunched on the barrel, the pad balanced on his knee, his head wreathed in gauze and pipe smoke. The gold nib of the pen flashed against the paper.

A poem.

Three wounded aviators, invalided out of the field. Discharged. They sit drinking tea beneath the lilacs of a summer afternoon, silent, withdrawn:

> Lest we let each other guess
> How happy we are . . .

After all, they're alive, sent home with "Blighty wounds"—injuries serious enough to remove them from combat, but not to kill. Million-dollar wounds. Meanwhile, at the front, their comrades are dying in droves. The aviators are relieved, yet ashamed of their relief. Among them is the Ace, who once stalked so godlike through the dawn with his hawk eyes and sun-painted hair. How he has fallen. His head is bandaged, his vision unclear.

Faulkner looks up, watching the women walk the sidewalk of the Square. They cast sidelong glances at the strange creature humped on the nail keg, scribbling beneath his gauzy headdress. They are untouchable as ghosts, these women. They drift so slender and silent beneath the lilac dome of afternoon, sliding their way into the poem:

> Smooth-shouldered creatures in sheer scarves, that pass
> And eye us strangely as they pass.

In the poem, the fallen Ace watches them over his cup of tea, half-blind, his world paled and ghostly behind the thin layer of gauze. Unreal. So much clearer was the night over Mannheim, when thin spears of fire rose from the earth, searching for the soft underbelly of his night-fighter. So much clearer, the memory of the dawn patrol:

Of going in the far thin sky to stalk
The mouth of death . . .

And nearly finding her, on the edge of a cloud forest, when the bullet tore through him, killing his machine, and he fell and fell.

One should not die like this.

Here he sits, the Ace, so cold and wan beneath the receding sun. The glory drained from his blood, a blanket over his knees. His brain concussed. He catches but fragments of conversation, shadows of movement. The very lilacs seem to bend toward him, like sympathetic heads, asking him how he died.

I—I am not dead.

So he tells them. He can hear their voices, as from a great distance, whispering among themselves, like the rustle of leaves:

He's not dead, poor chap; he
didn't die—

Faulkner gasps and looks up from the poem, as if surfacing for air. It's nearly dusk. The hardware store has been closed behind him, locked up, the sign flipped on the door. The old-timers are gone, shooed home from their keg perches. The Square has gone quiet. The motley ring of storefronts stares at this strange, scribbling creature in their midst. The bandaged count, the dashed flier, the hunched poet—the local boy bold enough to go to Canada, to return in the uniform of a Royal Flying Corps officer. His imagination seems too big to be grounded, his ambitions too lofty for gravity. His mind seeks truths far larger than points of fact. This local boy mad enough to say he wanted to write and then to do it—to stand into the wind.

18

Firewater

They were aloft again in late summer, hopping from barnyard to barnyard in their dying machine. They performed for the men of the Attapulgus Clay Company, diving into barrow pits fifty feet deep, vanishing between the layered cliffs of sediment only to roar nearly vertical from the far side, spit up from the throat of the earth. They slashed between mountains of overburden and explained the basics of stick-and-rudder to men who operated dragline excavators and steam shovels. They performed at a peanut festival, awarding a free ride to the sashed and crowned Peanut Queen. They watched men scramble after greased pigs in muddy paddocks and others juggle hatchets and flambeaux. A man played the harmonica and guitar at the same time, keeping time with a bass drum he wore on his back.

In early fall, they landed on highways lined with sugarcane mills. Mules, studded with flies, trod in dejected circles, grinding the cane, while the juice boiled in giant vats. Shoeless children played King of the Mountain on piles of ground refuse—pummy—or pursued one another through head-high fields of cane, each with a small knife under thumb to top the stalks and suck the juice. They rose from the roadside ditches, silent as apparitions, to stroke the taut skin of the flying machine. They did not harbor the same awe as the adults, for they'd been born into the age of flight. Instead, their faces were lumpy with determination, as if the touch of a wing might change their destiny, lift them out of this place.

Della searched the earth for their salvation. She searched for the crosslike shapes of other flying machines, factory-bright Wacos or de Havillands or Travel Airs arrayed like playthings on country airfields. She saw only the odd Jenny or clip-wing Canuck, ex–air circus veterans gone to seed, warped and skeletal as fossils. They maddened her somehow. She wanted to leap from the cockpit and dive sweep-armed, like Fury, to rip them from the fields.

They crossed the green slate of the Chattahoochee into Alabama. The longleaf pines had been clear-cut, the same as Georgia, and the land was stitched with rusty stretches of narrow-gauge rail. Dead sawmills rode atop bald red knees of hill, the topsoil bled away, the flatwoods stamped with polygons of cotton and peanut fields. Pickers waded through the white clouds of cotton in straw hats, back-bent, their fingers callused bullet-hard by the thorny clutches of the plants.

Money was growing thin, as it always did. They'd begun cutting out the bottoms of their soup cans to lick them clean, scraping their tongues over the jagged edges of tin to get the last slick of green peas or chicken noodle their camp spoons couldn't catch. Zeno was down to what he called "half rations," using one slice of bread for sandwiches, eating the peels of his oranges, chewing coffee beans to forget his pangs. Della was feeling caved, shaky, as though her skin were glued to her bones.

A small lake slid into view, bottle-green, banked by a neat grid of white cottages. Rowboats splintered the lake, shaded by parasols, while a swimming pool glowed between the buildings like a blue jewel. A health resort. White-haired folks milled about the place, their balding scalps pink beneath the sun. Zeno tipped the Jenny toward the place, as Della knew he would. The only thing that scared old people more than dying, he liked to say, was not having lived.

Attendants in white smocks descended the steps as the Jenny

bounced up the graveled drive, passing a sign that read: SEALY'S HOT SALT MINERAL WELL. The attendants formed a solid line at the bottom of the steps, like football players or legionnaires, behind which the slack-skinned antiquarians leaned and bobbed in their robes and bathing attire, trying to see. Now came the warden, a man in a white coat with a stethoscope hanging from his collar and a pair of wire-thin eyeglasses perched low on his nose. He stood unfazed before the shattering force of the propeller, as if it wouldn't slice him into a hundred bloody ribbons.

Zeno cut the engine and let down Sark, who leapt from wing to ground. The dog circled the warden, cautious. Zeno followed, lifting the goggles from his oil-blacked face. A paler mask across his eyes.

He swung his arms wide. "Rides!" he shouted. "Three cents a pound!"

The doctor marched forward. He stood just short of Zeno's outflung arms, as if waiting to be embraced, his face red. "Sir!" he boomed. "Sir! This is a *health* resort. I will not have my patients' air corrupted by the smoke of this detestable machine, nor their eardrums damaged by the racket."

Zeno withdrew a cigar stub from his coat pocket and stuck it in the corner of his mouth. "Fly before you die!" he roared over the man. "Good for the body, good for the soul! Let that high-altitude sunlight warm your blood, let those sweet clouds soften your skin. And the vibratory throb of that engine, ladies and gentlemen? You can take that to bed!"

At this, the crowd began to shift and mew, their eyes sparking man to woman, their cheeks flushing bright.

"Sir," said the white-coated warden. "Their hearts are not healthy enough for this!"

"For the bedroom?"

"For flight!"

"You hear that? The doctor here says you don't have the heart to fly!"

The crowd grumbled. A quivering of irate wattles:

The hell we don't.

The world ain't killed us yet.

We got more heart than that little prick.

Zeno looked at Della. "The scale, madam, if you please?"

She stepped over the side and handed down the battered bathroom scale, always good for an extra few cents.

Zeno set the device squarely on the ground at his feet. "Let's form a queue, ladies and gentlemen. Come now, come now. No need to be shy." The denizens were shuffling forward now, paying no mind to the smocked young attendants who stood wide-armed on the lawn, trying to hold them back, helpless before the slow stampede of thin legs and polished canes.

The warden was quaking visibly now, so red he might explode. "Sir! You will vacate this property at once, or I shall call the police."

The wedge of aged resortists was approaching the scale, sharpening itself into a queue. The first in line, a woman in her late seventies, strode smoothly past the warden, high-chinned, gently palming the white nimbus of her hair, as if preparing for a date.

The bespectacled doctor grabbed her arm. "Miss Pearl, I am your doctor, and I do not give you permission—"

"Unhand that woman," cried the man behind her, brandishing his cane. "I rode with Fightin' Joe Wheeler in the Cuban Campaign. Spaniards have felt the point of my saber!"

You show him, Colonel!

Stick the little prick!

Give him what for!

Miss Pearl ignored both the fuss and the bathroom scale. Instead, she stood before Zeno and lifted a silver-sequined pocketbook to her bosom, extracting a thick wad of bills. "Extra, for the weight of my heart," she said, laying the money in Zeno's palm, her varnished bloodred nails tickling down the length of his fingers.

Della grinned.

Now Miss Pearl turned to the machine and dropped her robe into a white pool at her feet, revealing the black rubber bathing suit she wore. Her legs were long, cured gold under the Alabama sun, the skin only slightly curdled over the blue and red spiders of her veins. Now she tilted her bottom beneath the cannonball gleam of her bathing suit, fluttering her eyelashes over her shoulder, coy. "I believe I need a boost, Captain."

Zeno was still staring at the money, watching the bills slowly uncouple in his palm.

Della stood on her tiptoes, her lips grazing his earlobe, and gently pinched his butt through the crumpled seat of his trousers. "Better hop to it," she whispered, taking the money from his hand. "*Captain*."

Zeno looked up, as if waked from slumber, and smoothed his mustaches. "Yes, ma'am."

Della sat basking in an Adirondack chair, eyeing the scale and collecting each passenger's money before their flight. They were so light, some of them, hardly the weight of children, as if their blood was slowly evaporating, rising heavenward in advance of their souls. Then Zeno would come sheering down from the sky, slipping the crosswind, and alight softly on the gravel drive of the resort, taxiing back to the front steps. The passengers would descend flushed and beaming from the cockpit, as if shot full of young blood, the years drained from their faces.

The warden, whose name was Dr. Graf, insisted on a postflight medical exam of each resident. He set up an examination table on the lawn, subjecting each air-rider to a battery of tests, prodding and inspecting them with a shining array of scopes and gauges and specula. He listened to their hearts, his thumb clicking away on a large silver stopwatch, and inspected the color of their tongues and cuticles. He measured the circumferences of various body parts, scratching down the figures with a silver-nib fountain pen, and pumped the rubber bulb of a blood pressure cuff, eyeing the thin needle of the gauge, his spectacles riding on the very tip of his nose.

"It can't be," Dr. Graf told himself. "It simply cannot be!"

Soon the doctor called for a secretary, who sat on the canvas seat of a folding stool, legs crossed primly, transcribing the findings into shorthand. Meanwhile an assistant stood by, handing the physician various instruments from a silver tray, cleaning them with cotton swabs and alcohol after every use.

"I cannot believe it," the doctor kept saying. "I simply cannot."

Only half the residents had taken their flights when the sun began slipping from the sky, balling red, shooting long purple shadows across the earth. Soon the fireflies were rising from the grass and Zeno shut down the motor on final approach, gliding featherlight from the dusking sky. The tires crackled along the gravel drive and Zeno pirouetted the tired machine before the front steps of the resort. Sark bounded from the cockpit, seeking his tribute of ear scratches and belly rubs from the assembled crowd.

Zeno followed shortly in his wake. "That's all for today, folks. Too dark now to fly."

Here came Dr. Graf, his face bright. "Please, Captain, you and your wife must stay the night. You will be our guests. Our accommodations are quite comfortable." His arm swung across the resort. The little cottages and dormitories shone church-white in the dusk, like some village of dream. Della thought of the cotton sea of a four-poster bed, in which you could swim for your lover's flesh, and the steaming heaven of an indoor shower. She was imagining those scalding spears of water raking the grit from her skin when Zeno removed the cigar from the corner of his mouth and spat in the grass. A hard *thwop*.

"Oh," he said, "I see them *gauges* of yours told you we were worth a bed." He pointed the frayed end of the cigar at the doctor, the chewed stub glistening with spit. "Well, *Doctor*, we don't need your hospitality. No sir, we'll be just fine sleeping in the fresh air, under the wing."

Della rose and walked away, as if she hadn't known what Zeno would say.

They camped on the edge of the lake, whose surface shone like a silver platter under the moon. It was man-dug, the curative waters sprung from a four-thousand-foot well discovered during wildcat drillings for oil and gas. Dr. Graf came walking down the lawn, his white coat floating behind him, his stethoscope draped like a steely adornment from his shoulders. An attendant trailed in his wake, pushing a wooden cart through the grass, the silver domes of the dinner service rattling on their plates.

Della was sitting on the grassy bank, raising and lowering her white feet in the shallows, watching her toes turn liquid beneath the water. Sark lay beside her, ears pricked, his eyes following the zip of Jesus bugs across the surface of the lake, the purple sway of cattails in the breeze. His eyes seemed darker here, clearer. Meanwhile Zeno stood above them, staring up at the stars. Alcohol was not allowed at the resort, but he'd managed to procure a pint bottle of rye from Miss Pearl, who sold whiskey and cigarillos and naughty picture cards out of her room.

Now he belched through his teeth, eyeing the doctor's approach. "Here comes the esteemed physician." He squinted one eye, as if aiming through a gunsight. "*Graf*, there's a Hun name if I ever heard one. There was a Graf in von Richthofen's squadron. MacMonagle sent him smoking down."

The dining cart rattled to a halt before them. The doctor stood chin-high, proud as a maître d', while the attendant lifted two silver covers from their platters. Steam curled into the night. There lay a meal of stuffed quail, grilled asparagus, and polenta.

"Dinner is served," said the doctor.

Zeno's face softened at the sight.

Soon they were feasting, eating like they hadn't in weeks. Months. They spooned the polenta steaming to their mouths, like golden batter, and white flakes of wing muscle rode the silvery tines of their forks, trailing the scent of rosemary and thyme.

The doctor spoke excitedly as they ate, recounting the results of his tests. He told of improved circulation and blood pressure among his patients, as well as fewer reports of melancholia and constipation. Heart rhythms were stronger, more regular, and he highly suspected that the morning surveys would note intensified night-vigor and deepened sleep, with a high instance of remembered dreams.

"It's uncanny," he said. "It seems that open-cockpit flight is a powerful stimulus for the constitution. The temperament. Even the digestion!"

Zeno forked a whole quiver of asparagus into his mouth. "You really want to stoke the bowels, put a Hun up there in a tri-decker to chase them. No laxative like a pair of Spandau machine guns."

"I'm serious, Captain. I have a proposition to make you."

Zeno looked up, his temples pulsing as he chewed.

Dr. Graf pressed on. "Stay here with us, Captain, you and your wife. Settle down. We shall make air-riding part of our treatment. A cutting-edge prescription, offered by no other health resort, promised to extend the life span and elevate the soul. Octogenarians shall come from all over the world, seeking our lofty curatives."

Zeno swallowed. He looked out across the grounds. Della knew he was taking in the white little cottages, so sturdy and square, and the purple sheen of lawn grass mowed slick. He looked down at his fork, twisting it slightly. This warm treasure of fowl and cornmeal. A life so easy, in which you might live a hundred years. A dream.

He looked at Della.

She could see the vision rising before her, the days cycling so smoothly beneath the sun. The years. Hard roofs and regular beds. Hot showers and porcelain commodes. No hunger or thirst. No strange landings at dusk, descending into unknown worlds. No nights under the wing. No coffin factories or loggers' bets or farmers with leaf-spring knives—just the old-timers shuffling through their final years, back-bowed, as if the earth were pulling them slowly into its bosom, day by day. An unending stream of them, white-haired and sweet, until she and Zeno shuffled alongside them, dazed by the quick flash of decades. More likely, she thought, they would die the very first week—killed by the sheer irony of it.

Della cut her eyes to the west, hard.

Zeno nodded, his eyes flickering with new light. He looked at the doctor. "Snake-oiler," he said. "Quack."

Sark looked sharply at the doctor, who stepped backward a pace, as if shoved. His cheeks balled red.

"Me?"

"You," said Zeno. "You and your longevity prescriptions. What a crock.

Nothing can save these white-hairs from what's coming. You give them faith in a system, and you charge handsomely for it." Sark came forward, as if in reinforcement, settling himself beneath Zeno's hand. "There is no order in the world but the whim of God, cruel before the eyes of men."

"My methods are scientific, sir, I can assure you of that."

"Scientific? Is that what you call these healing waters?" His arm swung across the lake. "This fountain of youth in the Alabama pine barrens?"

"Scientists from Japan and the Middle East have been studying the therapeutic effects of medicinal springs for centuries. It's called balneology, the study of—"

"The study of baths," said Zeno. "Yes, I know. From the Latin *balneum*, for 'bath.'"

The doctor cocked his head. "You are a learned man."

"Enough to know a big puddle of snake oil when I see one."

"I beg your pardon, but those waters are infused with lime and chloride and iron, sodium and aluminum oxide. Even natural gas. The wellspring flows ten thousand gallons per hour, a gift from the earth. Long baths promote circulation, metabolism, even the absorption of essential minerals."

Sark looked from Zeno to the doctor, as if watching the toss of a hot potato or coal.

"Bunkum. And I'll tell you something else: to cling so tightly to life is to strangle it."

The doctor stepped forward and snatched Zeno's tumbler from his hand, slinging the whiskey into the grass. Before Zeno could protest, the man had descended the bank and squatted next to Della at the sandy edge. "Excuse me, ma'am."

Dr. Graf filled the tumbler from the shallows, then turned slowly on the bank. His white coat floated about the pressed creases of his slacks, his tie clip winking beneath the moon. He held the tumbler high before him. The disc of water quivered, as if blessed, and he produced a brass lighter from the hip pocket of his coat and touched the slender flame to the rim. The water ignited. A cone of blue fire, leaping and hissing inside the glass.

"Easy for you, who courts death, to speak of life." He set the burning glass back in Zeno's hand. "A damn sight harder when death takes your throat."

Zeno looked down at the glass, burning like a cobalt torch in his hand. For a long moment, he seemed dazed by the sight. Lost. His mind reeling through the darkness, toward distant flames. Then he looked up at Della and winked. Before she could protest, he hurled the blue wing of fire down his gullet, choking the firewater into his belly. He belched and raised his chin toward the doctor, smiling, as if offering up his throat.

Dr. Graf stood gape-mouthed. His eyes were wide behind the spectacles, as if magnified. Finally he shook his head and turned on his heel. He made his way back toward the white cottages, moon-bright on their little hill.

Della woke in the middle of the night, curled in her sleeping blanket beneath the meager roof of wing. She swiped the red scarf of hair from her face. There stood Zeno, waist-deep in the bright waters. Naked. His broad torso shone, strong as the flesh of some barkless tree. The vast ranges of scar glittered on his shoulder and arm. He was bathing Sark, scratching white valleys into his fur, massaging the healing waters into the dog's skin. These waters, which promised to quicken the blood, slow the years. Which held the blue mystery of flame. Zeno was whispering to the dog, kneading the tiny balls of muscle beneath his coat.

"You getting some gray in your beard, old man."

Sark looked up at his master. The heavy ax blade of the Scottie's beard, once the jettest black, was white-flecked at the edges, powdered with age. Zeno rubbed water into Sark's beard, coaxing and shaping until it grew long and glossy and sharp.

"There you go, old man. Ready to cleave stars and break hearts."

Sark's black eyes shone, slightly foggy, whelmed with starlight, and Della saw tears streaking down Zeno's cheeks.

His face was swollen, trembling, as if holding back some flood, some dark gush of love or pain. "You better outlive me, old man. A hundred years. You and your mama both."

He set Sark on the bank, gently, then staggered ashore himself, whiskey-swayed, trailing the sling of his ancient canteen, newly filled from the lake. His breath was labored and his steps heavy, as if he carried a lost calf or broken man on his shoulders.

Loss. The heaviest thing in the world.

Della mashed shut her eyes for the sake of his pride. She heard the crushed grass of his footfalls, nearing, and the whistle of his breath. She felt his knees drive into the earth before her, hard as pilings, and heard the gritty scrape of the canteen's cap. She felt his thumb, wet from the spigot, touch her forehead, scrawling the glistening symbol of his faith. Now it was upon her lips, the swale of her breast, and she wanted so badly to open her eyes. She wanted to rip the weights from his chest, the heavy stones he carried, blacked by the great fire of his heart. She wanted to crush them to ash in her hands, or sink them in the deep of the lake. She wanted to destroy them, cast them to oblivion, before they could pull him down from the sky, drive him into the earth.

Her eyes flicked wide, steeled with power, but Zeno was gone. He was lying flat in the grass, stark naked, snoring beneath the cool glare of stars.

19

Baby Buntin

OLE MISS, 1920

Everybody thinks I can fly," whispered Faulkner. "But I can't."

Robert Robson Buntin—"Baby"—didn't look up from his poker hand. The cards were spread like a sawmill blade before him, crisp and sharp. The parlor of the fraternity house was hazed with cigar smoke.

Baby cocked his chin toward Faulkner, growling from the side of his mouth. "You don't say."

Baby was short, like Faulkner, but well-built, with cannonball shoulders and a square jaw. His eyes were like a raptor's, clear and sharp. He'd been a test pilot in the Great War.

Faulkner burped, tasting gardenias in his mouth. He and brother Jack had enrolled at Ole Miss the previous fall—just in time for Prohibition. Liquor was scarce. The undergraduates were resorting to cheap perfume and cans of melted Sterno. Faulkner had had a snort of the former before coming to the fraternity house, where Baby was known to entertain entreaties and conspiracies during his poker hands, as if the high-stakes game didn't warrant his full attention.

"Teach me," said Faulkner. "I can pay you."

Baby didn't seem to hear him. His eyes were sweeping the tournament table, the green felt pocked and scarred like an old football field. The other Ole Miss law students sat smoking behind their flushes and busts, red-eyed from carousing, their ties yanked loose. Baby's eyes hunted for nervous tics and tells, the telegraphs of bid or bluff or fold. He saw the bulb of sweat on a man's temple, growing like a blister, or the nervous lick of a drying lip. The telltale twist of a mustache, the twirl of a coin or chip. These were soft-palmed planter's sons, most of them. Baby could pick their daddies' money like roadside posies. He had and he would.

"You pay me already," he said. "I'm making back your money three-fold tonight."

"Keep it."

Baby looked at him, then back at his hand, double-tapping the table for another card.

Faulkner sat back, watching this hard bantam of a man whose muscles slid and bucked beneath his shirt. Baby had crawled from the smoking craters of three separate crashes, when wing spars or tail rudders failed on experimental flying craft, and lived as a country barnstormer after the war, flying town to town in his double-decker ship, looping and rolling for the crumpled dollars of sharecroppers and woodcutters. A man of Faulkner's own stature, he played on the Ole Miss football team, charging and juking across the field, slipping and steamrolling would-be tacklers. Not born to wealth, Baby financed his studies through games of high-stakes poker and gin rummy and boxed in Memphis under an assumed name, not wanting his mother to hear tell of his bloody pursuits. Now he dated "the Pride of Oxford"—Mary Elmore—having swept her from the arms of the town's poetical eccentric and rumored air hero.

Faulkner.

Bill leaned forward, his lips nearly touching Baby's ear. He knew Mary Elmore, despite her new beau, must miss the long nights on the porch when he would regale her and her family and friends with the tallest of tales. When they would become entranced by his stories, their eyes glazed, and he would know he'd brought them inside the vast lands of his own mind, where fact paled before delight. Baby had borne witness to these flights on more than one occasion, his hawk eyes sparking with amusement, even awe. For Baby could do the deeds of tales, but he could not speak them. He could not call up his own past, resurrecting the wrecked machines or fallen pugilists or goal-line tackles, nor could he set them to ink, so that they lived on in the minds and mouths of men, never dead.

Meanwhile, Faulkner's poems and stories had begun appearing week after week in the *Mississippian* and the *Oxford Eagle*—tales of merciless beauties and marble fauns and bumbling air cadets.

Faulkner spoke softly into Baby's ear now, low and confident. "I'll write about you, Baby. Your kind." He lowered his voice yet further— barely a hiss. "You'll never die."

A vein jumped in Baby's neck, clear as a poker tell. He double-tapped the table for another card, then cocked his chin at Faulkner, speaking from the side of his mouth. "What if I don't like what you write?"

Faulkner shrugged, fitting a smoke into the long black tube of his cigarette holder. "Infamy, Baby, is a small price to pay for immortality."

Buntin worked his jaws, then laid his hand upon the table: a straight flush, which easily topped the two pairs and threes of a kind. The table groaned as Baby reached forward and enfolded the small castle of chips and bills in his arms, sliding them toward his heart.

He whispered from the corner of his mouth. "Sunday morning," he said, "while everyone's at church." Now he looked fully at Faulkner, his hawk's eyes blazing. "You kill us, Bill, and I'll find you in hell and thrash you so hard the devil will flinch."

Faulkner leaned back, smiling. He flashed a match, lighting the distant tip of his cigarette. "Deal."

The biplane sat raked and gleaming beneath the blue sea of Sunday sky, the wings glistening as if newly doped. It was a clip-wing Canuck, a Canadian version of the Curtiss Jenny with the wings bobbed outboard of the interplane struts. A stubby-winged machine, blade-quick and deadly. The ribbed skin of the fuselage still bore the mark of Baby's pre-university days, the words slightly faded now:

ROBERT "BABY" BUNTIN: BARNSTORMER

Baby himself stood waiting on the field, caparisoned in full flying regalia: leather cap and wool-lined goggles, heavy coat and riding boots. A white silk scarf stirred restlessly from his throat, as if eager to snap and flicker in the violence of flight. The sunlight slashed down from the blue yonder, sparking against his buttons and goggles, the steely eyelets of his knee-high jackboots.

Faulkner propped his bicycle alongside the airfield's hangar. He had pedaled here in secret, squeaking over the roughshod roads, his body cloaked in a giant borrowed greatcoat. He'd kept his head ducked low beneath a newsboy cap, hiding his face from the church traffic rumbling in from the countryside, the motorcars and wagons bouncing through the ruts. There were the farming families riding in their buckboards, so starched and scrubbed, their milk-skinned daughters with heavy breasts swaying beneath their dresses, their nails gouged clean, their cheeks blushed with the hampered fire of their sex.

All these country penitents, ready to sing hymns and eat the flesh of Christ, burned free of the weekly sins of haylofts and secret swimming holes. Faulkner didn't want them to recognize him, nor the highborn Oxonians in their Sunday best, sitting erect in their Model T Fords, riding high atop the toppled forests and cotton riches of their forefathers. Nor even his own brothers—Jack or Johncy or little Dean Swift, his heart. All these believers, who must not see the storied airman who could not fly.

Faulkner left his bicycle in the shadowed lee of the hangar and stepped into the light. He began unbuttoning his coat, shedding the shoddy black wool to reveal the sky-blue splendor of his Royal Flying Corps uniform. He stood glittering in the sun, medaled with stars and wings, an ace hatched from the woolen puddle at his feet. He strode toward the flying machine, this violent contrivance of blade and wire and wing that never failed to swell his heart.

Baby stood waiting, his face hewn wide and sharp. His blue eyes shone. "Bill, you're going to get oil all over that pretty costume of yours."

Faulkner raised the narrow point of his chin. "I have come for flying lessons, Baby, not sartorial advice."

Baby showed a slim smile of amusement. He clapped Faulkner on the shoulder. "I read your story in the student newspaper. The one about the air cadet?"

"'Landing in Luck.'"

"Yes," said Baby. His square hand worked on Faulkner's shoulder. The same hand had steered clip-winged fliers between the clouds and busted the wag-tongued mouths of Memphis welterweights. "Damn good, that story. Authentic. You must have had some instruction, yes?"

Faulkner nodded, his mouth dry with thrill. "That's right. Cadet Wing, outside Toronto." He licked his lips, trying to unstick the words from the flypaper of his tongue. "Honestly, it isn't the flying I'm worried about."

"No?"

"It's the landing."

"Ah, like the cadet of your story."

"Like him."

"Don't let your imagination overpower you," said Baby. He cocked his head toward the craft. "She's like a woman. You can't force anything. You have to be smooth, gentle. You don't land her. She lands you."

"Right," said Faulkner, as if he knew how to land a woman. As if Estelle Warren had not gone to live at the foot of an oceanic volcano four thousand miles from Mississippi. As if Mary Elmore had not left him for this bantamweight god.

Baby squeezed his shoulder. "You ready, Bill?"

Faulkner looked at the bob-winged flier sitting so high and haughty in the grass.

La belle dame sans merci.

This merciless beauty, which could slash the bonds of earth, lifting him high over the postage stamp of Oxford. Which could kill him coming down.

"I'm ready."

20

Panhandle

*T*hey followed the white thread of the coast, flying over single-street fishing villages huddled at the sea's edge, looking down on salt-weathered shacks built in the age of Osceola, king of the Seminole. Great mullet nets hung drying in the sun. Pods of dolphins patrolled the shoreline and snapper boats bounded through the inshore swells, returning from long weeks of fishing the Yucatán reefs.

Pensacola Bay hove into view, where they planned to winter. There were the great wharves and coaling docks, quiet now, and the ship channel where the odd freighter steamed in lazy commerce. The inner shoreline was built on the discharged ballast of old steamers and square-riggers. Bluestone from the quarries of Italy, red granite from Sweden. Crumbled tile from the blasted mansions of France. The city was largely Spanish, with red-tile roofs and wrought-iron railings jutting over sandy streets, where even the flies dozed during the siesta. A great five-sided fort guarded entry to the harbor, the guns pointed seaward.

They landed on one of the outer keys, raking the sand with their wheels and skids. They left their boots standing beneath the wings. The Gulf, cold as slate, rumbled over their feet. They stayed in the vacation house of a lumber family, former friends of Della's father who used the place only in summer. The cedar shakes were rimed with salt. The sea wind howled against the windowpanes; the house timbers groaned like those of a sailing ship, rattling the nautical decor on the walls. The power was cut off in the winter and they burned wads of old newspaper and dried antlers of driftwood—anything they could for the light and heat and comfort of it. They drank wharf-bought Cuban rum, staring into the bright knives of heat, and made love on a pallet of blankets on the floor.

The Jenny sat hunkered in the side yard, anchored beneath the blown palms. The engine was covered in a green tarpaulin, like the head of a blinkered racehorse, and the wings rocked and shuddered against their moorings. Della drank her coffee in the morning and watched the machine tremble nervously in the wind. Sometimes she wished it would snap free of its anchors and go tumbling through the scrubby island forest, wrecked and scattered among the trees.

The naval air station was just down the coast, across from the coastal fort. Flights of shiny new pursuit planes rumbled overhead, silver-winged, fat as bumblebees, trailing faint whispers of smoke. Their bodies gleamed bright and vicious against the winter sky, barbed with guns, ready for war. Della and Zeno and Sark would stop, their feet in the cold wet sand, and watch the machines peel from formation, one after the next, to practice their gunnery.

"Too bad we can't take one of *those* to California," said Della.

Machine guns crackled over the bay.

"They'd shoot us to pieces before we even slipped the tarmac," said Zeno, watching them pull up from their strafing runs. "Jenny's all we got for now."

They removed the cover from the Model A Ford in the garage and bucked and sang over the toll bridge into town. An eight-story stucco hotel dominated the waterfront, lit like a giant gambling boat at the edge of the bay. Young sailors and air cadets strode beneath the streetlamps, their uniforms starched crisp, stretched tight across their proud chests. They sat drinking sangria in a street-front cantina, the windows thrown open in celebration of the Repeal. Zeno's tongue and teeth were red, as if he'd been drinking blood. He was watching the white teeth of these youths, bared in glee. The unlined skin. He was thinking, Della knew, of the boys he'd watched burn or fall or crack into a thousand shattered pieces.

A pair of young air cadets crashed into the bar beside her, chuckling, ordering double rums. The nearest one side-eyed her, belching through his teeth. "You ever made time with an aviator, honey?"

Della sipped her sangria, not looking at him. "Once or twice."

The second cadet laid his head nearly flat on the bar, so he could see past his friend. "How 'bout two at once? A double-decker?"

Zeno straightened slightly from his stool. "How 'bout three?" he said.

The cadets squinted up at him, as if trying to discern his breed.

"You with that old foghorn?" asked one. "There's gray in his hair."

Zeno swirled his bloodred drink, the chipped ice jingling. "And whiskey in my prick. You want a draft?"

Della could feel their young bodies go rigid beside her. She sat hunch-shouldered between Zeno and them, one hand on her drink.

"Some mouth you got, old man. Careful you don't find a fist in it."

Zeno's tongue swirled over his teeth, slowly. His next words could bust bottles and overturn tables, split knuckles and knock jaws out of hinge. He didn't know but to fight.

"You little know-nothings—"

Della's hand found him under the bar, cupping his groin. His voice caught. She gripped him like a control stick, unseen, sipping her sangria with her free hand. Another drink and he might not have felt her, might have shot off his mouth like a gun. Now he stood there, silenced, his neck tendons flexed. The cadets stood wet-mouthed, like dogs before their master, awaiting command. Della stroked him with her thumb.

She looked at the two cadets. "Zeno was in the Lafayette Escadrille."

Both their heads cocked at the same angle.

"No," said one.

"Yes," said Della.

"Whiskey 'n' Soda," said the other. "You knew them?"

He meant the squadron's mascots, a pair of African lion cubs known to tumble and paw about the airfield.

"Knew them?" said Della. "They licked his face." She squeezed him. "Didn't they, honey?"

"They licked my face," said Zeno.

The cadets turned toward the bar.

"Get this man a whiskey-soda, a double on the double!"

They stopped one hundred yards short of the air station gate, parked in the darkness between streetlamps. It was nearing dawn. The cadets lay snoring in the rumble seat, one head propped on the other's shoulder. The four of them had drunk until the cantina closed and then found their way to the speakeasies of Palafox Street and finally to the sailors' taverns near the coaling docks, where tattooed stevedores and merchant seamen swam in flickering red light, their teeth flashing like knives.

The vast tarmac of the air station lay on the other side of the fence. Naval biplanes gleamed metallic under the moon. There were Curtiss Hawk fighters, sharp-beaked as raptors, built to fly from the flattop islands of aircraft carriers. There were Sparrowhawk pursuit craft, each designed to hang from the trapeze of a dirigible airship, and a squadron of brand-new Goshawk bomber-fighters. Their stainless steel propellers shone like giant scimitars, cocked before engines the size of wagon wheels, the cylinders arrayed like iron spokes.

"Wright radials," said Zeno. He might have been looking at a painting in the Louvre. "Nine cylinders, seven hundred horsepower."

The gleaming planes seemed to be taunting them almost, so close yet out of reach, protected by razor wire, barricades, and roaming patrols of military police armed with canines and submachine guns. An impossibility. The Jenny seemed so fragile in comparison to such machines, a plaything of balsawood and parchment and glue—a craft as delicate as their own dreams, held together with faith, chance, endless maintenance.

Still, staring at these warplanes, Della felt a tenderness for the Jenny, which had carried them so far already and kept rising, morning after morning, season after season, ready to start bounding westward again once the days warmed and they could earn their bread and fuel from the crowds. Despite the winter hiatus, Della had the feeling they were finally heading someplace instead of circling—that they were pulling out of the old spin.

She touched Zeno's back. "We better see if we can wake them."

He nodded.

Della shook the cadets gently, watching their eyes open slowly, hazed with dream, trying to discern their whereabouts. They fumbled and hic-cupped, trying to extricate themselves from the vehicle. Zeno righted each man, gripping him by the shoulders, while Della fixed their hats and neckerchiefs.

One of the cadets held up his hand in salute. "Whisky-soda," he slurred.

They stood behind the cadets, aiming them, then set them walking like windup toys. A wind had begun to blow in from the sea, shoving the aspirant fliers off course, but they succeeded in correcting them-selves again and again, zigzagging toward the air station gate, tacking against the wind like sailing ships.

Della watched them closely, willing them along with her heart. She was only slightly older than they were, but they seemed so young to her. Still boys. Young men who'd yet to be truly afraid, to realize they could die. They were fearless, cocksure, their shoulders pinned high and tight. She hoped such reckless faith would keep them alive through the months to come. She hoped they would settle safely to the earth, softly, each and every time.

Zeno stood beside her, his shoulder touching hers. She looked up at him. He, too, was willing them along, his arms crossed, his thumbs sticking up. She knew he was seeing not just these fliers but all the oth-ers he'd known. The boys with their caps set so rakish and bold, their collars popped careless, their cigarettes smoking before their spotless cheeks. Young men with wings pinned over their hearts, so sure of their immortality, who now lived only on mantels and bedside tables, inside attic trunks and cellar albums and in the broken hearts of mothers and wives and sweethearts, in the bent postures of fathers behind plows or the tills of country stores.

The guards stood on either side of the gate, stony with duty, their mouths grim beneath the white domes of their helmets. The cadets passed with little drama. Then they were gone, vanishing into the vast night of the airbase.

Zeno spat. "Cocky little bucks."

But his eyes gleamed. He put his arm around her, squeezed.

The wind came cracking across Pensacola Bay, slamming the body of the Ford. The automobile lurched on the three-mile bridge, hunting for traction, the windshield clattering in its frame. Dawn was coming—a rumor of light in the east. Gulls raced landward on the gales, quick as bullets, and waves crashed against the bridge piers, spitting foam high over the rails. Zeno fought the wheel, a cigar hanging from his teeth.

This wind had come whirling up from Cuba and roaring across the Gulf, unchallenged but for the odd freighter or cutter or fishing trawler. Now, land-fallen, it seemed angry, bending trees and banging shutters, scalping dunes and shoving automobiles off course. Della thought of the great thunderheads that might follow on such a wind. A squadron of them, like great hydrogen airships, bellied with fire and war. Her belly sang with anticipation.

She rode with one hand on Zeno's thigh, her feet tucked beneath her. Her white canvas shoes lay dirty and limp on the floorboards, coated with the filth of barroom floors. The thin line of Santa Rosa Island rose into view, like a long ship in the Gulf. Deckhands were on the bayside docks, double-lashing yachts and teak-decked cabin cruisers, their hulls jostling on the swells, and the flags of the coastal fort snapped hard in the gusts. There was a wild electricity in the dawn, an apocalyptic hum that stirred the blood. It made Della's thumb work back and forth on Zeno's thigh, as if shaping the clay of his flesh.

When they reached the house, Sark was watching through one of the front windows, his ears perked for their return. They parked in the garage and shuttered the windows of the house and built a fire in the potbellied stove. Soon they had a mouth of coals going, cozy and red, as the wind skirled about the house. The nautical decor shuddered on the walls, the braided halyards and ships' wheels and porthole mirrors. The lifeboat compass rattled on the captain's desk, as did the harbor bell and the engine order telegraph, the needle quivering at FULL STEAM. The floors seemed almost to sway. They might be riding high in the cabin of a galleon or man-of-war, their cannon bristling over rising mountains of seawater.

Zeno stood wide-legged before the stove, the poker dangling at his side. He was staring into the red fury of the coals, entranced. As if these were the most precious of gemstones, glowing with unearthly power.

Della walked up behind him, unseen, and unzipped her jumpsuit, slipping the sleeves. The metallic suit fell away from her like the thinnest armor and she stepped fully from the legs, emerging white and naked from the crumpled metal, as from a wrecked machine.

She knelt and wound herself between Zeno's spraddled legs, coiling herself around one of his great thighs, and then began climbing the front of him, grasping his trouser pockets and his belt buckle and the lapels of his leather flying coat. The firelight slithered up the narrow valley of her spine, flowing like lava against her skin. She could feel the heat rising through the curls of her hair, glowing, her chest swelling.

She set one foot against Zeno's knee, spreading her body wide against him. She grabbed hold of his leather collar and hauled herself from the ground, scaling his body like a tree until she hung in his branches, her feet hooked around his trunk. She felt child-light in his arms, weightless. A creature immune to gravity and loss.

"Baby," he said, his voice deep, happy.

Della pressed her face into his neck, scratching her cheek against his jaw. Then she brought her lips to his ear, taking the lobe between her teeth. Outside, the wind howled.

"Captain," she said.

Della woke to silence. Her flesh felt viscous, melted like candlewax into the pallet on the floor. Her limbs glowed. Zeno snored peacefully beside her, clad in a wrecked toga of blankets, his stocking feet pointed dead upright. Sark lay curled at the foot of the front door, sleeping, while thin spears of sun shot through shutters and doorjambs, suspending lazy mobs of dust motes. Della watched them. How strange for the world to orbit the fiery ball of the sun, like a moth about a flame. So close to being consumed. A long finger of sunlight slipped through a chip in the nearest shutter and ran slanted across the floor. She watched for the minutest shift in this beam, like the sweeping hand of a clock. Some sign of the great wheeling of the earth. The velocity that sustained them.

She slithered from the tangle of blankets, silent, and moved featherlight across the floor, stilting on the balls of her feet, her heels high and round and small. She wanted to see what new world lay beyond the walls, struck bright and clean in the storm's wake. Zeno would twist and writhe and groan beneath the blast of light, but she didn't care. She wanted to come slinking back into bed with him, bathed in sun. Spend the day crawling over him, burrowing herself into the nooks and corners of his flesh. She wanted to lick the whiskey-sweat from his neck, bury her nose beneath his chin.

She lifted the nearest window and swung open the shutters, closing her eyes against the glare, feeling the blast of light on her skin. She could feel herself glowing, her face lifted high to the sun. Her heart was a warm engine, running steady when she opened her eyes and looked down at the yard.

The Jenny. She lay smashed beneath a fallen palm tree, her cleaved wings sprung nearly vertical, like a cricket's legs, the spars and ribs stabbing through the painted canvas of her skin. The wheels were splayed flat beneath her belly, her propeller shorn from its hub. Their home for so long, their world. She seemed so fragile now—like a dragonfly, a dream—a world wrecked, exploded into this tangled mess of stray wood and wire.

Della staggered back from the sill, as from her father's study. She sank to the floor, her chest full of lead.

21

Mayday

NEW ORLEANS, 1925

Faulkner dipped his pewter stein into the tub of Pernod. The milky blond liqueur swirled around a single great chunk of ice. He watched the afternoon sun stream through the windows of the apartment at 625 Orleans Alley—otherwise known as Pirate's Alley—illuminating a vast galaxy of dust motes. These tiny particles, gold-struck, darted and swirled over the heads of the partygoers, erratic as flies, as if engaged in aerial battle. Beneath them, the writers and artists of the Quarter babbled on and on, their teeth rattling like chipped ice in their jaws.

"What is it you do, Mr. Faulkner?" asked a newspaperman, an editor for the *Times-Picayune*. The man was prim, his tie knotted just so.

Faulkner kept watching the dust. He was deep into a novel—his first—his typewriter clacking away like a machine gun, the carriage release ringing down the narrow alleys of the Quarter. In the rising pages, the fallen Ace of his poetry, thought dead in the war, had surfaced on a homebound train, blind and nearly dumb.

"I run a launch," said Faulkner. "In the Gulf."

"A launch?"

"That's right. Go fishing and come back with a load of five-gallon cans."

"Cans?"

Faulkner peered through the smeared windows. He wrote on the narrow balcony in the mornings, sitting hunched over the cobblestones where General Andrew Jackson had conspired with the pirate and contrabandist Jean Lafitte—"the Terror of the Gulf"—enlisting his guns in the Battle of New Orleans. Across the alley glowed the sculpted greenery of St. Anthony's Garden, where men had engaged in affaires d'honneur, dueling with rapiers and sabers and pistols, murdering each other over slurs and mistresses and games of cards. Christ rose in white marble from the hedges, his arms lifted high and winglike, as if conducting the motley rabble of drunks and vagrants who milled outside the wrought-iron palings, hacking and screaming over the wet little mouths of their bottles.

"Cans of Cuban rum," said Faulkner. "What else? There's a Prohibition on, you know."

The rear of St. Louis Cathedral rose behind the marble Christ, a mountain of stone whose triple black spires seemed to pierce the heavens. Before the church, the old parade ground of Jackson Square, renamed again and again by successive conquerors: *place, plaza, square*. Here had been the site of public executions, where the condemned danced and swayed from the gallows. Now Andrew Jackson, dead and triumphant, reared his war steed upon a block of stone, his saber slung long from his hip, one hand doffing his bicorne hat to the crowds.

The newspaperman hiccupped. "You mean you're a smuggler?"

Faulkner's eyes cut him hard. "Jesus, bud, keep it down. You want to get me incarcerated?" He lowered his voice. "The Cuban schooners bury them in the sandbars for us. It's like buried treasure. A little creosote and bourbon, it sells as Scotch whisky in the Quarter."

"I thought you were a writer."

"A writer must eat, man."

"Do you still fly?"

Faulkner thought of Baby Buntin leaping from the cockpit after one too many rough landings outside Oxford. The fearless and unflappable Buntin, who'd survived the experimental death machines of the United States government, throwing up his hands in surrender.

Faulkner shook his head at the editor. "Not often," he said. "I wadded up one too many crates in the war. Lost my nerve."

"That's too bad," said the editor. "The Gates Flying Circus is coming to town. We need someone to write a feature on them."

Faulkner nearly choked. The *Gates*, the most famous of the flying circuses. Already he could see himself loop-the-looping over the bright scrawl of the Mississippi, the riverboats and barges small as bath toys beneath him, the doomed city huddled in the very belly of the river, leveed against flood on every side.

Faulkner placed his hand on the editor's shoulder, steering him for the balcony. "The Gates Flying Circus? I'm your man, sir. Let us step outside to discuss."

The man allowed himself to be led. "What about your nerve?"

"My nerve as a pilot, bud. Not a passenger. No one could cover that circus like me."

"No?"

"Who else of your writers is a flier, tell me that? Hell, I'm writing a novel about an aviator as we speak."

"A novel?"

The balcony neared. The doors were thrown open, letting the apartment breathe. Flower boxes hung from the rail, overrun with green fountains of shrubbery. Hidden amid this jungle stood the small iron table where Faulkner sat hunched over his typewriter day and night, a tall glass of water or alcohol at hand. They approached the threshold.

"That's right," he said. "I have a mistress, bud, and she's thirty thousand words long."

"And what are you calling this mistress?"

They stepped onto the narrow ledge of the balcony, hardly wider than a ship's plank, and Faulkner saw her for the first time. He froze midstep, nearly dropping his stein. She sat cross-legged on the very edge of an iron chair. A creature so thin and elven, her crow-black bangs cut careless across the hard-jawed beauty of her face. Her bald knees were sun-reddened, her linen dress crinkled over the boylike angles of her frame. She looked so fragile, so sullen—her tendons strung thinly against her skin, like those of a fiddle, her veins a cool blue. Faulkner's mind, in a flash, went tripping and tumbling over the miracle of her. The pale ridges and dark hollows of her frame, seen and unseen. The black hair. How starkly her ribs must buttress the rosy knobs of her breasts.

She sat wreathed in smoke, not giving a damn for her own beauty, nor the shining eyes and wagging tongues of the party. So it seemed. She lifted a cigarette to the bloodless slash of her mouth. Her jaw protruded hard into the air, proud. She sucked until the ash glowed bright.

Faulkner was seized in a fist of desire, squeezed breathless, his own ribs curling and crackling around his heart. He couldn't get enough air.

The editor was still waiting, his question hanging with the dust motes. "The title?" he asked again.

Faulkner's eyes never left the girl.

"*Mayday*."

He wore a rope for a belt that summer, walking barefoot on the sugary beaches of Pascagoula, onto the long fishing piers of the Mississippi coast and into the dark caverns of the shrimpers' taverns. His cheeks were hollowed with desire, shadowed with stubble. His hair was sunstruck, carrying a reddish glint. His heart an ember, searing in the mad darkness of his chest.

Her name was Helen Baird. Helen, the name that launched one thousand ships. Her people were from Pascagoula. She was twenty-one years old. An artist. In her mother's house, the vast menagerie of her work: featherweight sculptures of horses and men, wire-framed, skinned with crepe paper and paste. So fragile, they were, hollow as bird bones, as the skeletal machines of wood and wire that sang through the heavens. So like herself, thin-boned in her baggy painting smocks, sweeping the ragged bangs from her face, caring nothing for men or what they thought. She possessed her own gravity, it seemed. She drew the world into her orbit.

Faulkner was summering at the Camp—the bayside retreat of the Stone family. An oak tree grew through the very middle of the place, rising through a cutout in the floorboards and twisting through the rafters. The green crown hung over the house like a giant umbrella. The waters of Bay St. Louis tongued the shore. The wind rattled the bright sabers of palmetto, whispered through the gentle fronds of wild palm. Faulkner found a great oak shading a bluff, the trunk encircled by an octagonal bench. Here he would sit in the long afternoons, banging two-fingered on his portable typewriter, sucking on his meerschaum pipe.

Helen. She was fire in his blood. He would look across the bay, seeing the white scrape of wind on the water, the thousandfold dash of sunlight, and the world was singing his desire. His pain. They would lie sometimes on the sun-warmed stone of the jetties, talking above the gray crush of waves, and she would wear one of the swimsuits that did nothing to hide the ghastly scars of her girlhood accident, the terrific wasteland that covered one shoulder and leapt down her back like a geologic formation.

"I was burned," she told people. That brusque, even proud.

Faulkner's heart would blaze in his chest, fanned by her words, her breath. His blood ran scalding beneath his skin, so hot it could kill him. How badly he wanted to run his hands over that terrible country of scar. To know her pain. Her secret fears and desires. How badly he wanted to be there that day of her childhood, catching the boiling pot on his own thin shoulders. His own flesh bubbling, so they would be twinned in agony. Then, perhaps, he might be allowed beneath the cold shield she wore against the world, into her warmth. He might be worthy of her regard, allowed into the specific gravity of her heart.

They would lie flat on the jetty stones or rock themselves beneath the creaking chains of porch swings, and he would regale her with his stories, trying so hard to lift the light into her eyes. It was there, there, there—but only in sparks, moment-bright, like the strike of flint and stone. There was never the deep coal-burn, the madness like his. The desire to burn. To melt their flesh into one, their blood tangling. Siblings on the last island of the earth. Sometimes he found her looking at him wistfully, even sadly, as if he were something trapped in a jar. A firefly, perhaps, who wore the red coal of his heart hanging in the wind.

A specimen.

He wrote sonnets for her, like so many of his heroes had written. He wrote lovingly of her *boy's breast* and *plain flanks*, the *scarce-dreamed curving* of her thigh. The *brown and simple music of her knees*. In these poems, her breasts were *twin timorous rabbits*. He was a man accursed with *the gift of tongues*.

He was not one of the Baby Buntins of the world, he knew—not an ace—but he was something. A creature rarer, perhaps. He could feel it now, burning hot inside him. A gift. The furious vision, the thunder of tongue. Like the Holy Ghost but hotter, wilder, lifting him from the meager station he held in the eyes of women and mothers and kin. He wanted her to recognize the fire inside him, the whelming ghost. He launched his entire fleet, composing a book of sonnets in her name, hand-lettered and hardbound.

Helen: A Courtship.

Fifteen poems, cut bloody from his heart, bled across the parchment.

Soon thereafter, on a midnight beach, she rejected his marriage proposal.

She said she didn't know he felt that way toward her.

Faulkner rose to his feet, slowly, against the full weight of the stars.

He turned and made for the dunes, whose folds might hold some remnant warmth of sun. He didn't want her to see his tears. He withdrew a glass bottle from the heart pocket of his coat, as if drawing a gun.

He finished editing the manuscript of his novel, *Mayday*, on the octagonal bench of the great oak over the bay. This back-bent vocation, so like prayer, became his only respite from the broken thing in his chest. This pain, undreamed. He wrapped up the typescript and mailed it off to an agency in New York, hoping against hope the story might find wind beneath the stony towers of that city. Then he booked passage for Europe, with only his wrecked heart and busted shoes and twenty dollars from his Aunt Bama sewn into the lining of his one-elbowed coat.

In July, he stood at the rail of the steamship, surveying the long blade of the Gulf coast, the white sands burning beneath the blue wash of sky.

He practiced his line again and again, as if the repetition would make it true. Turning seaward, eastward, toward his destination, he whispered it again, like a mantra or hymn, burning on his lips.

Je suis un poète. Je suis un poète.

I am a poet.

Book III

22

Super Tramp

W e can't," said Della. "They were friends of my father."

"*Were*," said Zeno. He was sitting behind the wheel of the Model A Ford, which he'd rolled from the garage for post-storm inspection. A loose beam had landed across the machine, busting one window and slightly caving the roof.

Della stood in front of the automobile and crossed her arms. "It ain't right," she said.

"It's more *right* than that," he said, cocking his thumb at the Jenny, a tangled wreck of wood and fabric and wire. Della could hardly look. The sight of the smashed machine made her feel panicked, desperate. She could hear the ticking of cedar shingles, drying in the sun. The rasp of palm fronds. She could hear Sark panting between them, waiting.

"Listen," said Zeno. "We knew this day was coming. The old girl was on her last wings. We're lucky she went down like she did, that her wings didn't fold over the Alabama flatwoods at two thousand feet. I don't like it, either. But these homes out here, they're owned by timber and steel and turpentine barons. Top-hatters all, with rings on their fingers and butler bells on their bedside tables. These are houses born to drown or blow over, and everything that goes with them. It's all insured, honey."

"Still."

"You want to walk to California?"

"We could hitch," said Della.

Zeno looked around them, his jaw hanging open. "With *whom*?"

"Don't be a bastard."

"Listen, we'll leave a note on the seat—make sure this little buggy gets returned to the rightful owner." He worked his teeth back and forth. "You want to stay a groundling?"

Della looked down at Sark. His ears were spread wide, his pink tongue glistening in the sun. His head was slightly cocked, awaiting what she would say. The sky curved cloudless above them, unreachable, a blue its own. Her shoulders felt naked beneath the sun, her bones weighted with lead shot instead of marrow. So heavy. She wanted to crumple joint by joint into the earth, crushed like the Jenny. She wanted to raise her head from her skirts and bawl and scream.

Instead she straightened her spine and set one boot on the bumper and leaned far across the hood, looking Zeno dead in the face. "We ain't taking this automobile. You hear me? I'm not putting that on my daddy's name. You want this car, you'll have to run me over with it first. Listen to the crunch of my fucking bones."

Zeno raised his hands from the wheel, as if held at gunpoint. "Baby," he said.

Della had already whirled about. She strode from the yard. Sark trundled along in her wake, not waiting for his master.

The earth fumed, dreamy and prehistoric, shuddering beneath the distant crash of surf. Wrack littered the road, as if a parade had passed in the night. Green fans of saw palmetto and gray clumps of Spanish moss, the white sands wind-piled against the seaward edges of trees and porch steps. They walked past the stilt-legged complex of the Pensacola Beach Casino, still hibernating, the chimneys snoring beneath the faintest breaths of smoke. Della imagined the three-hundred-person dining room, huge and dark, echoing with the odd clang of a winter tourist's fork or glass or plate, the picture windows holding the silent Gulf like a giant aquarium.

In the lot, a scattered row of automobiles, sand-covered like dunes. Old Glory hung limp from the flagpole, exhausted from the night's blow. Della and Sark kept on. New sand had been driven across the road, soft and snowlike. It squeaked beneath their feet. The whole island seemed alien and deserted, as if God had become bored or hurt, looking askance of the place.

They wheeled the motorbike from the shed. It was a Harley-Davidson Model V, olive-green, with a sidecar the shape of a small motorboat. The handlebars were wide and low, the engine shaped like a mechanical heart.

"Side-valve motor," said Zeno. "Forty-five cubic inches." He squeezed tires and thumped carburetors and fingered chains, as if examining an infirmary patient.

A vacant beach house, to which the shed belonged, stood silent beside them. Lazy sentinel palm trees leaned about the place. A slink of chain lay coiled in the grass, whose padlock Della had picked with a pair of bobby pins—a skill Zeno had taught her.

Now he stood from the machine, setting his hands up on hips. "You done good, girl."

"You haven't tried starting it yet."

"We had these bikes in France. She'll run."

He primed the carburetor and set the choke and spark advance and leapt on the starter lever. The motor fired on the third kick, an explosion of power. The bike rattled in place, whelmed with smoke. The twin hammers of the pistons beating in a heartlike rhythm: *whump-whump, whump-whump, whump-whump.*

They donned their goggles and scarves. Della and Sark settled into the leather seat of the sidecar, snug as a cockpit, the dog panting his excitement. Sark, like his masters, needed to be in the wind. Their canvas duffel of gear was stuffed at Della's feet, the rest of their things strapped in a bundle over the rear fender. They'd tied their canvas tarpaulin in a roll across the handlebars, just above the coiled spring of the fork.

Zeno looked down from the saddle, his mustache spreading wide over his teeth. "Next best thing to wings," he said.

He cracked the throttle. They went bouncing through the yard and turned onto the beach road, zigzagging between storm debris. Soon they were on the three-mile toll bridge, hard on the throttle, racing thirty feet above the bay. Della leaned back and closed her eyes, feeling the thunder of power, the wind buffeting her face. She let herself fly.

They camped in the lee of the machine, stringing the tarpaulin over their heads for cover. They slept in roadside woods or fallow fields or abandoned filling stations, the floors scarred with the fires of past migrants. Black puddles of melted tires, charred spindles of burned chairs. Bottles burst glittering on the floor. Vagrants were walking the roads in busted shoes, their backs canted from years in the fields. Their possessions bobbed from the ends of bindle sticks, knotted up in flour sacks and bandannas or bulging from splitting valises with muddy bottoms. Whole strings of extended kin, Black and brown and white, marched through knee-high blooms of dust, their eyes glazed dumb with toil.

Here was the migration they'd seen from the air, the human herd headed west, filling the sinewy roads and highways. This river of the bankrupt and orphaned and workless, the once-rich and the lowborn walking side by side, laboring behind wobble-wheeled baby carriages or wheelbarrows or pushcarts overburdened with the remnants of home. Some rode bicycles, their thin tires weaving through the ruts, or trudged hunchbacked in the traces of crude rickshaws.

Della looked into their faces as they passed, their eyes. She was searching for the steely glitter she saw so often beneath the Jenny's wings. The awe and pride, the fight. But she saw no spark. She felt she was failing these people, unable to lift the light into their eyes. She feared she would fail Zeno, too, her love insufficient to keep him alive. Aloft. Her power had waned. She no longer walked across the sky nor swung from the wires of heaven.

A sudden dread bored through her hollows, as if her bones and organs had been poured full of molten lead—a fear she would never again rise from the earth. She thought of her father, whose melancholia had proved too heavy, a weight that drove him out of his head, into the ground, and she thought of her aunts, bitter women who sloshed themselves so full of gin they could almost float, almost forget their dead husbands and empty homes.

And Della knew what she feared most: that she would end up just like them, a sad story, a mortal ruin. A creature crumpled beneath the world's weight, crushed as sure as the Jenny. She feared it could be in her blood or destiny. She'd tried so hard to escape, to leave such a fate behind her, beneath her, but here she was, staring it in the face. And, looking at Zeno, she knew more clearly than ever what she could not bear. She was heart-bound to a man whose loss would wreck her beyond repair—a man who, at times, seemed to want to lose himself.

She shivered and wrapped a blanket over her shoulders, hiding the name stitched blood-red across her back. The words stung like a wound.

They camped the final night of 1933 in a hobo jungle on the edge of the Flora-Bama border, a vast city of tin and burlap shanties that shivered and flapped in the slightest breeze. Broken-down jalopies lay beached beneath the spindly pines, their tires cannibalized for fuel, their hulks sheltering whole families of vagrants. Strings of laundry snapped ragged in the wind. Colorless dogs weaved from fire to fire, whining for scraps, their ribs sharp as knives beneath their shrunken skins; people shooed them with sticks and firebrands.

Della knew they lived so close to this same fate, surviving on the thinnest margin of wind and fire. The motorbike could seize a piston or blow a tire or throw a rod and they would remain here, sucked slowly back into the earth, dusty and bent, unable to break free of gravity or poverty or fate.

They squatted about a fire of burning trash and lightwood. There was no understory; the grounds of the camp had been scavenged for every last stick of kindling and tinder. Children came walking in from the distant darkness, carrying armfuls of brushwood they traded for rolled balls of government bread or stunted cigarettes. The fire crackled and sizzled, boiling sap from the pine, eating greedily through the dry soft-wood and belching a sooty smoke that blacked the cheeks of those it warmed. Their faces hovered dusky and raceless, their skins allowed to mingle in the darkness.

Many were migrant fruit pickers come south for the citrus harvest. They'd hoped to pick the vast universe of fall-fat oranges from their groves only to find the orchards filled already with local laborers. Former clerks and shopkeepers and tradesmen thrust into the fields. In the distance, the iron thunder of trains, rumbling and whistling through the night, hurtling the dimpled orbs far across the continent.

A man sat cross-legged at the head of the fire, stoking the coals with an iron poker. He wore a weather-beaten top hat perched high atop his head like a thundercloud, and his patchwork coat glimmered vari-colored in the firelight, as if composed of feathers or scales. He leaned toward the fire, showing his face. He had a long gray beard, curled like a question mark from the point of his chin, and his jaw was slightly crooked, misaligned with the upper half of his face. A crowd had gathered around him, their heads bobbing to the rhythm of his voice.

"Name's Sammy Super Tramp," he said. "I been to forty-six contiguous states. That's right. Been hopping freight since I was knee-high to a fly. Rode grainers and gondolas, boxcars and reefers and coalers. Caught them on the fly and in the yards, on the sidings and under the stars. Rode suicide on tanker porches, hung monkey from the rods. Escaped many a brakeman and bull, and some I sure didn't. Been clubbed and stabbed and pot-shot. Seen freight-hoppers thrown from cars, sliced double on the tracks, beat pulpy with billy clubs and ball bats." He cocked his head toward the distant tracks. "I wouldn't never stop, though. I got iron singing through my veins, got steam whistling out my heart. Can't stay in no place long. Got to keep drinking wind and spitting strong."

He leaned toward the fire, his face glowing red, and spat into the coals.

Della saw that his coat of many colors was not a random patchwork—each piece of cloth had been scissored into the shape of a separate state.

A jumbled map of denim and muslin and twill, gingham and canvas and flannel—motley badges loose-sewn like feathers or fur.

He saw her looking.

"Map of the Super Tramp," he said, clapping his chest. "My own US of A. States strung in order of visitation. Rode the rails out of Louisianne in my thirteenth year." He touched a red, boot-shaped patch over his heart. "Across the big star of Texas and through the New Mexican winter, across the red rocks of Arizona and up the California coast." He fingered the various states, twisting his right arm into the light, hopping from milestone to milestone of his life, down one sleeve and up the other, looping through the Pacific Northwest and racing east across the Upper West, crossing the Great Divide in the valley between his shoulder blades. "I seen five-wived Brighams in Salt Lake, seen tommy-gun Tonys in the Big Windy. Seen black rollers big as the Rockies rise over the Great Plains, and twisters turn cornfields upside down. Seen Holy Rollers swagger through West Virginny, necklaced with live rattlesnakes. I seen near all there is to see, and I'm seeing it still. I got to keep rolling, or I'll catch ill."

He paused, inhaling, and the words rushed from Della's mouth, too quick to stop.

"What's California like?"

Super Tramp turned his face upon her, eyes glittering. Della could feel her own eyes dream-bright now, like so many others that hovered around storytelling fires, or under wings or stars or steeples.

"What is California like?" asked the tramp. "Why, what are you?"

"Me?"

"You carry your own weather inside you. Storm or sun between your ribs. The weather without reflects the weather within. The Golden State or the Manifest Death. The same terrain, storm or sun, is two countries out of kind. But I will say this of California among states: it is the edge, to which men go who seek such brinks, and some keep going. Some to silver, some to sea. Some to a thousand pieces each."

Zeno lowered the bottle from his mouth. His lips shone, bright and wet. "Some to sky," he said. "Some to ground."

The tramp cocked his head. "The priests say both."

Zeno nodded. "Though some say if you go high enough, beyond the atmosphere, you might orbit forever, never coming down."

"They say the sun will devour a man at such heights."

Zeno sipped again from the bottle. "Better ash than dust."

The tramp's eyes seemed to flash. "You are a flier, sir?"

"Once. I have been clipped of my wings."

"Then, sir, you must be headed to La Nouvelle-Orléans. City of absinthe alleys and bone-laden levees, where madness lurks like smoke."

Della leaned forward. "Why New Orleans?" she asked.

The tramp spread his arms wide, the states feathering his sleeves.

"The air show, don't you know? This Mardi Gras. Barnstormers and air racers will abound, ribbon-cutting the new airport built on the banks of the lake." The tramp leaned toward the fire. Embers rose before him like burning flies, as if to alight on the tattered nation of his coat. "What better place to hop aboard the rails of heaven or fall burning from the sun?"

23

Soldier's Pay

NEW ORLEANS, 1926

Faulkner strode beneath the ironwork balconies of the Quarter, a cobblestone jungle where hanging plants and ferns exploded from their planters, cascading down the stucco facades with tropic abandon, and the wrought-iron galleries were filigreed like interwoven vines or lace. This city within the city, where the very bricks sweat like flesh in the night and even the street names moved the blood: Rampart and Royal, Bourbon and Burgundy and Dauphine. These narrow rues crowded with brothels and taverns and town houses, where bottles and hearts shattered night after night and foghorns boomed lonesome through the alleyways.

Faulkner passed painters with spattered faces and wild eyes, absinthe-drunk, their brains crawling with wormwood. He passed trench-coated rumrunners, their collars snapped high around their cigarettes, and jake-legged drunks whose soles slapped the sidewalks, their hands ever raised for alms. He passed unseen through reeling bands of seamen who chattered in strange tongues, their faces spiraled with tattoos, their bellies awash with bootleg rum doctored to taste like bourbon or rye or gin.

Men who carried blades in their boots, women with razors dangling between their breasts on lengths of twine. None seemed to see him.

Two weeks ago, he'd stepped shabby and wild-bearded from the train in Oxford, setting foot on home soil for the first time since departing for Europe. His mother and brothers and Mammy Callie were waiting. At sight of him, the women raised their hands to their mouths while his brothers whispered and grinned. His clothes were rumpled and soiled. His beard spiked wild from his cheeks and chin and neck. His coat was split-seamed, slowly disassembling itself, revealing pale slashes of his underlying shirt, the pockets square-bulged here or there with bottles. His eyes were red-shot.

He'd strode down the cobbled rues of Paris in his patchwork coat, the wet stones echoing his hurt. He peered through the golden windows of the literary cafés, once glimpsing James Joyce at a table. He watched the cloudy-eyed genius from afar, afraid to approach. He toured the battle-fields where his brother Jack and so many of his kind had fought, their bones ten years buried beneath the endless fields of chiseled stone. He journeyed to England, where he saw flocks of sheep standing shaggy and soiled on the greenest hills of the earth, posing as if for poets or painters, and spent his precious few pounds purchasing the golden light of Scotch whisky in the stony caverns of rural public houses where every man's face looked like a pie left out in the rain.

He'd gone to Europe with a wish on his lips, a dictum. *Je suis un poète.* His heart split like stone, if stone could ache. He'd strode through the gray rains of Paris, sad and wet and haunted by the ghost of Helen. The vision of her walking beside him, her cigarette burning cherry-bright beneath the black trees of the city, beneath the stained facades and narrow balconies. The dark caving of her cheeks, sucking smoke, and the blue of her breath, curling beneath the careless slash of her bangs. Her knees so bald and white and fine. Her narrow heels clicking beneath the lean swivel of her hips, stepping in time to his own. The firmness of her haunches, so slim and hard, which he wanted to know. To touch. To test beneath his teeth, as if for ripeness. This pale fruit. This flesh. The heart and bone and spirit of her, which haunted him like an infection. A fever he could not shake.

The family watched him come hobbling toward them from the train, his satchel dangling sleeves and yellowed socks from its busted seams and zippers. His typewriter tucked beneath his arm. Their heads were slightly cocked, their eyes slit narrow under the sun. Their smiles held in tremulous suspension. Perhaps they were trying to discern some change of fate upon him. Some golden strike of sun, glowing about his tousled hair. For their prodigal was returning to Oxford a changed man.

A novelist.

A letter from New York had been waiting in Paris after he returned from a weeklong stint on a Breton fishing boat. He said his hands were still red-raw from the labor, his sea legs still swaying, when he sliced through that envelope in the *bureau de poste*. His novel, *Mayday*, was to be published by a New York house. Retitled *Soldier's Pay*. Enclosed was a check for two hundred dollars—his advance—which he walked all over Paris trying to cash. Finally, he slapped his RAF dog tags on the counter at the British Consul, who cashed the check in pounds sterling, which he used to book his passage home.

His mother hugged him first, then his brothers, oldest to youngest. Jack and Johncy and little Dean Swift, his face alight with pride. Lastly there was Mammy Callie, whom he loved like a mother. She stood slightly apart in her head wrap and apron, the cotton starched hard as parchment, knife-creased on the ironing board. Her round face beaming, buttered by the sun.

She drew him hard into her bosom, the starched apron scratching his face. "Lawd, Mimmie," she said—her pet name for him since boyhood. "You need a bath." She laughed, and he could hear the deep bellows of her lungs, her little body rumbling with joy.

Faulkner looked up finally, his cheek red-printed, as if emerging from a long nap against her chest. He looked at her, then to the rest of them. "Where's Daddy?"

"Not fit to read," said Murry Falkner. He snapped open the *Oxford Eagle*, the newspaper pulled taut between his hands. "That's what I heard."

His eldest son was standing in the living room before him, his hands held at his sides. Murry glanced at his son's feet. Billy's old twelve-dollar shoes were soiled and shattered—busted, no doubt, from countless drunken marches through the decadent alleyways of New Orleans or Paris, where sin and dissolution clung to a man like mildew.

He shook his head, quoting a line from Billy's book. "'His yellow eyes washed over her warm and clear as urine.'" Murry's own eyes skated along the stamped lines of newsprint, as if he were reading verbatim from the headlines. His voice was cold. "'She lay . . . running her fingers lightly over her breasts, across her belly, drawing concentric circles.'" He shook his head again, not deigning to raise his eyes.

"*Smut*," he said.

He could almost hear his son's hands balled into fists, the knuckles crackling with impotent fury. He turned the page of his paper.

"I heard the university library would not even accept a gifted copy."

His own library of Zane Grey novels stood stacked on the table beside him. *Riders of the Purple Sage* and *The Lone Star Ranger*, *Nevada* and *The Day of the Beast*. Stories of masked gunslingers and magic valleys, villainous Mormons and damsels in need of armed men. Their thick spines gleamed gold-lettered from the stacks and shelves like an indictment.

His son cleared his throat. "The substance of your library could be written upon the back of a postage stamp."

"And what would you know of stamps, a boy could not even keep his job as postmaster of this little town? Who failed even at that?"

"I will make something of this little town."

"I'd like to see that."

"You are mean, Daddy."

Murry Falkner felt his face flinch. His flesh had never failed him, this body that had shoveled countless tons of coal and eaten a pair of 12-gauge shotgun slugs. He felt the hard sting of his son's words, the barbed truth of them. His blood raged wild beneath his skin; his words rose bitter and fast.

"And you, my son, you are a disappointment."

Murry Falkner's eyes slashed upward, quick and steely as blades, keen to see what blood he'd drawn. But they softened, confused. His son was already gone, vanished like a ghost. No echo even of his shattered shoes. Their thin-worn soles. Murry Falkner's pupils grew, as if to catch the last light from the room.

Faulkner walked the Quarter where he had known her, and he feared and desired her presence around every corner, down every alley, beneath every streetlamp and electric sign. *Helen.* He thought he saw the lean blades of her hips moving beneath the red lights of speakeasies, cutting against the bellies of other men, or the red ash of her cigarette dancing like a firefly from high balconies he could not reach. He'd thought a book might raise him in her estimation, high enough to be loved, but he heard she was seeing a young attorney. A man of status. Wealth. Influence. A man who, surely, had heard those longed-for words from the father of his world: *This is my beloved son, in whom I am well pleased.*

Faulkner's steps rang down the narrow alleyways, their cobblestones grouted with a century's worth of blood and urine, whiskey and vomit and vice of every stripe. His heels echoed off the stone walls, hard and sharp, like the staccato crack of typewriter. And those very stones and cobbles seemed to be speaking to him. The Quarter itself. The city telling him to do the only thing that could save him, the one act that might lift him above all the agony and pain of loss, making him a creature to be desired, even loved.

He must write.

24

Stack-o-Lee

*T*hey crossed the state line at dawn, hunched against the wind, crossing the green-dark sheen of the Perdido River into Alabama. The iron heart of the motor throbbed beneath them, beating fire. Della rode in the sidecar with Sark sleeping curled in her lap, his tiny shoulders twitching with dream. She still wore the blanket over her shoulders, as if to mask the name stitched red across her back.

They rode west along US 90, the Old Spanish Trail. Conquistadors had blazed this sweeping canyon through the land, cutting a swath through white ridges of scrub pine. Endless armies of softwoods, their trunks arrow-straight, sprang from green explosions of palmetto, the under-story sliced here or there with pale jags of game trails. Here were the paths of tusked hogs, whose ancestors had ridden huddled in the bellies of Spanish galleons, and the gray flicker of whitetail deer. The heels of vagrants pocked some of the trails now, the smoke of their fires whispering atop the ridges. Belts of creekwater swung beneath the highway, sun-glittered, their banks knuckled with the broad roots of cypress or mangrove. Black men fished the shadows of the trees with cane poles, their metal pails churning with bass or bream.

The sun rose bright into the winter sky. They nooned on the banks of a small creek, squatting to eat catfish coal-roasted in corn husks, picking the flaky meat from the bones with their hands. The fisherman, ancient as a statue, squatted beneath the yellow brim of his straw hat, his toothless gums sucking like a fish's. His bib pocket jingled with the change of vagrants and travelers.

Zeno chewed in one side of his mouth, letting Sark lick the juice from his fingers. He nodded at the fisherman. "Good," he said.

They rode on. Vast truck farms swung outward from the highway, their rolling fields torn treeless from the pines. The old-growth timber had been felled by ax and crosscut saw, their stumps burned or dynamited from the earth. Some torn free by stump-pulling mules, their great haunches whip-scarred, quivering with power. A single tree could cost a man a week of his life. The furrowed beds, bare beneath the winter sun, awaited the seeds of tobacco or peanuts or cotton. Zeno wrung the handlebar, throttling them past slow-moving produce trucks, their tarpaulins flapping in the wind like broken wings.

The highway wound through pecan groves and citrus orchards where the trees stood in strict formation, the fruit in their branches like sweet bright planets in a universe as orderly as man could ever hope to lord. Pickers stood on stick-built ladders, their bodies half-lost in the green tangles of leaves, dropping oranges into canvas sacks strapped across their shoulders. Some worked in brogans and slacks, their shirts rolled to the elbow, their forearms stringy, rippling with sweat. They looked flat-bellied, unfed, their trousers hanging loose from their suspenders.

Della leaned toward Zeno, shouting through the wind. "How much cash have we got left?"

Zeno grimaced like she'd jabbed a finger in his side. "Spent our last nickel on that catfish!" he shouted. "We're out."

Della felt the air go sudden-thin, a cold edge slicing between her ribs. Her heart shivered in place. They'd been penniless plenty of times before, stone broke, but they'd always had the Jenny. A means of getting airborne, away, and earning at least something to eat. Someone would always feed you supper for a ride, a loop, or a dangle from the under-carriage.

Now she felt the soggy lump beneath the sole of her foot: the secret pair of greenbacks she kept folded in reserve, like a last set of tawdry wings. Her father had given her the money for her twentieth birthday, the week before he shot himself. He'd called her into his office and slid an envelope across the desktop, her name scrawled carefully in large cursive script. His eyes appeared sad and wet and distant that day, as if he could already see the fate headed his way.

"Happiest Birthday, Del. Open it later, will you?"

Inside was a note, the black handwriting bent slightly jagged:

TO MY DARLING DAUGHTER, ADELLA ROY, WHO IS
TWENTY YEARS ON EARTH TODAY. MAY YOU SOAR HIGH
AND TRAVEL FAR, MY SWEET ONE.

There were two sawbucks with the note. Twenty dollars. What must have been so much to him then. It was all she'd kept of her own money that first day Zeno came to the sawmill, when she bought the workers their rides.

Now Della felt the bills beneath her foot. She kneaded them with her toes.

She was not there. Not yet.

She leaned toward Zeno, talking close to his ear. "I could always pose for dirty pictures."

Zeno grinned, not taking his eyes from the road. "As much as I'd like to see those."

He did not pass the next produce truck. Instead, Zeno fell into the wake of the machine, trailing it from the highway.

Foley, Alabama. The southernmost terminus of the Louisville & Nash-ville Railroad. The end of the line. The rail platform stood level and plum, the yellow pine lumber gleaming beneath the sun. The metal roof hovered high over the wall-less depot, long as a chicken barn, sheltering stacked bales of late-picked cotton and endless crates of winter oranges.

Della could not but imagine the place from a god's height, as upon a map—the endless parades of trucks and wagons converging from every corner of the countryside, top-heavy with their mountains of cargo, crawling the roads like ants, ready to deliver their swollen payloads of citrus to the great iron slugs that would chug them north, ice-cooled in ventilated boxcars, where they would be peeled by schoolboys with penknife and thumb, their tongues jammed into the corners of their mouths, or crushed in the chromium juicers of big-city kitchens, their pulpless juice squirted into breakfast glasses.

When she was a girl, her father had taught her the trick of sucking the juice from an orange. A winter treat. He would carve the navel gently with a paring knife, then insert a peppermint stick. Della would squeeze and suck with all her might. The red ribbon of candy would soon develop cavities, allowing the juice to be sucked minty and sweet from the citrus meat. She would leave the once-round fruits in the slop bucket, shriveled and misshapen, their guts uneaten. Once she opened the door of the pantry to find the maid bent over the discarded fruit. The woman looked up, wide-eyed, a wedge of rind gleaming against her teeth.

The growers' trucks lined the elevated depot. Men with heavy shoulders stood among crates of citrus, knee-deep, chucking them one after the next onto the platform. Their bodies gleamed beneath the winter sun, tireless as machines, oiled with sweat. Their skin was black and brown and white, their blood standing in bluish rivers from their muscles. They paused only to swipe the salt from their eyes. They swabbed their brows against swollen biceps or forearms, as if their hands were too tired for the task, stiff-clawed with labor.

A small Black boy stood at the corner of the platform, juggling a trio of oranges. He wore an overlarge shirt and trousers, the cuffs rolled high over his bare feet. A tatty newsboy's hat lay upturned in the dust before him, a few red cents glittering in the folds.

Zeno slowed the bike alongside him, shutting off the motor. He leaned on the handlebars, sticking his last cigar between his teeth. His eyes moved down the row of trucks and wagons, the working men.

"Say," he said. "Who's the cock of the walk here? The king loader?"

The boy didn't hesitate. "Stack," he said.

"Stag?"

The boy shook his head, his eyes darting between the wheeling globes of citrus. "Stack-o-Lee."

Lee Stackhouse stood high in the bed of the citrus truck, surrounded by crates. The straps of his overalls strained sweat-bleached against the wide yoke of his shoulders, his flesh polished a lustrous brown. He wore a tattered railroader's cap turned backward to shade his neck. Sweat ran like tears down his cheeks and his chin, gathering into a silver medal at the hollow of his throat. Veins zigzagged across the heavy globes of his shoulders, cascading like worms down the lengths of his arms, as if born from the clay of his flesh. He looked malformed almost, such was the swollen power of his body, every muscle bucking against the exquisite web of tendon and sinew and vein. As if his strength might jump his skin, busting bright and bloody into the sun.

The driver of the citrus truck spat in the dust of the road. His face was long and red beneath his straw hat. His chambray shirt wore a dark apron of sweat. "Stack, you best murder this damn Gypsy. I want that bike in my barn."

"Easy work, boss. Easy work."

Zeno stood in the bed of a second truck, surrounded by his own fortress of citrus crates. He was unbuttoning his leather coat. The crowd watched him, fixated, as though he were a woman undressing. As if they were cutting away his clothes with their eyes. Their money was out, the dirty greenbacks flapping with anticipation. Zeno took his time, sliding the coat from his shoulders and catching it on the hook of a finger. He jutted his hip suggestively, tossing the coat into the crowd, who cheered.

Twenty minutes before, he'd parked the motorbike before a ring of men in straw hats who were warming their hands over a barrel fire. They were the drivers and foremen, overseeing the work of the loaders.

Zeno had leaned far over the handlebars, removing his cigar. "I can outwork any beast born of man."

The men looked him up, down. Their eyes were long-accustomed to appraising flesh, the swell of working men.

"The fuck you can."

"Fancy a wager?"

Stack-o-Lee's driver stepped forward. "What you got to bet?"

Zeno leaned back, sticking the cigar between his back molars, and rapped a knuckle on the fuel tank of the machine. "Forty-five cubic inches of Milwaukee iron."

The man's eyes had brighted, as Zeno knew they would.

Now the trucks were parked side by side, backed flush to the platform. Their beds held one hundred crates apiece, each weighing forty-two pounds. The lift from bed to platform was three vertical feet, the height of their waists. Each man, if he emptied his truck, would have moved more than two tons of crated citrus.

Zeno was unbuttoning his shirt now. When he slipped from the yellowy cotton, the crowd gasped. His burns screamed beneath the sun. The vast country of scar, ridged hard, like badlands erupted from his flesh. The men on the platform were accustomed to disfigurement. Fingers pinched off by drag chains or heavy crates, healed knobby at the first or second knuckle. Eyes burst milky from the glance of fence staples. Pockmarks of rash and infection, which could crater a man's flesh like Swiss cheese, and the gnarled limbs of polio, so like the twisted shillelaghs of old men. Still the burns arrested them, stealing the breath from their throats.

Zeno grinned, his cigar stuck from the corner of his mouth. Della's heart flew. A bloody balloon, straining against her ribs. Swelling, rising. Sark sat at her heel, watching him, too. Their man. Zeno's chest was broad, lightly furred, his shoulders built thick over the broad brown barrel of his belly. His belt was cinched just below his navel, high and tight. His body never seemed to alter, no matter the famine or glut. As if his form, like his soul, were unmoved by circumstance.

He set his legs straight together and raised his arms, squeezing his muscles like a vaudeville strong man, tooth-grinning beneath his dark mustache. Now Stack-o-Lee struck the same pose. His sides flared like the wide hood of a cobra, his arms balling and quivering the size of ostrich eggs. His eyes were hooded, his nostrils wide. His mouth grim and straight and sure.

The bets flooded his way. The smart money. It was only a matter of odds now. Three-to-one. Four. Five-to-one he would outmatch this mustachioed newcomer. No man could touch Stack-o-Lee, even if he'd been touched by fire—exempted, somehow, from lesser pain. Stackhouse was King Loader of South Alabama. He clasped his hands before his waist and squeezed, elbows out, making a wreath of his arms. A bulging wheel of power, vein-strung. He grinned, cocking his head.

"Stack-o-Matic."

Ten-to-one odds.

Zeno looked at Della, winked.

When all bets were placed, the starter raised a pistol. A heavy revolver, like a cowboy might carry. It cracked against the sky.

Afterward, Zeno lay flat on his back, heaving like a landed fish. His eyes were lost, gone to some unseen distance. Saliva gummed the corners of his mouth. His breath sounded like a whipsaw. Della knelt over him, slapping his face, while Sark turned the black hatchet of his snout this way and that, keeping the onlookers at bay. They'd climbed the sides of the truck, hanging from the bedrails and squatting on the platform, their mouths slack with awe. This Gypsy man who rode into town on a motorbike, challenging the great Stack-o-Lee to a duel of citrus crates. This once-burned man who might have worked himself right out of the world, blowing his heart apart. The bed was empty about him. Two tons of oranges sat on the platform, beaming bright. His wife knelt astride his naked chest, slapping his cheeks, calling him home.

Finally she was able to lift him to a sitting position. A strange angel of sweat where he'd lain, light-winged and vaporous, as if part of his soul still clung to the bed. His breath skirled ragged through his teeth, foamy and thick. His eyes blinked awake, returning from wherever they'd gone. He looked at his wife.

"Did I win?"

She rammed a fist of crumpled greenbacks into his chest.

They stopped at a crossroads on the edge of town, the motorbike chugging beneath them, and the boy who juggled oranges rose from the ditch. Zeno peeled off forty of the one hundred dollars they'd won. Four sawbucks. Far more than Stackhouse's boss would've given him for winning.

The boy set the bills inside his cap and planted it firmly on his head, then stepped back out of reach. "Stack said you ain't had to sell it so hard. Said he thought you done kilt yourself."

Zeno grinned. "Didn't want him to hurt his pride too bad."

The boy didn't smile. He pulled his cap down tighter. "Pride don't eat."

25

Brothers

Faulkner sat behind his typewriter, fury-eyed, as if hunched in the cockpit of a flying ship. His elbows were tucked close to his sides, his hands jabbing the keys two-fingered, punching letters hard and black and wet across the paper. The words came in tight groups, again and again, stringing into long chains that banged against the carriage return. The thin metal hammers of the typewriter kept rising and falling, moving in time to the bones of his hands, the machine clattering like an engine atop the thin-legged writing table his mother had given him.

A whiskey jug sat beneath his stool, forgotten. His pipe lay cold, ha-loed in ash. He was no longer on the porch of the family home. He was high over France, his body cradled in the wood-and-wire skeleton of a pursuit plane, his face set hard against the blasting wind. His eyes were coal-hot, his aim true. Planes were abuzz on every side of him, machines cut sharp and dark and fast against a paper-white sky. Hard, lean pilots dodging swarms of machine-gun fire that erupted from the ground like fiery hornets or rained down from the guns of enemy fighters. He flew in a squadron of his own making, free of the red clay and cotton fields of Mississippi, soaring instead over the green fields of France, his characters falling into formation around him.

There were the Sartoris twins, Johnny and Bayard, sprung from the fictional county of Yoknapatawpha, Mississippi—based on Faulkner's own home. These brothers, grandsons of partisan rangers, had been raised in an atmosphere that crackled with mythic cavalcades, flashing sabers, the blue-black thunder of gunpowder. Forebears who died rakish on horseback, chancing enemy guns for a can of anchovies or walking straight into the pistols of their rivals, accepting their deaths uncowed. The boys sucked the wind and smoke of such stories, growing tall and glory-haunted, burdened by the names of their ancestors.

As schoolboys, they would come home bloodied in the afternoons, having fought their way through whole packs of bullies who said they looked like girls with their long, tawny curls bouncing on the backs of their necks. The brothers would not let their hair be touched—they had more slaughter to accomplish, more boys to whip. Later, they would become pursuit pilots in the Great War, the winged cavalry of a new age.

Johnny was the best-loved of the twins, his spirit warm and bright. A crack shot and fearless pilot. A golden son. Then there was Bayard, the darker, brooding and surly, who tried to stop his brother from going up one fateful morning over France. The sky was thick with clouds and the Germans would be swarming high over the pale layers of cover, ready to pounce. Johnny, ever willful, sent a burst of fire across his brother's nose, warning him back, then pulled back his stick, climbing for a fight.

Soon he was surrounded, hemmed, and the Huns were sending tiny hot fists of lead into the thin skin of his machine. Young Bayard watched from his own machine, helpless, as Johnny's paperweight fighter ignited beneath the guns of a German ace. His wings sprouted long feathers of fire. The flames were whipping and cracking, crawling toward the cockpit, soon to reach him, and Bayard could only watch.

What would his brother do?

Bill and Dean slept that summer on the screened side porch of the Falkner home. Bill, home from New Orleans, and Dean Swift, now nineteen, lay side by side on matching cots, listening to the scurry and croak of the Mississippi night. Dean, sun-kissed gold, slept barefoot and unhaunted— the way he lived. He could cut a two iron hard against the wind, bending the white world of the ball to his will, landing it softly at the foot of the flagstick, or pop a quail on the wing with his .22 rifle, dropping it neatly from the sky. He could shoot the branch from beneath a squirrel at one hundred yards, his tongue tucked under his bottom lip. His smile could curl the corners of the prettiest girl's mouth. He carried the warmth of summer like an aura—a golden light. He slept reckless beneath the sheets, his limbs hanging out at odd angles. His breath unhurried, like that of a sleeping saint.

Faulkner would watch his littlest brother sometimes, his pipe puffing in the night, his eyes burning through the smoke. This tousle-haired angel of a boy. This handsome colt, whose middle name was Swift. The boy seemed incapable of sitting at a school desk. His heel would jump like a telegraph button in the classroom, tapping out the SOS signal of his soul, his eyes seeking the skitter of squirrels beyond the schoolhouse windows, the wheeling flicker of game birds. He could be caught staring one-eyed at high wedges of geese, arrayed like squadrons against the sky.

"*Dean Swift*," a schoolteacher might say sharply. "What is *your* opinion on the topic?"

Young Dean turning toward her, his cheeks gilded with sunlight. "Opinion, ma'am?"

"'Whether 'tis nobler in the mind to suffer / The slings and arrows of outrageous fortune, / Or to take Arms against a Sea of troubles—?'"

Young Dean cocking his head, one finger twirling the bleached curls of his hair. His smile whipping bright across his face. "Why, ma'am, I think Mister Hamlet 'struts and frets' too much 'his hour upon the stage.'"

The most iron-jawed of schoolteachers could not but grin before this boy—this face which seemed to carry the sun in afterglow, a basketful of light. More often, Dean could not be found in class. He was a truant of the grand scale, a schoolboy's ghost. His appointed seat shone beneath the slanted rays of morning sun, empty, the wood unburnished by his bum. The same for his tower room in the Falkner home. That high room ever-vacant, as if awaiting return of the wild prince. The same room where brother Bill once lived.

Meanwhile, the world was changing about them. Their middle brothers, Johncy and Jack, were both married now. Wedding bands flashed on their ring fingers, bright and heavy and sure, while Faulkner's own eyes could still well up with tears, remembering the burning sands of Pascagoula, the glittering bay.

Helen.

Brother Johncy was the city engineer now, overseeing the crews who were paving the muddy streets of town, pouring a moat of gravel and tar around the courthouse and lining the streets with white sidewalks. Soon the Square would click beneath Oxonian heels. Brother Jack, meanwhile, had become a federal agent—one of Hoover's G-men. He'd stiffen whenever older brother Bill drew a pint bottle of bootleg liquor from his coat, setting the stopper between his teeth. A sly grin across his face. A knowing wink. This oldest brother, still their hero, who'd written and sold a second novel, *Mosquitoes*, set in New Orleans. Soon to be published.

Dean Swift enrolled at Ole Miss, but rarely showed his face in class. More often he could be found barefoot in the woods, a rifle strapped across his back, or walking the green pastures of the golf course, carrying his canvas quiver of clubs. The family worried what he would make of himself.

Faulkner made vocabulary lists for his littlest brother and corrected his rollicking short stories, tales of hunting and fishing gallivants in the bottomlands of the Tallahatchie River. A land where young black bears rolled like boulders through the brush and a giant brown bear was still storied to tread, his flesh bearing the old injuries of arrowheads and musket balls and bullets. Old Ben. Dean, hunched over Bill's vocabulary lists, dug his tongue into his cheek: "*Apotheosis? Ratiocination? Quietude?*"

Faulkner sat in the stands during Dean's pickup games, cheering when his brother's baseball bat cracked in the dusk, wielded like the scepter of a young god. The ashwood flashing a ring of power about his body, whipped so hard the bat seemed to curve in his hands, twisting with power, and the baseballs sailed high against the purple summer sky, pale as moons, denting hoods and smashing windows when they fell.

That summer, lying aback their porch cots, Dean Swift wanted to hear again and again of his brother Bill's flying exploits during the Great War, when he crashed his Sopwith Camel biplane through a hangar on Armistice Day while doing a loop the loop—or was it a French-built Spad fighter, as Jack remembered him saying? No matter, Dean's eyes would fill with light, watching the whispering halo of the overhead fan, so much like an aircraft propeller spinning against the haint-blue sky of the porch ceiling. Faulkner could almost see the swelling heart of his littlest brother, yearning to slip the bony cage of his breast, to fly.

26

Point Clear

MOBILE BAY, 1934

*T*hey rode west out of Foley, passing shabby arrays of turpentiners' shacks that slouched tin-chimneyed at roadside, spitting thin spires of smoke, and orchards picked naked of fruit. Meatless cattle ranged across the road, lowing unfazed before honking automobiles. Zeno weaved the motorbike between their lean flanks. They had some money in their pockets now, but nowhere to break the bills. More than once they paid a whole dollar for a chicken, which they wrung and quartered and roasted on sticks. The pickers and turpentiners did not have change to break larger bills. They stood strong-jawed on their slanted stoops and porches, cupping their elbows, as if posing for the itinerant photographers of the WPA. They watched the strange trio of riders passing down the road, man and woman and dog all goggled against the wind, riding the clattering heart of their machine through the pines.

The riders finally made change with the ferryman at Fish River and paid a quarter to cross, then rented a fishing cabin for the night. Their first roof in days. The walls were adorned with the fat bodies of redfish and sheepshead and saltwater trout, their scales enameled bright. The beds were iron-framed and narrow, with wool blankets and white sheets. They crawled into one together, too tired even to fire the stove. The three of them lay notched and twined, their breath rustling in the dark. Della woke once in the night, seeing the glass eyes of the trophies bulged strangely around her, hovering bodiless from the walls, as if she slept in the river's deep. She closed her eyes against them, sinking back into Zeno's embrace. Sark breathing against her breast, a black satchel of warmth.

They rode west again at dawn, riding until they reached a high bluff over Mobile Bay. Here they stood and stretched, gazing across the noontime glitter of the place. Freighters and oilers throbbed against the expanse. Vessels sized like whole factories afloat, their stacks pouring bent pillars of smoke. A few sails on the water, wind-bloomed, dragging hulls through the blue ridges of chop.

Zeno shivered. "Boats," he said. "I could drown in a bathtub, I bet."

Della squatted on the bluff, looking west. "You're too good at floating for that."

Zeno's eyes were full of the bay. "It ain't the way I'll go down."

A maddening in Della's chest, an angry spark. She thought of her father. These men who thought they could steer their own way into the next world. Who thought the privilege of being men extended that far. "You know, Zeno, you might not get to choose."

Zeno looked at her. The wet of his eyes shone sudden-hard, like the glass eyes of those fish on the wall. He kicked the starter of the bike. The motor fired like a gun over the bay.

They rode north through gnarled skeletons of oaks, the branches bearing gray sweeps of moss. The bay flashed in and out of the trees, bright enough to pain the eyes, the road following the high shoreline bluffs. Della peered across the water, imagining the pale shimmer of shore across the bay and the Gulf coast beyond, wheeling westward in slim bands of islands and scattered villages, curving toward New Orleans. She imagined all the wings that would be gathering in that city, a vast flock of hope.

The road wound toward a small bluff where an old resort sprang from the oaks, double-winged against the bay. The Point Clear Hotel, salt-weathered, wearing a greenish film of former glory, as if waiting for a new heyday to arrive. Zeno steered them up the loop of drive, the tires crackling and weaving over the bleached shells of the path. The bell-man stood in his box cap, his golden shoulder epaulets dulled with age. He eyed them suspiciously. These dusty riders, with their loud machine and goggled canine.

Then Zeno laid a dollar in his hand. "Ye ole cherry tree–chopper," he said. "More if you can lead us to sustenance."

The bellman beamed. Soon they were standing in a bar called The Texas, a gleaming behemoth of mahogany and mirrored glass. The place looked like the old haunt of Wild Bill Hickok or the Texas Rangers. Men who wore ivory-handled pistols and shearling jackets, their curls rolling uncut beneath swan-size hats. The windows held the blue glitter of the bay, big as oil paintings of sails and steamers. Bottles of every stripe and caliber lined the walls, each filled with spirits newly raised from the basement, shining proudly in the wake of the Repeal.

They took a wide round table by the window and ordered two dozen oysters, which arrived slimy and tonguelike on a bed of shaved ice, their juices gleaming in the upturned hulls of their shells.

Della looked at the gorgeous ring of them, arranged like a giant necklace. "We're going to spend all our money before we get to New Orleans."

Zeno took up a lemon half wrapped in cheesecloth and squeezed it over an oyster, then freed the meat on the tines of a tiny silver fork. He held the offering under her chin. "For you, baby."

"I'm serious."

"So am I. I prepared you this delicacy."

"You're not listening to me. You want to spend all our money so we can't get anywhere or go west and we just keep circling around like big damn buzzards. Going nowhere."

"Just eat this oyster first, then we'll talk."

She frowned at it, her stomach longing despite.

"Come on," said Zeno. "Some noble oysterman picked this out of a cold creek this morning just for you."

When she didn't answer, he lowered the fork and touched her forehead lightly, right between the eyes. She felt her brow unfurrow at the touch of his thumb.

"You worry too much," he said. "You'll give yourself lines."

Her eyes flashed. She slid the oyster from his fork with her teeth. "I ain't old as you yet, old man."

Zeno grinned. "Give yourself time."

They drank gimlets from silver cups and slurped the oysters' liquor from their shells, tasting the salty shoals of the beds. The bay shone. The wood of the bar felt warm as flesh. Everything danced bright. When they finished, Zeno paid the tab from their dwindling roll.

Ten dollars. A green fan of George Washingtons.

"A cherry tree of presidents," announced Zeno, grinning.

Della did not really care. The gin was singing in her temples, telling her she sat in a great fortress of light. She set her elbow on the table, her chin on her palm. "Oh well, wasn't like we had enough to buy a new set of wings anyway."

Zeno belched through his teeth. "Who said 'buy'?"

27

On Eagle's Wings

OXFORD, MISSISSIPPI, 1927

*F*aulkner floats high against the sun, watching the stricken ace.

Johnny Sartoris stands from his cockpit and steps out onto the burning stage of the wing. His gloved hands grip the banshee wires ten thousand feet over the earth while the fuselage flashes and roars behind him, streaming flames. Brother Bayard is circling in his own machine, helpless. Watching. Even the Hun has quit firing, staring stone-faced over the skull and bones that mark his fuselage. Waiting. All is held in suspension, stilled, the flying machines dangling by unseen wires, balanced like the tin-metal stars over a baby's crib.

This terrible constellation of men.

The flames are licking all around Johnny, tearing at his back and boots, soon to engulf him. He has no parachute. He looks at Bayard and lets one hand from the wire and thumbs his nose at his twin brother, as if he were about to dive from the high ledge of a rock quarry or speak to the prettiest girl in class or sock the school bully in the face. As if they were still boys, and this was the same game as ever, only with higher stakes. Then Johnny lets his other hand go and steps from the wing.

LIEUT. JOHN SARTORIS, R.A.F.
KILLED IN ACTION, JULY 5, 1918.
'I BARE HIM ON EAGLES' WINGS AND BROUGHT HIM UNTO ME'

Bayard would live only two years after his brother's death. Two years of roaring reckless through the North Mississippi countryside in an over-powered roadster, tempting death at every bend, his guilt hounding him like a pack of wolves, ever nipping his heels. He should have been the one to die, he thinks. Johnny, the best of them, should have lived. Two years of drinking too much whiskey and leaping aback crazed stallions and throwing empty bottles at traffic police. Two years of replaying his brother's death again and again, watching him step from the wing, his body busting gut-first through the cloud deck on the way to the ground.

In the end, Bayard would become the test pilot for a new type of bi-plane—an experimental design with no wing wires or interplane struts. On the maiden flight, the machine would rip apart in midair, torn wing-less over the government field as if by the violent, wrenching force of his own hands. As if he willed its destruction. At last, his gravestone would be set alongside Johnny's on the town's cemetery bluff, the dark fuselage of his coffin lowered inch-by-inch into the red earth of Yoknapatawpha County, Mississippi.

The page proofs of *Mosquitoes* arrive from New York. Faulkner's second novel, set aboard a yacht of New Orleans artists and bohèmes whose words are many, small and biting, whining over Lake Pontchartrain like a mob of mosquitoes.

Faulkner sits sharpening his pencil nub, dropping tiny curls of cedar onto the white block of pages. His jaws pulse. The shreds build like a little pile of tinder. He licks the tip of the pencil, as if testing a knife, and brings the honed point to the dedication.

TO HELEN, BEAUTIFUL AND WISE.

He does not cut these words for spite or because he no longer believes them. He cuts them because she is to marry Mr. Guy Lyman, Esquire, of New Orleans, and Faulkner will enchain her inside his heart no longer.

He will have her happy and free. This woman who might have loved him. He wants her to feel no guilt. No regret.

He stares at the strike of pencil lead, shining like a bullet's graze.

The hardest cut he has ever made.

A darling, killed.

He feels strangely light. He thinks of Estelle. His first love, who's back in Oxford now. She's home with her daughter, Cho-Cho—"butterfly"—to wait out the probationary period of her divorce. She has had enough of life abroad with Cornell.

Faulkner feels blossoms, tiny and white, springing beneath the storm of his heart.

28

Ghosts of Alabama

MOBILE BAY, ALABAMA, 1934

They left the hotel after lunch, riding on along the shore road. The afternoon light cascaded down through the oaks, scattering the pavement with light. They felt dazzled, sun-shot. Their tires burned through a brown fire of fallen leaves. Della closed her eyes, feeling the wind hum on her mouth, playing across her lips like a lover's thumb. She could feel the hard pulse of the motor in her chest, the fiery throb. Zeno sat erect on the saddle, holding the wide handlebars in his leather gauntlets, his trousered knees hugging the warm stove of the engine. Sark sat clutched in her lap, his ears feathering the wind. Della closed her eyes again, her thoughts drifting, scattering like the leaves in their wake.

She woke to the exhaust pipes popping and crackling as Zeno decelerated. Before them an upturned wooden canoe was scuttling across the road on several human legs like a giant beetle. The bearers stopped when they heard the bike, tilting the canoe so that their faces appeared between the thwarts. Two were teenagers, brown-skinned. The third was a Catholic priest. A rosary hung from his neck and his black trousers were hacked into shorts, frayed like those of a scalawag or castaway. His knees were knobby and white, his toenails square and trim, bluish with cold. His eyes sparkled as if filled with the bay.

"Please excuse us," he said. "Just portaging our way home."

On the side of the road, a sign: ST. MARY'S HOME FOR CATHOLIC ORPHANS.

A white chapel peeked between the trees.

Zeno leaned on the handlebars. "Room for three more, Father?"

They sat around the campfire with the orphans, a ring of them listening to the stories of Father Tom. The fire spat and cracked. Della stared through the night at the chapel, standing like a great hunk of ice through the trees. The fortress of some winter queen. She thought of her own self reigning there, her blood cold as stone. Her heart blue, needing nothing beyond itself.

The priest was telling them of the ghost storied to haunt the shore road between Point Clear and Battles Wharf. He sat wide-kneed as he spoke, leaning toward his audience. The white planes of his face crawled with firelight. He was thumbing the glass beads of his rosary, each glowing in his hand.

"They say the man stole a horse. A prize Thoroughbred."

Della thought she saw the priest glance toward the motorbike beneath the trees. She looked at Zeno, but he didn't seem to notice. His head was cocked at the same angle as the other orphans'. His mouth hung slightly open, as if breathing in the priest's words.

"So they sat him aback the horse he'd stolen and ran a string beneath the belly of the beast, lashing his ankles each to each. They threw a rope over the limb of a high oak and slipped the noose over his neck, cinching it tight." Father Tom looked from one face to the next, each of them waiting openmouthed for the rest of his story. "Do you know what they did next?"

No head moved.

"They slapped that horse's *rump!*"

The priest lifted his rosary, snapping a bead with his thumb.

"Popped his head right off."

The orphans gasped.

"Now he rides the high bluffs over Mobile Bay, night after night, back and forth, on a horse the color of smoke. Looking for the head he lost."

Della watched the shoulders of the children hunch, as if from a passing chill.

A quiver across Father Tom's lips—nearly a smile.

"You just have to hope yours isn't the head he finds."

The children's heads shivered on their necks. Some glanced over their shoulders, looking for the ghost high upon his horse, headless, a black hollow between his shoulders. Zeno smiled wide and pleased, as if he knew the name of the ghost. As if he and Father Tom shared the same secret.

Della licked her lips. "Do you think ghosts know they're dead, Father? Or do they just keep living the past over and over, unable to see beyond one single stretch of time?"

Father Tom cocked his head, rolling a bead between his fingers. "Ghosts are only stories," he said. "Told again and again and again."

Della looked out at the black candelabra of trees, moss-hung. The white frame of the chapel. She looked at her own pale hands, which had grasped the very sinews of heaven, holding her high against gravity and death.

"Stories," she said. Sometimes she could hardly believe her own. Sometimes she wondered if she held the threads of her own story or if there were another hand out there, unseen—god or author or fate—pulling the strings and banshee wires of their world. Or no one, only the wind. Sometimes she wondered if they were not haunted but haints themselves, turning endless circles over the land, performing the same acts over and over, replaying the same deaths—unable to move on.

29

The Pear Tree

OXFORD, MISSISSIPPI, 1928

*F*aulkner sits at his table. He feels as if he has swallowed light. He can see the scene so completely, burning in his mind. Three brothers, boys, are standing at the roots of the pear tree beside their home, staring up. The grass buzzes below their feet—the electric hum of April, searing with life—and the tree has exploded into bloom, the snowy blossoms purring and shivering in the breeze, as if a cloud of tiny white birds has alighted in the branches. The brothers are Jason and Quentin and the youngest, Benjy, an idiot.

They are watching their sister, Caddy, seven years old, who's climbing the tree, braving a whipping to see the party going on inside the parlor. Their grandmother Damuddy has been living in the room for weeks—ever since she took sick. All of the grown-ups are in there now, together, but the children aren't allowed in the house. They can see silhouettes rising and falling against the light of the window. It's a party full of moaning and singing, they've been told, called a funeral.

Benjy worries the buzzards will undress Damuddy, like they did the horse that fell in the ditch that had to be shot. He remembers the buzzards circling, circling, flapping black and slow over the bones. But

Caddy says the buzzards can't get into the parlor. She says their father wouldn't let no buzzards in the house. Caddy doesn't even believe it's a funeral. That's why she's climbing to look.

"I'm going to tell on her," says Jason, watching her.

They tried to stop her, but she wouldn't heed. She's the bravest among them, the wildest. Earlier that day, she stripped off her dress in front of them and went splashing near-naked in the creek, muddying her underclothes.

"We'll get whipped now," said Quentin.

"I don't care," said Caddy. "I'll run away and never come back."

Benjy moaned, as if he knew the meaning of her words.

Now Faulkner stands beside the three brothers, who watch their sister's small hands seek the man-thick limbs of the pear tree, pulling her higher and higher from the earth. It's as if the tree is stealing her from them, luring her into its arms, its clutches. They are maddened and afraid, but cannot say why. This tiny sister, who hangs so high above them, is ascending beyond their grasp, their protection. So high now they can see straight up her skirt, between the soft white flesh of her young thighs. They can see the muddy seat of her drawers hanging over them, crusted as with the dried blood of a wound.

They stare teary-eyed, transfixed, as if in worship. Then she is gone, swallowed into the white cloud of blossoms. There is only a thrashing in the crown of branches, bodiless, and the fear of the bough breaking and their sister falling to earth, dewy and ripe, landing with a smack before them—the white flesh of her bottom brown-bruised, as if by a strange man's thumb.

"Caddy, Caddy," says Benjy.

Caddy, who smells like trees in the rain.

Faulkner looks up from the paper, tears in his eyes. His heart trembles with the fury of creation, as with a thousand quivering wings.

The pastor's wife answered the door, her arms stained to the elbow with blackberry juice. She looked at the young man and woman on her stoop.

Sunday-dressed, when it was only Thursday afternoon. She knew what they must want.

"The pastor is taking his afternoon rest," she told them.

William Cuthbert Faulkner bowed slightly, apologizing for the intrusion. He was wearing his powder-blue flier's uniform, his cap tucked neatly under one arm. His gaze fell upon the woman's arms, the long gloves of blackberry juice. Now he looked up, smiling into her face.

"I do apologize most sincerely, ma'am, most sincerely. We did not wish to disturb your making of blackberry . . . ?" His voice trailed off slowly, like a sinking hook.

"*Preserves*," said the pastor's wife firmly.

"Ah," said Faulkner, smiling, not saying *wine*.

The woman wiped her hands on the towel at her waist, swabbing it dark. "I'll wake the pastor," she said. "Most marrying is done *by appointment*, you know."

"Why, thank you, ma'am. We would be ever so grateful."

He felt Estelle Franklin, his childhood sweetheart, tilt her hip into his side.

"You are magic," she said, her breath tickling his neck.

Faulkner's lungs swelled, sucking her words deep into his chest.

They named their baby Alabama after the aunt who once sewed twenty dollars into the lining of Bill's coat for his trip overseas. She was born in the bitter cold of January 1931—two months before she was due. She bloomed tiny and beautiful from the womb, pink and slightly blue, her dice-size fists curled like a boxer's against her chest. The tiniest seed of being, born unripe into the world. She hardly even cried.

There was no incubator at Dr. Culley's hospital on Van Buren Avenue, so they brought her home to Rowan Oak, the run-down antebellum manor Faulkner had bought. He'd named the place for the rowans, the mountain trees the ancient Scots believed to have magical powers, warding off witches and fairies. Here the newborn could be attended by Mammy Callie and a trained nurse and receive daily visits from her physician, Dr. Culley. How she suffered. Her digestive tract was underdeveloped—she could not keep down any milk. Faulkner asked Dean to find a goat. The brothers took turns milking the animal, their sleeves rolled despite the cold, their breath mingling in the barn-dark while they squeezed and stroked the blue-white fluid into a small pail, their brows gathered as they funneled the warm milk into a tiny glass feeding bottle.

It didn't help. The tiny babe spat up everything they tried to give her.

Without milk, she would die. Her body needed energy to grow, to keep warm. The fire was roaring in the hearth, but the old house was drafty—the sharp sting of a North Mississippi winter jabbing at the walls, darting through every chink in the joinery and casements, so cold the brothers could feel it in the toes of their boots.

Desperate, they went to Memphis for an incubator. Dean Swift drove, earning his middle name as he straddled the centerline at top speed, weaving his brother's roadster in and out of the slower traffic, his hands and feet dancing deftly between the gas and clutch and gearshift, keeping the engine in the power. Faulkner rode shotgun, his tweed hat jammed low, his neck and chin wrapped in a scarf that whipped and snapped in the wind. They flew past farm trucks and tractors and dusty sedans like they were standing still, racing between cold brown fields and quiet country hamlets, racketing into the brick and glass canyons of Memphis in record time.

It wasn't enough.

Baby Alabama died in her crib early one morning, as if some vulture had swept down and plucked the spirit from the tiny cage of her bones. She'd lived ten days, fighting every minute, and now she was gone.

Faulkner blamed Dr. Culley. The man had been indifferent, he said. His hospital should have had an incubator. *The bastard deserves to die*—so he was heard to say. Rumor was, the physician had hung up on Faulkner the previous night, telling him there was nothing more he could do for the child. Then Faulkner, finding his baby daughter cold in her crib, had taken his revolver from an oily sock in the bureau drawer and climbed into his roadster and roared to the Culleys' home on South Eleventh Street. The dawn light, cold and pale, was shafting down through the winter skeletons of the trees when he got out of the car and stood before the man's house. The birds fell silent. A feral tomcat watched from across the street.

"Dr. Culley, I'm calling you out!"

There was a rumble and curse in the house. The sound of creaking hinges, moaning floorboards, slippered feet. The doctor—a handsome man—opened the front door in his night-robe, red-eyed with stubbly chin, his eyeglasses perched low on his nose.

"Mr. Faulkner, I realize you're upset—"

Faulkner shot Culley in the shoulder, dropping him there in the threshold of his own home, where he cursed and pled for mercy—such was the story told. Other townsfolks said the shooting had occurred not at the doctor's home but at Rowan Oak. They said Culley arrived that morning to check on Baby Alabama and Faulkner shot him right through the screen door of the house—or tried to, said others, but narrowly missed. Such were the rumors that hissed through Oxford, swirling through town like the powder-smoke of battles past.

Many Oxonians would claim no shooting ever occurred. They claimed the story was another in a long line of fabrications, another fiction sprung of the no-count scribbler's fanciful imagination. No charges were brought against the grieving father, after all, but Dr. Culley was not seen outside his home for two weeks after the baby's death. Some people said the doctor had received, there on his front porch, the only payment he was due—in a hot gobbet of lead.

Less heard was the story of the horse-drawn wagon that arrived at Dr. Culley's hospital not long after Baby Alabama's tiny casket went into the ground, having ridden to the cemetery in her father's lap. In the wagon's bed was a brand-new Hess incubator from Chicago, top of the line, designed for premature babies unable to maintain their own body heat, who needed the womblike warmth of the heated cabinet to grow and survive. The unit, donated by Alabama's father, was to be made available for any premature infant, no matter if the parents could afford the bill.

30

La Batre

ALABAMA GULF COAST, 1934

*T*hey stayed three days at the orphanage, paddling canoes and sleeping in bunks. Father Tom drank sparingly at night—two fingers of Irish whiskey, neat—and Zeno did the same. He told stories to the adolescents of the first time he looped a biplane or met Whiskey and Soda, the lion cubs of the Lafayette Escadrille. He told of flying so high over mountains they looked like ocean swells far below—a vast green sea of earth—and how cows liked to face into the wind, as if to watch what weather was coming. He never spoke of the war itself or of his own time as an orphan before going south to live with his uncle.

Then, the third night, he woke Della without warning, prodding her shoulder where she lay on the top bunk. "It's time," he whispered.

"It's after midnight, Zeno."

"We have to go." Something like fear in his eyes.

"Why?" she asked.

"I had a bad dream."

"A bad dream?"

"A memory," said Zeno. "Something the older boys used to do." He looked over his shoulder, as if a ghost or monster might be hovering behind him, listening. "In a place like this."

Della reached out from under the covers, touching his ear. "Okay, honey. Do you want to tell Father Tom goodbye?"

Zeno shook his head.

They wheeled the motorbike a mile down the road before cranking the engine. The exhaust pipes crackled under the oaks, fracturing the night. They rode north along the bay. Long fingers of fog bloomed before the single headlight, wheeling and flashing in strange forms. Della could feel the vapor grazing her neck and cheeks like the touch of spirits. She squinted, watching for the headless rider of the priest's story to rear from the fog, high on his stolen horse.

A story, she told herself. Only that. Still, she reached out and touched Zeno's knee, as if to make sure he was still there, not a ghost she'd picked up along the way.

They passed through the town of Fairhope in the muddled light of dawn. Roadside cottages bloomed soft and pale on either side of them, like the remnants of dreams. They crossed the bay causeway with the sun rising at their backs, glittering across the Port of Mobile. The Alabama dry docks, where Great War minesweepers had been built, lay like empty concrete canyons along the bay while banana steamers smoked at the wharves, unloading their green bunches by the thousands.

The buildings of Mobile huddled against the sky, sun-spangled and squat, housing the offices of fruit brokers and shipping agents and men who traded in cotton or timber or turpentine. Men who woke up to alarm clocks or screaming children, their happiness dictated by broad sheets of numbers they could only dimly control. Men like her father. Their hair graying early, as if to hurry them toward peace and rest.

Soon the riders were cracking through the city on the motorbike, the streets hissing black and damp with dawn. Men were sweeping storefronts in canvas aprons while newsboys tromped toward street corners, their papers warm as fresh bread loaves beneath their arms. The smell of coal and wood fires stung the nose, sharp and blue, while the alleyways exhaled a reek of piss and whiskey. Then they were out of the city, throbbing through a brittle jungle of winter scrubland. The sun gleamed down the railroad tracks that paralleled the highway, the rails bright with wear. Soon they were overtaking a freight train. The caboose was steel-built, bloodied with rust, the boxcars rocking and clacking through the trees, strung coupler to coupler beneath the black storm of engine smoke, the letters L&N stenciled on their wooden sheathing. The Louisville & Nashville line. Della thought of the Super Tramp as she examined the train. She knew freight-hoppers were being killed in droves on the western lines, shot and clubbed by railroad bulls, thrown from moving boxcars.

They passed an open-top gondola, the sides bowed from heavy use, and Della saw three heads peek over the edge of the car, peering as if from the rim of a giant bathtub. Boys, she saw, but with faces knotted hard against the world, fistlike. This was not the storybook world seen from the sky. Here was the hard land, which would dash any body fallen from high.

Della raised a hand to the boys. They ducked.

Zeno turned off the highway, throttling them toward the nearest town. The sun was still climbing the sky, wingless and white, and Della couldn't help but envy its rise. She felt the red letters of her name burning between her shoulder blades, like wounds or lies.

The blacktop road slithered through the pinewoods, making for the coast. They saw an alligator basking on the roadside, open-jawed, sunning his tongue. Overhead, geese honked southward in their squadrons, bottle-bellied, braving the eruptions of lead shot that would punch them bloody from the sky. High above them, a single bird wheeled and darted with violent abandon, as if to shed itself of wings. A raptor. The bird snapped and rolled against the sky, looping and twisting with aerobatic ferocity. Catching insects on the wing, perhaps, then kiting for short moments, spread-winged, to eat. The raptor trailed a long black fork of tail, which scissored open and closed, shearing through the sky.

Della was about to ask Zeno if he knew the name of the bird when the road turned and broke from the trees onto a small fishing village built on the banks of a bayou. The cottages and storefronts were huddled close, their roofs streaked and soiled beneath the ever-present flurry of gulls. The bayou ran dark through the middle of the town, shouldering a fleet of shrimp and oyster boats whose masts bobbed along the waterfront. Their hulls thumped on the water, rusty and old. Pale bluffs of oyster shell cradled the bayou, coughed out by the canneries that lined the banks. More boats were anchored downstream, towing barges of piled oysters, each awaiting its turn at the docks. A salty musk pervaded the place, thick in the nose.

They rode down to the waterfront in search of food, pushing through the door of a dust-windowed shop. The proprietor eyed them suspiciously from behind the counter. Her hands were thrust inside the front pouch of her apron, balled into fists. Her face looked like meat pie.

She jutted her chin. "What brings you two to Bayou La Batre?"

Zeno raised his eyes over a shelf. "Just passing through," he said. "Headed for New Orleans."

The woman shuddered at mention of the city. She crossed herself. "A damned city."

"Damned?" asked Zeno.

Her lips squirmed against her teeth. "City that sheltered him," she said.

"Him, who?"

"The Terror of the Gulf." The woman lowered her voice, as if speaking the name of a demon or ghost. "Jean Lafitte."

"The privateer?"

"The *pirate*, and nothing higher." She squinted one eye at Zeno. "We get us a lot of foreigners come through, hunting after that treasure of his. You one?"

"I was born in Connecticut," said Zeno.

"Hmm," said the woman.

"Listen," said Zeno, "why would he bury his treasure here?"

"Him and them Baratarians of his made these bayous like the bank," she said. "Buried they Spanish gold and plunder all throughout. When my gran-mammy was a child, the people used to anoint their doors with holy oil to keep him away. Some say he still walks the bottom of the bayou, in that red doublet of his and feathered hat. Say if you dangle your bare feet in the water, he'll think your heels is doubloons and snatch you down to the dark."

Zeno sat a wheel of cheese and box of crackers on the counter. "We'll keep that in mind."

The woman worked her jaw, making change below the counter. "You ought."

"Say," said Zeno, "there isn't an airfield around here, is there?"

The woman sat back on her stool, thrusting her hands back into her apron. "This ain't Connecticut."

They sat at the edge of the bayou, making tiny sandwiches of crackers and cheese. Zeno made his with the cheese on the outside, two slices for every cracker.

"High cotton," he said. "*Double* rations."

The docks were weathered and rickety, the tarred posts canted out of plumb. The oyster boats creaked at their moorings, their rubber tires bumping and squeaking. Della looked at Zeno, who'd reclined onto his elbows. A mess of cracker crumbs down his shirtfront. He lifted his face to the sun, shutting his eyes. His boots stood beaten beside him, unpolished. His white feet were crossed one atop the other. His nails, somehow, neat and trim.

Della sat cross-legged, erect, chewing a cracker. She pressed Zeno's knee with her finger. "Tell me about your dream," she said. "From last night."

Zeno scrunched his nose at the sky. "No."

"Please."

"You don't want to know."

"I do."

"Ain't fit for a woman's ears."

Della sniffed. "I can judge that for myself."

He opened one eye in her direction. "I know."

Sark was clucking about, cleaning the scene of crumbs. Meanwhile, the gulls screamed and swung overhead, countless, like a feather pillow had detonated in the sky. Zeno lay below them, faceup, unafraid of the squirts that coated the village.

"You might think different of me after," he said.

"I won't."

Zeno sat up slowly, brushing the crumbs from his shirt. He seemed to be moving with effort, as against a wind or tide. He scooted to the edge of the dock and hung his legs over the side, dipping his bare feet into the bayou. His shoulders slumped.

"The senior boys," he said. "They were the ones who did it."

"At the orphanage?"

Zeno nodded.

"Who did what?" asked Della.

Zeno's shoulders rose, fell. He thumbed the tip of his nose, then straightened his shoulders, breathing in. "They made sure every new boy got a *thumbs-up*."

"Thumbs-up?"

Zeno nodded, wiggling slightly on his seat bones, showing what he meant.

A plunge in Della's breast. "God, Zeno, I'm so sorry."

Zeno didn't answer. He stared down into the bayou, wiggling his toes beneath the water, as if daring Lafitte to rise. His brow dark, like he might jump after the ghost himself. Della reached out and touched his neck, threading her fingers through his hair. Zeno's eyes softened, released from the spell. Soon he was standing and yawning, his body stretched wide as a tree beneath the sun.

"We best not be skylarking," he said. "We got places to get to."

Della rose. She tilted her face to him, passing the last slice of cheese from her teeth to his.

"Let's go," she said.

31

Hawks

Howard Hawks stood before the mahogany behemoth of his desk. A desk as big as an altar, set on wooden lion's paws. This was Metro-Goldwyn-Mayer Studios, after all—MGM—whose maned lion, Leo, roared on silver screens across the land. Hawks smiled. He was a paper baron's son who'd grown up racing stripped-down speedsters in the whirling dust of California dirt tracks, then attended an elite eastern university, only to leave behind the smoky parlors of Cornell to train as a squadron commander in the Great War. Now he was the Grey Fox of Hollywood, a man who'd directed a rash of silent films before his brother was killed flying a camera plane over Santa Monica Bay, a fiery midair collision from which men fell burning into the sea. The wreckage was discovered by a minesweeper at fifty-three fathoms, the bodies raised by naval divers.

Hawks identified his brother's shattered remains, then went on to direct *Dawn Patrol*, the flying epic that drove billionaire Howard Hughes nearly mad. Hughes tried to buy up every existing fighter plane of the era so the film couldn't compete with his own *Hell's Angels*. Hawks had flown in *Dawn Patrol* himself, piloting one of the Wichita Fokkers—a Kansas-built plane painted to look like a German fighter.

Now he stood tall and lean before his desk, blue-eyed in a gray suit. His office walls were lined with books, their titles glittering on their spines. The brass cigarette cases on the tables shone, polished daily. The emerald leather of the couches glowed.

"Mr. Faulkner," said Hawks, extending his hand.

Faulkner strode across the office. "Mr. Hawks," he said. "I have seen your name on my check."

Hawks gestured to a small tower of checks, sitting unsigned at the corner of his desk. "The mighty pen."

Faulkner was dead broke. He'd traveled to California in a lower berth, having bought his train ticket with a five-dollar loan from his grandfather. The house that published *The Sound and the Fury* had gone bankrupt, defaulting on thousands of dollars in royalties he was owed, and no one would extend him credit—not even the sporting goods store in Oxford where he'd recently shaken a signed three-dollar check before the shop-keeper's stony face.

"My autograph will be worth more than this one day!"

Meanwhile, his father was dying. Murry Falkner, who'd survived coal shovels and shotgun blasts and balloonitics, had recently been seen sitting in his porch rocker, holding a head of iceberg lettuce in his lap—as if this rabbit's food, recommended by his doctor, could unclog his failing heart, clearing his arteries of a lifetime of fried okra, fatback, and streak o' lean.

When he died, Faulkner would become the family patriarch. His mother would need her grocer's bill paid and the monthly mortgage, and someone would have to cover Dean's tuition if he wasn't expelled for truancy. Then there was Estelle, whose eyes turned so often these days to tiny pins, as if staring across the ocean. To Shanghai, Hono-lulu? Those old days of opulence, with her first husband? Sometimes, it seemed she could see nothing so small as a price tag, as if the trees of Rowan Oak bore leaves with the faces of presidents.

Faulkner, like so many writers before him, had gone west.

He'd stood, suitcase in hand, before the vast acreage of MGM Studios, where the soundstages stood in their rows, high and windowless like the hangars for Zeppelins, housing the dreams of the republic in their cavernous vaults. The ships of pirates and swashbucklers slept beneath those roofs, set against giant murals of the high seas. Nearby, castles of pasteboard and painted stone awaited their damsels and knights. Vast wardrobes held the costumes of gunfighters and gladiators, corsairs and generals and nuns. Every officer's uniform from every army that ever existed, each bearing service medals and braids of distinction.

Faulkner, standing across the street from these studios, had shifted his briefcase to his other hand. Dried blood clung to his temple—he was not sure how it got there—and he could feel the whiskey-sweat stinging beneath the arms of his rumpled tweed jacket. The Santa Ana wind came burning down from the brown haze of mountains, whistling desert-dry through alleyways and across shingles, whipping trash and dust down the sidewalks, burying grit in ears and necklines. Across the road, a pistoled guard stood at the east gate of the place, checking cars before they passed beneath a gold-lit sign that read: METRO-GOLDWYN-MAYER STUDIOS. Beside this, the roaring face of Leo the Lion.

Within these gates, Joan Crawford and Douglas Fairbanks and Clark Gable strode before the glass eyes of movie guns, their skin shot porcelain-white beneath the stage lights, their faces projected giant-size before a billion moviegoers each year. Now the producers and agents wanted flying films, tales of reckless aces who drank hard and loved harder, dying in romantic places like the French countryside or waking to find themselves in the cottages of Bavarian farm maidens who healed their wounded bodies and broken hearts.

Faulkner had straightened his spine, drawn the Californian dust into his lungs, and walked across the street.

"I don't remember a woman in the story," said Faulkner. He was sitting on the emerald green leather of the couch, his briefcase between his knees. He was discussing the script he was to write, based on his short story "Turnabout," set among bomber pilots of the Great War.

Hawks, sitting behind his desk now, made a rough steeple of his hands. He cocked his head, a gentle crossing his lips. "This is Hollywood, Mr. Faulkner, there is always a woman."

Faulkner looked at the briefcase. Inside, a check for $500, to be followed by another every week until the picture was done. Signed by this man, Hawks, whose signature was worth untold sums. Enough to raise a man from the slop of financial woe, high enough to head his family. Perhaps, even, to fly.

"Five days," said Faulkner.

"To take the job?"

"To complete it."

32

Singing River

They crossed the Mississippi line at dusk, going places, whirring through a purpling jungle of oak and pine. Sharp thickets of saw palmetto and Spanish bayonet sprang through the trees. Della wondered how many of the old black bears and red wolves still moved through these Gulf forests, cutting white jags of trail through the understory.

The sun died red into the horizon. Night came curling along the road like smoke. A sortie of bats rose wheeling and slashing from the eaves of a barn, seeking prey. The headlight of the motorbike burned down the blacktop, illuminating the ghostly scurry of possums and raccoons, hunchbacked on their errands, while moths fluttered above the road, briefly luminescent. These popped against the riders' fists and goggles, shoulders and chests. In the morning, they would rise gut-streaked, the wings of tiny fliers pasted to their breasts.

Fields broke from the side of the highway, here or there, and Della looked for places to stop. They had a loaf of French bread, cake-soft beneath a hard brown crust, along with a white stick of butter. Her belly was hollow, thrilling for the meal to come. The moon rose in a white slash, bluing the landscape. An empty pasture rolled into view, where a lone tree stood crooked and vine-draped, big as a dilapidated house.

Della squeezed Zeno's thigh.

Zeno nodded, wheeling the bike from the highway. They rode bobbing and sputtering across the field, as if heading home.

The tree was covered in a brittle veil of kudzu, winter-thin, which rasped in the shifting night. They passed through a narrow vent, like a secret door, into the great hollows of the place. Heavy oak limbs rose over them like rafters, holding up the shroud of vines. The three of them stood wide-eyed beneath this shelter. Even Sark seemed awed, his tongue hanging slack and pink. Della's eyes traced the hoary arms of oak, her heart quickening with gratitude. The place felt hallowed, almost, like the weird church of a druid or witch, perhaps some shaman of the Biloxi or Pascagoula tribe—or maybe just a spot that an old farmer held sacred, a lunch place of blessed shade.

They laid out their sleeping blankets and sat cross-legged, cracking the loaf of bread, dropping flecks of crust in their laps. They slathered the shreds in butter, chewing from the sides of their mouths. The place warmed around them, like the chamber of a cave, and the stars winked in and out of the branches. Sark ate from their hands, his tongue warm and gritty, and Zeno opened the bottle of red wine he'd bought in Bayou La Batre. The wine pulsed like blood in their temples and Della's vision began to bleed. The stars turned sickle, each a tiny scrawl of moon. Soon they were shifting and purring beneath the blankets, breathing each other's breath, notching their bodies this way and that. Della looked over Zeno's shoulder, seeing the wild skeleton of limbs high above them, like the bones for wings.

Della lay spent, watching the stars pulsing through the vines. For so long, she'd thought of home as a myth. A veil. The most tenuous threads of security, no more substantial than the fibrous veins of a fly's wing. A structure that could be exploded in an instant, scattered broken to the four winds. This vagrancy they saw on the roads, the vast shifting of souls, seemed but a return to the natural state of their kind. Nomadic, rootless. Alone but for small and infrequent knots. Shuffling under the sun, as if wing-shorn.

West, she thought, was not so much a place on a map as a point in the geography of their souls. A place that might calm their manic sorties, field to field, before they burned out of luck or time or desire. They would know they'd given this entire nation the chance to undo them, challenging them at every ridge and river and thunderhead, and they'd survived. They would know they deserved the home they carried between them, clutched like a secret ember in their hands. They were so close now, she thought. If they could just cross the vast scrawl of the Mississippi River—that wild border—she felt they could make the rest of the journey. She closed her eyes, her chin tucked on Zeno's shoulder, her heart thumbing his skin.

The winter sun broke ground, chasing night from the pasture. Soon they were riding west along the Old Spanish Trail, crossing piney ridges and brown brooms of marsh, the creeks racing like tar snakes beneath the bridges. Pascagoula assembled before them, built on the banks of the Singing River. Double-masted luggers lined the waterfront, unloading silvery mounds of red snapper from their live wells and iceboxes. The fish were wheeled into the long wooden buildings of the seafood companies where they would be gutted and packed in barrels of ice, shipped north by rail. Half-finished schooners sat cradled in the shipyards, long-ribbed like the skeletons of beasts long extinct, while gulls wheeled overhead, scrawling batlike shadows across the ground. Della and Zeno sat on one of the rotting wharves, watching the river move beneath their boots. The surface shivered, bark-ridged under the sun.

"Bees," said Zeno, crunching his teeth into an apple. "A swarm of them."

"More like a hum," said Della. She set her hand on the wooden planks of the wharf. "Like a church organ, felt through a heavy door."

Zeno nodded. "That's very specific," he said. "And good."

They were discussing the sound of the river, the mysterious song that gave the Singing River its name. Scientists had posited a wealth of theories. Streams of fish muscling upstream, their fins whistling in unison, or ribbons of sand scraping along the slate bottom. An underwater cave, moaning in the current like the blown mouth of a bottle.

"You know what the old people say," said Zeno, rotating his apple for the next bite.

Della knocked her shoulder against him, her long red hair wrapped around her neck. "People old as you?"

"Even older." Zeno smiled. "They say it's the death song of the Pascagoula. Rather than be enslaved by the Biloxi tribe, they chose to walk hand in hand into the river, chanting. They say it's the voice of the braves, rising from the river."

Della removed her hand from the wharf plank. She looked at the crisscrossing lines of her palm, pink and slightly jagged. So like old wounds, made by banshee wires or struts. Then she set both hands back against the wood, flat, feeling the hum of the river rise against her palms. She closed her eyes, imagining wind beneath her hands.

Zeno stopped dead in his tracks, looking at the handbill blown fluttering against his boot. The paper was green and weather-curled, soiled like a giant greenback dollar. Zeno bent down slowly and picked it from the cinder sidewalk, holding it by a single dog-eared corner. They were standing before the green lawn of the Pascagoula courthouse, the flagpole ringing now and again in the lazy shift of wind. They were planning to sleep that night on the white beaches south of town, where the high-powered motors of rumrunners could still be heard throbbing in the night, inbound from Cuba, no matter the Repeal.

Zeno unfurled the handbill and held it close to his face.

"What is it?" asked Della.

Zeno spread the poster against a nearby telephone pole, as if tacking up a bounty reward.

DON'T FAIL TO SEE
~ ERNST UDEN, GERMAN ACE ~
IN AERIAL COMBAT WITH
~ AN AMERICAN PILOT ~
THE THRILL AND HORROR OF THE GREAT AIR WAR,
FEATURING DEATH-DIPS, IMMELMANN TURNS, AND
OTHER DOGFIGHTING MANEUVERS OF THE GREAT ACES

Beneath these words, the crude picture of a biplane, the fuselage bearing the Iron Cross of the Imperial German Flying Corps.

Zeno looked over his shoulder at her, his eyes bright. "Wings."

33

Today We Live

OXFORD, MISSISSIPPI, 1933

*T*he Lyric theater stood on Van Buren Avenue, the white brick facade unadorned but for the stepped parapet of the roof, which
boy-Faulkner once imagined as the battlements of a castle wall. His
own father, Murry Falkner, railroad coaler and liveryman, had owned
this building in the early days of the century, when he ran a stable for
carriage horses. The window casings were painted black now, as were
the great carriage doors through which tired draft horses once passed,
sweat-rimed from pulling buggies through the dusty streets of the
Square. Beasts of burden, sunk-headed, waiting to be combed and hoof-
picked by the coal-eyed boy, son of a stableman, who strode among the
veined colonnades of their legs with wonder in his heart.

That boy's father was dead. Murry Falkner's heart had killed him,
giving out after nearly sixty-two years of hard service and abuse. Six
decades of failed businesses and high-proof whiskey and chicken-fried
steaks the size of catcher's mitts. Four wild sons, two of them yet uncor-
ralled. His eldest could not be reached at the time of his death. He was
panther hunting with Howard Hawks and Clark Gable on Coronado
Island.

Oh, you are a writer, Mr. Faulkner?

Yes, Mr. Gable. And what do you do?

When Faulkner arrived in Oxford, having ridden the long miles cross-country in the silver missile of a streamliner, his father was already in the ground. Faulkner sat at Mack's Cafe near the rail platform, sipping a mug of black coffee, whiskey-hardened from the bottle in his coat, and read the obituary, squinting through a blue wreath of cigarette smoke. The newspaper had spelled his father's last name *Faulkner*.

A crinkling at the corners of his eyes. His father would've hated the spelling applied to his own surname—a fancy of his wayward son, a maddening affectation, as if his born name were not good enough, not highborn enough for his lofty ambitions. And yet a hard, begrudging pride would have choked the old man to his teeth, threatening to bust through his eyes. This son of his, who could hardly paste a stamp to an envelope, had stuck his name in ink and lights, on bookshelves and library annals and the lips of people in New York, France, Hollywood. He'd made a name for himself, bolder even than his father's.

Now Faulkner stood across the street from the Lyric, watching the townspeople bustle and chatter beneath the theater marquee. The avenue lay before him, paved by Johncy's crews. A river of asphalt, still warm with the day's heat. Radiant in the dusk. His wife stood on one side of him, pregnant again, and on the other stood young Dean Swift, who'd lately changed his surname to match his brother's. Young Dean, his favorite, whose eyes were full of awe. Across the street, the marquee read:

PREMIERE: "TODAY WE LIVE"

A FILM BASED ON THE STORY BY AUTHOR WILLIAM FAULKNER

The film starred Joan Crawford and Gary Cooper as an English girl and American fighter pilot caught in a love triangle during the Great War, combining the "fiery headstrong personality" of the female star with the "eager romantic nature" of the male—so said the taglines at least. Faulkner had written the script in five days but been forced through endless rewrites with a dizzying array of screenwriters, each with his own ideas and style, adding and excising and reworking scenes and storylines until the film threatened to become a complete farce of its original form, a gluey melodrama with only the well-shot aerial dog-fight scenes to commend it.

Still, the author felt unafraid of the step he was to take, striding across the street and through the white flak-bursts of camera light, entering his father's old stables to watch the film he wrote silver-beamed through the theater dark. His nerves were steady, even calm. It seemed so easy a maneuver in comparison with the one he would face in the days to come, strapping himself into the hard chair of the cockpit alone. The Hollywood checks, after all, had afforded him flying lessons. In one week's time, he was to make his first solo flight, putting wind beneath his dreams.

34

Uden

MISSISSIPPI GULF COAST, 1934

*T*hey narrowly missed him at Gautier and Fontainebleau, following the pointing hands of sharecroppers and swampers in rubber
boots, finding fields with sodden handbills stuck fluttering in the weeds.
They roared over rickety bayou bridges and through pecan orchards
where the trees stood in their rows, aligned like gravestones, their naked branches fissuring the lower reaches of sky. The long corridors were
swept weedless, littered with the cracked shells of nuts the pickers had
missed, the meat stolen by foraging squirrels or crows or vagrants. They
looked like the empty halls of some lonesome manor.

More than once, Della looked heavenward to see biplanes wheeling
in combat against the clouds, only to realize they were just turkey buzzards circling or knife-winged raptors with forked tails, slashing and
scissoring through the sky. People spoke of machines buzzing low overhead, nearly slashing off treetops with their propellers, or chasing one
another across the heavens in spinning ribbons and rolls. They might be
speaking of some rare and mythic species of bird, thought Della, which
alighted only in the odd barnyard or pasture, high-nosed and puffing
castor smoke.

The second day, a storm came brooding from the Gulf, high and dark as a city skyline, booming and pulsing with threat. Zeno wheeled the bike into a pecan grove and they made camp in the lee of the machine. The ground rumbled and the sky turned dark gray, the branches shivering overhead. The wind whistled through the orchard, kicking up leaves and dirt, stinging their faces. They hooked the tarpaulin to the handlebars and fender of the motorbike and pegged it taut, huddling beneath this makeshift shelter as the rain came shattering through the trees.

Sark trembled between them, his ears laid back like a rabbit's, and Della raised her hand to the sunken roof of the tarp. The waxed canvas, rain-thrummed, tickled the palm of her hand.

"You think they're headed to New Orleans? Same as us?"

"Got to be," said Zeno. "For the show."

"You think they're in it?"

"I bet."

The wind blew cold through the tarp, flecking them with spray. Zeno lit a cigarillo in the cup of his palms, then passed it over. She sucked the wet end of the cigar, once and deep, filling her lungs. She raised her chin, fighting the urge to cough, and blew a long torrent of smoke, watching the wind rip it curling from her mouth. She passed the cigar back to Zeno, already feeling a tingle in her scalp from the smoke, a hum in her temples.

She cocked one eye at him. "You know him, don't you? This Uden."

Zeno sucked on the little cigar, the ash flaring between his lips. He exhaled through his teeth. "Got drunk with him once. Over There."

"France?"

Zeno nodded. "He was one of Richthofen's protégés. Another one of those blue-eyed baron types, descended of Prussian cavalrymen or some such. Forefathers' portraits on the walls, bearded hounds at the heels. All that rot. MacMonagle shot him down near Saint-Mihiel. Lit his Fokker on fire and he jumped. Huns had parachutes, you know. We went out in the squadron car and got him from the Tommies. He was sopping. Face like his mother had tried to drown him in the bathtub. I mean, pretty broken up. It wasn't just the rain, I don't think. Looked like the landing had wrecked something on his insides."

Zeno pulled on the cigar, his free arm wrapped around his knees.

"We took him back to the château and broke out the champagne, but he said he didn't want a drink. Kept talking about *die Läuse* and *die Ratten*, the lice and rats. Seemed he just couldn't believe how the guys in the trenches were living. Like this was the first time he'd ever been on the ground. Finally we mixed some brandy in warm milk and gave him that. He sucked it down, asked for another. Started talking about how we're all brothers, and he doesn't understand why we're killing one another. Told me he always respected the American pioneer spirit. Told the Frenchies he liked their bread. This boy-Hun with purple bags under his eyes, like somebody socked him in the face. Kid was weeping by the time we put him to bed. I slept in the same room. He whimpered in his sleep."

Zeno ashed his cigar.

"We sent him back over the lines in the morning. Customary. Figured we'd never see him again. The Huns would ship him home on a medical. Or, more likely, put a rifle in his hands, force him to the front." Zeno shook his head. "Instead he turns up two weeks later in a new fighter, a blue-eyed skull painted on the fuselage. Goes on to have seven victories. An *Überkanonen*. Top gun."

Zeno looked out at the storm, the rain slashing slantwise beyond the flap.

"Two of those kills were my friends. One was MacMonagle, the same day I went down. The one I saw burn. I guess whatever was broken inside him that night got fixed."

"Or didn't," said Della.

Zeno nodded. "I had a dream once that I smothered him in his sleep. Silenced those whimpers." Zeno looked at her. "It wasn't a nightmare."

They woke to a sodden earth. The trees were wet and black, their branches strung with dew. The sky was white and low, hovering just over the jagged crowns of the trees. The sun had risen unseen, diffused through the fog. They'd slept in their clothes. Their leathers were board-stiff, groaning as they buckled and strapped themselves against the weather. The bike was coated in a sheen of moisture, like a cold bomb. Zeno kicked viciously for ignition, again and again, mouth-breathing. The motor caught fire, finally, in a cacophonous roar, then settled into a stammering idle. Soon they were on the road, the wet pavement hissing beneath the tires.

They detoured north on the word of a filling station attendant, finding nothing, then looped back toward the Gulf, riding through a broad sweep of virgin pine, the trees passing like shadowy towers in the mist. They were rounding a bend, the motor throbbing along, when an animal leapt curling into the middle of the road. A red fox, torch-bright in the fog. Zeno hit the brakes. The three-wheeled machine skidded sideways along the wet tar of the road, the handlebars shuddering in his fists. Della clung hard to Sark, her fingers digging between his ribs. They stopped just short of the fox, turned broadside, the engine stalled. The fox stood frozen, round-eyed with fright, one lower fang hooked outside her lip. Her shoulders were bunched, quivering. Her lower legs black, as if she'd walked through a pool of ink. Her tail was bushy, big as a firebrand.

She didn't move.

Della, closest, reached out her hand, slowly, as if to shoo or pet her—she wasn't sure which. Just then, the fox bolted into the mist, as if fired from a gun, and Sark went rigid in Della's lap, a knot of muscle. He was looking in the opposite direction. Zeno was kicking the starter when a cry of hounds pierced the fog and the animals burst from the trees themselves, a flood of them tumbling across the road, brown-spotted and white, their tongues slung wild from their mouths. They forked around the motorbike, roiling and foaming, hard on the fox's scent. On their heels came a rider in a scarlet coat, high-hatted on a horse the color of steel. Horse and rider reared together in the road, as if posing for a monument. Now more red-coated riders broke from the trail, wheeling and rearing their horses, churning at the foot of the road. They couldn't pass the master of the hunt—the rules forbade it.

Della didn't understand why the huntsman had stopped in the road until she twisted in her seat to look back at Zeno. He was standing on the pegs of the motorbike, his big English revolver leveled at the man on horseback.

"Good, sir," he said, "I'd kindly ask you to call off the hounds, which gave the lady here quite a fright. At least until we have our motorbike out of the way."

The huntsman looked down from the high saddle of his horse, his mouth grim beneath his top hat. His riding breeches were white, bowed into black riding boots. "I would hardly call this a kindly request, sir."

Zeno cocked the hammer. "I could make it unkindly."

The huntsman raised the brass horn to his lips. A series of long, lonesome wails, rising and falling through the trees. In the distance, the hounds howled their disappointment, high and haunting, like grieving spirits.

Zeno looked at Della, nodding his head toward the kick lever. "Would you do us the honor, my sweet?" He smiled at the riders, speaking through his teeth. "And take your time about it."

She stood and removed her coat, slowly, revealing the words stitched across her shoulder blades. She set her boot on the kick lever and stretched to kiss Zeno long on the lips, reaching down to cup him between the legs, hearing the gasps of the huntsmen. She inhaled Zeno as she kissed him, his breath and scent. She'd hardly loved him so much in her life.

"My pleasure," she said.

They rode out of the pinelands, striking the two-lane blacktop of the Old Spanish Trail and turning west to speed along the Gulf. They passed into Ocean Springs at noon, bumping along the waterfront. The shrimping fleet was strung along the wharves, their green nets hung from their outriggers like mossy drapes. In the long, open-doored canning plants, the pickers were working over troughs of ice-chilled shrimp, doing what looked like sleight-of-hand, peeling the shrimp in single hard twists. Their finger bones knuckling, rippling in sequence. They would dip their hands in buckets of alum water to cleanse the acidic residue of the shellfish.

At Della's bidding, they turned onto a dirt lane after passing through town. A sign was hammered to a tree there: SHEARWATER POTTERY. A workshop rose from the woods, gray and windowless, kiln smoke churning through the branches. Inside sat a man in a white cotton shirt rolled to the elbows, a pair of canvas pants. His forearms were thin and sinewy, his hands wielding a fettling knife. He was trimming the clay cast of a man on horseback. The beast was arched beneath the rider, who clutched the base of a torch.

"Lamp base," the shop woman told them. "Cast in a plaster mold. The clay is leather-hard, ready to be trimmed. In the morning, we'll fire the piece in the kiln."

They watched the potter, who was consumed in his labor, the thinnest feathers of clay curling beneath the gleam of his knife. He didn't seem to know they were there. His head was bent close to his work, his chin cut sharp across the apple of his neck, as if carved by his own blade. The shelves and tables were lined with ceramic figurines, vases and lampstands and bookends shaped like pelicans or crabs or skimmers. A coastal menagerie, glazed and fired. A single raptor perched on the edge of a shelf. A hawk or kite, with a white head and long dark tail, forked like a pair of daggers. The same bird of prey Della had seen darting and wheeling over the coast, high and aerobatic. She started to ask Zeno if she could buy the piece, but he already had out their thinning roll, freeing a pair of bills with his thumb.

They motored out of town, spinning across the two-mile concrete bridge toward Biloxi. Sark stood high in Della's lap, drinking the wind, his tongue fluttering from his mouth. The ceramic bird rode in the inner pocket of Della's suit.

"It's a swallow-tailed kite," the shop woman had told her. "One of the great aerialists, they snatch insects on the wing and snakes from the trees."

"Are they rare?"

"Somewhat. Most of the ones on our coast are migrants. They cross the Caribbean in the fall, winter in South America, and start arriving back here this time of year."

"They go all the way to South America, really?"

"Sure. Scientists say they travel up to ten thousand miles in each direction."

"Gypsy fliers," Zeno had said. "Like us."

The bay gleamed, sun-dashed beneath the winter sky. Shrimp and oyster boats plowed the waters, their engine stacks chuffing smoke. The light poles of the bridge whipped past, again and again, each adorned with a single seagull, his wings hunched for warmth. Men stood fishing from the bridge, their poles quivering like antennae in the wind, tin pails and tackle boxes at their feet.

Della saw one of the fishing poles curled like a shepherd's crook, bobbing and thrashing with a hit, but the fisherman was paying no mind. Instead he was standing with both hands on the railing, his eyes cast heavenward. Della saw other fishermen poised in like fashion, their bellies pushed against the railing, and she followed their gaze. High over the bay, a pair of fliers orbited the sun. Then, one after the other, they rolled belly-up and dived from this height, slicing and spiraling for the bay, twist-turning, as if to braid a rope to the earth. They seemed conjoined by some gravity their own, expanding and contracting through the sky, growing tail fins and wires as they neared, the translucent disks of their propellers shattering the air. They were biplanes, saw Della, slicing and barreling for advantage. The higher plane sparked fire, trailing twin tendrils of smoke. Zeno cut the motorbike's engine, rolling to the shoulder to watch. The sound of machine guns came whip-cracking across the bay, stuttering in and out of earshot.

Della found herself at the rail. The machines were zigzagging downward, crisscrossing, screaming fast for the water. Her hands were curled on the concrete, knuckled bloodless. She was holding her breath. They were too close to pull out. They would crash white-spumed into the bay, leaving shattered litters of wreckage in their wake. Rainbow blooms of oil and pale shreds of canvas.

At the last moment they pulled up, bouncing like butterflies from the surface—that quick—the brassy dust of spent shell casings glittering in their wake. Firing blanks for the crowd. Climbing now, looping and twisting, and Della saw people standing in boats and grouped along the shore, looking up. The traffic on the bridge had stopped. People were shielding their eyes from the sun, watching, their mouths slack. The machines sang at the edge of destruction, their wires screaming with tension, the wings threatening to rip free of their bodies. Their bellies flashed as they rolled, their control surfaces torqued like fins, the sound of guns and engines surging wildly on the wind.

Della felt a green burn in her blood, like swallowed poison. Envy. She was no longer a Daughter of the Sun flashing blood-red and silver across the sky, riding wings her own. She wanted to pull these fliers to the earth, close enough she could grasp a wing wire and be yanked back into the air. The machines performed a high loop, one after the other, as upon a carnival wheel, and dived again for the bay. They pulled up again at the last moment, hard and fast, and this time the violence of the maneuver ripped free the wing of one machine. The craft went cartwheeling across the water, tumbling and shattering, leaving a long puzzle of wreckage in its wake.

Zeno slammed his palms hard on the rail. "Christ," he said. "Jesus Christ."

The surviving machine circled like a grieving swan as a tugboat smoked toward the wreckage. The deckhands used a gaff to hook the belt of the pilot, who was floating facedown in the bay. They hauled him over the side of the boat and knelt around him, as if in prayer. One of them rose and staggered toward the gunwale, vomiting over the side. Another of the men stood in a frayed sweater and removed his cap, shaking his head at the orbiting craft.

The machine peeled away, heading west, crossing over the bridge. The sun blazed across the fuselage as it passed and Della saw the blue-eyed skull painted on the ribbed body of the craft, the Iron Crosses on the undersides of the wings. The pilot sat grim-faced in goggles and scarf, as if carved from stone.

Uden.

She thought the German ace might turn and land on the white strip of beach alongside Biloxi in order to bury his fallen comrade, but the biplane continued straight and level, flying west down the coast, shrinking against the sky. The motorbike roared to life behind her. She turned to see Zeno with his goggles already donned, his eyes set on the diminishing speck.

He revved the throttle. "Travel Air 2000," he said. "Wichita Fokker."

35

NC13413

*I*t's too many thirteens in the name," said Aunt Bama. "Like your mama said."

"Shoo," said Dean, who stood barefoot in the field beside her, his suspenders crisscrossed between his shoulder blades. "She's the most beautiful thing I ever seen, is what she is."

The Falkner clan was gathered in a brown field on the outskirts of Oxford, staring at the large red biplane Bill had flown down from Memphis, freshly bought. The machine sat nose-high in the grass, blood-red, the wings staggered for speed. The cabin was enclosed in glass, the stainless steel propeller silvering in the sun. The red machine gleamed as if painted in a slaughterhouse. That bright. The registration number—NC13413—was stenciled on the tail in white.

"The numbers don't have a thing to do with how she flies," said Faulkner. "And she flies like a dream."

"What is she again, William?" asked his mother.

"Waco C Series," said Faulkner. "*C* stands for 'cabin.' She's got a 210-horse Continental radial, with spruce spars and aluminum-sheeted leading edges."

He stood looking at the ship, awed that it was his. He'd soloed in April, rising alone in an open-cockpit biplane, feeling the invisible towers of heat shouldering his wings. The speed-hardened stairs of wind lifted him higher. These bulwarks of flight, invisible as faith. The countryside was exploding beneath him, the lovely paroxysm of spring, the pink confetti of azaleas and magnolias cheering him on. The white blossoms of dogwood and fruit trees, wind-shivered, like gathered flurries of peace doves. The whole city of Memphis, where he took his training, smoked in the distance, crawling with the shining beetles of passenger cars. The Mississippi River shone like a banner beneath the sun.

His blood had hummed that day, as if infused with the ascendant magic of Christ. The holy breath of his stories had carried him aloft, the ceaseless drive of his pen, the stuttering fury of his typewriter. This black-eyed boy, small for his age, who'd watched balloons float high over the land like warped moons and built his own aircraft of newspaper and paste. This young man who'd dreamed of aces. He'd been knocked to the earth again and again. By fathers and lovers and townsfolk, by editors and critics and Hollywood men. He'd written despite. Beneath his name now could be found towering stories of ink, high and gothic and heretofore unseen in their architecture. Stories that could elevate readers high into the atmosphere of a vision, fierce and true, from which they could look upon a whole universe the size of a postage stamp—the world of Yoknapatawpha County, Mississippi. This man, who'd changed his name to Faulkner.

He had risen.

Now he stood in the field among the rest of his clan. The patriarch. There was his mother, who fed him tea and whiskey when he was sick with drink, weaning him sober; and his wife, Estelle, who was holding their baby girl against her breast, little Jill. There was Johncy, who was a pilot himself now, working on his transport license, and somewhere, far afield, G-man Jack might be piloting his Monocoupe from station to station.

A brotherhood of fliers. All but one.

The best of them, young Dean. Their star. His light had waned in recent years, it seemed, as if he couldn't find the right direction to project it. He was twenty-five years old, working at the Gulf service station in town. He'd tried construction jobs and illustration courses but nothing stuck. Nothing could hold the fierceness of his light. He would sit sometimes at home now, high in the tower room of his parents' house, unsure what to do with himself. Which wall to look at. His bat had begun making less of a crack. Squirrels could escape his aim. Sometimes, in public, he told people his brother would write the Great American Novel, his eyes burning with faith. His hold was too tight on the tails of his eldest brother's coat, which was not his nature. He needed a life commensurate with his potential, thought Faulkner. His light.

"She's really yours now?" asked Dean.

Faulkner set his hand on his littlest brother's shoulder. "Under one considerable condition."

"What?"

"I keep her up in Memphis, where you can learn to fly."

A few weeks later, Faulkner stood outside the pilots' lounge at the Memphis airfield, watching the sky. His heart was glad. Dean Swift, who once made baseballs leap from his bat, as if sprung from his own jaunty spirit, and ran barefoot through the woods with a peashooter across his back, shooting birds on the wing and pan-frying them over a campfire—he was a genius at the stick. This young man who fluttered the hearts of schoolteachers and town daughters had found his direction at last. He'd pointed his nose into the wind and taken flight.

Aircraft wings seemed to dance beneath his hands, slicing the sky with scalpel-like exactitude. Still a student, just weeks aloft, he could fly in a twenty-knot crosswind, slipping his ship sideways from the sky, and stick the wheels on the grass with hardly a bounce. He could weigh lift-versus-distance in a single glance, flying out of strips no bigger than barnyards, and the braided steel of control cables seemed but extensions of his hands, the fine tendons of his fingers. Such was his precision, greased easy beneath his smile.

Faulkner would drive up to Memphis once a week, taking a suite at the Hotel Peabody, and have a few turns behind the stick of his red Waco. He would spend the rest of the time in the airfield lounge, sitting amid spirals of pipe smoke, listening to the stories of the old pilots. *Bench flying.* They would be looking out at the clouds, talking of rough landings or near misses or names passed into the ground, and Faulkner would watch them pause, no matter the story's momentum, to watch the grace of the upstart marvel, Dean Swift. They would lick their lips as he conducted a crosswind landing or short takeoff or low orbit of the field, his wings flashing in the sun.

"Hey, Cap, who's instructing who up there?"

Captain Omlie, who ran the Memphis Flying Service, pulled on a cigarette, watching the red biplane swing around for final approach, sliding smoothly from the air. "Most natural pilot I ever taught. He'll earn his commercial and instructor's rating with the ink still wet on his private license. His transport rating soon after that."

The captain pulled again on the cigarette. The straps of his leather flying cap hung loose from his chin; his striped tie was tucked into the lapels of a worn flying sweater.

"He reminds me of Phoebe—only pilot I've known that gifted in the air."

Captain Omlie's wife, Phoebe, held the record for the highest parachute jump by a woman—15,200 feet—and was the first licensed female transport pilot and aircraft mechanic. She'd flown for Hollywood films and her own air circus and now held a federal aviation position in Washington, DC, appointed by President Roosevelt himself.

Faulkner felt the swell of pride in his chest. The red biplane touched down with hardly a bark of the tires, the propeller wheeling like a silver shield in the sun. Dean at the yoke, smiling through the greenhouse windows of the cabin. His instructor dozing beside him, rocked gently to sleep.

"He's something," said Faulkner.

Captain Omlie mashed out his cigarette and reached into his chest pocket. "By the way, something came in the mail for you today."

He handed Faulkner an envelope. Inside was his permanent license, issued by the Aeronautics Branch of the Department of Commerce, certifying him as a PRIVATE PILOT OF AIRCRAFT OF THE UNITED STATES. Faulkner stared at his own picture, set there in black and white. The narrow chin and graying temples, the yet-dark mustache. The bright black eyes, which had seen so much, their corners sprung with the silvery crow's-feet of age, torment, irony. The yellowy cardstock trembled in his hands, weighty as any one of the clothbound novels on his study shelves at Rowan Oak, which bore his name in golden script.

He was thirty-six years old.

A pilot.

Captain Omlie saw the license trembling in his hand.

Faulkner quickly folded it away in the inner pocket of his tweed coat, tucked next to a small bottle of whiskey. "Captain Omlie, I advise you to set some days aside around Mardi Gras."

"Why's that?"

"Because I am going to fly us down for the opening festivities of the Shushan Airport, all expenses paid. And we are going to have us a time."

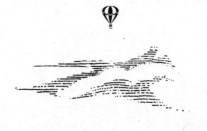

Book IV

36

Conquest of the Air

*T*hey crossed the Louisiana line in the slanting light of afternoon.
Since Biloxi, they'd stopped only for gas, passing through Gulfport
and Pass Christian at speed, towns where the pavement raced right along
the beach. Della had watched the pelicans heel over like dive-bombers
and plunge from the sky, twisting and folding their wings, stretching
their bodies into long javelins the moment before impact, emerging with
fish wiggling in their bills or gullets. Shrimp and oyster boats rocked
on the swells, harried by screaming flutters of gulls, and large white
houses stood on the landward side of the highway, windows gleaming,
as if watching for ships to appear on the horizon. They passed through a
region of second-growth pineland, the spindly trees catfaced for turpentine, before crossing the Pearl River into Louisiana.

Now the woods broke onto broad prairies of salt marsh, treeless
and winter-brown, specked with white wading birds. They passed fish
camps perched high on stilts, like offerings to the gods of flood, while
the hulls of forgotten trawlers and pleasure boats lay beached in the
reeds or cradled on blocks. They jolted over the curling black bayous on
iron swing-bridges, their trestles scabby with rust, and the immensity

of Lake Pontchartrain shimmered in the distance, cut with the white fins of sails.

The city of New Orleans rose before them, a Gothic skyline emerging as from the swamp itself. The buildings looked preposterous, rising as they did from below the level of the water. A city held captive by its own geography, the floodwaters shoved back by a dizzying array of man-made floodwalls and levees and dikes. The place held a sinister attraction for Della, a city born from the mixed blood and tongues of a thousand seaports across the world—Caribbean and African, European and Asiatic. It was so alien to her own home, where some families could trace their blood in unbroken lines to the original Scottish Highlanders who founded the town. New Orleans promised to be stranger, muddier, more exotic. Narrowing her eyes, she thought she could make out the tiny flecks of birds wheeling over the wharves and canals—perhaps some of them were planes.

They passed from the rickety watchtowers of fish camps into the oak-lined streets of the city itself, riding past shotgun shacks set like boxcars beneath the trees. People of every color were in the streets, dancing in feathered masks or top hats or tin-metal crowns, strings of beads or sequins or metallic scales rattling against their chests. Whole throngs of flesh, moiling and surging, strung across sidewalks and knotted at the mouths of taverns and corner stores, kinking and lurching and weaving, their teeth shining, and Della could hear the ocean of their voices even above the throb of the motorbike. The streets glittered with shattered bottles and glass beads and wooden doubloons the size of dollar coins. Here a puddle of blood, heel-pocked, worming itself toward a gutter drain. There a man wearing the hooked beak of a plague doctor, bone-white, urinating into a potted plant.

These revelers, they seemed at war if war were something joyous and bright. Their bodies tangled and thrashed with wild abandon, scaled and shimmering, while plumes and banners reeled and bobbed above their heads. They slapped one another and roared, holding aloft strange scepters and brass-capped canes, their eyes sparking behind golden masks. Their skulls were crowned with ox horns or antlers or donkey ears, some with the belled hats of jesters or the pointed caps of dunces or queens. Glass exploded at their feet, in shimmering starburst, and confetti spumed from balconies. Their lips glowed like fireflies, smoking in the dusk. These fallen children, their bodies strung with the wild raiment of dream.

Zeno turned left onto the wide avenue of Elysian Fields, weaving the bike through the stamping forests of boots. People began stepping back from the machine, gently, parting before the round moon of headlight. They seemed enchanted by the presence of this throaty conveyance. Some reached out to touch the finned heart of the machine or the hot tube of the tailpipe, burning themselves. They stuck their scalded fingertips into their mouths, grinning wickedly, as if sucking on candies. The oaks of the avenue hung low over the street, glazed with the flickering glow of streetlights and flambeaux. Zeno zigzagged from block to block, following some path of his own, rattling over cobblestones and jumping curbs. People handed them bottles whose spigots stuck out like pistol barrels from paper sacks. The riders sucked down stinging ribbons of whiskey or gin, now and then a bloody mouthful of port wine. They nodded in gratitude, handing back the bottles. The people grinned.

They followed the tracks of a trolley line. A streetcar came rumbling past, the wires clacking overhead. A bell heralded its passage down the grassy neutral ground of the avenue. The windows of the car glowed like a café's in the night, peopled with strange gods and beasts and kings, their teeth shining beneath their masks and crowns.

The streetcar passed on, sliding like a submarine into the night. Della found the people on the street seemed to move more slowly than before, their bodies stretching into wild-struck poses, rampant and gay, as if they might swim their way to the stars. These creatures sprung from below sea level, experiments of every kind—feather and tail and beak— that might beat the weight of flood or doom. She found herself reaching out, letting her fingers graze them in passing, touching the split tails of their coats and their sequined dresses, their skirts made of feathers or coins or beads. To swim, she thought, was only to fly underwater.

They pushed deeper into the night, the crowds growing thicker, the buildings taller. Then they broke from the concrete jungle of the business district, looking upon the giant ring of Lee Circle. The pavement haloed a white column of stone, floodlit, high upon which stood the bronze figure of the Confederate general, greened with age, like the dulled point of an ancient spear. His shoulders and hat brim were streaked with the airy defecations of pigeons.

Around this circle, as if on a merry-go-round, paraded floats depicting the "Conquest of the Air"—the year's theme. A whole mythology of the sky. Winged creatures and contrivances built on rolling platforms, each towed by a team of mules. There was the brightest angel, Lucifer, the light-bringer, thrust burning from heaven, his flesh scalded red by his fall. He rose six-winged from his parade float, glowing like a giant red lantern in the night. The thin wires of his armature were just visible beneath his papery skin. There was Icarus, who flew too close to the sun, his spread wings constructed of feathers and wax, showing the long death-drips of their melt. Here came the first kitelike flier of the Wright brothers, which seemed too fragile for the hard shoves of the winds aloft, and here the silvery tarpon of Lindberg's craft, which crossed the ocean to find the searching spotlights of Paris. Now the flying boats that triumphed over sea and sky, floating like winged passenger liners through the night, and the great barrels of the speed racers, whose stubby fins slashed around the pylons of race courses throughout the land. They rocked and trembled over the rough street, as if from turbulence.

Della watched this carousel of fliers trundling through the night. She reached out to take Zeno's hand and lead him closer. But Zeno's arms were crossed hard against his chest, his hands tucked flat against his ribs.

He wiggled his thumbs and frowned. "Not a goddamn thing here that's flightworthy."

Remember that thou art dust, and unto dust thou shalt return.

Dawn light streamed through the cathedral windows, waving smoky and bannerlike above the hundred bright points of candle flame. The words drifted on the perfumed air, steady as a chant.

Remember that thou art dust, and unto dust—

Della's chin bounced from her chest. She was trying to stay awake in the pew. Failing. They'd spent the night bouncing from tavern to tavern, jostling and twist-turning through the bodies of the Quarter. They bellied against scarred bar tops, again and again, and braved wet dark alleys where masked gods weaved and hissed, pissing their names on the walls. They smoked beneath flickering gas lamps and arched carriageways that held the ghostly echo of hooves, and they never slept. They were on their way to the river, ready to crumple on the soft grass of the levee for an hour's rest, when a broadside of church bells came peeling across the city.

Zeno straightened, as if called.

Ash Wednesday.

Soon he had them standing before Saint Louis Cathedral, a three-towered castle built in sight of the river. Della looked down at herself. Her silver jumpsuit was dusty, dulled an iron gray. Her boots ashy and unpolished, their soles sticky with tavern floors and gutters. Leaves and confetti dangled from the ragged red mane of her hair, like the decorations of a wood witch or battle maiden. Zeno looked only slightly better, his leather flying coat adorned with the pasty streaks of dead insects, his trousers spotted with oil and grease and wine. Sark, sitting in the sidecar, was the only one of them who looked somewhat reputable—thickly browed, bearded like a frosty old sea captain.

"You think they'll let us in?" she asked.

"Faith," said Zeno. He spat, pulling his lapel over the pistol draped beneath his arm.

Della raised an eyebrow at the gun and Zeno returned the look, unmoved.

"As if I'll be the only one armed."

Now she watched the people shuffling down the aisles, their hands clutched cross-palmed against their chests. The saints stood in their shadowy corners and alcoves, skinned in porcelain, tongues of holy fire painted atop their heads. The ceiling was high and vaulted, gilded like the courts of heaven. A river of believers lifted their heads to the black thumb of the priest, again and again, murmuring like flowing water.

Della thought of the tickle of that thumb, scrawling the sign of faith on her forehead. That touch, gentle as a father's.

Remember that thou art dust—

A gentle shake. She opened her eyes. There stood Zeno, a black cross of ashes scrawled on his forehead.

He swept the hair from her eyes softly. "Let's go, honey."

Noon found them standing on an observation deck, watching the opening ceremonies of the Shushan Airport. "The Air Hub of the Americas," as the papers billed it. Pennants snapped and flickered in the breeze, bright-strung like those of a medieval tourney. Governor Huey P. Long stood on a wooden stage, speaking into a microphone. His words came tinny and wind-broken across the gathered wings of his flock. The monoplanes of the Pan-American Air Races sat raked on either side of the stage, gleaming like the weapons of some war yet to come. They seemed caricatures of themselves, with bulbous motors and stubby wings, ready to cut a whirlwind around the pylons of the lake. Meanwhile, the speck of a single ship orbited at ten thousand feet, gnat-size against the sun, ready to drop the jumper whose blooming silk chute would open the show.

Zeno squinted through a pair of borrowed binoculars, scanning the tarmac. The crude smudge of ashes crinkled on his forehead.

Della leaned on the rail, arms crossed, bumping her hip against his. "What you going to give up for Lent, Captain?"

Zeno spat off the deck, not minding his aim. "Motorbikes."

37

The Comet

*W*illiam Faulkner stood before the grand edifice of the Shushan
Airport terminal, set against the bright expanse of Lake Pontchartrain. A two-story structure of tan stone, double-winged and
modernistic, with aluminum trim and pale green windows. The bright
metallic curve of the entrance portico seemed ready to accept the high-
speed duralumin automobiles of the futurist magazines—machines that
would stream silvery and silent along glass-smooth autostradas, con-
veying air passengers to flights on giant intercontinental flying ships.

Above this hung the stone-carved figure of a man, loin-clothed and
muscular, his arms spread Christ-wide beneath a pair of mechanistic
wings. A figure newly ascended from the lower stations of the earth. His
bare feet were cupped subtly in a pair of hands—the palms of an engineer or wing-wright or bank man. Above this, just visible over the roof
of the terminal, hovered the glass bubble of the control tower, tinted like
a Coca-Cola bottle. The heads of men could be seen inside this glassy
turret, their ears bulbed with headphones, their voices chittering invisibly across the sky.

Faulkner had circled the field once before landing, Captain Omlie perched beside him in the copilot's seat. The pair of them stared down upon this massive peninsula dredged up from the floor of the lake. An entire landmass, scooped and suctioned from the lakebed, built to cradle the most modern airport in the nation's history. An art deco masterpiece, built at a cost of $3 million and named after the head of the Levee Board, Abraham Shushan—one of the governor's men. Rumor said every fixture in the place was inscribed with his initials. Doorknobs and drawer pulls, pipe fittings and windowsills and even the silver handles of the commodes.

The Industrial Canal lay nearby, cut rifle-straight through the city's Ninth Ward, smoking with towboats and barges. The three runways of the airport formed a triangle with curved corners, each strip long enough for the long-range airliners said to come. The cruciform shapes of flying machines glittered along the taxiways, metallic and bright, like stars cut from tin. Flying boats and seaplanes floated in special slips, jostling on the chop, while the fighters of the Twentieth Pursuit Group sat in their squadron rows, yellow-winged, their propellers gleaming.

Faulkner worked the yoke and rudder pedals, feeling the cables of the ship slide smoothly beneath his touch. This delicate interplay of hands and feet, balancing the currents of wind and heat beneath his wings, the control surfaces ruddering this way and that, smooth as butter knives, slipping them gently from the sky. He described a broad arc around the field and turned for final approach. They descended over the lake itself, lower and lower, the sails of pleasure craft cutting beneath them like shark fins. The end of the runway sped beneath their wings. The wheels of the red biplane met the tarmac with a single high bark.

Faulkner leaned his head back, taking in the sunlight that fell through the glass roof of the cabin. "If that wasn't perfect, Captain, it was a splendid failure."

Now he walked up the curved front stairs of the terminal, the steps silver-trimmed to match the aluminum portico, and pushed open the glass doors. They gave way with a pneumatic suck, as if into a sealed laboratory. The lobby dazzled, a vast capsule of glass and sunlight. There were friezes in aluminum leaf depicting man's creation of the flying machine, and the furniture sat wire-strung and airy, the cushions seeming to hover weightless over the terrazzo floors. Men and women stood slant-hipped in stylish flying caps, their scarves flung over their shoulders. Figures as rakish and lean as the machines they flew.

Faulkner waded among them slowly, his head slightly cocked. His ears sailed along the murmuring river of their voices, the current of whisper and rumor. The same name rose again and again from these mouths, like a curse or chant:

The Comet.

The pride of the living in their voices, the hushed glee. The previous evening, after the opening ceremonies, a rocket-equipped airplane had crashed on the runway during its aerobatic performance and burned, killing the pilot.

I heard it was nine rockets strapped to the undersides of his wings.

I heard twelve.

Three hundred thousand candlepower, they say.

So bright you could hardly see.

Faulkner wended through the crowd of voices, the words rising violent and bright in the night sky of his mind.

I knew it was a bad idea from the start.

He was too low to start that loop.

They say he was still alive when she started to burn.

Faulkner's mind flashed quickly to Helen, his lost love, her flesh scarred from burning. How much he'd once wished to burn with her, no matter the pain or damnation. He shook the thought from his head and climbed the red-carpeted staircase to the second floor, finding himself on a broad gallery that overlooked the lobby, lined with murals depicting the pioneering flights of the age. He spun slowly on his heel, taking in the vast cyclorama of aerial conquest painted across the walls.

Lindbergh's *Spirit of St. Louis* soared high among the crisscrossing searchlights of Paris, watched by the stone gargoyles of Notre Dame. Nearby, a French biplane buzzed low over the crescent sails of Nile riverboats, skirting a pair of towering stone pharaohs—the Colossi of Memnon. Meanwhile, the white-winged whale of the *Santa Maria*, the Italian seaplane that circumnavigated the globe, floated in the pale haze over Rio de Janeiro, aiming deep into the green sea of the Amazon. Flying machines of wildly distinct design—like different species, almost—skimmed Himalayan peaks and Mayan pyramids and Hindu temples, transcending these highest works of god and man. Last, a trimotor transport ship, fat-bellied with wings of corrugated sheet metal, hung in triumph over the Manhattan skyline, floating over skyscrapers and bridges and passenger liners.

These winged boasts of man—he saw them all. Then he was walking toward the wide panorama of the observation window, framing the field like a mural itself. He was seeing, against that glass, the scene of the previous night, assembling his vision from the pit of babble beneath his feet.

He saw the Comet plane scream down the runway, trailing nine feathers of flame, and rise like a newborn star into the dusk, shooting up and up and up. It seemed unbelievable that a machine could rise so quickly, as if to pierce the black belly of heaven, floating bright among those highest reaches. But the machine bent from that course, leaning back upon itself, cutting a loop of fire in the dusk. Faulkner thought of the pilot, masked and goggled in his tiny aluminum cave, upside down, riding a nine-tailed demon of fire. The machine flashed belly-up beneath the moon and wheeled for the earth, trailing a braided garland of smoke. The Comet fell and fell, spitting flame. Her light licked across the thousand faces of the crowd, their thumb-smudged foreheads. She shot straight down, like a bolt thrown from heaven, and pulled out too late.

She struck the tarmac at a diagonal, sliding down the runway on her belly, trailing fire for three hundred feet before upending onto her nose, gently, before the crowd. She stood there a long moment, dark and strange, before tipping onto her back. The pilot—Captain Merle Nelson of Hollywood, California—spilled from the ship. He was squirming in his goggles and helmet, trying to crawl from the wreck, when the wings bloomed into flame, consuming him. He arose in the white brilliance of a god, his body crowned in fire. The rescue workers stood aback, the heat beating at their faces. He leapt and wheeled, as if trying to express some joy or agony. Finally he staggered, crumpling to the tarmac, and here came the fire trucks, too late, their sirens moaning through the night. The fabric was burning from the machine, the alloy skeleton twisting and curling with heat, writhing.

Faulkner blinked.

Daylight again, quick as a switch. He found himself standing at the observation window, bathed in a pale green glow. He was looking across the airfield, past the vast heraldry of wings, staring at the main strip of runway. There lay a black stain, broad as a house, where the Comet had burned. His eyes narrowed, as if he could glimpse the thinnest wisps of smoke still curling from the ashes, telling him their story.

38

Red Tears

"H err Uden!"

The German ace turned slowly from his machine. His face was skull-white, bloodless, and his blue eyes matched the eyes of the death's-head painted on the fuselage. He did not seem surprised at the shout of his name, nor the man who came striding toward him, barrel-chested in a leather flying coat, a cigar stuck between his teeth.

"Herr Uden," said Zeno. "You have kept the *Totenkopf*, I see." He gestured toward the blue-eyed skull. "Still quite the resemblance, it seems."

Della cringed. She was standing ten feet away, pretending to examine the wing trusses of a neighboring airplane.

That morning, she and Zeno had sat on the edge of the field, shoulder to shoulder. They'd watched the cleanup crew work through a waist-deep layer of mist, trying to scrub the black smudge of the Comet wreck from the runway.

"Just what is the plan?" she'd asked.

Zeno had kept his eyes on the cleaning crew. They were waddling strangely about, their shoe soles sticking to the superheated concrete.

"I get him to take me on a ride, like for old times' sake." He shrugged. "Then stick the Webley in his face."

"What if he won't jump?"

"He's got a parachute."

"What if he refuses?"

Zeno spat, crossing his arms. "He'll jump."

Zeno halted before the German, setting his fists on his hips. "Herr Uden, you might not remember me, but we spent a night together at an aerodrome near Bar-le-Duc in the summer of 1916, just after you were shot down." He extended his hand. "Captain Zeno Marigold, formerly of the Lafayette Escadrille."

Uden's eyes brighted a moment, then narrowed. He took Zeno's hand. "Captain Marigold," he said, "I believe you fed me milk."

"And brandy," said Zeno. "Though I'm not sure you knew we spiked your bottle."

Their hands remained clasped, their knuckles strung finely beneath the skin.

"There were many things I did not know, Captain."

Zeno looked at the skull and crossbones on the fuselage. "You learned fast, it seems."

Uden shrugged. "Didn't we all?"

Zeno's gaze hovered on the seven red tears painted below the eye of the skull.

Seven kills.

"Not all," he said.

Uden smiled, which seemed rare for him. Della could almost hear the crackling of flesh, as if his lips were breaking from a caul of ice.

"Is there something you want from me, Captain?"

Zeno grasped one of the wing wires, leaning away. "I thought you might give me a ride in this Wichita Fokker of yours. I never been up in a Travel Air."

Uden's blue eyes watched him. "I believe I could do even better for you."

"Oh?"

Uden extracted a thin gold cigarette case from his chest pocket and opened it. The cigarettes were packed like rifle cartridges, each bearing the gold seal of an expensive brand. He lit one with a windproof trench lighter, inhaled, then pointed across the tarmac with the cigarette, his hand smoking like a gun.

There, upon a giant drop cloth, sat a white biplane, newly painted. The wings blazed like a church house in the sun. A man in spattered overalls knelt beside the machine, painting the red and blue roundels of the Royal Flying Corps on the fuselage.

Zeno's mouth fell open. "A Gipsy Moth," he said.

Uden smiled through a blue scrawl of smoke.

"No," said Della.

They were sitting on the levee, sharing a thirty-cent shrimp po'boy from one of the food tents. Sailboats bobbed on the lake while a swarm of tiny racers whipped around the pylons, wasplike, buzzing in and out of earshot.

"It's five hundred dollars for a day's work," said Zeno. "You can't beat that."

"How many pilots has he run through already—you ask him that?"

Zeno bit into the sandwich and shrugged. "Sore subject, possibly."

"I'm serious, Zeno. You ever think it wasn't an accident? Biloxi? A few loosened screws in the night?"

"That doesn't sound like a profitable act, honey."

Della swung her hand across the lake, as if conducting the flyweight racers slicing around the pylons, their razor-thin wings trembling on the edge of control. The levee was lined with spectators, as were the grandstands and observation decks. Thousands of faces, each thrust into an imaginary slipstream.

"Not profitable?" she said. "Why do you think they come?"

Zeno's eyes tracked one of the racers while he chewed. "It's beautiful."

"Right, like most anything that hangs on a string. What if I fell off the wing one day, and you got somebody else? Think how many more would come."

Zeno chewed, peering out across the lake. "Nobody could replace you."

"The fuck they couldn't."

"It's five hundred dollars," said Zeno.

"So is a funeral. You going to leave me broke?"

"Big talk from you, who walks on wings for a living."

"And who taught me that?"

Zeno stopped chewing. He swallowed, set the sandwich in the paper, and looked at her. "Do you love it?"

Della felt her eyes widen, smarting. "I have to do it."

"What if I asked you to stop?"

"You wouldn't."

"What if I did?"

Della's eyes were burning. "I couldn't."

"You're asking me the same, pretty much."

Della leaned toward him, setting her hand on his thigh. "What if he's still adding tears to that skull on the side of his plane?"

Zeno's face hardened, a battered brown brick in the sun. The light licked along every wrinkle and crease. Della knew she'd said the wrong thing.

"Then I will bury him with it."

39

Dead Stick

Faulkner watched the air racer Roger Don Rae—a Michigan farm boy who'd worked his way from hoeing cornfields to carnival parachuting to air racing—lose his engine over the runway. His machine was a long silver javelin, with aluminum skin and stubby fins for wings, the nose louvered like the gills of a shark. A tiny blister of cockpit. Don Rae had come streaming in from the lake on his qualifying run, trailing the thinnest string of smoke, and slashed around the home pylon, quick as a blade. He was streaking low across the airfield, pushing two hundred miles per hour, when the 544-cubic-inch motor cut out.

Silence.

Faulkner, standing on an observation deck, thought he could hear the wind skirling against the thin blades of the wings. A whispered scream of suspension, just inches from the tarmac. Don Rae pulled up, peeling from the earth, trading speed for altitude, while the crowds held their breath. The racer shot heavenward, silent, shaped like a weapon against the sky, and disappeared into the brightness of the sun.

Faulkner grabbed Captain Omlie's forearm. He could hear the flags and pennants popping in the wind. The distant call of a foghorn. The whole city silent, waiting.

Now the racer reappeared, falling like a bead of mercury from the sun. It wheeled over the lake and came fast for the edge of the runway, engineless, making no sound. The wings shivered knife-thin, designed for speed, and Faulkner cringed, watching the undercarriage pass just inches over the concrete seawall at the edge of the field. The tires struck the runway, spitting little ribbons of smoke, and the machine came rolling across the tarmac. Don Rae stabbed the brakes just short of the grandstands, lifting the tail, bowing the machine before the roar of the crowd.

Faulkner exhaled, his vision crowded with silvery splinters of light. He realized he'd been clutching Omlie's arm and let go. "My apologies, Captain. These boys are hell on a man's nerves."

Friday, it was an Illinois barnstormer and air racer, Harold Neumann. He was flying a stubby monoplane called *Ike*, gull-white with hooded wheels, when the motor seized over the final pylon. Neumann slipped and flared, zigzagging in long scrawls over the airfield, bleeding speed, and plowed into a deep pool of water between the runways, a white blast of spray. The wings shot beneath the surface and the tail stood upright from the water. A diving whale. The tiny bubble of cockpit began disappearing into the foam. The craft was sinking, following the iron anchor of the engine.

Emergency trucks raced across the field, shedding white flutters of shirts and dark boots that tumbled end over end, the rescue workers stripping to their bronze chests and bare feet. The drivers swung alongside the bank, and the workers dived directly from the truck beds, their bodies spearing the surface in white trails of foam. Their arms and feet thrashed toward the wreck, jutting this way and that from the water. Like buccaneers they swam, knives and chisels clutched in their teeth. The tail stood like a white tree from the water, canted and strange. They dived at its base, again and again, breaking glass and cutting straps. The pilot's goggled head broke the surface, finally, his mouth gaped for air. The rescuers swam him to shore on his back, floating him on their shoulders. He lay heaving on the bank like a caught fish, as if trying to suck back his escaping soul.

Faulkner sped toward the scene with a reporter from the New Orleans *Item*. They rode in the same car as the pilot's wife, her baby clutched red-faced and screaming in her arms. The man had rolled onto his belly and scrambled to the top of the bank, where he rose to his feet, wavering, his flight suit spurting water from various rips and holes, his gaze empty and far. The sight of his family brought him back to earth. He leapt for them. He embraced his wife, hard, lifting her heels from the ground, and then he held their babe aloft, teddy-sized and plump, as if for a christening, throwing a giant smile beneath the dangling feet. His wife's hands shadowed his every move, in case he dropped the child.

Now Faulkner sat on the fender of the car, a pint bottle on his knee. He had a whole crate of them stashed in the back of the Waco. Glass bottles of straight corn whiskey, best enjoyed at the foot of a shade tree or amid this heady atmosphere of rubber and fuel and smoke. They slipped nicely into the inner chest pocket of his coat. They had cork stoppers, their edges gnawed rough from the grip of his teeth. They were going fast.

He pulled the cork. His tie hung winded from his neck. The whiskey ran like a live wire through his chest. He watched the crowd gather about the risen man, the lot of them standing on land newly heaved from the bed of the lake. The workers wrapped the pilot in a blanket. He was beginning to tremble now, from cold or nerves, still cradling his child. Above them, the rest of the racers twisted and streaked around the pylons undaunted—each machine uniquely shaped, like the signature weapon of a god.

Faulkner watched.

These pilots, they died with the violence of saints or lived in furious suspension, steering machines that defied the unseen powers of gravity. He loved them for it. They lived on something like faith, he thought, held on trembling wings or beneath mushrooms of silk, crisscrossing the land like itinerant birds or moths, filling the hearts of those on the ground. Nothing but wind beneath their soles.

Faulkner sipped again from the bottle. A zag of lightning through his sternum.

He loved and feared for them. Not only for their death. He feared how such creatures, who strapped themselves into the stick-and-wire wings of angels, could live on the ground. To rise so high against the sun—so close to God, gifted with the highest planes of vision—and then to come down. Again and again and again. A heartbreak every time. A fall from grace. To scrabble in the dirt and filth, rubbing pennies and sleeping cold, feeling so alone. Living outside the safer constructions of men, ever grieving for the sky.

This he knew.

Faulkner sipped again from the bottle, a slug of warmth in his chest, and looked out across the field. The grandstands, full of strangers and friends, and the city against the river, where his heart had burned like a coal through the night-alleys, so alone.

To be apart from what you loved. Like Lucifer, who loved God most. Surely that was hell.

40

Gipsy Moth

Saturday, dawn. The sun lay buried beneath the eastern rim of the lake, just paling the sky. The pennants hung dew-heavy across the field, dripping like icicles. The lake was calm, colored like gunmetal. The gulls silent, hunch-winged in their roosts. Della slid from her blanket, leaving Zeno asleep. Snoring in the crook of his arm. Sark perked his head at her, but she stayed him with a finger. The dog seemed to nod, his head sinking again to his paws.

She pulled on her boots and coat and strode cross-armed against the cold, her heels grinding across the tarmac. The wings of the flying machines glistened with dew, their tails slick from the retreating night. She walked among their braces and struts and wires, the wood and steel twists of their propellers. She passed through this strange flock of flying machines and stood before the white biplane that Zeno was to fly.

A de Havilland Gipsy Moth, built in England. A favorite of the long-distance aviators. The Prince of Wales owned one, as well as the aviatrixes Amy Johnson and Jean Batten, who flew solo from England to South Africa, India, Australia. A machine that could traverse the endless skyway of the nation, over the yellow seas of wheat and craggy brown deserts, the shining banners of rivers and the purple thrust of the Sierras, delivering them to the Golden State. California. The wings hovered like thin layers of mist over the tarmac. The whole craft seemed vaporous in the dawn, slightly unreal. The nose sat high and jaunty, the prop cocked. A craft perched with the weightless beauty of a moth. The roundels hung like targets on the wings.

Della found herself on one knee, bent before the airplane. The red bunch of her hair framed her face like a hood, the long foxtail twisted around her neck. She held the ceramic figurine of the kite-hawk in one hand, her thumb rubbing the forked blade of tail. She was trying to pray. Not to God, exactly. To whoever would listen. To this machine, perhaps, which would pluck Zeno from her reach, lifting him high into his past, and to the clay-fired figurine clutched in her fist, whose edges of beak and talon and tail threatened to break her skin. To the kite-winged raptors of true blood and bone, who slashed and soared over the land, as if to cut their stories into the sky. As if they knew truths she did not, and were trying to speak to her in some language their own, the slash and scrawl of flight.

She squeezed the figurine harder. The tendons stood wirelike from her wrist. Her knuckles popped like gravel beneath the skin. She had the sense that she and Zeno were standing on the edge of the world, cold and sharp as a knife—a world that took down both killers and saints without compunction. If she bled now, perhaps her blood would give satisfaction. Enough violence for the day. The red ooze would sting like a potion in her hand, protecting Zeno.

The clay edges of the figurine drove deeper into her palm. Della mashed shut her eyes. She could feel her shoulder blades sprung sharp from the bend of her spine, wanting out. She was holding her breath now, trying to picture Zeno safe on the ground, the pair of them with a folded deck of bills—enough to buy themselves a new set of wings.

A path west.

A home.

A voice behind her said, "*Gott mit uns.*"

Della bolted upright. She looked over her shoulder, blinking the stars from her eyes. There stood Ernst Uden, white-faced in a leather jacket, smoking one of his fancy cigarettes.

"What?"

Uden held out his hand, saying nothing. A brass device, perfectly round, lay in his palm like a timepiece. It was a trench lighter, made from a pair of Imperial German Army belt buckles soldered together. The Kaiser's crown was stamped in the center, surrounded by an inscription: GOTT MIT UNS.

"What does that mean?"

Uden closed his hand over the lighter. "God with us."

Della cocked her head. "Didn't seem like God was with that last American pilot of yours, the one we saw go down in Biloxi."

Uden blew a rag of smoke from his mouth. "Perhaps just the opposite."

Della stepped closer, her hands balled white at her sides. "There ain't even a second name on your handbills. How many pilots have you been through before Zeno?"

The man jutted his bottom lip. "It is a dangerous job."

Della sniffed. She could feel her hair burning wild in the gray of dawn. "I walk on wings for a living, motherfucker."

"Then you know."

"I know if something happens to him up there today, I'm coming after you. You'll be a puddle when I'm done."

Uden smiled—a grim line—and looked over the field. The first birds were aloft, chittering dark-winged over the runways. His blue eyes led them, as if he held a shotgun. "And what if he does something to me?" He looked at her. "I have no red-haired heroine to avenge me."

Della licked her lips. "You'll have to do it yourself, then. You can haunt us if you like. We have plenty of ghosts as it is. What's one more?"

Uden dropped his cigarette half-smoked, stamping it under his boot. A vague mist touched his eyes—or maybe it was just the light. "I do not think they will let me out of hell that long." He turned and strode away, his bootheels clicking on the tarmac.

Della exhaled, dizzied, and sank to her haunches. She felt a sting and opened her hand. There lay the ceramic bird, wreathed in blood.

41

Speed Kings

Hot as a .44 pistol and twice as fast.

So they said of the Model 44, the racer that won the Unlimited class. A snub-nose cannon of a machine, it boomed around the pylons with incredible velocity, bearing the tiniest bubble of a cockpit. The whole sky over the lake cracked with the power of the unlimiteds, whipped to fury. Faulkner watched from the observation deck, leaning on the rail, sipping from his pint bottle. His chest sang at the sight, his blood spiked with lightning.

These finned barrels of thunder, which held the power of five hundred charging horses. He thought of the pilots so small in their cockpits, surrounded by a fearful array of quivering gauges and switches and dials. Aluminum skin shivering on every side of them, feverish with speed. They cut open the blue belly of the sky, leaving long trails of smoke in their wake. The world bleeding beyond their canopies, blurred with power.

Faulkner saw that they would never stop, this race of men. They would rope the sky with crisscrossing contrails and tassels of smoke, as if to cinch the very heavens to the earth. They would war in the air.

Thousands of bombers, arrayed in battle formations, blotting out the sun like sudden weather. An aluminum overcast. They would rain destruction from their bellies, turning whole cities to ash, and fall like burning tears from the sun.

Still, that would not be enough. They would need to go faster, higher, piercing the blue bubble of the earth. No matter if they darked the sky or muddied the sea or burned alive. These were creatures careless with their lives. They breathed smoke and drank fire and put the power of whole stampedes into canisters they rode across the sky. They had learned to overcome fear, and they had to do it again and again and again, like sharks that could never quit swimming lest they die.

Faulkner wondered, *would they ever learn?*

He sipped from his bottle, the whiskey searing his tongue.

Captain Omlie was called back to Memphis early for work. To save money, Faulkner moved from their hotel to the home of a reporter he knew from the *Times-Picayune*. His suitcase bumped his leg as he rode uptown on the streetcar. The porched houses of St. Charles Avenue swung from the trees, grand and broad, the curbs and gutters still thick with the motley detritus of the Mardi Gras parades. Beads and feathers and shattered glass. Puke and beer and chicken bones. A wild slop.

How he loved this city, so doomed, even if the very houses menaced him, pregnant with danger. In their very paint seemed to lie the distillates of his destruction, waiting to be sparked. In one of them, surely, lived Helen. Still he couldn't think of those days in Pascagoula without tears seeping into his vision, burning, his breath fluttering strange. She was behind every curtained window, kneeling in every flower bed. Smoking on every porch.

He left his suitcase in the spare room of the house and returned to the airfield.

The Model 45 racer was revealed. A team of men drew the veil from this silver pistol of a flier whose propeller grinned evilly beneath the sun. This greatest of speed ships, as if a cruel wind had streamlined the racers of the past, shaping this machine. The pilot and designer was the speed king himself, Jimmie Weddell—an orphan who'd left school in the ninth grade to open a garage behind the family home. He cobbled together his own early biplanes, taught himself how to fly, and smuggled rum over the Mexican border during Prohibition, wearing a Colt's .44 revolver on his hip. He became the first pilot to break three hundred miles per hour in level flight, battling Jimmy Doolittle in pylon races across the nation. He held records for timed flights between New Orleans and various cities of the South, achieved while delivering *Times-Picayune* photographs of Tulane football games in time for the Sunday paper.

Faulkner watched the man pilot the 45 to a new world record, averaging 266 miles per hour around a hundred-kilometer course. The air cracked in the wake of the machine, as if lightning-split. The wings shone so bright they hurt the eyes. Here was the prototype of the fighters of wars to come. An uncompromising machine. An aerial predator. Three months later, Faulkner would read that Jimmie Weddell was dead, killed while giving flight lessons in a de Havilland Gipsy Moth. His Model 45 would vanish. In years not far off, navy pilots would encounter swarms of high-powered machines that looked strikingly similar to the 45, their ghost-colored wings painted with the red suns of Imperial Japan.

Faulkner drew the white scroll of his program from his hip pocket and uncurled it. Next up was a parachuting exhibition, followed by a mock air duel between a pair of Great War aces.

The latter he didn't want to miss.

Faulkner left the observation deck—too crowded—and went wandering down the terminal halls, cowlicked and harmless-looking, sipping now and again from his bottle, his eyes set to distant visions. At last he found the stairwell to the roof. He sat among the whirring turbines of the ventilation system, cross-legged like a boy, and fired his meerschaum pipe. The biplane of the parachute jumper puttered higher and higher, as if climbing the endless steps of an ancient temple. The sun warmed Faulkner's cheeks. He thought of young Dean Swift, whose face was like warm gold.

How much he would have enjoyed this show. He would ache to fly inside the tin stars of these racers. These stainless machines, riveted from the airy dreams of men. Not so much to win as to revel. He would want to flash the sky for the crowds, writing his joy with the rocking of his wings, the dash of his tail. Perhaps, someday, he would. For now, he couldn't take the time off for the show. He was building hours for his commercial license, after all. Steering ships all over Memphis and the North Mississippi hills, their cockpits aglow with his smile.

Faulkner watched the biplane, nearly at its zenith two thousand feet over the field. A low-level parachute exhibition. Perhaps, like the Balloonitic of days past, the jumper would pop his chute just feet from the ground, low enough to buckle the knees of even the hardest-hearted onlookers. Now the jumper stepped out onto the wing, hunchbacked. His survival a thin sheet of silk, folded neatly in his canvas rucksack. The program said only of the man: BEN GREW—PARACHUTIST.

He was holding on to the middle strut two-handed, still sidestepping for the outer edge of the wing, when the chute popped unexpectedly from his back. A long white bulb of silk, shooting into the slipstream. He was ripped from the wing, slung behind the machine, but the parachute caught on the tail. He snapped taut at the end of the line, dangling spraddle-limbed in his harness, his hands flapping wildly.

The crowd cooed, thinking this was an act, a part of the show. But Faulkner knew. He knew the pilot's stick and rudder would be frozen now, the tail surfaces clutched in a vast net of parachute lines. The machine began nosing toward the lake. The pilot wriggled and twisted in the cockpit, his shoulders jumping with effort. His hands yanking the stick this way and that, so hard his fingernails would be cutting into their own quicks, bleeding beneath his gloves. The dive steepened.

At last the pilot stood from the cockpit, his scarf snapping in the wind, and looked back at his friend. Faulkner watched them falling for the earth. The men reached out to each other, as if they could touch across the blue rift of sky. As if their fingertips could graze. Their hands hovered there—imprinted on the blue sky of his mind—and then the parachutist fell away. He fell flapping through the air, trying to fly. His body struck the lake in a white bird of spray. The pilot bailed out, falling alongside his ship. They smacked the water at the same instant, a violent fountain in the lake.

Faulkner stood on the roof of the terminal, clutching his chest. These men, heretofore strangers, whose names he would now never forget. He was no better than the rest of his race, he knew, who loved the dead more than the living. Who killed their sons and stars and gods, as if to love them better.

Rescue launches motored toward the wreckage, bumping through the chop, while observation planes orbited the scene, watching for bodies to rise. The sun rolled west, slanting gold across the lake. The Great War air duel was canceled. Faulkner left the roof, descending back into the terminal. He wore a mask of tears, hot as moonshine on his cheeks. He staggered and bumped and excused himself through the throngs, their every gaze set on the lake.

He was crossing before one of the large observation windows, trying to blink his vision clear, when he saw her. *Helen.* On the other side of the glass. She was standing on the observation deck, small and angular in a black dress, her husband's hand hooking the exquisite cinch of her waist. She turned, as if someone had called her name. *Had he?* Their eyes met through the sea-green glass. There was no sting. Just a vast ocean of days between them, full of strange and unknown memories. She pressed her hand to the window, her eyes wet and red. Faulkner felt for a moment like a creature preserved in the green glass of a bottle or jar. Unreachable. That her tears were for him.

He pressed his own hand to the glass, against hers. Warm against his palm. They nodded to each other, welded for the briefest moment in the same agony. The dead thousands of days. Then Faulkner removed his hand and walked out of the terminal, down the steps and under the blue-gold dome of sky.

42

Night in the Vieux Carré

"*A*re you going to the Quarter, by chance?"
Quart-uh.

Della and Zeno, sitting aboard the motorbike, looked at the man. He was small of frame, wearing a tatty tweed coat and a loose knot of tie. His hair stood slightly unkempt, windblown. His eyes were dark worlds, warm and wet and bright.

He bowed slightly. "I would be ever so grateful for a ride."

Della and Zeno looked down at themselves. Zeno was aboard the single saddle of the bike while Della sat high-kneed in the sidecar, Sark perched in her lap. The Scottie's head was cocked slightly, watching this strange newcomer.

Where does he think he's going to sit?

The man, receiving no response from the riders, slapped the white scroll of his program against his thigh and reached into his coat, drawing a glass pint from the folds. He shook the bottle. The failing light seemed to gather within the substance, silvery and lucid.

"Stumphole juice, straight from North Mississippi. It will run this motorized cycle of yours, if not your mouths." He smiled.

Della watched Zeno's eyes soften, as with love. Then Sark twisted to look at her, tongue out. Smiling. She sighed, scooting her bum slightly sideways in the seat. She nodded at the sliver of room.

"Hope you ain't had your supper yet."

The man patted his thin belly. "Not a bite since breakfast," he said.

They motored alongside Bayou St. John, which crawled like a thin river through blocks of houses, harboring alligators right in the heart of the city. Daylight was faltering, turning pink, the grassy banks purpling beneath lonesome palms. Their passenger, who said his name was Bill, sat beside Della in the sidecar, his knees crammed against his chest. She couldn't believe how little space he actually took up, as if there were only wind beneath the folds of his coat. He passed her the bottle and she drank, breathing fire.

She passed the bottle to Zeno. "That will clean your teeth."

Zeno kept his right hand on the throttle, reaching across his body for the whiskey.

Della watched him. The air duel had been called off after the crash of the pilot and jumper. Zeno had been belted into the cockpit of the Gipsy Moth, checking his stick and rudder, when the screams came rippling across the tarmac. Della, holding Sark, had looked up in time to see the white blast of spray in the lake, as if a depth charge had been detonated. A terrible answer to her prayers. She staggered but kept her balance, squeezing Sark to her chest.

Zeno, meanwhile, rose from the cockpit, pulling himself by wire and strut until he was standing in the seat, high enough to look across the top wing.

"Sweet Jesus," he said.

The pilot was from Ohio, a country barnstormer who'd arrived without invitation, hoping to land himself a place on the bill—just as she and Zeno had done so many times before, flying into carnivals or air shows, landing in barnyards or cow pastures or fairgrounds. The pilot's wife had watched him plummet to his death from the grandstands. The boats were still out there, dragging the lake for bodies.

Now Zeno swigged from the passenger's bottle, exhaling through his teeth. He was still dressed for the canceled air duel, his white scarf snapping in the wind. His gaze distant, as if he were seeing long into the past or future. Della squeezed his knee, trying to bring him back to her. He smiled, handing back the bottle.

The bayou narrowed alongside the road, straightening through a jumble of houses. They passed a golf course cut dog-legged from the oaks of the city park. The players labored beneath their canvas bags of clubs, hurrying to finish before dark. Then they were on Esplanade Avenue, passing through a shadowy hall of trees. Tricycles stood forgotten on the sidewalks, abandoned when dinner was called, and dogs hovered at doorways and stoops, waiting for scraps. The sting of woodsmoke hovered over the city, blue-risen from tin chimneys and stovepipes. Sark leaned toward their passenger, his tongue a-loll, letting the man scratch him absently between the ears.

The man seemed in a trance almost. He held his chin high, his dark eyes gliding over the city, nostalgic. His head rocked softly over the bumps, chin-cocked, accustomed perhaps to bad roads or good horses. There seemed the slightest grin beneath his trim mustache, pained, as if he were floating through a dream or memory. His hands remained tucked between his knees, elbows pinned to ribs, except when Della passed him the bottle. Then he would seem to perk to life, surprised at every new sip.

They turned on Royal Street, entering the Quarter. The high pink walls of houses rose on either side of them, spilling yellow light from their casement windows, the balconies scrolled with black iron railings. Plant boxes hung swollen, trailing dead sweeps of vines, the varicolored buildings set one against the next like mismatched bricks. Their upper porches curved around the street corners like theater balconies, looking down on people stomping jake-legged through intersections or staring into the dead eyes of bottle mouths, their cigarettes burning close to their fingertips. The electric streetlamps were on, perched like old gaslights over the sidewalk.

They passed a church garden where a white statue of Christ stood wide-armed, floodlit, his shadow thrown huge against the backside of the cathedral. The crumpled forms of winos lay against the wrought-iron fence, cloaked in shadow. Now the buildings grew taller on either side of Royal Street, surer, their sides zigzagged with catwalks and fire escapes. This narrow canyon of light, carved through the darkness of the city.

A tall white building rose from the street, bright as the marble Christ, higher than anything in sight. Every bulb seemed alight in the place, blazing. The front of the building was carved and filigreed with ornate designs, and flags of various nations fluttered over the sidewalk. Zeno stopped the motorbike directly beneath the awning of the place, which read: HOTEL MONTELEONE. A bellman stood before the polished brass doors of the lobby. Zeno cut off the motorbike.

"What are you doing?" asked Della.

"Getting a drink."

"They won't let us in there."

Zeno swung off the bike and stretched, his scarf fluttering in the breeze. "Relax, baby. The circus is in town."

A valet materialized from between a pair of potted shrubs, ready to take the key.

Their passenger extracted himself from the sidecar and waited politely beside Zeno, hands clasped, as Della followed. There was something about the man, thought Della. He seemed shy, slightly bemused, yet also sure of himself, his place in the world.

"May I buy you two a round of cocktails to express my thanks?" he asked.

Della and Zeno looked at each other. "Most certainly."

Zeno removed his flying cap, hooked his arm through Della's, scooped Sark against his chest, and the four of them entered the white dazzle of the lobby. Chandeliers gleamed like shattered stars over the checked marble floors; heels rang like shots through the place. Zeno strode tall across the floor, smiling this way and that, as if brandishing a knife. They entered the plush cavern of the Swan Bar, where barmen were cracking cocktail shakers over highball glasses, spearing olives and cherries on long toothpicks.

They took seats at the bar, three abreast, Della between the two men. She shivered and rubbed her palms together, trying to drive the chill from her bones—a lingering sting from the brisk ride through the winter dusk, the aerial tragedy they'd witnessed that afternoon.

"I know just the thing," said their passenger. One of the bow-tied bartenders soon appeared, wiping down the bar and setting three linen cocktail napkins before them.

"Three toddies," ordered Bill. "*S'il vous plaît.*"

The barman bowed. "Yes, Mr. Faulkner."

Della looked at their passenger, whose surname was apparently known by the barmen of the Monteleone, but the man's gaze was elsewhere. He was watching the thin blue whisper of a woman's cigarette. The smoke rose uncoiling over the bar, blooming. His eyes traced the smoky threads and curls, the ghostly filigree rising from the idle tips of the woman's fingers.

Della leaned into the bar. "What is it you do, Mr. Faulkner?"

The man's gaze remained on the smoke. "I write."

"Are you going to write about the air show?"

He looked at her and cocked his head, his eyes newly alight, his lips parting. "Why, yes, I believe I will."

Their drinks arrived. Three toddies in clear glass mugs. The burnt-yellow amalgams of whiskey and lemon steamed beneath their noses. They clanged their glasses.

"To all the dead pilots," said Faulkner.

"Amen," said Zeno.

They drank. After the toddies, an experimental cocktail of the head bartender's, a mixture of rye and cognac and vermouth. He said he was thinking of calling it the "Vieux Carré"—the French name for the Quarter.

The writer spoke little, but his very presence seemed to charge the atmosphere. There was an electricity in the room, as before a storm.

Della could sense it. A quickening, as if they stood in the proximity of a lightning rod, distant thunder tickling the soles of their feet.

They left the hotel and ventured deeper into the Quarter, roving with the human tide of the cobbled streets, following the little man into dark hole-in-the-wall haunts and slate-roofed Creole cottages, drinking whiskey and listening to tales of the pirates and contrabandists who once plied their trades in these dim candlelit warrens, where their ghosts were said to lurk yet in the shadows.

"This tavern was once a smithy," said Faulkner, "owned by none other than the pirate Jean Lafitte."

"Ah," said Zeno, "our friend from Bayou La Batre!"

"Precisely, Captain. Now, did you know the Quarter burned not once but *twice* in the late eighteenth century, and this old blacksmith shop was one of the few buildings to survive both great fires? They say bucket brigades were formed all the way from the Mississippi River to here, a quarter of a mile right up St. Philip Street."

"Lafitte's Baratarians?" asked Della.

"Indeed, my dear. Can you picture them?" Their passenger swung his hand down the long street. "A line of dusky banditti swinging pails of Ole Man River through halls of fire, perhaps singing piratical chanteys while they worked. They couldn't let all their hard-won plunder perish in the cellar, could they now?"

They traveled on, trading stories, gesticulating wildly, their hands cutting through the air like wings. Shadowy figures danced and reeled on the ironwork balconies above them; electric signs sizzled against patinated walls. In a dim old warehouse with a copper-topped bar, they watched the bartender drip water from a brass faucet onto sugar cubes dropped in milky slugs of outlaw absinthe, which Della had never tasted. A green-black burn, from tongue to belly. Soon her blood was leaping newly inside her, thrilling with drink and hope.

They swung from bar to bar, Della hanging from Zeno's arm like one of the Jenny's interplane struts, the writer zigzagging expertly through the crowds, leading them through the night. They followed him into bright cafés with vaulted ceilings and aproned waiters, into old speak-

easies so dark and narrow their shoulders brushed the walls. For supper, muffuletta sandwiches from a corner tavern with uneven tile floors
and paint-flaked walls covered in portraits of Napoléon. A many-faced
shrine. Zeno eyed the paintings suspiciously, squinting in the dim light,
as if the plump Bonapartes might be staring back at him as he chewed.

"What is the meaning of Little Boney upon these walls?"

Their passenger wiggled in his seat, spreading his hands across the
table. "They say this was to be Napoléon's home in the New World had
he escaped exile. None other than our friend Lafitte hatched the plot to
rescue him from a remote hunk of volcanic rock in the middle of the
Atlantic. His Baratarians would pilot a high-speed schooner built especially for the task, the *Seraphine*, scaling his island home with daggers
in their teeth. Alas, *l'Empereur* perished before they set sail. The God of
Clay was dead."

"Ah," said Zeno, clapping one big palm on the man's arm. "You know
Byron!"

The writer smiled and nodded to Della, quoting the poet: "'She walks
in beauty, like the night.'"

Zeno smiled broadly, a few bread crumbs glued to his lips. "That she
does, my good man. That she does."

They pitched themselves back into the electric darkness, the wild jos-
tle of the old streets, veering between gutters of snarled bunting and
serpentine, moving through gangs of merrymakers shouting in English
and French, Creole and Italian. Curses and howls, blessings and ballads.
Now and again, the pop of fireworks or gunshots.

They found themselves in an old Spanish armory with a stand-up bar
built for tired horsemen and teamsters to stretch their legs—not a single
stool or chair. The three of them stood at the bar drinking creamy green
cocktails, a specialty of the place.

The writer gestured to the grand panel of tarnished glass behind the
bar. "That *mirruh* was shipped here from a Parisian bistro a decade before the Civil War, already ninety years old at the time. Fashioned a
decade before our Republic itself. What wild cinemas must have shown
upon that screen."

The man's words seemed to crack open the world for Della, his tales illuminating the vast histories hidden in a portrait on the wall, beneath a layer of paint, in the very ground beneath their feet. Not just here but anywhere. Expansive realms of possibility, the world so much wider and deeper than it appeared at first sight.

Breathless almost, she found herself telling the man of her dream. Going west. The life they might have in a place like Hollywood, where the very air seemed to carry the faintest particles of gold. Where they might have a small bungalow, thick-walled as a desert fort, the plot shaded by green fronds of palm. A place where they would be paid in paper money for exploits shot in black and white, burned onto 35-millimeter reels, and stored in cast-metal drums. She did not expect perfection in this new place, nor immortality through the thin witness of film. She wanted only a lengthening of wind and light—beyond tomorrow—and perhaps the wonder of a wooden floor, hard and sure, after a day on the wing.

"Easier said than done," said Zeno, a fine green foam perched on his mustaches.

"We'll get there."

"But afterward. A lot of people arrive in the Golden State with plans to work in pictures."

"So?"

"So, most of them end up drinking in lounges."

"We have to have faith, Zeno. Nothing in the world is sure. But we have a chance, and that's all anybody can ask. Chance enough to stand on. It can't be slimmer than what we have out there." She cast her hand out, gesturing toward the pastures and barnyards of their past.

Zeno grunted, nodded. "True. But we still need wings."

The writer seemed to be listening keenly, as he had to all their stories, but said nothing.

In the wee hours, the three of them circled back to the Hotel Monteleone, resolved on a nightcap. In the last hour, Della noticed their passenger had become quiet. Nostalgia, perhaps, or loneliness, or some dream of his own. Perhaps he didn't want to say goodbye. Back at the hotel, she saw him gazing again at the blue haze over the bar, as he had when they first arrived. His eyes, black and bright, climbed the curling blooms of cigarette smoke, as if reading meaning in their loop and drift, in the strange shapes of their ascension. His temples pulsing, rumbling, as if he could bend such airy forms to his will. He reached into the pocket of his coat, withdrew a fountain pen, and removed the cap, a golden spear of nib. He was sliding a cocktail napkin toward his chest, his pen poised to write on the white fabric, when Zeno bolted upright from his stool, nearly knocking it backward.

There, across the bar, stood Uden. He smiled thinly, white-scarfed, and raised a glass of milk in toast. Zeno stiffened. Sark's ears perked like daggers.

Della knew, sure as steel, what was going to happen.

Her glass crashed against the bar.

43

A Breakfast Tale

Faulkner rose over Lake Pontchartrain in his red biplane. It was Sunday noon, cloudless and bright. Sails sprang like winter blossoms from the lake, wind-swelled. New Orleans lay beneath a bluish veil of wood and coal smoke. A city of ghosts, each wanting its story told. The airport terminal shone, faceted with steel and glass and stone. A black smudge on the main runway, where the comet plane had burned. That afternoon, the pilot's ashes were to be scattered over the lake. The faintest shower of stardust, pitting the surface like the feet of Jesus bugs. That light. Faulkner banked the biplane, watching the machine's shadow ripple across the surface.

He couldn't stay. He had to get home to Rowan Oak. He had a new book to write. The characters were already wheeling and buzzing in his mind, rakish, slightly larger-than-life, ready to loop and soar through the story.

He'd awoken early that morning in the front yard of a home on St. Charles Avenue. He was fully clothed, propped upright against the trunk of a crape myrtle. The naked branches gleamed with dew. A small dark-green bottle lay in the grass beside him, empty. He raised the spout to his nose and sniffed. *Absinthe.*

He rose slowly, swiping the grass from the damp seat of his trousers, then set out for the home of the *Times-Picayune* reporter where his luggage was stored. The early streetcars shuttled past him. His legs felt thin and willowy beneath his trousers. His head was full of crashing thunder and smoke. He zigzagged block to block, following the names of streets tiled blue and white on sidewalk corners, the letters fractured and gummed. The birds were squeaking and cheering, stringing themselves tree to tree while feral cats gathered lean and notch-eared at kitchen stoops, waiting for dishes of milk.

He was famished. He couldn't remember his last meal. Perhaps he'd eaten breakfast yesterday, or told someone he had. There was so much attrition in memory. So many casualties, whole hours and days sucked into the black oblivion of the mind. Forgotten. The voids filled with the stories that were called the past, crowding the very air of the living. Tales told again and again and again, as if the telling kept them alive, sure as breath.

Sunlight was jeweling the avenues, raising the wild reek of the previous night. The thick miasma of this city, like an atmosphere its own. He lifted his arms, his coat spread tatty and frayed over the sidewalk. His shoes weaved along the fractured concrete, between the stains of urine and wine. He looked at the sky, white-gold with morning light. A bird swiveled over the trees, throwing its shadow across the street.

He felt, sometimes, that he kited on the very breath of some beast or god, snatching words from the wind. They came gentle as mayflies or strange as moths. They pricked like mosquitoes or stung like bees. They grew legion, filling the pages of books.

Mary Rose—the reporter's wife—opened the door at his first knock. She held one hand to her breast, clutching a silver pendant she wore. She was already dressed for church.

"Why, Mr. Faulkner, I was worried sick when you didn't come home last night."

Faulkner bowed slightly. "I do apologize, ma'am. Extenuating circumstances."

Mary Rose didn't budge from the doorway. She lifted her nose slightly, flaring her nostrils. Scenting him. Still holding the pendant like some amulet of protection.

"Extenuating?"

Faulkner eyed the sliver of space between her hip and the doorjamb, tensing his muscles as a wingback would. Like Baby Buntin, perhaps, who once juked and cut through mazes of bodies. But Faulkner had his own strengths to play.

"I accepted a ride from a pair of motorcyclists last night, a man and a woman, performers from the air circus."

Mary Rose worried the pendant beneath her thumb. "Performers?"

"Oh yes. Barnstormers, wingwalkers." Faulkner leaned forward, lowering his voice: "Gypsy aerialists, ma'am. Flying daredevils. We did us a little riding, drinking, carousing."

Mary Rose shifted slightly in place, licking her lips. The door hinges groaned slightly. "Flying daredevils?" she asked.

Faulkner straightened. "That's right, Miss Mary. Theirs is quite the story, I can assure you." Now he cocked his head, smiled. "You really ought to hear it."

Mary Rose looked dazed, spellbound. She moved aside, letting Faulkner into the house.

"I shall tell you the whole tale," he said, entering. "Over breakfast."

44

Dawn Duel

*T*he Gipsy Moth sat on the tarmac, bird-white in the predawn gray. A machine so fragile, thought Della. A contrivance of tissue and wire, light as the winged tickle of a butterfly. The roundels lay on the thin wings like blue and red eyespots, ready to shiver across the sky. Della crossed her arms hard beneath her breasts. Her ribs felt brittle beneath her hands, as if she could crack them with a squeeze.

No, she thought. *No no no.*

"Please," she said.

Zeno didn't seem to hear her. He was staring at the pale wonder of the craft, his lips slightly parted. His scarf rustling in the breeze. Uden stood before his own machine, his pale face mirroring the blue-eyed skull on the fuselage.

The show was over, but not their duel. They would fight at daybreak. If Zeno won, they would get the Travel Air. If he lost, they would join Uden's act.

"Please," she said again. "Don't."

Zeno's cheek twitched, a ripple across the graying stubble. He said nothing.

"This isn't the way," said Della.

Zeno's head cocked slightly. He seemed rapt, entranced. Slowly, he licked his mustache. "We need wings."

Della shook her head. If he went up against Uden, she knew, he may never come down. He could keep circling his past, town to town, dueling again and again until one of them fell. Sark was looking up at her, foggy-eyed, his ears perked. She bent and scooped him, one hand beneath the warm keel of his belly.

"If you go up there," she said, "don't bother coming back."

Zeno's eyes stayed on the Gipsy Moth. "Why not?"

Della hitched the dog against her chest. "Because we'll be gone."

"Gone?"

"*Gone*, man. We'll take the train if we have to."

"The train?"

Della's free hand crept to the pocket of her jumper. She felt the square of linen there, folded the size of a postage stamp, which she'd been carrying since the Swan Room.

"We don't need wings," she said.

"We can't arrive in California naked."

Della pressed the folded square beneath her thumb. "We won't," she said, taking it from her pocket.

When Della had spilled her drink at the Hotel Monteleone, the barman's rag had whipped to the scene, sweeping the mess into a stainless steel bucket. Zeno had paid no attention, still staring at the rival air ace across the room. Meanwhile, Della had finally lifted her hand from the bar, finding a white linen cocktail napkin stuck to her palm. She peeled it from her skin slowly, finding words written there. She looked to the writer who'd been sitting beside her, but he was gone. No sign of his presence but the ringed sweat of his drinks on the bar top, the blue ghost of his last cigarette, and the words left scrawled on the soft square of linen. Faint clues, like those of a spirit passing in the night.

Now Della held out the folded note. "He left this."

"Who did?"

"Our passenger."

"So?"

"So read it."

Zeno sighed, taking the napkin. He unfolded it corner by corner and stretched it tight between his hands to read. The corners fluttered in the wind, the words scrawled jagged and black between his thumbs. Then his palms snapped closed, balling the words in his fists.

"The man was a fake, honey. A charlatan. Did he even pay his bill?"

"They knew his name."

"To be known by a hotel barman," said Zeno. "The highest of distinctions."

"We have to have faith." Della could feel the sun burning beneath the horizon, soon to break. "Please."

Zeno looked back to the Gipsy Moth. The wind skated across the field, black and chill, gently rocking the flying machine. The wings shivered, pulling at their tie-down cords. Zeno's eyes tracked the movement, as if hypnotized.

Della pulled Sark closer against her chest. "Don't leave us, Zeno. Do the hard thing. Let go."

Zeno shook his head slowly, as if in trance. "I could never leave you."

"You could die."

Zeno wet his lips with his tongue, his eyes on the Gipsy Moth. "I'm not afraid."

Della leaned toward him, so close she could've taken his earlobe in her teeth. "*How very selfish of you.*"

Zeno blinked, his eyes wet. Della thought she'd triumphed. That her words had broken the spell. Then he blinked a second time, hard, as if to cut the tears from his eyes. His face was stone. He set his goggles in place and clapped the wad of napkin back in her hand.

"Wait for me," he said.

A white sun blistered the horizon. Dawn came flooding across the lake, a vast nation of light. Zeno walked toward the Gipsy Moth, his bootheels grinding across the cinder. His silhouette grew strange against the impending light, like a wisp of smoke.

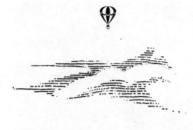

Book V

45

The Flying Faulkners

*T*he handbills were orange, rained fluttering on the town square like a lost squadron of monarch butterflies. The people of Ripley, Mississippi, stooped to pick up these strange missives from the heavens. They set their reading glasses on their noses to inspect the lines stamped in the heavy block script of a country print shop.

WILLIAM FAULKNER'S

(FAMOUS AUTHOR)

AIR CIRCUS

STUNT FLYING

by

William Faulkner and Capt. V. C. Omlie

SATURDAY AND SUNDAY

April 28th–29th

Parachute Jump Sunday—5 p.m.

PASSENGER RIDES

These ships will burn that GOOD GULF GAS

The people of Ripley knew the family name. Their town had been the home of the scion of the line, William Clark Falkner—the Old Colonel. The Hero of the Black Plume, who led the First Mississippi Partisan Rangers into the killing storm of First Manassas. Some whispered that it was the Old Colonel himself who stood "like a stone wall" against the enemy—not that Virginia upstart, Stonewall Jackson.

On these very streets, a man had attacked the Old Colonel, believing W. C. Falkner had blackballed him from the Knights of Temperance. When the man's revolver misfired, Falkner killed him with his Bowie knife. Later, he shot another man dead in an argument over a house rental. There were other duels and altercations, known or rumored or narrowly averted. There was the first narrow-gauge railroad in North Mississippi, which he built, and the best-selling riverboat romances he wrote. There was the day a former business partner threw down on him in the public square with a .44-caliber revolver and shot him dead. An eight-foot-tall statue of him stood in the Ripley cemetery, chiseled from Italian marble.

The townspeople folded the handbills and slid them into their handbags or shirt pockets. They'd read them more carefully than any book of the "Famous Author." Perhaps they would see what strange birds had sprung of the Old Colonel's line.

On Sunday afternoons, the Faulkner Air Circus descended on the communities of North Mississippi. Captain Omlie did the stunt flying in his Waco biplane, twisting and looping and diving to the moaning chagrin of local cattle, leaving convoluted entrails of smoke hanging on the breeze. A local Oxonian, George Goff, performed the parachute jumps, springing the silken bloom of his canopy low enough that spectators were known to faint at the sight, their bodies falling faster than the dainty touchdown of the parachutist. Often, Dean Swift would run the show from the ground, collecting money for air rides and acting as the master of ceremonies, announcing the stunts and exploits to the crowds. He stood on a milk crate or washtub or hickory stump— whatever was handy. The people gathered around him, drawn toward the beaming gold of his face, the rich thunder of his voice. The young man's vast and unexpected vocabulary.

Faulkner himself gave rides in his Waco cabin cruiser. More than one passenger would descend green-faced and sickly from the red biplane after enduring one of the author's signature landings, when the Waco would stab for the ground, again and again, bouncing off the soft turf of the field.

Black Eagle, brother of the family wet nurse, did most of the mechanical work. He assisted Faulkner around Rowan Oak, painting fences or forking hay or accompanying his employer to a distant shade tree, there to drink from a jug. Other times, he drove Faulkner to the airfield in Memphis, where they would fly the Waco or change the oil or polish the wings to the bloodiest red gleam. Black Eagle's big hands roamed the swells and contours of the machine with the greatest tenderness, as they might the flesh of a prized racehorse. Sometimes Faulkner would turn the controls over to the Black man during a passenger ride. The planters' sons or cotton queens in the back seat would quake in terror, their hands pawing the cabin windows, while Faulkner lit himself a cigarette, the creases sparking at the corners of his and Black Eagle's eyes.

In June, Dean Swift sat at the soda fountain in Chilton's Drugstore on the Square. His feet were hooked beneath his stool, his head bent to a tall glass of Coca-Cola. The soda popped and fizzed beneath his nose, tickling his nostrils. His air license rode in his shirt pocket. He could feel it there, badge-size against his chest. He'd noticed a new gleam in the eyes of the townspeople since he started flying. Pride for a rising son, perhaps, who'd proved himself more than a crack batter and winning smile.

Dean lifted the Coca-Cola to his lips. The sweet elixir crackled on his tongue. The chips of ice shifted and popped, an arctic landscape emerging from the thick bowl of fountain glass. The stormy tonic cracked sweetly down his throat. As he set the glass on the zinc countertop, the door of the drugstore jingled open. A bloom of summer heat reached across the room, touching his face. He looked up, seeing the girl who entered. His eyes rounded, boylike. His mouth went dry. He thought of the thermals that rose invisibly from the earth, the soaring columns of lift.

The soda jerk appeared across the counter. "You want another one?"

Dean Swift licked the fizz from his mustache, looking at the girl.

"Two," he said.

Her name was Louise Hale. She was sun-bronzed, with muscles that swam beneath her skin like seals. Her face was a golden torch. Her people were from the Tallahatchie bottoms north of Oxford—the land of brown bears and smoke-colored deer and Chickasaw wraiths. She was fearless as a feist dog, and she smelled of the outdoors. Dean loved to bury his nose in her neck, scenting the deep forest of her body, the silvery creeks of sweat. The tawny hills and swales of her, like a homeland. She could shoot birds on the wing and field-dress deer and crack a drive down the fairway like the long draw of an Indian bow. She had such faith in the man he wanted to become. The head of an air service. A flock of planes arrayed before the silver dome of a Quonset hangar, his name snapping taut on the windsock.

Louise was working as a secretary for the Works Progress Administration in Oxford. The WPA. She'd worked in a Memphis department store, photographing children on Santa's knee, and as an assistant to an Ole Miss professor. She'd taken classes at "the M"—the Mississippi College for Women. She was as unafraid of hard work as she was most everything else.

She loved to fly. On cross-country ventures, she would curl up in the copilot's seat. A golden coil of arms and calves, the crescent nails of her bare feet pressed against his leg. She would smile in her sleep, as if cupped in a warm palm. Even the heaviest turbulence failed to rouse her. Awake, she met tumult with a glowing eye. She'd beg Dean to loop and roll the plane, watching the earth spin beneath the skilled ministrations of his hands, the angular patches of cotton fields rolling over their heads. The scrawls of great rivers and highways hanging from the ceiling of an inverted world. Her mouth slightly parted, her eyes aglow.

Such faith.

Dean had moved in with Captain Omlie in Memphis. He'd follow the railroad tracks home to Oxford, buzzing low over the WPA office on the Square, drawing Louise out to the airfield on the edge of town. Other days, she would drive up to Memphis with a friend, the pair of them sitting in the hangar's shade alongside Bill and Black Eagle. Together, they'd watch Dean take up passengers, the Waco passing like a bright red star over the city skyline.

They married in September, in the town of Batesville, where Dean was flying passengers for an air show, charging a dollar per ride. They couldn't leave the field until dusk. The fireflies were rising along the road in tiny streamers of light. Dean convinced a jeweler to open his store, paying for the ring from the day's wad of bills. Together they sought out a justice of the peace. The man answered the door in his dinner bib, ready to shoo another doe-eyed couple from his porch as he'd done so many times in the past. Instead, his face went butter-smooth, as if he'd seen something for the first time; his supper hung for a moment un-chewed. After doing the honors, he refused to take their money.

Later, an announcement party at Rowan Oak. Bill lifted his glass be-fore dinner: "To the best wife and best flier I have ever known." The next day, the brothers drove out to the airfield. There sat the cabin Waco, pride of the Faulkner Air Circus. The wings were staked down with rope, as if the machine might leap into the sky of its own accord.

Bill set his hand on Dean's shoulder. "Damned proud of you."

He removed his hand and lit his pipe. He spoke with his teeth clamped, pushing his words through the smoke.

"What do you think of your new ship?"

Dean's eyes rounded. "Mine?"

"Wedding gift," said Bill. "From now on, our air circus will be called The Flying Faulkners."

46

Sunset Limited

Della stood before New Orleans Union Station, the glass cupola shining like a beacon in the rising sun. The terminal's four chimneys whispered smoke, the platform archways swallowing early passengers with overstuffed suitcases and one-way tickets. The automobiles on Rampart Street clattered and lurched, crisscrossing, motoring uptown and down. Della's heart careered in her chest like a small animal in flight, fleeing a hunting raptor or hound.

She hadn't waited on the tarmac. She'd swiveled on her heel and walked away, just like she'd said she would. She'd heard the engine of the Gipsy Moth catch fire but didn't look. Sark bounced along at her heel, his head thrust forward like an ax. This black diehard, determined to defend her from stray dogs or winos or railroad bulls or whatever may come.

She looked at him and stopped. She took him up and cradled him and kissed him in the ruff of his neck. He squirmed, rigid with duty. She set him in the seat of the sidecar, massaging him behind the ears. His smoky eyes stared at her, his lower jaw slightly open, his little teeth white and sharp. His head was cocked, as if asking a question.

"I'm sorry, sweet boy," she said. "But he'd die without you."

Behind them, the roar of machines running up their engines. She had to hurry. She couldn't watch. If she didn't know what happened, she could imagine whatever she liked. She could imagine Zeno descending from the duel intact, some part of him purged or healed. He could pass into the realm of story, of dream.

She buried her face again into the ruff of Sark's neck.

"Take care of him," she said, her forehead against the jumping throb of his jugular. Then she snapped a chain to his collar and rose, walking fast from the motorbike. She didn't look back. She could almost hear the desperate inflation of the dog's lungs, like a bellows sucking air. His ribs stretched quivering beneath the black coat of his fur, trying to contain his hurt.

Della pulled off her boot in front of the ticket window, digging out the pair of sawbucks her father had given her so long ago. Twenty dollars. The bills were moist and rank, like tropical leaves. She laid them on the counter, spreading them flat beneath her palms.

"California."

She stood on the rail platform. The early sun slashed down through the skylights, illuminating the great trains of the Southern Pacific Railroad. Their engines shone cannon-black, oiled like giant artillery guns. Their boilers throbbed and hissed. Shoe soles clacked in the airy space. People spoke in hushed voices, as they would in some holy place. Della clutched her ticket to her chest, looking for her train.

There. The Sunset Limited. The great transcontinental express, which steamed out of the flooded country of the bayous and across the vast brown rangelands of the West, passing miles of pumpjacks and starving cattle, crossing the purple mountains of the desert and arriving in Los Angeles in seventy-two hours. The very name of the line moved her blood. The Sunset Limited. She felt her cheeks flushing, a singing pressure in her ears.

She moved. She strode past dark green sleeper cars with PULLMAN painted gold on their sides. People in suits and dresses were boarding, grasping brass handrails as they mounted small step stools. Porters in uniform caps waited with the passengers' luggage, their shoulders bowed like yokes. They looked as if they could sling the bags through the roof. Della strode on, her bootheels ringing like shots beneath the skylights. The sound seemed sharp enough to shatter the glass, a sudden blizzard over the place. Her heart was beating red in her face. Her cheeks were hot. Her breath whistled through clenched teeth.

She stood before the coach car. The sides were made from wooden planks. Iridescent streaks and thumbprints on the windows. No boarding stool. Della looked at the gap, a scant few inches between platform and train. A mile. She had walked on a thousand wings, but never stepped so far. The whistle blew, a blast of jetted steam.

Della stepped from the platform, onto the train.

47

Pylon

*W*illie "Suicide" Jones stepped onto the wing of the biplane, his body hunched against the wind. His jumpsuit ballooned in the slipstream, threatening to tear him from the interplane wires. Far below, the handbills of The Flying Faulkners hailed his appearance over the North Mississippi countryside: THE ONLY NEGRO WINGWALKER AND PARACHUTE JUMPER IN THE WORLD.

Suicide Jones would cling to a braided hemp rope hanging from the tail of a biplane, holding fast as the machine looped six times in succession, his body slingshotted through the sky with incredible violence. He would switch planes in midair, descending the rungs of a thirty-foot rope ladder that snapped and twisted in the slipstream, and he would open parachutes just feet from the earth, as if to preserve every moment of free fall. He'd been traveling with air circuses for more than a decade, field to field, earning his living from the sky. Now he'd come to Mississippi.

Dean watched from the cockpit, slowly circling the field.

The previous fall, he'd earned his commercial pilot's license, making only one error on his written examination. When listing a pilot's essential equipment, he failed to include a timepiece. The family roared at the news. They would tell the story again and again.

Dean don't need a watch. He lives every day by the sun.

He was a partner in Mid-South Airways now—Omlie's outfit in Memphis—thanks to Bill's gift of the Waco. People began to recognize his bright red flying machine. When the motor swallowed a valve just one thousand feet over the Mississippi River, motorists on the Memphis Bridge would report seeing a red biplane drop like a feather into the high brush of a midriver island, undamaged. Dean's three passengers from Kansas City emerged without a scratch. It would take a six-man crew three days of work to cut a makeshift runway for the repaired airplane to take off from the tiny island in the middle of the river.

Dean flew air shows in Mississippi, Tennessee, Missouri—giving as many as sixty passenger rides a day. Louise came along, curled next to him in the cabin. They lived light, hopping from town to town, springing fresh-clad from their suitcases each morning. When they returned to Memphis, they might dine at the Skyway, the rooftop restaurant of the Peabody Hotel, burning their pockets clean. The liftman said the hotel's elevator would fly up the floors whenever they were aboard, the pulleys singing, as if they were more buoyant than normal passengers, their spirits lifting skyward.

Bill joined them often for air shows. He would appear at the field in his powder-blue uniform, his Royal Flying Corps wings buffed bright. This man once known as Count No-Count, who now had a flying circus to his name. He might fly the odd chock of passengers. More often, he simply watched from the ground, his swagger stick tucked under one arm, his pipe clamped between his teeth. His face beaming through the smoke.

So proud.

Dean watched for the black storms of drink that could descend upon his eldest brother. They seemed to come most often in the wake of a book. Once they flew to Clarksdale to visit brother Johncy, who'd also earned his commercial license. Bill circled the field again and again. His breath whelmed the cabin, hot as nitro. After twenty minutes, Dean took the controls gently, landing them on the grass strip with the softest bounce.

Johncy met them on the ground with a questioning look.

"Just practicing some low-speed turns," said Dean.

No irony in his smile. No wink.

Suicide Jones swung in and out of the wing wires, easy as a child at play. They said he'd earned his name in a government experiment in Arkansas where he night-jumped from ten thousand feet to test the searchlights of the national guard. The antiaircraft lights roared from the earth, crisscrossing until they targeted his falling form. He was blinded by their power, unable to see the ground. He estimated his descent, counting off each second of free fall, pulling his rip cord just one thousand feet over Little Rock. His vision took three days to return.

Six white jumpers had turned down the job, calling it "suicide."

Dean watched the man leap and swing toward the end of the wing. His moves so deft, as if choreographed. Dean thought of Louise, watching from the ground. Her family had never owned an automobile. She'd been learning to drive, sitting in his lap while they rumbled through the Memphis streets in his Buick roadster. Just days ago, on her first cross-city solo, the car had stalled in the middle of a railroad crossing. A train was coming hard down the tracks. The roadster wouldn't start. Louise leapt from the car and set her back against the bumper, straining, her flat shoes skidding on the pavement. A pair of stevedores, walking to work, ran to help. Together they pushed the car from the tracks just seconds before the train boomed past. Louise drove home and collapsed, shivering, straining for breath. Never had anything given her such a case of nerves, no matter how close the call. At the doctor's office, they learned why. Louise was pregnant. She and Dean were going to have a baby, due in the spring of 1936.

Suicide Jones reached the outer strut of the wing. He somersaulted onto his head and caught the nearest wires with his boots. He braced his legs and pushed himself into a handstand one thousand feet over the state of Mississippi. He turned his head and looked at Dean, his inverted mouth breaking into a grin. Dean tried to smile back but couldn't—he was already smiling as widely as he could.

At five o'clock that afternoon, Suicide Jones performed his parachute jump. He opened his canopy at two thousand feet and dangled there, smiling, while his right hand passed surreptitiously beneath his chest rig, cutting away the first chute. The crowd gasped, thinking they were witnessing the man fall to his death. They couldn't look away. Jones fell another eight seconds, far beyond the pale, only to open a reserve chute less than one thousand feet from the ground, bouncing as if into the light. A spectator once tried to sue him for this act, having suffered an infarction at the sight.

Another successful show.

As a lagniappe, Dean circled high over the field in his red biplane, dropping a gift for the crowd. A signed copy of Bill's most recent novel, *Pylon*, set during the opening of the Feinman Airport in the city of New Valois—an obvious echo of the Shushan Airport in New Orleans. A trio of barnstormers were at the heart of the novel, a love triangle. The signed first edition floated down beneath a tiny silk parachute. The crowd jostled and elbowed for position, each hoping to catch the famous author's book.

48

West

Della looked out the window of the coach car. The bright shield of the Mississippi River shone through the glass. No railroad span ran west out of New Orleans. Instead, the railcars rolled onto a thousand-foot ferry and floated across the river, rocking and clacking beneath a black storm of engine smoke. Meanwhile, tugboats chugged back and forth between the banks, throaty and snub-nosed, pushing freighters the size of toppled office buildings.

Della touched her forehead to the window. This wasn't how she'd imagined crossing this mighty river that cleaved the nation from east into west. Not so low to the surface, scant inches from getting wet. Not hungry and penniless. Not alone.

She folded down the wooden tray table in front of her seat and reached into the small front pockets of her jumpsuit. Her hands remained there, bulging and knuckling, making fists beneath the silver sheen of fabric. Now she brought them out, emptying her pockets on the table. There was the ceramic figurine she'd bought in Ocean Springs, the swallow-tailed kite. The black scissors of the tail gleamed. From her other pocket, the folded cocktail napkin. These articles of faith, which shivered slightly with the throb of the ferry. They held no power on their own, she knew. But she could believe in them more fully than coins and paper money, which came and went, went, went.

Slowly, she unfolded the napkin, corner by corner, spreading the creased and wrinkled linen like an ancient treasure map. She smoothed it again and again, gently beneath her palms, then bent her head, reading the words scrawled jagged and black.

<u>HOWARD HAWKS</u>
MGM STUDIOS
WASHINGTON BLVD, CULVER CITY
SAY BILL FAULKNER SENT YOU

Della placed both hands over the napkin and interlaced her fingers, as if to keep her arms from flying apart, from punching and clawing her way out of this railcar. She'd given her word. She'd told Zeno she would leave, and now she had. There was no going back, nothing but to lean her head against the back of the seat and try to breathe, to calm the roaring engine of her heart. She mashed her eyes shut against the rising tears. They seared beneath her lids, as if they could blind her. She kept her eyes closed until the ferry bumped the far bank of the river.

The Sunset Limited rattled across steel trestles, crossing the black slink of bayou creeks and skating high among the crowns of cypress and oak. Silver moss swept down the long chain of passenger windows. The train roared out of the swamp, crossing causeways between sugarcane fields and the shallow seas of crawfish farms. Once a flight of pursuit planes passed over the train, an echelon of steel stars. Della closed her eyes. Her bones felt fragile, full of gas or air.

They crossed into Texas, chugging high over the Sabine River. Soon they were passing whole forests of oil derricks sprung from clear-cut plots, one or two spurting black plumes of crude. They passed Houston in the evening, the skyline lit like an electric castle against the violet sky, then through the heart of Texas at night, the central plains, the vast fields of darkness. The odd campfire or farmhouse, lone torches in the void. Knots of migrants, westbound on broken boots, squatting around burning temples of twigs. Ranch hands resting on their saddles while their starving cattle nosed the burned prairie grass. Black boulders of dust, big as whole cities, were rolling across the west—so Della heard. No rain to tamp down the earth, to divide soil from sky. She heard men were speeding across the Midwest in high-powered automobiles, peddling rockets and dynamite to the dry hamlets and hovels. *Rainmakers.* As if the heavens could be blown wide, spilling the hoarded gift of rain.

Near dawn, the train stopped for twenty minutes in San Antonio. Then the iron groaned, urging itself on. *Chick-a-chick-a-chug.* Della leaned her head back on the bench. She crossed her arms against her ribs, hard, closing her eyes. She drifted.

She was there again, the airfield at dawn. The wind skirling over the dull steel of the lake. The pair of biplanes set twenty paces apart, trembling and vaporous. Their propellers like twisted cutlasses, gleaming. Their wings so fragile they could be crushed in a man's fist.

Della opened her mouth to call to the pilots, but the machines vanished at the sound of her voice. She found herself alone on the tarmac but for Sark. The dog stood rigid beside her in the sidecar, looking up. Now she could hear the planes circling high overhead, hunting in the dawn. Here was the fight she'd not wanted to witness. The sound of gunned engines and screaming wing wires. The looping, twisting braids of smoke. The shadows lancing across the earth. She feared the crippling thunderclap of a crash, which could echo inside her for years, bouncing off bones and tearing through guts. Her insides shredded, bleeding. Never to heal.

No.

Her spirit rose in her chest, fuming against her ribs. Her sweat burned like kerosene on her skin. She clicked the red dart of her tongue, and her body burst into flame. She was a finger of fire risen from the earth, terrible and bright. A blazing torch. She would draw them from the cold corners of the sky, into the throbbing glow of her power, then deeper, into the red ember of her heart. She would burn them alive and breathe their dust.

They would never die.

Sark, dark and hard, quaked like a black rock beside her. His belly swelled, his ribs rattled. His throat pulsed, trying to hold back his pain. It couldn't. His snout rose, his body bucked like a pistol. His pain exploded from his chest, high and sharp, fracturing the sky.

Della bolted awake, hearing the scream of iron beneath the train's wheels. The Sunset Limited was skidding and sparking across a winter prairie, sliding toward some new chasm or fallen bridge.

49

Armistice Day

PONTOTOC, MISSISSIPPI, 1935

*T*hey fell on the town like some kind of weather, a cloud bursting into a thousand fluttering feathers. Children ran back and forth in yards and fields, trying to catch the leaflets before they touched the earth. They alighted white and strange in their hands. They read:

> *MAMMOTH ARMISTICE DAY AIR PAGEANT*
> *TWO DAYS—NOV. 10–11, TWO O'CLOCK.*
> *FEATURING DEAN FAULKNER AND NAVY SEWELL.*
> *THRILLING EXHIBITION OF STUNT FLYING*
> *AND AERIAL ACROBATICS.*
> *DEATH-DEFYING PARACHUTE JUMPS.*
> *SEE PONTOTOC FROM THE AIR.*
> *LONG RIDES, ONE DOLLAR.*

See Pontotoc from the air. There were three farmers who wanted to see their land from the sky, to survey the green polygons of their fields, the work of their plows stamped like destiny into the earth. The farmers' names were Red and Bud and Henry. They piled into the cabin of the red Waco. They rubbed their hands between their knees, as if to summon fire. Their bottoms wiggled. Their tails would wag if they had them. Red, who had several hours of flight time as a student pilot, took the copilot's seat.

Louise, five months pregnant, had driven down from Memphis to surprise her husband. She sat cross-legged at the edge of the airfield, barefoot, holding an apple. The roadster's motor ticked in the background, still hot. She watched the red biplane disappear over the trees, rising fresh and bright into the afternoon. The flesh of the apple cracked in her mouth.

Faulkner was building a grape arbor in the yard at Rowan Oak, a wooden trellis for the vines to climb. He had tenpenny nails clamped in his teeth. The telephone rang in the house like a shot. The hammer fell from his hand and stuck deep in the earth, as if its weight had multiplied.

Brother Jack would fly home from North Carolina in his Aeronca. Brother Johncy's cropduster would nose over on takeoff, forcing him to drive. Faulkner would speed to Thaxton, Mississippi, straddling the painted lines of the highway. The same as Dean had done, those years ago, racing to Memphis for an incubator.

Faulkner left the road and sped across the field for the single giant oak, big as a house. He whipped the car broadside and leapt from behind the wheel. Men were working beneath the tree, their hacksaws gnawing through the failing light. Their cutting torches burned like blue fireflies, hissing through the dusk. The Waco was a bloody fist in the earth, half buried between the roots of the oak. The tail stood tall and canted and red.

Faulkner approached. The sawteeth stilled before him. The torch flies froze. The men in their heavy boots stepped back, silent, allowing his approach. He walked through a narrow valley of men. Firefighters and neighbors and kinsmen. He could feel the goo of time passing through his fingers, thick as atmosphere. He could hear distant sounds. The leathery whisper of a bat's wings. The cool speech of leaves. The metallic prick of the first star, tapping the dusk.

Night, falling over the field.

The impact had forced the motor through the cabin, into the men. Three of them had been removed. The passengers. They lay on the back of a flatbed truck, covered in a bedsheet.

Only the pilot was left.

His blood so bright in the dusk, like something that could never die.

Faulkner bent over the sight. His hands were at his sides, his head slightly cocked.

"Dean," he said, "is that you?"

50

The Daring

*T*he Sunset Limited sat motionless on the tracks. The passengers straight-backed in their seats, looking nervously at the world be- yond the windows. A wind-burned rangeland, vast and treeless beneath an iron sky. The old lands of killers and stars who stopped trains and pistol-whipped travelers. Lands once haunted by Geronimo, war chief of the Chiricahua, who died a Christian in Fort Sill, Oklahoma, and Billy the Kid, heart-shot by an old friend in a New Mexico shack.

The passengers didn't rise from their seats. They waited, hoping to out- last this strange hitch in time. As if, soon, their world would start to turn again, and they could return to their newspapers and dime novels, wor- rying over what lay behind them, what was to come.

Della rose from her seat.

Her metallic jumpsuit rasped down the aisle. One passenger, in a news- paper article, would say she sounded in her passing like "a knife against a whetstone." She unlatched the door of the car and hopped down from the train, her bootheels clacking in the railbed. The Sunset Limited lay along the horizon, curling out of sight. Ahead hung mountains of the palest purple, as if made of smoke or dream. The sun was diving toward them, balling the color of fire.

Della began to walk toward the head of the train. She passed the lounge car, with its barbershop and shower-bath. A man with a thin black mustache watched her pass, his razor stropped bright, as did the pre-supper patron beneath him, wearing his white beard of cream, ready to have the day's shadow bladed from his throat. She passed the dining car and the first-class sleepers. The porters were ducking to their windows, peering out. Men in ties were setting down their papers and glasses of sherry, reading the name stitched blood-red across her back.

DELLA THE DARING.

She strode past conductors who hung slanted from the steps of their cars, squinting into the distance. Past the baggage car, windowless with twin sliding doors, and the postal car, where the clerks had gathered beneath the iron hook that caught canvas bags of mail dangling from stations. She walked faster, faster. Her lungs were starting to burn, her hair flaming long from her head. Later, she would remember how the winter ranges burned gold.

She passed the engine itself, aimed cannon-black down the rails. Before this sat the white shape of the Gipsy Moth, perched bird-light over the rails. This seeming creation of wire and paste, featherweight, which had stopped the greatest passenger train of the land. The pilot leaned against the fuselage, smoking a cigar. He spoke to the conductor and fireman, smiling, shrugging. One fist perched casually at his hip, revealing the curled butt of the pistol beneath his coat. A black terrier stood over his shoulder, watching bunny-eared from the cockpit.

Zeno saw her, his face rounding bright over the rails.

Della began to run toward them, west, as if racing the sun.

Epilogue

Eagles' Wings

*I*n Oxford, Mississippi, a granite headstone stands twin-columned from the earth, supporting a triangular pediment. The heavy base is littered with tarnished pennies and unsmoked cigarettes and half-empty bottles of bourbon whiskey left like tributes for a god. A single name has been chiseled into the stone face of the die.

FAULKNER

Nearby lies the grave of Dean Swift Faulkner, who was buried on Armistice Day, 1935, in a closed casket, at the age of twenty-eight years. His three surviving brothers, who were pilots, lowered his body into the muddy earth. His marker is small, unadorned. His epitaph, chosen by his eldest brother, is the same as that of doomed Johnny Sartoris, the darling of Yoknapatawpha County, who fell to his death over France.

I BARE HIM ON EAGLES'
WINGS AND BROUGHT HIM
UNTO ME

Dean Swift's daughter was born four months after his death. Years later, on her wedding day, her Uncle William—Pappy—would walk her down the aisle. That night, after the reception, when the guests were home in their beds and the dark autumn trees creaking overhead, Faulkner would return to the church, collect the altar flowers, and carry them out to the churchyard, laying them to rest upon his brother's grave. He arranged the flowers just so, as if the wind would never blow them away. Then he walked home to Rowan Oak, through a dark path in the woods, alone.

In Thaxton, Mississippi, a tree stands in the middle of a field. Leafless, storm-struck, spread like a crown of bone against the sky. Now and then, the roots of the tree spit up scraps of twisted metal or painted canvas, like shrapnel from a wound. The fragments lie naked beneath the sky, gleaming, asking for their story to be told.

Author's Note

This book is a work of fiction, an imagining of the lives of the two barn-stormers who crossed paths with William Faulkner during the Mardi Gras festivities of 1934. Nevertheless, the Faulkner chapters are based on true events, stories, or biographical anecdotes—outlandish as some may seem. For instance, a "balloonitic" did land in the Falkner family's lot, causing Murray Falkner to shoot a pig; the Falkner boys did build an airplane out of their mother's beanpoles and wrapping paper, launching it off a bluff behind their house; William Faulkner and a friend did forge a letter of reference from a Reverend Mr. Edward Twimberly-Thorndyke of London for the RAF enlistment office, calling themselves "godfearing young Christian gentlemen"; Faulkner did return to Oxford after the Great War wearing the uniform of a Royal Flying Corps officer, affecting a limp and telling tales of a metal plate in his head; and The Flying Faulkners did perform over the North Mississippi countryside in 1935. Surely, if I were to fabricate such tales, they could not be believed.

Whenever possible, I have endeavored to remain true to the historical and biographical record, and I would be remiss not to mention some of the sources most helpful in illuminating the lesser-known parts of Faulkner's life: Joseph Blotner, *Faulkner: A Biography* (University Press of Mississippi, 2005); Robert Harrison, *Aviation Lore in*

Faulkner (J. Benjamins Publishing, 1985); John "Johncy" Faulkner, *My Brother Bill* (Trident Press, 1963); Murry C. "Jack" Falkner, *The Falkners of Mississippi: A Memoir* (LSU Press, 1967); Dean Faulkner Wells, *Every Day by the Sun* (Crown, 2011). What's more, I am greatly indebted to Dr. Hubert Horton McAlexander, Professor of English Emeritus at the University of Georgia, who first steered me toward my love of Faulkner, and to my late father, Rick Brown, who took me to our local airport so many times when I was a boy to look at the airplanes. Blue skies and tailwinds, old man.

Acknowledgments

To my mother, Janet Brown, who could've discouraged me from stepping onto my own wings but gave me her faith instead—you are the best mom a writer could have.

To my late father, Rick Brown, who steered us through all kinds of weather with a steady hand and stout heart—you are still my copilot.

To my love, AJ, who makes my heart fly and my boots jump—you are my home.

To my English professor, Dr. Hubert McAlexander, who made lightning crackle through the classroom and illumined my path to Faulkner—you lit the fire.

To my friend and agent, Christopher Rhodes, who's ridden beside me through all the storms and kept the faith burning—you have my love and immense gratitude.

To my friend and mentor, Jason Frye, whose insight, advice, and spirit have lit the way time and again—you are the man, and your friendship is one of the great gifts of my life.

To my team at St. Martin's, who've taken me on this journey—I'm honored to work with such brilliant people, and I hope we have miles and miles more still to go.

To all the booksellers, near and far, who've ever put a book of mine in the hands of a reader—you are the wind beneath my wings, and your friendship is one of the unexpected delights of the writing life.